A Great
and
Glorious
Gift

A GREAT AND GLORIOUS GIFT

A FARM FRESH ROMANCE 3

VALERIE COMER

GreenWords Media

A Great and Glorious Gift

FARM FRESH MARKET ROMANCE 3

VALERIE COMER

GreenWords Media

In Memory of Paula...

James 1:17: Every good and perfect gift is from above, coming down from the Father of the heavenly lights, who does not change like shifting shadows. (NIV)

Romans 8:28: And we know that in all things God works for the good of those who love him, who have been called according to his purpose. (NIV)

T hese forest creatures are just the cutest things
ever!"

Juni O'Neill huddled inside her rain jacket
and smiled at the young woman who'd entered her booth
at the Farm Fresh Market. She might not be able to stand
Quincey's big brother — the jerk — but that wasn't the
girl's fault.

"All the kids at the farm have some of these." Quincey
fingered the felt creations dangling from the display. "If
not foxes and badgers, then the ranch set or the mermaids
or the dragons. You have the greatest imagination."

"Thank you." It was nice to be complimented, even by
someone who clearly wouldn't be buying a set at this
week's market. Or, to be honest, ever. Juni's target audience was not young adults, unless they had nieces or
nephews. Quincey Shirkowski did not.

"Sure is a miserable day, though." Quincey glanced out

from beneath the striped overhang of the market canopy. "Was it busy earlier?"

"No. Most people are smart enough to know they can get the same items on other Saturday mornings when it's not cold, windy, and wet."

"I guess." Quincey looked down the row of booths.

All Juni saw was brightly colored canopies with their side curtains down in a misguided effort to keep out the wind and rain. Why, again, had she bothered to come today? Because she was stubborn, that's why.

Quincey turned back, huddling deeper into her raincoat. "Though I guess they might be out of beets or lettuce by next weekend, and who's to say the weather will be nicer?"

Beets and lettuce, maybe. But not what was basically designer stuffed animals. Toys. Juni designed and sewed toys. It had seemed a good idea back in spring when she'd moved in with her sister in Galena Landing. A short-term position wasn't sufficient to contain her energy and imagination, even if teaching assorted classes in the high school's arts department beat teaching math or one of the sciences all to pieces.

The locals had snapped up her designs from the first week. Tourists flocked to the town in northern Idaho all summer long. Many of them had been charmed by the felties. Juni had barely been able to keep up, sewing her fingers to the bone most evenings. But now it was mid-September. The visitors were long gone, and the locals had either bought their sets or were waiting until closer to Christmas.

Juni was praying for the latter, plus she wasn't a quitter. That temp teaching position had turned into a permanent job, but Juni still needed something to fill her empty evenings, especially now that her starry-eyed sister spent so much time with her boyfriend and his kids.

"Hey, didn't you go to SIU?" Quincey tilted her head. "Did you know my brother Zay there?"

And there it was.

Juni stared at the girl, suddenly aware of Zadok Shirkowski playing a jig on his violin in the minstrel booth across the way. Could she lie and say no, that her degree was from some other college besides South Idaho U? But she'd been challenged to live out her Christian faith since her return to Galena Landing, and didn't that preclude flat-out lying?

She'd managed to skirt the question other times, with other people, but there was no one here but Quincey and her, and the girl's expectant gaze was fixed on Juni. Short of the canopy collapsing — *please, Lord, that would be great* — she had no choice but to reply.

"We, uh, met once." On a blind date. A mistake Juni would never make again.

Quincey brightened. "Oooh, tell me about it!"

Juni shrugged. "There's not much to tell." At least, not once she'd stripped out all the details of a desperate co-ed whose roommate had talked her into expanding her horizons.

You won't regret it, Tracie had vowed. *Trust me. I've got someone amazing for you to meet.*

An amazing jerk, that's what. As for trusting Tracie, Juni had never done so again.

"I can just see you guys together." Quincey managed a dreamy expression. "You're both so talented and creative."

Juni coughed. "Thanks, but no thanks. I'm not planning to date anyone for a very long time." If the someone was Zadok? Never.

"Aw, why not? Xavier said you got the permanent job now that Ms. Jones didn't come back after her baby. So, you're not planning on moving away, right?"

"I'm not sure." And why couldn't the girl leave her alone? Juni needed to turn the tables, or she'd have to resort to *over*turning hers to precipitate a change of topic. "Are you seeing anyone? You're working out at Green Acres Farm this fall, right?"

"Yeah, but all the men there are ancient. Some are married, and the other interns must be at least five years older than me. No offense, but..."

Juni laughed. Maybe at the age of 19 it would seem like 25-year-olds were gray-beards. She'd likely once thought the same thing. "There are other guys in town, aren't there?" Not that she could think of any in Quincey's age range. There weren't many in hers, either.

Quincey scrunched her freckled nose. "I don't think so. I'm just here for my internship at the farm, and then I'm back to college for the winter term."

"What's your major?"

"Marketing. At Green Acres, I'm doing whatever needs doing on days when it's all hands on deck which, honestly, is oftener than I thought it would be. But I'm also working in the office with Gabe Rubachuk on ways to expand the farm's reach."

"Marketing, huh?" Juni eyed the girl. "Do you think I could sell these online?" She swept a hand to take in her displays.

"I'm sure you could! They're lightweight and unbreakable, so mailing them would be easy. Have you thought about an Etsy shop?"

"Not really. I sold nearly everything I could create over the spring and summer just from the market here. But lately, well... you can see how few people are shopping on days like today."

Quincey picked up a stuffed mermaid and examined it. "We could do a photoshoot. Gabe set up a fish tank for his girls to play with their mermaids over in the office. They hang out with us nearly every day after school. They all love it. It's such a cute backdrop."

Juni's heart warmed. See? She might not be doing anything big and important in the world, but kids loved her toys. She was expanding horizons and imaginations. That was worthwhile, right?

Tell that to her father.

Although, nothing would convince him. Dad was the main reason she'd left Boise last spring when she found herself between positions. He persisted in thinking women should be barefoot and pregnant, like Wife #2... and preferably giving birth to boys, which Wife #2 also excelled at compared with Juni's mom.

Mom had come to grips with a life free of Grant O'Neill. Not only that, she was thriving in her receptionist job at the Galena Landing Town Hall. Her liberty hadn't inspired her to start dating again, though.

Juni's sister had also managed to put Dad in the rearview mirror, but it hadn't been easy. Dad's views on women kept interfering when Arleigh began dating Mitchell Ackerman a few months ago. But Mitch wasn't narcissistic like Dad. He'd just been hyper focused on trying to rein in two rambunctious boys as a single dad.

"Juni?"

She refocused on Quincey. "Sorry. What did you say?" Please let it not have been more about the girl's older brother. The guy was a conundrum, though maybe that was in Juni's mind. If men were shy and unassuming, they weren't worth her time. If they were confident, they were probably narcissists like Dad.

See? It was all in Juni's head.

"I can help you, if you like. Another portfolio to turn in to my prof would be helpful."

"Um, sure?" Was she really going to do this? But, why not? It wasn't like she had to keep the shop going for years and years unless it turned out to be her life passion. Which, to be honest, was highly unlikely. She had far too many interests to buckle down to just one indefinitely. Maybe she could expand an online shop with other types of products, too.

"Where's your sister today?"

At Quincey's change of topic, Juni gave her head a quick shake. "Arleigh is at the farm with Mitchell's kids, so he could man his veggie booth." She pointed at the Ackerman Farms sign on a gazebo down the row. "There aren't a lot of fresh flowers right now — frost got some in the garden — so she just sent a few bouquets with me today."

"It must be so nice to have a sister." Quincey clasped her hands together.

"Some days it is." Juni laughed. "But then there are the other days. I'm sure brothers are the same." Drat, why had she brought the discussion back around?

"Maybe? But Zay is too busy trying to be my parent. I'm 19. I don't need my brother pretending to be my dad."

"I'm sorry."

Both Shirkowski parents had died in a car crash a couple of years ago, prompting their eldest child to return and care for his younger siblings. As conscientious as Zadok seemed, Juni could see he might overdo the control.

Quincey dashed away what might have been a tear. "And let's not get started on my little brother. Xavier is driving Zadok crazy with his lackadaisical attitude toward school. Is he in any of your classes?"

"He's in theater." And Juni definitely wasn't going to discuss the teen with his sister. Breach of confidence and all that.

An elderly woman, hunched over a cane and wearing a down parka under a clear plastic poncho, entered the booth. "Brr! How are you doing today, Juni?"

"I'm well, Mrs. Bowerchuk. What brings you out today?"

"Well, I can't stay cooped up every day of the week!"

"No, I suppose not." Though Juni wouldn't mind trying on miserable fall days like this.

"I'll leave you." Quincey fluttered her fingers. "I'll just go tell Zay we've got a marketing gig that needs his photography skills."

Wait. What? Juni held her hand out to stop the young woman, but Quincey had already tugged up the hood on her raincoat and dashed into the muddy area between the rows of booths.

"It must be nice to be so young and energetic," Mrs. Bowerchuk observed.

"Yeah, it must." But if that girl thought Juni was going to work with Mr. Blind-Date Jerk, she had another think coming.

Zadok Shirkowski's fingers danced over the strings of his violin, and he swayed to the music flowing from it. It was the only way to keep warm on this dreary, rainy September day. And had he mentioned cold? Because the temperature couldn't be much above forty.

He'd switch to his guitar for the next set, then maybe pull out his ukulele for a bit. A little variety was needed when a guy played for hours every Saturday morning.

Not that anyone was forcing him, or even paying him, though a few locals sometimes dropped bills into the instrument case he laid open on the table beside him. So, why did he come every single week, rain or shine?

Zadok couldn't answer that. Or, possibly, he didn't

want to. He'd played occasionally last summer at the market manager's request. Paula Dye oversaw the market, but she was also the part-time receptionist at Galena Gospel Chapel, and she'd encouraged him to use his talents for the community and not only on the church's worship team.

But this year, he'd kept coming because the market layout placed the O'Neill sisters' booth directly across from the minstrel booth, and that meant he could keep an eye on Juni.

Was that creepy? Nah, of course not.

So long as no one noticed, at least. Paula was too thankful to have live music every single week to even notice his... obsession.

If he watched a little closer through the downpour right now, it was only because his little sister was over there chatting Juni's ear off. Between the pounding rain and the music leaping from his strings, he couldn't hear their conversation. Probably just as well.

The market was all but dead today. Half the usual number of vendors were in attendance, all of them huddled in their booths under fluffy vests and hooded raincoats, rubbing their hands and stamping their feet in the cold. It was the final outdoor market of the season, and next week they'd be inside the Ackerman Farms' greenhouse until Christmas.

But, today... why had the sellers come? More to the point, why was Juni here? It wasn't like people couldn't survive without her toys for another week.

If he questioned her motives, he needed to ponder his

own, and that wasn't happening. He segued to a peppy worship melody they'd be singing tomorrow in church, closed his eyes, and poured his heart into it.

You are amazing, God.

And it was true. God had seen him through so much. His tumultuous high school and college years, the seminary training he hadn't even had the chance to put to good use, his relocation to Galena Landing after the deaths of his parents.

He'd given up everything for his younger sister and brother, and neither of them seemed grateful. It pinched, but he wasn't doing it for them. He was doing it because it was the right thing to do. He was doing it for Jesus.

Sounded noble, but he'd be lying if he pretended it was easy. He'd barely wrapped up his training. A church in Nevada had been courting him as their next minister of music. They'd even encouraged him to bring Quincey and Xavier with him.

Zadok couldn't do that to his sibs, especially Xavier, though God only knew, staying in Galena Landing didn't seem to make much difference. The kid had done okay at first, but now, two years after their parents' passing, he was in a full-on funk. Nothing Zadok did pulled his brother out of it. No threats, no teasers, no attempts at camaraderie. Nothing.

"Why don't you call it a day?"

His eyes sprang open and took in the middle-aged market manager who stood before him. "Is it noon?"

Paula rolled her eyes. "It is *not* noon, but it might as well be. I think we should shut down the market early today. There have been so few shoppers due to the weather."

Elderly Mrs. Bowerchuk sloshed through the mud in her rubber boots, draped in what looked like a clear garbage bag. Likely only her cane kept her upright.

"You can't disappoint the ones who're still planning to come." But he did lower the violin into its case — no tips yet today — and massaged his chilled fingers.

"They'll get over it. But, either way, there's no need for you to stay. I'm sure there are things you'd rather be doing on a day like today."

Mrs. Bowerchuk ducked under Juni's canopy and engaged Juni and Quincey in conversation, not that he could hear them.

Paula turned to follow Zadok's gaze. Then she turned back to him with a grin. "Is that how it is?"

He tore his gaze away, his heart sinking. "Pardon me?"

Paula laughed. "Seriously, Zadok, go home. Save those hands and your voice for church tomorrow, and thank the Lord our markets will be indoors for the next few months. I still can't believe Mitchell Ackerman said yes to hosting."

"He's a good guy." Not that Zadok knew him well. The Ackerman brothers had inherited their grandparents' farm a few miles north of town. Treyan worked at the town office, but Mitchell had poured his focus into creating a sustainable market garden. His wife had passed away several years ago, leaving Mitchell to raise two little boys while managing his struggling business. Grief might cause some people to reach out but, in Zadok's experience, the opposite was true. He'd put his head down and focused on what was smack in front of him, much like Mitch Ackerman had done.

Only, the other guy had emerged from his heartache to find love with Juni's sister. Zadok expected to hear of an engagement any time, quite frankly.

Whereas Zadok had emerged from his own mourning to discover the woman he'd encountered on a disastrous blind date years ago had moved to his new town. He'd nearly managed to forget that night until Juni had blithely shown up at both the market and the church months ago.

Quincey darted toward him across the muddy verge. "Zay!"

"Hey, Quince."

Paula backed up a step. "Go home, Zadok," she repeated. "I'm going to call it for today. It's only an hour early."

Quincey tugged on his arm. "I need you to do a favor for me."

It was rare she asked anything of him. "Sure. What's up?"

"I'm going to set up an online shop for Juni, and I need you to take photos."

"Photos of Juni?" His voice stuttered.

A grinning Quincey swatted his bicep. "No, silly. Of her felt thingies. But, you know what? Headshots are a good idea. People will also want to see the creator."

"No." He licked his lips.

"You already said yes." Quincey giggled. "You can't back out now. We'll set up a time over the next week or so.

The sooner the better. Your work hours are the same this week?"

Zadok tried to keep his sigh contained. "Yes, just like always." Taking over his dad's tire shop had never in a million years been his dream. But what else was he going to do in small-town Galena Landing? With Dad gone, Zadok either needed to sell Tires and Treads or manage it. If he sold it, what was he going to do to fill his time? He needed to put in nearly two more years until Xavier graduated. Then he'd be free to sell the business and resume the life he'd put on hold.

Right now, he was shackled to his siblings, and the bubbly one wanted him to do a favor. He sighed again.

"Sure. Whatever. Set something up. You know my schedule."

He was so, so going to regret this.

CHAPTER
TWO

Pastor Ron's sermon the next morning came from James 1:17, but Juni wasn't convinced. Sure, the words sounded good.

Every good and perfect gift is from above, coming down from the Father of the heavenly lights, who does not change like shifting shadows.

It wasn't that she didn't believe the Bible. Or... maybe it was that not all gifts were good. The good ones were from above. The other ones... were not.

Right? That must be it.

Except then he threw Romans 8:28 in the mix.

And we know that in all things God works for the good of those who love him, who have been called according to his purpose.

Ugh. That didn't leave much out, frankly.

Juni shifted restlessly in her seat on the lightly padded pew, causing Arleigh to give her a questioning look.

No. She didn't want to talk about it with her sister.

Arleigh didn't have the kinds of doubts Juni did. She was stronger. She'd seen through Dad from the beginning and cut all ties with him after their parents' divorce. Sure, Arleigh had struggled to get Dad's voice out of her head in the intervening years — being repeatedly told her ideas were adorable but of no real value had done a number on her self-esteem — but she hadn't been the fool Juni had been.

Juni had seen how Dad treated her big sister and determined to be the better daughter, the one who could meet his expectations. The favored one.

Look how that had turned out. All she'd gotten from the experience was the college degree he'd supported until she'd stepped out of line in her senior year and funding had been cut off. Dad mentioned that his son Galway wanted to play hockey, and it was pretty expensive. *Sorry, Juni. Can't do both.*

What he'd really meant was that she wasn't worthy, after all.

How was Dad a good and perfect gift? He wasn't. As far as Juni could tell, he also wasn't something that God had worked for her good. Maybe the common denominator was Juni. She didn't love God enough. She wasn't called according to His good purpose.

Yeah, it was her at fault. Always and forever.

"You okay?" Arleigh whispered, nudging her lightly.

Juni forced a smile. "Sure." She looked down and twisted the rings on her right hand. Then the ones on her left hand.

From her sister's other side, Mitchell stretched his arm

across the back of the pew and rubbed Arleigh's shoulder. They smiled at each other before turning back to face Pastor Ron.

Juni shifted down the bench lest Mitch touch her shoulder by accident and make it awkward for everyone. Being around the lovebirds was a bit sickening at times. She was happy for her sister. She was. But watching the pair of them only served to remind Juni of how alone she was.

Like Mom, who sat on her other side, but Mom had been a wife and a mother. Yeah, she'd been married to Dad, which was far from ideal. Juni got that. But Mom had had the experiences Juni longed for.

The key was finding someone who wasn't like Dad. Also, someone not like Zadok Shirkowski.

Galena Landing was a small town. There weren't tons of single men in their mid-to-late twenties or early thirties. If the guy also needed to be a Christian — he did — and not weird, she was down to few options.

Well, there was Simon Melnychuk, the fire chief. He seemed nice-ish, but she couldn't get rid of his occasional attention quickly enough. He was too smooth. Too something.

Thanks to Green Acres Farm opening up a whole new set of opportunities for the region with their farm school focused on sustainable living and food production, the town was in better shape than when Juni had been a teen.

But nice, single men? Nowhere to be found. She could sympathize with Quincey on that lost cause.

She blinked as Pastor Ron left the platform. Keanan

Welsh lifted his guitar strap over his neck as he took his place behind the microphone. Wasn't Zadok leading music today? He had led the earlier set.

Keanan fingered the strings and looked out across the sanctuary, meeting the gazes of many. Juni looked down. He was too perceptive, plus he was a friend of Zadok's. She didn't want to know what the man might think of her. See in her.

"Pastor Ron asked me to sing this song for you this morning. It's called *As Long as You are Glorified*, and it goes like this." Keanan picked an elaborate rhythm before launching into the questions the song posed. Basically, the songwriter asked if he should only love and trust God when times were good.

Juni winced. The questions hit too close to home. On the other hand, it seemed she wasn't the only one who felt this way. It wasn't as comforting as it ought to be, though, because the lyricist had come to the conclusion that God was still God, regardless, and that nothing else mattered if God were glorified.

Did she really believe that? Could she sing this song with a straight face? It wasn't asked of her, since Keanan sang it as a special number. But, still. She'd look it up on YouTube later and ponder the words.

Zadok joined Keanan onstage and the two of them led the closing number together. Juni had always loved Matt Redman's *Blessed be the Name of the Lord*. Guess she'd never thought too much about the words, though. Blessing God even in the darkness and desert places? She hadn't been doing that. Not from her heart.

And she called herself a Christian? She was so far from living that life the right way. It wasn't that she didn't believe Jesus had done His part. He had. But she failed utterly at responding appropriately.

The song finally ended, and Pastor Ron offered a closing prayer and a benediction.

If Juni could muster up a flying carpet to whisk her out of the building — preferably all the way back to the basement apartment she shared with Arleigh at Ackerman Farms — she'd have jumped aboard without a second thought.

Instead, Mom wrapped an arm over her shoulder. "Wasn't that a lovely message? It was just what I needed to hear today."

Juni managed a smile. "He's definitely got a way with words."

"We're so blessed to have him as our pastor. Are you coming over for lunch? I've got chicken in the slow cooker." She leaned around Juni. "How about you, Arleigh? Lunch?"

"I told you not today, Mom." Arleigh laughed. "Mitchell and I have plans with the boys, since the weather finally cleared."

"Well, next week, you should all come."

"Maybe. We'll fit it in soon, okay?"

"So, that leaves you and me, honey." Mom smiled conspiratorially.

Great. She'd seem selfish if she begged off, but she felt so off-kilter lately. With Arleigh out of the suite, she could indulge in some painting or crafting and lose herself in the creative process.

"Juni?" Quincey touched her shoulder from two pews behind. "Can we meet at two o'clock instead of five at Lakeside Park? It looks like it's going to rain again later. Bring all your stuff. I've been getting props together, and Zay is free to shoot photos."

"I..." Juni took a deep breath. She'd asked Quincey to help her, and the girl was running with it. Perfect, right?

"What's this all about?" Mom's open smile took in both of them.

"Quincey is helping me set up an online shop for my felties."

"Isn't that marvelous! And it gives me an idea. Quincey, why don't you and your brothers come for lunch? Arleigh had to bow out, and there's too much for just Juni and me. That way you don't have to worry about cooking a meal, I'll get time with my daughter, and you can zip off from my place for your photoshoot."

Wasn't that just perfect?

"Oh, wow!" Quincey beamed at Mom. "That's so sweet of you, Mrs. O'Neill! I'll run ask Zay right now, but I'm pretty sure we don't have any firm lunch plans. Hold that thought!" She darted away.

Juni focused on her mom, managing not to watch Quincey hop up on the platform where Zadok was nestling his guitar into its case.

Mom patted her arm. "They're such a nice family."

"Aren't they, though?" Juni managed a smile. Monday morning at Galena High couldn't come soon enough.

THIS WAS SUCH a bad idea on so many levels, but Zadok couldn't exactly refuse without explaining far too much to too many people. Was he gratified or not that Mrs. O'Neill didn't seem to know anything about him? He wasn't sure.

Grant O'Neill, on the other hand, knew a lot...

Nope. Not thinking about that man. Zadok had had a handful of years to ponder that entire debacle and, the more he thought about it, the more he doubted the man had been up to any good despite his pious demeanor and his fine standing in the church they'd both attended.

He turned off his car in guest parking beside the apartment building, and both siblings leaped from the vehicle before he'd pulled his key. "Hey, calm down! You don't even know this woman. Be on your best behavior."

Xavier shoved his hands in his jeans pockets and glared at him across the roof of the car.

Quincey, as usual, was bouncing around like an energizer bunny. "I'm always on my best behavior. You know that, Zay. I'm excited about this opportunity. Juni's got a great shot at a terrific online shop. Her stuff is so stinkin' cute!"

Their younger brother rolled his eyes. Zadok felt like doing the same, but ten additional years had its uses. He could control those impulses now. But some things he couldn't control, like his kid sister's enthusiasm.

He was glad she was home this summer and fall. He was. She kept him and Xavier from either deathly silence or snarling at each other. But, man, where did she get all this energy from?

"Come on! We're headed to the third floor. Juni's car is already here, and time's wasting if we want to catch the best daylight at the lake." She jogged to the door and pressed the intercom button while Xavier ambled up behind her.

She wasn't wrong. Plus, Zadok had already agreed to it all, so it was too late for cold feet and grumpiness. He followed the two of them up the carpeted steps in the slightly musty building.

Donna O'Neill swept the door wide at their approach. "Welcome! I'm so happy you could join us."

The delectable aroma of chicken and... pesto?... found Zadok's nostrils as he inhaled. "Thanks for the invitation. That smells amazing."

She beamed. "I hope it will taste the same. Come on in. Juni's just fixing a quick salad."

"Is there anything I can do to help?" Quincey stepped forward.

Zadok swelled with pride at how much she'd grown up. But then, shouldn't he have offered, himself? Too late now to be first, but that didn't mean he shouldn't. "Put us all to work, if you like."

Xavier mumbled something behind him, but Zadok ignored him. The kid was going through something and refused to talk about it. Either way, his attitude was getting on Zadok's last nerve.

"Oh, no. We're ready in a jiffy. Have a seat at the table, and Quincey, if you like, you could fill the water glasses."

"I'll do it," Zadok said quickly. He needed to counteract Juni's impressions of him.

Donna looked between them, her smile seemingly frozen on her face, but Quincey nudged him and winked. "Go for it."

Grr. It wasn't that way. He was just tired of Juni assuming what he was like without giving him a chance to prove differently. It wasn't like they were going to return to square one and get a redo.

He wouldn't be completely against that option, but on the other hand? A woman who jumped to conclusions like she had wasn't someone he could trust with his heart.

No hearts were involved. None were going to be. He was a nice guy, steady, honest, polite, and he simply wanted her to realize that.

Like the fish that got away?

No. Not like that.

"...the fridge dispenser."

He blinked. Man, he needed to quit spacing out. "Sure, I'll wash up and get right to it."

"The restroom is the first door on the left."

After washing, he passed through the corner of the living room where his siblings sat on the sofa like two bumps on a log. He entered the kitchen and scanned the scenario. A glass-doored cupboard beside the fridge with its inline water dispenser made his task obvious.

But he couldn't stay silent and still be polite, right? "Hi, Juni. This sure smells good."

She didn't meet his gaze. "Mom got the slow cooker started first thing this morning. It's all her. She's a great cook."

"Aw, thank you, honey. I love having people to cook for."

"So, uh, five glasses of water? With ice?"

"Yes." Donna laughed. "I'm not hiding any other guests in the closet."

"No, of course not." He reached into the cupboard and began filling glasses. He should still be making small talk, right? That's how these sorts of visits went. "Have you lived here long?"

"Since I moved back to Galena Landing after my divorce. I guess that's been about fifteen years now. Grant and I raised our girls here for a time, but then..." She fluttered her hands.

Ugh, why hadn't Zadok thought through that question before it left his mouth? "It's a nice town to return to."

"I was so sorry to hear of your parents' passing." Donna patted his arm. "It seemed they'd just moved to town and bought Tires and Treads from Roger Sharp when they had that terrible accident, but I guess they'd been here a couple of years."

"It was tough. They were so excited about their move from the city. They'd been working toward that for years."

"You'd already left home by then, right?"

"Yes." Could he have prevented the accident had he been here? Of course not. But it still seemed he shouldn't have been so far away. "Okay, all the water glasses are ready. Want me to take them out to the table now?"

"Sure. I'll just finish getting the chicken into a bowl. Juni, have you got—?"

"Yes, Mom. The salad is ready, the dressings are out, and I'll get the rice now."

"Thank you. I don't know what I'd do without you."

If Zadok hadn't glanced her direction, he wouldn't have caught Juni's eyeroll. Did she have any idea how much Quincey was missing, not having a mom who fussed over her like that?

And that wasn't a fair thought, either. Juni may not have lost both parents like the Shirkowski siblings had, but her parents were split up and not on speaking terms with each other. There was more than one way to have a challenging nuclear family situation.

Donna pointed out where she'd like each of them to sit and, before he knew it, Zadok found himself beside Juni along the curve of the round table.

"Zadok, would you mind asking the blessing?" Donna reached for Juni's hand on one side and Quincey's on the other.

No. Not hand-holding-for-grace people. But here they were. He held out his own hands to Juni and Xavier. Both felt strange to his touch, but Juni... wow. He was overcome with the desire to make things right with her, but how?

He managed to bless the food without tripping over his words, and both hands were yanked from his loose grasp a fraction of a second after the amen.

Quincey had no idea how much her random offer to Juni at yesterday's market was affecting him. How it was pulling him into Juni's orbit, a place he'd vowed to steer clear of since his shocked gaze had settled on her in Galena Gospel Church last spring.

She'd pretended not to recognize him, and he'd been happy to reciprocate. Until he hadn't. Until he wished he'd met her for the first time now, without the baggage of that nasty blind date in their history.

Clearly, Juni had not changed her mind. It was all him. And he wouldn't pressure her by trying to get in her good graces now.

Though, a genuine apology might be a good start.

THREE

Could this get any more awkward? Juni couldn't think how, but sitting across from Zadok would have made it harder to avoid eye contact. His hand under hers at grace, though. Had Mom done that on purpose?

Probably not. Mom was big on physical contact. Hugs, casual touches, holding hands for prayer — Mom would take any legitimate excuse for touching.

Another way Juni was her mother's opposite. The list never ended.

"This is so delish, Mrs. O!" Quincey gushed. "Is it an easy recipe?"

"So simple." Mom beamed. "I'd be happy to share it with you. Do you have a slow cooker?"

Quincey looked at her brother. "Do we?"

"Uh... I'm not sure. We can buy one if not."

It was his mother's kitchen, but shouldn't he be acquainted with it by now? Men.

"I'll look in the basement," Quincey said. "It seems like something Mom would have had."

Mom patted Quincey's arm. "My slow cooker makes all the difference. It's great coming home after work to a hot meal ready to eat."

"I'm sure! We're always scrambling." Quincey grinned at her brother. "Hey, I was going to tell you, Allison and Liz out at the farm are offering a fill-the-freezer meal prep day. The price sounds reasonable, especially with my employee discount. What do you think?"

Juni cast a furtive glance to Zadok, whose brows had pulled tight at his sister's suggestion.

"We could look into it, I guess, but I don't have time to do a prep day."

Quincey stared back. "I work full-time, too."

"Busy people need a prep day more than anyone," Mom said blandly. "Anyone want more chicken and rice before dessert? I have apple crisp in the oven."

Juni managed not to smirk. But maybe she or Arleigh should do the class. They both put in long days, too. Arleigh and Mitchell worked on the farm, so they could adjust their hours somewhat to fix meals, but harvest was in full swing, and there'd been more takeout than usual lately.

"I'd like the info, Quincey." Juni met the girl's gaze across the table. "My sister and I should look into it. Mom's right. The busier people are, the more they need to have a plan."

"I've got a plan," Zadok muttered.

She raised her eyebrows as she turned to him. "That's not what Quincey said."

"Sisters."

"What do you think, Xavier?" Quincey asked.

"Don't look at me." The teen held up both hands. "I'm not gonna cook."

"It's important for everyone to know their way around a kitchen." Mom rose to her feet, lifted the salad bowl, and carried it to the kitchen.

Hot-button issue with Mom, after all the years Dad had carefully divided their household with men's work and women's work. Color Juni shocked if Dad knew how to set up his own coffeepot, let alone cook a meal with a protein, a carb, and a vegetable. Even grilling wasn't manly enough for him. No surprise he'd married Genevieve so quickly after divorcing Mom.

"I agree." Juni couldn't resist poking the situation. "Food preparation should be a basic human skill. No one would expect someone else to brush their teeth for them, either."

Xavier glowered at her.

Tough luck, buddy. I said what I said.

"You sold me on it."

Juni pulled back as she took in Zadok's words and expression. "Pardon me?"

"You're right. No adult human can expect someone else to always be there to cook for them."

"I'm not an adult," Xavier mumbled.

Quincey elbowed him. "Coming soon, ready or not."

He glared at her.

Juni stifled a chuckle but turned back to Zadok. "So, you're going to sign up for the meal prep day?"

"I'll look into it, at least." His brown eyes — or were they hazel? — challenged hers. "If not, I'll look for a different kind of plan. How about you?"

Oh, no way, buster. He wasn't going to lure her into a shared experience like that. "It's a great idea for those who don't live on a farm. Mitchell raises meat and vegetables. In our situation, it makes the most sense to come up with a plan of our own that uses what we already have available."

"I suppose so."

Was that disappointment on his face as he looked down? Because Mom was right. Juni wasn't ever going on a second date with a guy who thought a woman's place was automatically in the kitchen. She'd seen enough of that mindset with Dad.

The fragrant aroma of warm apples and cinnamon heralded Mom's return to the table.

Juni leaped out of her chair. "Let me get the ice cream."

"Thank you." Mom smiled at her. "Xavier, would you mind gathering the plates and setting them in the sink?"

The teen scowled as he stumbled to his feet. "Yeah, okay."

Juni dug the carton of vanilla ice cream out of Mom's freezer then found the scoop, listening to the clank of dishes from the dining area just out of sight. She turned back toward the table and nearly bumped into Zadok, who carried the slow cooker insert. She managed not to snort. Someone was taking Mom's hints to heart.

"Where should I set this?"

"Wherever." Avoiding eye contact, Juni waved the scoop toward the sink. She dodged around him then Xavier with his stack of plates.

Quincey bounced a little in her chair. "This apple crisp smells amazing, Mrs. O. Wouldn't it be great if we could bottle up the aroma?"

"Aw, you're sweet." Mom scooped a serving into a bowl.

Juni added a dollop of ice cream as the Shirkowski brothers resumed their places at the table. She passed the first bowl to Quincey, who beamed, then the next to Zadok.

"Thank you."

Was he trying to catch her eye? She was having none of that nonsense. It was bad enough she'd been tricked into letting him come to Mom's for lunch. She'd also been tricked into letting him shoot photos of her creations. Doubtless Quincey had snuck that one past him as she'd done to Juni, because there was no way he'd have volunteered if he hadn't been cornered.

Except then why was he being nice today? Juni had stayed off of his radar for over five months, cautiously optimistic she could keep it that way. He ignored her. She ignored him. Easy peasy.

So, yeah, she enjoyed his music at the market far too much. Enjoyed the glimpses of his lanky frame, his brown hair, and handsome face — fine, she could admit it — as much as the toe-tapping tunes and his smooth tenor.

Juni would enjoy the music just as much if the

minstrel were female or elderly. It had nothing to do with Zadok Shirkowski.

She watched the edges of her ice cream melt into rivulets on the apple crisp for a moment. Right. She could keep arguing with herself forever, and she would.

Because this was not a man who would handle her heart wisely. He'd already proved that on a January evening nearly four years ago. She wasn't dumb enough to give him a second chance. Not that he wanted one.

No, they'd survive the next few hours, she'd get her photos, and then they'd go back to ignoring each other. If that became difficult some day in the future, she'd give her notice and look for a teaching job elsewhere.

Odds were, he'd move away first, though. Hadn't he been attending divinity school when his parents passed away? Once Xavier was through high school, all of the Shirkowski siblings would likely vacate Galena Landing.

Juni liked living near Mom and Arleigh. Surely she could ignore the guy for two more years.

Mrs. O's gentle rebuttal at lunch had stabbed Zadok's conscience. Of course, he knew cooking wasn't women's work. He knew Quincey worked as many hours as he did. If she were a part-timer, asking her to take over meal prep would make sense. But, the real question was, would he have made the same assumption if his siblings' roles were reversed?

What about if Xavier was 19 and working out at Green Acres while Quincey was a junior in high school?

Zadok winced inwardly. He knew exactly how that would look. He'd confirm that his brother's hours were as long as his and that Quincey could start meals after school.

Why hadn't he made the same thought progression with Xavier? Yeah, the kid was surly and seemed to be getting through school and life with the least amount of effort, so engaging him would be an uphill battle. What kind of guardian was Zadok to let Xavier's attitude dictate family dynamics?

You're not my father.

How many times had Xavier flung those words at him? Too many to count, like Zadok needed the reminder or something. But that didn't mean his brother's attitude should be allowed to rule.

"Thanks so much for the lunch invitation, Mrs. O." Zadok smiled at their host. "I hate to eat and run, but the forecast calls for rain again later, and we've got a photo-shoot on the agenda before then."

She waved a hand. "I knew that when I invited you. It will only take a few minutes to clean up. The dishwasher will handle most of it."

Xavier pushed his chair back a little. "Just drop me off at home."

"Aw, Xav, you can come, too," Quincey wheedled. "I could use your help."

"With what? A bunch of toys? I don't think so."

"Do you have any homework due tomorrow?" Zadok asked.

Xavier glowered at him. "No. I just need a break from all this togetherness."

Probably online game time. How did a man step in to parent a half-grown kid? Most men grew into fatherhood with babies and toddlers. Taking on a teen had never been Zadok's plan, but here they were.

Was this the time and place to start arguing with his brother, though? Nope. Zadok needed to come up with a plan for that, too. He'd let too many things slide lately. Meals. Xavier. Making things right with Juni.

He forced the thoughts to the back of his mind and rose, stacking several dessert dishes as he did so.

Quincey took a few things into the kitchen as Mrs. O protested. Xavier stood awkwardly behind his chair, shifting from one foot to the other, fingering the phone outlined in his pocket.

"I have everything in my car," Juni said. "I'll meet you down at the park."

Quincey popped back into the dining area. "May I ride with you?"

"Sure."

That left Zadok with a little privacy to deal with Xavier in the truck. Not that he knew what to say.

"Have a great time." Mrs. O kissed Juni's cheek. "I can't wait to see the photos."

Yeah, he only hoped his sister's trust wasn't misplaced. Noel Kenzie out at the farm was a way better photographer than he was, but Zadok did have a camera with all the settings he barely knew how to use. He'd do his best.

For Quincey.

Tell yourself that, Zay.

Fine. Totally for Juni. Happy now?

Nope. He wasn't happy about it. Not even a tiny bit. Juni was the sort of girl he could get interested in, for sure, but he'd had his chance and totally blown it back several years ago.

He'd taken advice from the wrong person, but how could he have been expected to have known that?

A little research — a little thought — might not have gone amiss. He'd been so full of himself. No wonder she'd run.

"See you there, Zay." Quincey wiggled her fingers at him as she followed Juni to the door.

He turned to their host. "Thanks again, Mrs. O."

"We'll have to get together again soon."

"That would be nice." Kind of, anyway. He smiled and gestured to Xavier to precede him. Was Mrs. O matchmaking? If so, that could only mean that Juni hadn't told her mom what had happened.

That might not be surprising, actually. She seemed a very private person beneath the sociable veneer. If Zadok were a betting man, he'd put money on Arleigh not knowing, either. What sibling would be so friendly and gracious to the guy who'd stomped on her sister's heart? Not an O'Neill, from what he'd been able to figure out.

By the time Zadok made it down to the truck, his

brother already sat in the passenger seat with his head-phones in his ears. Zadok started the vehicle then reached over and tugged one out. A drumbeat blasted into the vehicle.

"Hey! I was listening to that."

"Be sociable for another five minutes, bro."

"Whatever." Xavier fumbled with his phone, and blessed silence soothed the air. "Happy now?"

"Man, what's going on?" Zadok backed out of the parking space and turned onto the street.

"What do you mean? I'm fine."

"You're not fine. You're snappier than a starving wolf pup. Is something going on at school?"

Xavier shrugged. "Same old. I can't wait to get out of this berg."

"Oh, yeah? What do you want to do then?"

"Anything but this."

"You'll need to study to get into college."

Xav snorted. "Who said anything about college?"

"Fair enough." Zadok focused on the tree-lined street in front of him. Some of the leaves were turning yellow already. "You can get a trade." Good grades wouldn't go amiss for that, either, but he wasn't going to push too hard right now.

"Anything but the tire shop."

Like it had been Zadok's first choice. Not Dad's, either, come to think of it. They'd been looking for a small busi-ness to buy, and this had become available in a town that appealed to them.

"I hear you."

"Then why do you do it?"

Zadok glanced sideways at his brother. "It's called taking responsibility." Which led down a whole tangent he'd better not traverse at the moment. "There aren't a ton of jobs in Galena Landing, especially not for ministers of music."

"No kidding," Xavier mumbled.

Zadok ignored him. "But there was a tire shop in need of a manager. People in this town depend on Tires and Treads, to say nothing of the families who rely on our jobs."

"Yeah, yeah."

"It was a valid consideration. I needed something to fill my time and put food on our table, too."

"We don't have to be stuck here."

"Oh?" Zadok glanced across the car. "What do you think we should do?"

"Get the heck out of Dodge."

As if the teen had a clue what that saying meant. "The school year just started. Your second-to-last one. We'll talk about selling out in a year and a half."

"It doesn't matter. Who cares about school?"

"I do. You should." He nearly missed the teen's grimace. "What's really going on, Xav? Is it one of your teachers? The football team? A girl?" *Please not a girl.*

"Told you. It's nothing."

Zadok put the truck in park in front of the bungalow his parents had bought only four years back. "When you're ready to talk, I'm ready to listen."

Xavier shoved the door open, stuffed his headphones

back into his ears, and shuffled up the walk without a backward glance.

Was there any relationship Zadok was not failing at? Quincey, maybe. And to keep in his sister's good books, he now needed to head down to the lakefront and help her stage Juni's felt toys.

He knew how Xavier felt, at least in part. Everything was too much, with too few actual choices. Some days — today — he felt like a pinball getting whacked around inside an arcade game.

When could he get a break?

FOUR

N o." Juni touched her windswept hair. "It's a photoshoot for the toys, not for me."

Quincey laughed. "Isn't there always a bio for the crafter or author? And that requires a headshot."

Juni glanced toward Zadok, who stood at the end of the pier, holding his camera, staring out across Galena Lake. She couldn't very well reveal that the problem was the photographer. She couldn't smile for Zadok, and the thought of him having dozens of photos of her on his computer screen to touch up was, at the very least, creepy.

"You look great." Quincey angled her head to one side. "That sweater is the perfect color for your blond hair and sets off your figure. Your hair is beautiful."

"It's messy from the wind."

"It's artlessly casual and makes you relatable."

Was that even a thing? Maybe Juni didn't want to know, because either way, it felt like she was losing. Quincey was nothing if not determined.

"We've taken enough of your brother's time."

"Better to do it all at one time than to drag him out again later. Besides, who knows how many more gorgeous days we'll have this fall?"

October was generally full of them, but Quincey was right that they couldn't count on one landing on a day everyone was available. And they *were* here now. Still...

"I don't think I need headshots. Maybe a logo or something." Argh, she needed a website. She needed far too much. Maybe she should just forget the whole concept. Except for the fact that Zadok and Quincey had already given up an entire Sunday afternoon to stage and shoot dozens, if not hundreds, of photos in creative settings.

They'd done the mermaids in an aquarium on the end of the dock and on the rocks and sand of the beach. The cowboy sets had been staged amid low weeds along the lake trail, as had the forest creatures. And the dragons had roosted in the rocks — Quincey had even brought a small wooden treasure chest with gold-foil-covered chocolate coins as a prop.

And now Juni balked at headshots? It wasn't like she had to use them. *Just get it over with already.*

"Maybe if I put my hair in a messy bun?" Juni wound her locks, twisted and pinned them, then secured the look with two pencils she kept in her purse for just such an occasion.

Quincey stared at her. "How do you even do that?"

"Do what?" Juni used her phone camera in selfie-mode to check the look. It was casual, but so were her toys. It was a better look than down and tangled.

"You put that together in under a minute flat."

"Yes?" She tucked the phone back in her purse. "Teachers are required to wear buns. It's a law, so you get good at it."

Quincey narrowed her gaze at her.

Clearly the girl couldn't figure out whether Juni was kidding or not. Juni wasn't sure herself. It was likely nerves talking. Nerves knowing that Zadok stood twenty feet away and was watching her. Probably close enough to hear the conversation.

"Can you show me how to do that?"

Juni blinked. "A bun?"

"Yeah. Is my hair long enough?"

"Sure." Not that Juni wanted a bonding moment with any of the Shirkowski clan, but a hair demonstration or two wasn't going to develop into a long-term thing.

"My mom always kept her hair short. No fancy styles for her."

Juni's heart twisted at the brightness in the girl's voice as she attempted to cover the hurt of her loss. "My mom favors short as well. I didn't learn bun-making from her."

Quincey grinned. "Any kind?"

"Good one. She does bake dinner rolls sometimes." Mom had baked all their family's consumption of baked goods when she was married to Dad. She'd been the perfect housewife. According to Dad, not as perfect as Wife #2, but Juni figured Mom's bread was superior to Genevieve's. It was more Mom's attitude that Dad couldn't stomach long-term. Mom had real-ized Dad was gaslighting her and had managed to break out. Genevieve was still caught up in it, and Juni cringed to think how her five young half-brothers and -sisters were being taught that the guy was always the boss and always right. Even if he clearly wasn't.

"Just stand over there."

Juni refocused on Quincey. "Pardon me?"

"That Japanese maple will be a great backdrop." Quincey raised her voice. "Don't you think, Zay?"

He'd moved closer while Juni's mind had wandered. She could feel it even though her back was to him. She could smell him, that unique blend of musk and forest she associated with him.

"Sure. Let's take a few and then try the lake in the background."

"After that, the playground!" Quincey exclaimed. "That will show Juni has a childlike heart."

"Okay. You call the shots."

Juni managed to squelch her protest. At least Quincey had said childlike and not childish. But would some people think she was immature and silly because she made kids' toys?

It didn't matter what other people thought. No one had voiced those ideas. The locals and tourists loved her creations. Maybe others would, too.

"Say cheese!"

Juni managed to smile toward Quincey. Was that where she was supposed to look? Because smiling at Zadok would be so much harder.

"Oh, you can do better than that!" the girl called.

"Think of a silly knock-knock joke. Or imagine little Zoey playing with the mermaids."

"Look over here," Zadok said.

Juni flashed him a big smile. There. That one was for what he'd lost the moment he opened his big mouth on that stupid blind date. This one was for a future he would never see. This one proved she was just fine, that she'd never harbored a moment of wishing things had gone down differently. This one was for...

"And now turn with your back to the lake."

In Zadok's eyes, this was all a session he was shooting as a favor to his sister. It had nothing to do with her, about what they could have had if he hadn't messed up. He'd probably forgotten all about it by now. At least, he'd never shown a single flicker of recognition or interest in all their many run-ins at the Farm Fresh Market.

Neither had she, but then she was a professional trained in drama and acting. Not good enough for Hollywood or Broadway, of course, but plenty for keeping a casual smile in place— like this — in a small town where no one suspected anything.

Juni tossed a flirty smile over her shoulder toward the camera.

Click. Click. Click.

"Now we're talking!" Quincey yelled.

Juni turned slowly, smiling at Zadok, then Quincey, then off into the distance.

Click. Click. Click.

"Oooh, we got some good ones, I think! What do you say, Zay?"

"Yeah." He cleared his throat, sounding a little gruff. "Pretty sure I can work with what we've got." He lowered his camera and studied Juni as though she were a lab rat exhibiting unusual behavior.

She raised her eyebrows and stared back.

Was that a flush forming on his stubbled cheeks? Maybe. And maybe it served him right if he had a regret or two. Juni wasn't above rubbing his face in it. She smirked.

His jaw tightened, and he looked down at his camera. "I'm done here."

Message received, loud and clear. He was done setting his day aside for the likes of her. Well, she concurred. She was done playing nice with him, too.

Except... well, he wasn't getting anything out of this. It was all a favor — not to Juni, but to his sister. And didn't that deserve some sort of recognition? Gratitude?

"Thanks, Zadok. I really appreciate it."

"You're welcome. I'll go through them this evening and get the best of them to Quincey."

Not to Juni. Right. Had she expected him to ask for her email? Of course not. She wasn't the one building the online store. That was all Quincey.

"Okay, well, thank you."

"No prob." He glanced at his sister. "Ready?"

Quincey stuffed the props she'd brought inside the aquarium. "Need a hand packing up the rest, Juni?"

"No, I've got it. Thank you." The felties had been placed back in their boxes as they wrapped each set. She just had a few random props of her own left.

Zadok carried the aquarium, his long legs eating up

the distance back to his car as Quincey jogged alongside him, gesturing and chattering.

Juni couldn't make out the girl's words, but she didn't need to. Quincey's enthusiasm was all that had made this afternoon bearable.

It had been years since that stupid blind date. Why couldn't she forget it ever happened?

ZADOK ABSOLUTELY SHOULD NOT BE TAKING this long studying every single headshot he'd snapped of Juni this afternoon.

She was beautiful. Quincey had been right about the rusty tones of the sweater against the vibrancy of the Japanese maple. For that brief moment, the sky behind had been a pure autumnal blue. Clouds had roiled to the west — and now dumped more rain on the already soaked valley — but that angle at that moment had been perfect.

He'd captured it.

Her hair in that bun. He'd been as gobsmacked as his sister at the speed in which Juni had altered her look. Her casual updo revealed her autumn-leaf earrings. Revealed the smooth line of her neck.

Zadok should not be staring at her neck, even in his photo editing software. Not examining the curve of her jaw and wondering how it would taste.

Enough. He clicked the X at the corner of the program

and surged to his feet, and a sense of dread trickled down his spine.

He hadn't saved the edits he'd spent half an hour slaving over. Not that it had been a hardship. Had he really done that much, or had he mostly stared at her?

He was acting like a lovesick teen, and he was neither. A lot of guys were married by the time they were twenty-six. Might even have become fathers. And didn't everyone have to go through the lovesick phase before they emerged into a firm, solid love?

But that was the problem. There'd be no happy ending with Juni, because today's interlude — this whole summer, really — was Act II of a tragedy written by Shakespeare.

Everyone dies.

Zadok gave his hair a quick scrub with both hands and shook his head as he left his study and headed down the corridor to the kitchen.

Xavier sat at the table with a large spoon stuck into a carton of ice cream. He looked up with guilt plastered across his face. "Uh..."

As if Zadok didn't have enough problems of his own. "Hey. A little hungry? Save some for the rest of us."

Not that Quincey would dive into a bucket of frozen sugar. Her internship out at Green Acres included health and nutrition with Jo Nemesek and Sierra Rubachuk. Jo was a registered nutritionist who worked at Galena Hills, a nursing home. Sierra was a naturopath who'd sworn off sugar and even honey and was influencing Quincey in that regard. Maybe a little too much... she was becoming the sugar police.

Whatever. She wasn't going to fight Xavier for that ice cream, but Zadok might. He'd picked that carton up on yesterday's trip to Super One, planning to drown his own sorrows in it.

"Here. Go ahead." Xavier pushed the carton toward Zadok.

What on earth? The thing was half-empty. "You're going to have one heck of a bellyache."

Xavier shrugged. "Whatever."

"You're going to school tomorrow even if you do."

The teen stared back with dull eyes. "Who cares?"

"I do." Zadok pointed at the carton. "Put that away, please. And let's talk."

Xavier snapped the lid on the container and dropped it into the fridge's freezer drawer. "There's nothing to talk about."

"You used to like school."

"That was then."

"What happened?"

Xavier eyed him. "Like you don't know."

This was about Mom and Dad's death again. Still. What was a reasonable time to mourn? What was a reasonable process? The three of them had done some sessions with Pastor Ron and his wife, Wanda, an accredited counselor. It had helped Zadok a lot. Quincey, too. At the time, Zadok had assumed the same for the youngest Shirkowski sibling. Apparently, he'd been wrong.

And, yeah, he'd known Xavier was struggling. It would

be impossible not to notice. He'd prayed for his brother, tried to put in an encouraging word when he could. Tried to normalize life as much as possible.

"Quit trying to be my father. You're not." Xavier stormed out of the kitchen and stomped down the basement stairs. A few seconds later, the door to his bedroom slammed.

Zadok dropped into the chair his brother had just vacated and, elbows on the table, sank his head into his hands. "God, what do I do? How do I get through to him?"

Maybe he should go talk to Pastor Ron. They met monthly with Keanan Welsh and a few other musicians to plan out the schedule for leading worship, but that was no time for a more personal chat.

Pastor Ron was so busy, though, and always looked tired. The congregation had grown in recent years as the valley became reinvigorated with small-scale, sustainable farming practices.

Thanks again to that crew out at Green Acres. They'd led the way, proving there was a market for both their products and for their knowledge. Their farm school was a happening thing. Quincey was loving her internship there.

None of that solved the problem of Xavier, though. The kid was resigned at best about school. Probably Zadok should talk to the principal, but wouldn't the woman call him if there was a problem? The balance was hard. He might not be his brother's dad, but he was his legal guardian.

Taking time from the tire shop wasn't always easy. The guys who did the actual mounting and balancing had no clue about meeting customers or any of the other things Zadok did in the office. He'd have to lock up the street entrance to meet with the principal.

Why did Xavier have to wallow and drag Zadok down with him?

Aargh, it was hard being the oldest in a parentless family. If only Zadok could glean from his dad's wisdom one more time. Of course, if he could do that, the problem wouldn't exist. Dad could handle his own rebel teen then. He'd guided Zadok through the tumultuous years just fine.

Too bad he hadn't been at South Idaho U that fateful day four years ago, though. Dad could have saved his eldest a lot of grief in that blind date.

Zadok had trusted the wrong advice, and he was going to pay for it the rest of his life.

FIVE

J uni?"

She looked up from her book as her big sister stuck her head around the bedroom door. "Hey. How was your big date?" She couldn't help smirking.

Arleigh laughed as she settled cross-legged onto the foot of Juni's bed. "Is that what you call it when you take two kids to the playground and try to wear them out so they'll sleep well?"

"Aw, you love it. You know you do."

Arleigh's boyfriend, Mitchell, was a widower with boys in second grade and kindergarten. Lincoln and Hudson had been a wild pair before Arleigh had become their nanny last spring. Arleigh had been at her wit's end after her flower farm on rented land had flooded out and been destroyed. She and Mitchell had hammered out a deal where she could use half of one greenhouse for her flowers, watch the boys part-time, and live in the basement suite rent-free with Juni.

"I didn't mean to fall in love." Arleigh's voice was filled with dreamy wonder.

Juni laughed and threw a pillow at her sister. "Neither did Mitchell."

"I know."

"You guys are so adorable. Although, you know, a little sickly sweet."

Arleigh smiled softly. "You, too, could be this happy."

"Right." Juni snorted. "Because amazing guys grow on trees and can be picked like apples. Oh, there's a nice round one, perfectly red, no blemish."

"I didn't think Mitchell was amazing or perfect at first. And he's still not perfect."

"But he's learning."

That got Arleigh's attention. "Are you suggesting I'm turning him into the man I want him to be? Because that's not at all true."

Juni spread her hands wide. "What can I say?"

"He's turning to God for changes from within, and I'm trying to do that, too. It's not some outward change so I'll like him better."

"I know." And Juni did know, but it was still hard to believe. There was her father again, telling her what kind of woman to be so that a man would appreciate her.

Arleigh leaned forward and tapped Juni's temple lightly. "Dad's in there; am I right?"

Juni sighed. "How did you know?"

"Because he lives in my head, too. I've got him locked in the dungeon in the far back corner, but he still gets his fingers through the bars and tries to latch onto my brain."

She shuddered. "And you call me the dramatic one."

"You know it's true. He trained us. Conditioned us. It's really hard to evict everything he said, because it's part of the fabric of our lives. Who are we without those threads?"

"You tell me." Juni eyed her sister. "Who are we?"

"Loved by God. Infused with vibrant hope for a better future. The trajectory is different now."

"Because Mitchell."

"Because Jesus."

Semantics. Okay, that wasn't quite fair, but still. Wouldn't it be much easier to fully trust God if there was a gorgeous guy walking the same path beside you? Not that Juni would ever let Arleigh know she thought Mitchell was gorgeous. Also, it wasn't actually Mitchell Ackerman lurking in the sidelines of Juni's imagination when she thought that.

Not only did she need to banish Grant O'Neill from her head, she needed to toss out Zadok Shirkowski. She'd thought Zadok was different, but she'd been naive, seeing only what she wanted to see.

He'd been an upperclassman, a college senior to her sophomore. She'd seen him around campus for an entire semester. She'd attended several of the music department concerts just so she could sigh over the tall, lean, talented musician without anyone noticing.

Her best friend had caught on, though. Tracie had pulled some strings, strings that should never have been pulled. And the blind date that had thrilled and delighted Juni for the first few minutes had unraveled so quickly she hardly knew what had happened before she'd bolted from the coffee shop.

Zadok Shirkowski spouted the same nonsense as Dad. In a slightly more palatable way, maybe, but the end result would be the same. Men who expected their women to be perfectly demure little homemakers, worshiping their man as the head of their household, and delivering baby after baby to be indoctrinated the same way? Nuh uh.

Dad's perfect wife — the second one, since Mom had figured out his game-plan and divorced him — had been pregnant with their fifth that winter.

"Juni?"

She pulled her focus back into the basement suite with its familiar yellow walls and looked into her sister's concerned eyes. "Yeah?"

"Dad may be an elder of his congregation, but he isn't Jesus. He isn't even a little bit like Jesus."

"I know. That church is way crazy."

"But remember what you said to me a few months ago when I was panicking over Mitchell?"

Juni forced a chuckle. "Which time? There were so many..."

Arleigh pitched the pillow back at Juni's head. "About how he's not like Dad. I was so wary of any tiny slip that smacked of misogyny that I couldn't even see Mitchell for who he actually was."

"I remember." The problem was that Zadok had done far worse than a wee gaffe. Arleigh had suspected Mitchell, but Juni had all the evidence on Zadok. It was so clear that if Galena Landing had another evangelical church, that's where Juni would be attending, even if she had to go without her sister and mother. Did Pastor Ron know how misguided Zadok was? Maybe she should tell him.

"I worry about you."

Juni straightened her spine. "Well, don't. Mom is doing perfectly fine without a man in her life, and I can, too. I have a great career, making a difference in the lives of many teenagers. Thanks to you and your bright ideas, I've got a nice little toy manufacturing business happening on the side. I'm fulfilled." Also a great liar, at least if her sister would bite.

"How did the photoshoot go?"

"Pretty well. We spent a couple of hours down at Lakeside Park before the wind and rain blew in again. Quincey had some fun ideas of how to display the sets."

"Is Zadok a good photographer?"

Juni managed a casual shrug. "I don't know, to be honest. I guess I'll see the results when Quincey gets them to me."

"You didn't even have a peek in the review setting on his camera?" Arleigh's eyes widened.

And get that close to Zadok Shirkowski? Not a chance. "Nope. I can wait."

"He's cute."

"Who, Zadok?"

"Well, I'm not talking about his little brother."

"Aw, Xavier is cute, though maybe a little too young for me."

Arleigh's grin was nearly feral. "But Zadok isn't."

Great. Juni had played right into her sister's hand. "I don't like him that way. Or at all, really."

"Why?" Arleigh angled her head and studied Juni. "Honest question, actually. You two seem aware of each other, but I don't know as I've ever heard you exchange five words. I sure wish I could have been at Mom's for lunch today and watched you interact."

"There was nothing to see. Nothing to hear."

"But... why?"

"Seriously, Arleigh! How many guys have you met since you were sixteen that you never bothered to give a second glance to? If there's no spark, there's no spark."

"Other times there's a spark, and no one acknowledges it."

Juni raised her eyebrows. "Are you speaking from experience?"

"You know I am."

Caught again. "Except there's a major difference."

Arleigh leaned forward, elbows on her knees. "Yes?"

"You and Mitchell *had* a spark. You just drove each other crazy because you were so different."

"And because I wanted his greenhouse."

"Which you now have unlimited access to for the rest of your life, so you got what you wanted. Right?"

Arleigh laughed. "I absolutely did. But the greenhouse was only a surface thing. I wanted—"

"It wasn't a surface thing at the time. You were devastated by the flood. You were *this* close to being homeless. You were in the depths of despair."

"It wasn't that bad."

56

"It *was* that bad. I don't know how you could have forgotten so quickly."

"Hope and love are an amazing combination. You should try it."

Juni rolled her eyes. "I have hope. I have love."

"In what? Or should I say, in whom?"

"Look, I'm a Christian, same as you. I know I'm loved by Jesus. I have hope in an eternity with Him."

"And that's a beautiful thing."

"It is." Maybe she'd finally made her point through her sister's thick skull.

"But there's more."

Of course, there was more. "Oh?"

"Wasn't it just this morning in church that Pastor Ron preached on the good and perfect gift?"

"Yes, salvation is God's glorious gift to all of us."

"Not just salvation, amazing as that is. But life here, too. Remember Brittany talking about how God led her out of her dark, tangled jungle and into a wide and pleasant place?"

"And you're back to talking about romantic love again. I don't need that."

"I am not talking about romance. It's a byproduct. A wonderful bonus. I'm talking about how she felt in her soul."

Brittany had married Mitchell's brother, Treyan, last spring. The couple lived across the farmyard with Trey's young daughter, Scarlett. Brittany knew what loss was like. Her own father had died in an accident a few years back and left her reeling. But Britt's dad sounded amazing, like the kind of man God should have kept alive. It would have been better if Grant O'Neill were killed by a drunk driver. There'd be some justice in that outcome, because then he couldn't poison other people with his narcissistic views anymore.

See? God couldn't be trusted. Not completely. He'd made some errors in judgment in the father department.

Then there was the Shirkowski family. A God who gave good gifts wouldn't have let Desmond and Myrna Shirkowski pass away and foisted the raising of their younger kids on their eldest. Right?

Arleigh yawned and stretched. "It's been a long day, and I'm headed to bed. See you in the morning. Think about what I said."

As if. "Sweet dreams." Someone might as well have them. It wasn't going to be Juni.

SO MUCH FOR thinking he could put off visiting the principal. When Ms. Atkinson called, a man did whatever it took — even locking up his place of business and taping a note to the door — and headed for the high school.

Zadok shifted uneasily in the guest chair. Ha. Delinquent's chair was more like it. And throughout all his own student years, he'd never once sat in this spot.

The same could not be said of Xavier.

On the one hand, Zadok's parents hadn't died when he

was 14. But even if they had, circumstances wouldn't have turned him into an aimless wreck. Nope. He'd been nothing if not driven.

Fat lot of good that had done him.

The principal gathered a stack of papers together, set them to one side of her massive desk, then studied him above her glasses. "Mr. Shirkowski."

"Zadok, please." His dad might have been gone for two years and his grandfather even longer, but he wasn't sure he'd ever feel like the title belonged to him.

"Your brother has not turned in any homework so far this school year, and it's been six weeks now."

He was aware of the timeline. He'd heaved a sigh of relief when the interminable summer break had ended. Surely all Xavier needed was to get back into a routine.

It had been a nice dream while it lasted. Zadok twitched in the chair. "I'll speak to him about it."

"I'm counting on it." Ms. Atkinson stared at him as though that would get her point across more seriously. "I know your family circumstances are... difficult."

He winced. Is that what people called it when parents died in an accident, leaving a 24-year-old to finish raising two teenagers? Quincey had wobbled, but she'd been nearly done high school and managed to keep it together long enough to graduate. Still, after one year of college in Spokane, she'd begged for a gap year.

He'd agreed to a gap *semester*, and then they'd see.

"Zadok? I asked what your plan is."

"My plan?" Great. He'd blanked for a minute.

"To see Xavier through this. Has he been in counseling?"

Zadok scratched his head. "Not lately. The three of us had some grief sessions over at Galena Gospel Church shortly after... the accident." Still hard to talk about. To put into words. He knew his parents were gone, but saying it out loud put a degree of finality on it. *Two years, Zay. They really are gone.*

"I'd recommend it. Perhaps for all of you, but definitely for Xavier. Also, I believe he needs a tutor. If he were on the football team or in the marching band, I'd threaten to revoke his involvement, but he isn't interested in anything."

"Except drama." Drat. He bit his tongue.

"Theater might be the only thing holding Xavier together." Ms. Atkinson shook her head. "As it's an accredited class, I won't curtail his involvement. Instead, I'm trying to be thankful there's anything at all he's interested in. Ms. O'Neill has been a godsend to the arts department."

Of course. Wasn't Juni a godsend to everyone but him?

"I recommend a tutor," Ms. Atkinson went on. "But you'll likely need to find a way to incentivize his participation."

Did the principal think tire shops made a ton of money? How was he to afford a tutor? And what kind of carrot could he dangle in front of his kid brother's nose to actually get the teen's attention?

The woman folded her hands on the desk and nodded

toward the door. "With that in mind, I've invited Ms. O'Neill to join us."

Wait, what? Zadok lurched to his feet, but it was too late.

The office door opened, and Juni stepped into the space. She wore a swishy, knee-length skirt with a soft-looking, blue sweater that matched her eyes. If possible, it looked better on her than yesterday's rust.

The room was too small. There wasn't enough air for all of them. Zadok caught himself fingering the crew neck of his T-shirt as though that would help.

Juni's gaze swept past him without lingering before she focused on her boss. "Yes, Ms. Atkinson? You wanted to see me?"

"Yes. I'd like you to meet Xavier Shirkowski's guardian, his brother, Zadok."

"Pleased to meet you." Juni stretched out her hand.

So, she was going to play it like she'd never noticed him before. Like they hadn't seen each other weekly at the market for months or spent hours together just yesterday.

Fine. He could pretend, too. "Likewise." He dipped his head over their clasped hands — how many rings was she wearing, anyway? — then pulled away as quickly as he could.

Her grip was stronger than seemed possible. Maybe it was a warning, not that he needed one. Zadok wasn't sure about her, but that blind date had scarred him for life. Or at least four years, not that anyone was counting.

"I was just telling Mr. Shirkowski — Zadok — that Xavier is in danger of academic probation. In looking over his class schedule, I see you are free final period, as is he. Would you be willing to tutor Xavier?"

Sitting tall and straight on the edge of her chair, Juni shot a quick side glance toward Zadok. "What classes does he need help with?"

No. This couldn't be happening. Xavier was his problem, not Juni's. Not the school's. And yet that wasn't quite true. The principal was stepping into the yoke beside him, helping carry the burden.

Or, maybe, assigning Juni to that position.

Ms. Atkinson eyed him shrewdly. "Did you have a different, preferred option, Zadok?"

Oops. He hadn't schooled his features as well as he'd hope. He forced out a brittle smile. "No, your solution is perfectly fine with me. I know Xavier respects Ms. O'Neill. Perhaps she can reach him where I can't." Man, those words cost him. A man's pride had to be worth something. Not his. His dignity was dust to grind beneath a steel-toed work boot.

"Excellent." The principal turned back to Juni. "Which classes? Well, everything, which is how we came to find ourselves in this boat. But, if we could focus on math, biology, and physics, that would be a good place to start."

Physics. For every action, there is an equal and opposite reaction. Sir Isaac Newton, right? That was about all Zadok remembered from physics.

"I majored in English and the arts." Juni's hands clenched in her lap.

"I understand, but I have utmost faith in your ability to help the young man." The principal leaned toward her.

"It's not that he has trouble with the concepts, or he certainly didn't in previous years. It's that he's lost interest in trying."

Zadok could sympathize, actually. There were a few things he'd lost interest in, as well. He'd achieved a degree in music and then enrolled in seminary with the plan of becoming a minister of music.

The dreams had popped like a poked balloon upon his parents' deaths. He'd never envisioned caring for two teenagers and taking over his father's tire shop in podunk Galena Landing.

But here he was. Sitting in Galena High's principal's office hoping Juni O'Neill could solve his problems with his brother.

The one person who swore to scorn him forever... and, so far, had proved to be a woman of her word.

SIX

Mornings deserved better than this. Even Mondays.

Juni tried to block Zadok's reactions from the chair beside hers. She'd done such a good job of pretending he didn't exist all spring and summer that she'd been lulled into thinking she could live that way forever. At least, until yesterday. If she'd suspected otherwise, she'd never have accepted the permanent position when Rachel Jones had decided not to return after her maternity leave.

Teaching at Galena High wasn't exactly Juni's dream job, but it wasn't bad. She'd log a few years of experience and then apply for work elsewhere if she wanted. But now with Arleigh and Mitchell getting serious, and Mitch's boys starting to grow on Juni, it would be harder to leave than she'd expected last spring. Especially if Arleigh added a baby or two to the family.

Juni had figured she could afford to wait and see...

because she could stick Zadok in her blind spot and ignore him.

Look how that was turning out. First the photography job, now this.

Math and the sciences? She might need to brush up. It would be good for her, though. Good for her resume as well. And if the tutoring happened on campus during regular hours, she wouldn't actually have to talk to Zadok.

How bad could it be?

"That works for me. Xavier's a good kid, and I'd like to see him turn around."

Beside her, Zadok stiffened.

She forced herself not to scowl at him. Shouldn't he feel relief? But maybe being thrown together affected him as much as it did her. Was that good or bad? It didn't matter. She had a job to do, and the guy could just go ahead and be grateful. It wouldn't kill him.

"Excellent." The principal glanced at the clock. "I'll speak with Xavier after school. Expect to meet him in the southeast corner of the study hall tomorrow at two. I'll have his other teachers acquaint you with his current lessons."

"Thank you." Juni rose. "If that's all for today?"

"It is. Thank you."

She strode out of the office, glad she'd worn a skirt and heels today. After all, the office had a glass door. Zadok could go ahead and see what he was missing.

No. That was exactly the wrong memo to send. That was a Dad-influenced message, that a woman was only as good as her figure and her ability to bear children, preferably male. Oh, she should also be sweet and demure.

Juni made it all the way through the reception area before he called her name from behind her. She froze, took a deep breath, and turned to face him.

"Yes?" The icy tone and the single, uplifted eyebrow had quelled many a teenager in her classes. The same should be true of Zadok.

"Thank you."

Juni blinked. "Trust me. I'm not doing it for you."

He winced.

Why did the guy have to look so good? Tall, slender, and handsome, with a slight scruff on his chin he hadn't worn in Boise. It suited him.

"Well, I'm thankful, anyway. Xavier has been... challenging."

"He's a good kid."

"Sure. I know that. But it's still been hard."

He'd called her in the high school corridor to cry her a river? A lot of kids had tough situations. She knew for certain some of them lived with domestic violence. Many had divorced parents who used them and their siblings as pawns. Poverty was a real problem, with kids not getting three squares at home. And Xavier wasn't the only orphan in the school.

Yeah, she felt sorry for him, but he was far from unique in his needs.

Juni took a couple of steps backward. Maybe Zadok would get the hint.

"Look, I'm sorr—"

She cut off whatever sort of apology he'd been about to make with a slice of her hand. "As I said, I'm not doing this for you. I'm doing this for Xavier. I'm doing this because it's my job, and I'll score points with Ms. Atkinson. You and I can go right back to pretending the other one doesn't exist. You did the photoshoot yesterday as a favor to your sister. I get that. If you want to delete your camera's memory card, go for it. I'll manage without your help."

Zadok blinked and stumbled back. "I just…"

"Save it. Now, if you don't mind, I have a class to get to." Juni pivoted on her heel and marched down the locker-lined corridor.

If he bothered to call after her again, she'd simply ignore him. Enough was enough. She already had to look at his face and hear his equally gorgeous singing voice at the Farm Fresh Markets on Saturday mornings and at church on Sundays. But then at least she didn't have to talk to him.

She angled into the teacher's lounge and nearly ran into Dennis Weebly on his way out.

"Whoa!" He pulled back, barely keeping his coffee from sloshing over onto her floral skirt. "Watch where you're going."

"Sorry," she mumbled.

"What yanked your chain?"

Juni scowled at the Math teacher. It wasn't like she could dump her frustrations out on him. "I'll be tutoring Xavier Shirkowski in math. I'm sure Ms. Atkinson will be in touch with you to send over what I need to know."

He smirked at her. "It's a little harder on the brain cells than twirling around onstage in a tutu."

"If I want your opinion on my classes, I'll ask you for it."

He chuckled and headed out of the break room.

Grr. He sounded so much like Dad. Her little teaching gig was a perfect way to pass time until she got married and began popping out babies. Both men would have been horrified if she'd dared to want to teach a heavy academic subject. What little female brain could handle that? Not hers.

Okay, fine. She hated math. She'd never wanted to teach it, but she almost wished she'd gone for it just to thumb her nose at Dad. Of course, then he wouldn't have paid for her degree, so there was that.

Too bad she couldn't even dump the angst of the past hour onto her sister. Arleigh already suspected something or thought she did. So far, Juni had managed to keep Arleigh from finding out there was any history between her and Zadok.

Arleigh was only going by the way Juni reacted — or tried not to react — to Zadok's mellow tenor at the market and at church.

Juni wasn't about to fill her sister in now. No. There'd be too much explaining to do, and Juni would not come up smelling like roses. She couldn't blame everything on Dad, though she'd certainly try. In her own head, it mostly worked.

The buzzer rang, signaling the end of first period. Immediately the noise level in the corridor surged as the teens flocked to their lockers. Voices. Laughter. Clanging metal doors.

Juni needed to get her attitude adjusted before she made her way to the visual arts classroom. Today she had tenth grade art. Thankfully she could teach the students about perspective and vanishing points while her own perspective was skewed.

Maybe she could visualize sending Zadok down the train track she'd use to demonstrate vanishing points. He'd become a tiny dot in the distance before disappearing completely and permanently.

She could only wish.

Meanwhile, time for a bright, happy face as she entered the melee in the corridor and made her way to the second floor of the east wing.

"I DON'T WANT A TUTOR."

The kid wasn't the only one. Zadok eyed his brother. "You should have thought of that before you blew off all your classes so far this school year."

"They can't make me."

"Ms. O'Neill might have some tricks up her sleeve to change your mind about that." If she did, she'd win over both Shirkowski brothers, and Zadok would love her forever.

It was only a figure of speech.

Tell that to his heart. It had picked up a bit of erratic rhythm there for a few seconds.

Whatever.

"Look, Xav. What's going on in your head? Talk to me."

The boy offered a loose shrug. "There's nothing to talk about. Life is dumb, okay?"

A tendril of actual fear took hold inside Zadok. This wasn't disinterest or lethargy anymore. It was deeper. "You miss Dad and Mom. I get it." Or, at least, he was trying to.

"You don't get anything."

"So, explain."

Xavier leveled a glare at Zadok. "What happens if I skip tutoring?"

"You'll probably get kicked out of school."

"That wouldn't be so bad."

"Then you can learn how to change tires." Zadok thumbed to the work bay visible through the office window where Bobby and Austin were putting winter tires on a pickup truck.

The kid wrinkled his nose. "As if."

"Look, life isn't a free ride. You're a teenager in school. My job as a—"

"Don't say parent."

"Okay, I won't. My job as your *guardian* is to make sure you have an education and a safe, welcoming home."

Xavier raised his chin and crossed his arms over his chest. "Yeah?"

"My job is to turn you into a responsible, respectable

adult. And people who aren't students need jobs so they can pay their own expenses."

"So?"

"So... what kind of a job do you think a sixteen-year-old high-school dropout can find?"

Xavier stared at him.

Zadok stared back.

The teen heaved a sigh. "Like I said, life is dumb."

"It doesn't have to be. God gave everything—"

"Don't."

"But it's true."

"God took away our parents. I'm through with Him. Don't try to tell me how much He cares."

This was more passion than Xav had shown for any topic in a while. Too bad it hewed at the very core of everything Zadok believed in. At the heart of who their parents had been, as well.

"You know how when you're in the family room in the basement, you can't see what's going on outside?"

"Because there are no windows. Duh."

"Exactly. And what can you see from the backyard?"

Xavier shrugged. "The houses up the street."

"Can you see the top of the hill?"

"No. The houses are in the way." He glowered at Zadok.

"What about if we drive to the top of the mountain up from Green Acres Farm? What do you see from there?"

Xavier clenched his jaw. "I don't know what you're trying to prove."

"I'm trying to prove that there are places with limited

vision, and there are places with wide open vistas in front of them. Right now, you're stuck in a small, dark room, and you can't see the panorama. But buddy, the expansive view is still there, just waiting for you to come up to the lookout and see for yourself."

"You're full of it."

"I hope so."

"What?" Xavier reared back.

Good. Zadok had gotten through, at least a little. "I'm full of hope, bro. Because God is the giver of good gifts, like Pastor Ron talked about in his sermon yesterday. Yeah, life sometimes stinks, and it's hard to imagine anything good coming from Dad and Mom's deaths, but without faith in God, our perspective is as narrow as that basement room with no windows."

"I don't think there's anything better out there to see."

"You're wrong. There's lots." Man, he needed to hear this pep talk, too. "Want to take a drive to the top of the mountain?"

"Now?"

"Sure, why not now?"

"Aren't you supposed to be here until five o'clock?"

The world had not exploded when Zadok locked up for an hour to meet with Ms. Atkinson this morning. He doubted it would if he took off early this afternoon, either. Not that he could afford to skip out all the time any more than Xavier could afford to skip school. But sometimes more important things came up.

"You know what? Let's go." He grabbed his keys from the top desk drawer. "I'll just tell Bobby and Austin to call it a day when they're done with Mason Waterman's truck."

When he got done with that, he came back into the office to snag his ball cap off the hook. "Come on."

"Okay. If you're sure."

"Oh, I'm sure, all right. We don't have that many good days left this fall before snow hits at that elevation." Zadok locked up the office as they left.

Xavier stood at the hood of the truck. "Can I drive?"

Zadok's body froze but his mind raced. The kid had taken driver's ed at school in spring and earned his learner's license. They didn't drive many places, and Xavier hadn't seemed all that interested in practicing. But now, headed onto a narrow, rutted logging road with steep drops? Not a good time. Yet, how could he squelch the one thing his baby brother showed any interest in for several weeks or even months?

"Sure." He tossed the keys at Xavier. "Are you comfortable backing out of the parking space?"

"No sweat." Xavier didn't look as confident as he sounded, but Zadok had to let him try. There wasn't much back there to hit unless he tried really hard.

Lord, please let him not try to hit anything. And I pray that this will be the breakthrough we need around here.

Zadok couldn't remember the last time he'd sat in the passenger seat. Never in this truck.

Xavier shoved in the key and cranked the engine. He gave Zadok a lopsided grin. "Last chance to change your mind."

And lose that flicker? Not a chance. Zadok snapped his

buckle in place and prayed he wouldn't need to test its effectiveness today, to say nothing of the airbags.

The truck lurched backward then slammed to an abrupt halt.

"Easy does it. Gentle pressure is all you need."

"Right." Xavier eased back in an arc before applying the brakes again. "Better?"

"Yeah. Good job."

A fleeting grin swept the teen's face as he shifted into drive. Progress was rough and intermittent at Galena Landing's lone stoplight. Then Xavier guided the truck across the bridge and past the plot of land where Arleigh's flower farm used to be before the February flood had destroyed her greenhouses and ancient mobile home.

Zadok had managed a few breaths by the time the truck was headed toward the valley's edge. They passed Ackerman Farms and bore down on the forestry road at the end of Thompson Road going a little faster than necessary.

Was this how Dad had felt when he taught his older two to drive?

Zadok had never figured just how much his parents had done for him. Kids took a lot for granted. No wonder Xavier was struggling. Zadok didn't even know all the pieces he should be picking up, but were they all his responsibility? As Xavier liked to point out, Zadok wasn't actually the parent. But the kid obviously wasn't capable of managing on his own at 16. Zadok had been far more responsible, and so had Quincey.

But neither of them had been orphans at that age, either.

He'd never prayed as hard as he did as Xavier guided the truck up the abandoned logging road. Finally they came to a stop at the lookout, and Zadok held out his hand. "I'll drive the return trip."

Xavier laughed and slapped the keys into it. "You're such an old man."

"Maybe so. I really like living."

Xavier snorted and jumped out of the truck.

Zadok pocketed the keys and followed his brother to the edge of the precipice. "Quite a view, huh?"

"There's the Canadian border, right? That slash line cut through the forest?"

"Yup."

Xavier looked the other direction. "Galena Lake looks pretty small from up here."

"Perspective is everything."

The kid rolled his eyes. "Yeah, yeah."

The contrail from a jet gleamed in the blue sky way above. "I wonder where they've come from and where they're going."

Xavier shrugged. "Dunno."

"What does Galena Landing seem like to the passengers looking out the windows?"

"Just some dinky little town beside a puddle. If they can even see it at all."

"I think you're right." Zadok wasn't quite done. "But it's really important to us."

SEVEN

I don't need a tutor."

Juni looked to the study hall door where Xavier Shirkowski stood framed in the rectangle of light. "Hi, Xavier. Come on in."

"Did you hear me?"

"Sure. Did you hear me?"

He sighed and took a couple of steps. "Seriously."

"Have a seat." Juni pointed at the chair around the corner of the table. "If you don't want a tutor, then all you have to do is prove you don't need me. It will take a few weeks to catch up, but maybe less if you apply yourself."

He slumped into the chair and sighed again.

"Or, you can make it difficult, and we'll be seeing each other three times a week until the end of the school year, unless you get suspended before then. It's your choice."

The teen snorted a bitter laugh. "You make it sound so appealing."

"Here's the thing, Xavier. I looked back in your school

records. You've been a B student all along, so my bet is that this situation isn't because you don't understand the material. It's because you don't feel like performing."

His eyebrows flickered, but he said nothing.

"You're in my fifth period drama class."

"Yeah?"

"What have we been learning there?"

Xavier gave his head a little shake. "Is this part of the tutoring?"

"Not at all."

"Then... why?"

At least Juni had his attention. "Humor me. What have we been practicing in drama?"

"How to pretend to be someone else."

She chuckled. "Okay, sort of. And how do we do that?"

"By trying to think what it's like to be that person and then acting like them."

"Who have you pretended to be?"

"You mean in theater?"

He was catching her drift already. Maybe this wasn't going to be as painful as it had seemed it was going to be. "Let's start there, yes."

"A female zoologist."

"Was that easy or hard?"

Xavier shifted in his chair. "I never tried to think like a girl before."

That was what he'd absorbed from the practice? "How about the rest of the character?"

"She's smart. She cares about animals."

Juni was crawling out on a shaky limb. "So, in those ways, she's like you."

Xavier narrowed his gaze at her. "Sure."

"So, tell me about the Xavier Shirkowski whose report cards called him a team player." She glanced down at her notes. "Personable. Conscientious."

He crossed his arms over his chest, slouched deeper into the chair, and glowered at her. "His parents died."

"I'm sorry. That must have been extremely difficult for you."

"You think?"

She'd received a degree in education. There'd definitely been some psychology mixed into that, but it hadn't been the focus of her studies. She needed to tread carefully. "Yes, I can see how it would have been. My parents divorced when I was your age. That was rather traumatic, too."

"Not the same thing."

"I agree, partly because the hurt never had a chance to heal. My dad continued to jab at my mother for years afterward. There was no reprieve. Ever."

Xavier stared at her, clearly unimpressed.

"What other kinds of trauma have kids your age experienced?"

"Davy was in a car wreck that broke his back."

"Oh, man. That must be hard. How is he doing?"

"They moved to Boise to get better medical care. I haven't heard from him in a while."

Boise. The place Juni wished she could forget, but it

was still the state capital as well as the business and medical hub of Idaho.

"I don't know what this all has to do with algebra." Xavier shot her a glance.

"Not much," Juni admitted. "But it has a lot to do with you and why you don't feel like caring about school."

"What's the point?"

Twenty trite retorts danced on the tip of Juni's tongue, but she held them back. What would actually get the teen's attention? It was hard to know.

She could gain insight from Zadok. But... could she? If the teen's older brother held the keys to Xavier's motivation, wouldn't he have used them already? Sure, he would have.

"For today, I'd like you to do some play-acting."

The boy's eyebrows tipped up.

"Pretend you care about algebra. Pretend you're a smart kid — not much acting required there — and can ace this assignment in forty minutes." Juni tapped the paper in front of him.

"I don't want to."

She leaned closer and looked him in the eye. "I don't want to flunk you, either. I know you can perform if you choose to. You've proved it in drama class. So here." She nudged the paper. "Show me your acting ability on paper."

Xavier scanned the paper then offered her a woebegone look.

Juni held her breath. *Lord, please help me find the way to motivate this kid. He thinks he has it worse than anyone else, and it definitely hasn't been a stroll in the park, but he's alive and has people who care about him.*

Strangely, she was one of them.

With a sigh he must have pulled clear from his toenails, Xavier picked up the sharpened pencil and began to work.

Juni opened her bag and pulled out the felt raccoons she'd cut out last night along with embroidery floss. If her online store took off, she needed to be ready.

ZADOK ARRIVED at Ackerman Farm half an hour before the start of the market on Saturday. It was only to make sure of the setup. Mitchell had assured Zadok that Arleigh played classical music for her flowers via speakers he'd mounted for that purpose, and it would be easy to redirect the input from her tablet to his guitar pickup and microphone.

Okay, fine. He hadn't come early only for the setup. It was to see if he could catch Juni before things got busy to see how she was doing with Xavier. And to see what she thought of the photos and the work Quincey had been doing on a website.

Or maybe he just wanted to see Juni.

Which, of course, was the opposite of what she wanted. She'd made it abundantly clear that she'd prefer he didn't exist. She was a theater teacher, and she knew how to act out that preference.

Paula's car was already parked beside the greenhouse when Zadok turned in the drive. He pulled in beside her so he could offload his equipment. He'd move the truck beyond the barn to open access for shoppers before the market began.

Zadok grabbed an armload of instruments, headed for the greenhouse, and stopped just inside the door in surprise. "Whoa. This looks better than I expected."

Laughing, Arleigh came toward him wearing a green gardening apron. "I'm not sure how to respond to that! Either your expectations were low, or this is absolutely amazing." She turned to survey the space. "My bet is on basement-level expectations."

"Well, maybe. This greenhouse is bigger than the one you used to have." Last fall's market had been held at her former place that had been flooded out in February.

She smirked. "Yeah, I've come up in the world."

Had she and Mitchell made things official yet? Not that Zadok had heard of. A surreptitious glance at Arleigh's left hand did not reveal a diamond, so maybe he hadn't missed an announcement. It was coming, though.

And the thought created longing in his own heart, not that he was jealous of Mitchell or the man's newlywed brother, Treyan. No, Zadok had had no designs on Brittany Santoro or Arleigh O'Neill. His thoughts had been consumed by Juni O'Neill since she dropped back into his orbit last spring.

Truth? He'd never quite quit kicking himself since that

disastrous date. Why had he taken his professor's advice and gone against his own better judgment?

Juni might not have known ahead of time exactly whom she was meeting in the coffee shop, but Zadok had. His best friend, John, had been dating Juni's roommate, and Zadok had taken the opportunity to beg Tracie to set something up.

And then he'd wondered if his theology prof might be related to the girl with the same last name.

He should never have wondered. History had been turned with that one question.

Zadok scoffed under his breath, causing a questioning look from Arleigh. He shook his head. "Where am I setting up?"

"Halfway down the left side. See the gap in tables?"

He did. He also noticed that the table directly across from the opening was loaded with bouquets, and his breath stuttered. Was that Mitchell's idea? Arleigh's? Or maybe Paula's. The market manager was a creature of habit, after all, and might have simply duplicated the layout of the outdoor market. That was probably it.

There was a whole lot less room between the rows of tables in the greenhouse than between booths in Lakeside Park, though. Unless Juni had her own table... no. A cardboard box labeled mermaids sat on top of another labeled dragons beside the bouquets. Juni would be directly across from the minstrel station. It would be like he was singing to her.

Zadok laid his instrument cases on the low bench at

the back of his designated area and pivoted for his next load, nearly running into Paula.

"Hi, Zadok. Is this okay?"

"Sure. I'll grab the rest of my stuff and do a sound check with Mitchell, unless there's something else you need me to do first?"

"No, that's fine." Paula drummed her fingers on her ever-present clipboard. "Do you really think people will drive all the way out here for the market?"

He suppressed an eyeroll. They'd hashed this out in vendor meetings over and over and *over*. "They showed up in droves last year to Arleigh's greenhouse."

"That was much closer to town."

"True, but it was also far enough they had to drive. This is only a couple of miles further."

"Four point three miles further."

"So, five minutes. They'll be here, Paula. You'll see."

Brittany Ackerman bustled in, carrying a tray of salted caramel cupcakes.

Zadok's stomach growled as she went by.

She tossed him a saucy wink. "Didn't you have breakfast?"

"Coffee and a doughnut from the drive-through."

"Which is *not* the breakfast of champions."

"Maybe I was holding out for a cupcake?"

She set the box on the table beyond the O'Neill sisters' display. "I'm not allowed to sell any until the bell rings to start the market. Paula's rules."

Paula cleared her throat. "You could donate a couple to the cause. Taste testers, you know."

Zadok laughed. "I will totally volunteer. I'll even make a donation later, if you like."

"Are you all set up and ready for the market to open in —" Brittany glanced at her watch "—twenty minutes?"

"Busted. Save a cupcake for me." Zadok turned back toward the door that had been propped open with a bag of potting soil just in time to dodge Juni as she entered with more boxes. "Need a hand?"

She glowered at him. "I've got everything, thanks."

Of course, she didn't require help. At least, not from him. This time he made it all the way to the truck and returned with his booster and box of music. Not that he needed it for much of anything, but he was working on a couple of new songs for Sunday worship, and those would be better with focused practice. He didn't have to explain to anyone what he was playing, especially if he wasn't singing along out loud. A few astute souls might recognize the music on Sunday morning.

He moved his truck to the other end of the parking area, noting that Mitchell and Juni had done the same. Even Arleigh's vibrantly painted VW van was out of the way of the incoming tide of shoppers.

Unless Paula's panic was not in vain. Could she be right, that town residents wouldn't drive this far for fresh produce and other market goodies? It was only the beginning of October. Most weren't thinking of Christmas gifts or decor yet.

Mitchell had placed a mound of huge pumpkins in the back corner of the greenhouse and shone lights on it from several angles. Now his boys clambered all over them while Arleigh snapped a few photos. Huh. A fall photo op? Someone was thinking.

Zadok selected his guitar for the first round of music and tested the sound system. After Mitchell's thumbs-up, he let his fingers do the entertaining while he watched the vendors position their wares on the wide greenhouse tables.

Jean Stedman had brought her church-potluck-sized coffee urn and set it up with foam cups, a box of sugar cubes, and a carton of half-and-half. She arranged a few plastic-wrapped puffed-wheat squares in a nearby basket.

The most recent addition to the market, pottery, sat next to Jean's booth. Nila was new to town and created a colorful array of mugs and bowls. Zadok eyed them as his fingers danced over the guitar strings. Maybe Quincey would like one of those mugs for Christmas.

Green Acres Farm had a double booth loaded with honey, eggs, frozen chickens, apples, and nuts from their farm. Zadok had never wondered what nuts grew in any particular area, but the market had taught him this climate was good for hazelnuts and walnuts.

Mitchell's table, next to the O'Neill sisters, was heaped with squashes, tomatoes, and root vegetables. Interesting that there wasn't much overlap with Green Acres. Was that purposeful on either side?

And then there was Solaria with their freeze-dried soup mixes, developed from their own vegetables, Radish Farm with their fermented pickles and kraut, Mrs. Kozak with her jellies and jams, and Risen with their amazing sourdough offerings.

Zadok didn't know what the market had looked like a few years ago when Paula had first been tasked with reviving the long-dormant institution, but it was certainly a bustling place now. Even if the plastic-canvas toilet-paper covers made his eyes bleed. Mrs. Drummond must sell enough of the things to warrant coming back week after week.

There'd likely be more crafty creations as Christmas approached — his perusal landed on Juni's table — but none could compare to the creativity Juni exemplified. A guy didn't need to have little kids to see that her toys were works of art.

With a start, he realized he was staring at her. Even stranger, she was looking straight back at him with her eyebrows tipped up. He must have been making it weird, or she'd never challenge him back like that.

He bobbed his eyebrows at her and found the fingering for Chris Tomlin's catchy tune *Gifts from God.* It wasn't really a congregational sing-along for all its message reminded him that the best things in life were straight from God's hands. And wasn't that a worthwhile reminder any day of the week? The lyrics spoke of looking back and realizing things had maybe turned out the way they should, that God's plan was bigger than the songwriter's own.

Zadok's fingers faltered as the lyrics paraded through his head. It was a peppy country-style tune. Maybe he should just sing the words out. Maybe it was okay for her to hear the message.

The bell rang to indicate the opening of this Saturday's

market. A dozen people swarmed in and began taking in the wares.

Juni still watched him.

All right, then. He nodded to her, stepped up to the mic, and began to sing.

And later, he'd make it a point to talk to her. To go way back to that January night and apologize. Would she accept his attempt at amends? No way to know if he didn't try. At least then she'd know the whole story, such as it was.

EIGHT

J uni hadn't been sure what to expect from the first indoor market, but it was a little underwhelming. More people had come than last week outside in the cold rain, though.

"Don't worry. It will pick up by mid-November." Arleigh fiddled with her fall flower bouquets again. Some of the gerbera daisies, mums, and ornamental grasses stood in pottery vases Nila had crafted. The potter had taken one of the floral arrangements to her own table.

Cross-promotion sounded great, but Juni couldn't see any other vendor she could reciprocate with. Didn't stop her from scanning up one side of the greenhouse and down the other. Anything to keep from looking at the musician no more than ten feet in front of her.

Because every time her gaze slid past Zadok, he seemed to be watching her, and that was all kinds of creepy. It might simply be because of the proximity, but she doubted it. It seemed he'd made up his mind to talk to her, if Monday at the school had been any indication, and she needed to be increasingly on guard to prevent an opportunity.

"I love those lyrics." Arleigh perched on her tall stool and swayed from side to side with her eyes closed.

What song was Zadok playing? Juni wasn't familiar with it. She shook her head. "I don't think I know it."

"As Long as You are Glorified." Arleigh hummed along. "Such a great reminder that it's not all about me, you know? God isn't good only when I'm doing well. He's good when I'm good, but also when I'm struggling. I love that He doesn't change. I need that in my life. Well, you know."

Juni did know. She felt the same. Aside from Zadok and his reminders of the past, she could be really happy here in Galena Landing. It was a joy to see her mother several times a week and to share a home with her sister. Of course, that was likely to change sooner rather than later, the way Arleigh and Mitchell were so starry-eyed over each other. Eventually Arleigh would marry the farmer and move upstairs.

And would Juni still be content to live in the basement suite after that? Um, that would be a big, fat no. By the time the wedding rolled around, she was going to need a plan.

Find a place of her own? Find a job in some other town?

Drat Zadok, anyway. If he weren't an increasingly large part of her life — market, church, and now school — she wouldn't give another thought to moving away. She liked it here. And she'd like it even more when she had a baby niece or nephew to spoil, plus Mitchell's kids were growing on her.

The only solution was to keep on avoiding Zadok as best she could. Maybe she should pray *he'd* be the one to move away. He was the one who didn't belong.

She couldn't, in all good conscience, pray that before Xavier graduated from high school, and that was still 20 months away, not that anyone was counting.

Fine. She'd keep ignoring Zadok. She'd managed okay for the first few months she'd been here. She could shore up her defenses and make it through. Oh! She could pray he'd meet some other woman and marry her. That would help.

Wouldn't it?

Juni didn't want to think about how unsettled that thought made her gut. She leaned over to her sister. "When is Mitchell going to pop the question?"

Arleigh's eyes lit up. "I don't know. Also, why is tradition so firmly on the guy's side in situations like this?"

"Like you'd have the nerve to propose." Juni knew she wouldn't. Dad's indoctrinations of a woman's place ran deep.

"I could be tempted." Arleigh sighed. "I'm so happy, sis. I'm praying you'll find the right guy, too."

And here Juni was praying she'd *avoid* the right guy. The wrong guy. Any guy. Well, Zadok. Even her thoughts were jumbled with the man's strong tenor filling the sound waves.

Arleigh nudged her. "The Music Man would be amazing, I think."

"Nah. Not him."

Speaking of praying, Juni ought to get on with begging God for more shoppers today. Between her sister and the singer, she had altogether too much time to ponder the *could have beens*.

Like Arleigh, Juni had been conditioned to think the guy should be the leader in the relationship and then in their shared life. It sounded great, in theory. Biblical, even. But not when paired with narcissism.

Granted, not every man had that personality type, but Juni knew for a fact that Zadok shared it with her father. That meant there was no way she'd allow herself to be attracted to the man.

It hadn't worked. Wasn't working. She was already attracted, and chopping the attraction off at the knees wasn't working well for her. However, it must.

Arleigh's shoulder pressed against hers. "I don't understand why you reject him outright. You don't even know him."

"I know his type," Juni muttered.

"You don't know him well enough to know his type."

Juni hesitated. "Yes, I do."

"How?" Arleigh studied her through narrowed eyes. "Unless you've been out on a secret date and forgot to tell me."

Juni couldn't keep the snort completely muffled. If her sister only knew.

"Did I nail it?"

Lying was a sin that Juni didn't make a habit of. But

the hesitation seemed to be answer enough for Arleigh to pounce.

"When?"

Juni's eager gaze landed on a middle-aged woman approaching the booth. "Mrs. Nemesek! Thanks for coming out today."

The woman smiled. "Rosemary, remember? And how could I miss a chance for this little community gathering? I love the market."

"Me, too! It really is like its own community." One Juni mostly liked.

"I'd love two bouquets today, Arleigh. And Juni, can I get three sets of woodland creatures? I'm preparing shoeboxes for Samaritan's Purse, and those would be lovely additions, I think. They're small, lightweight, and whimsical. Plus, I think they transcend culture."

"Absolutely. What a great idea." Maybe she should come up with a safari set, too. Hmm. Juni wrapped woodland creatures while Rosemary chose which bouquets she wanted.

"How's Steve today?" Arleigh asked as she processed the payment.

Rosemary's husband had suffered from Guillain-Barré for years, from what Juni had heard. The viral infection had deeply weakened his muscles and balance but done nothing to quell his inner joy in the Lord.

"He's at the farm today, hanging out with Zachary and Jo's boys. John and Arthur always have a project on the go, and it does Steve's heart good to be part of the action."

"That's great!" Arleigh wrapped the stems in damp paper towels, then in a bag, and handed it over.

Rosemary tucked her purchases into her market bag with a smile of thanks and moved on to chat with Mitchell.

Arleigh wrapped her arm around Juni's shoulder, squeezed, and whispered right in her ear. "You are absolutely going to tell me the story of Zadok. Don't think I'll forget."

"Nothing to tell?" Too bad Juni couldn't pour more firmness into her voice.

"I'm not buying what you're selling. You. Me—" Arleigh waggled her finger between them "—we'll talk later."

Great. All that while Zadok crooned love songs from much too nearby.

ZADOK PLAYED on while Rosemary Nemesek made her way around the market. More townspeople arrived after that. Things never got busy, but it picked up and stayed steadier. Arleigh sold out of bouquets, the produce vendors' displays diminished, and Juni sold several sets, too.

Not that he was watching but, of course, he was. Because, having made up his mind to get to the bottom of this impasse between them, he wasn't going to let another day go by without an apology, even if it meant knocking on the door of the basement suite and begging Arleigh O'Neill not to send him away before he'd talked to her sister.

Only that kind of behavior would only make Juni even more certain of his misogyny.

Lord? It was handy he could pray while he played. Not so much while he sang, but he didn't need to use his voice for four hours straight. *Please give wisdom.*

He'd wondered if he should just let it go, like Juni seemed to want to do. But it wasn't doing her any good, either, from what he could see. She was sunny to everyone in Galena Landing but bitter toward him. He deserved it. He didn't deserve the gift of her forgiveness. But he wanted it, desperately.

Lord, please?

He glanced at the clock on the end wall. Today's market would close in ten minutes. He switched out the ukulele for the violin and swept into a jig to help the time dance by.

Finally, Paula rang her bell to signal the market's end. Across from him, Arleigh turned to help Mitchell pack the remains of his produce into crates while Juni swept her crafts into waiting boxes like she couldn't get out of the greenhouse quickly enough. Probably true.

Zadok set his violin in its case and fastened the clasps.

Juni rounded the end of her table and reached toward the box in the middle.

He pivoted toward her. "Here. Let me get that for you."

Her startled gaze met his. "Thanks, but no thanks. It's not heavy, and I've got it."

"Please let me." He lifted it. "Looks like you did pretty well for a fall market before the Christmas rush."

"I *said* I've got it."

"I heard you. Lead the way."

"Zadok, I—"

"Nice of you to help, Zadok," Arleigh said with a bright smile. "I loved your music choices this morning. I'm also thankful we're right across from you so we can hear the lyrics clearly. That one song, *As Long as You are Glorified*, gets me in the heart every time."

"Me, too. Thanks." He shot a smile toward Juni's sister and kept his grip on the box. "After you."

"Zadok..." Juni growled.

He met her narrowed gaze. "Please." What was he going to do if she grabbed it back? They had too much of an audience for a tug-of-war but, without their audience, he'd stand no chance at all. He might not, anyway. Could he accept that? Not without having his say.

She closed her eyes for a second and tightened her jaw. "Fine."

Zadok blinked and nearly asked her to repeat herself, but she was already halfway to the greenhouse doors while he stared after her like a lovesick puppy.

He wasn't one. It was just that others might see him that way. He hurried after her — no one would mess with his instruments in the next five or so minutes.

She veered abruptly to the left just outside the door. "May I have my box now that you've made your point and made me look like an ungrateful wretch to all the other vendors?"

Is that how she saw his insistence? "That wasn't my goal at all."

Juni crossed her arms over her coral-toned sweater.

That color looked great on her, but he couldn't let himself be distracted by her beauty. "May I have five minutes of your time?"

She glanced at the box he clutched then back at his face. "Whatever. Get it over with."

"Juni, I'm truly sorry for that night."

She closed her eyes and shook her head slightly.

His heart sank. "I begged Tracie to set up a blind date that week in college."

"Uh huh."

"I'd noticed you all through that fall, but I didn't think I stood a chance."

Nothing flickered on her face. She either had no thoughts on the topic, or she was drawing on her acting experience. Hopefully the latter. "And then I made a mistake. I asked my theology professor if you were related to him."

"So I heard." Her voice held no emotion.

"He told me what a girl like you would want in a guy..." Zadok swallowed hard. "He seemed so sure of himself."

Juni leaned into his space, eyes blazing. "Any man that parrots my father is no one I want to spend five minutes with. Got that? He's wrong on so many levels."

"I know that now." He'd sort of known it then, but he'd stepped out on a limb, trusting the older man. He'd been all kinds of a fool.

"That's great. I'm happy for you." She snatched the

box out of his arms. "But I in no way want a replay with you or anyone else. Got it?"

"I'm truly not that guy. Please forgive me."

Several vendors passed by, pushing hand carts and carrying baskets. Zadok stepped further off the path and into her space.

Juni backed up a few feet and held her box like a shield between them. "I understand the biblical dictate to forgive. Ephesians 4:32 says, *be kind and compassionate to one another, forgiving each other, just as in Christ God forgave you.* So this is me, forgiving you. Nowhere does it tell me to let you do the same thing to me again."

"I won't. I promise. Please give me a chance. Get to know the real me, not the college kid who was gullible and trusted the wrong advisor against his better judgment at the time."

But her head didn't stop shaking. "No. Just no."

How could he let it go? He needed to, or he'd become exactly the obnoxious, egotistical man she thought he was.

"Juni, I was a fool. Hopefully, I'm much less of one now than I was four years ago, but I can hardly blame you for not trusting my word on that."

She stifled a snort.

"So, let me just put this out there. You had my attention for months before that night. I blew everything in the blink of an eye. I've never forgiven myself for what I said to you. And I've never forgotten you. I've compared every woman to you for four years, and I was so sure when you moved to Galena Landing last spring that it was orchestrated by God to give me a second chance."

"Are you quite done?"

"Almost. Juni, I care for you. A lot. I would like to date you."

"As if," she muttered, her eyes rolling.

"But I can see you're not there yet. And maybe you won't ever be." That would be his cross to bear. "But please, if you find yourself changing your mind about me, *you* ask *me* out. I'll say yes. No question. But the ball is in your court. So we're clear."

She narrowed her gaze at him. "This is me taking that ball of yours and heaving it into the middle of Galena Lake, where — oh look — it's sinking without a trace. Just so we're quite clear."

Zadok took a step backward. "We're perfectly clear." He pivoted, and Mitchell Ackerman nearly ran him over with a loaded hand cart.

Juni marched across the yard, head high.

"Trouble in paradise?" Mitchell glanced between them.

Zadok snorted. "There never was a paradise."

"Those O'Neill women sure have a chip on their shoulders, huh? I mean, Arleigh's past that now, but it was tough going there for a while."

Zadok studied the other man. Was Mitchell telling tales out of turn? More to the point, was Zadok so transparent that everyone knew he had a thing for Juni, even though he thought he'd buried it? "You got any advice?"

Mitchell shook his head. "There are two sides to every

story. Arleigh and I were attracted to each other, but we both had hang-ups that made getting on the same page difficult. Seemed impossible at times, actually, and I wasn't always sure that was the goal I even wanted, if you know what I mean."

Zadok nodded. He understood far better than he wished he did. Why couldn't he put Juni out of his mind? There weren't a lot of single, 20-something, Christian women in Galena Landing, but nothing was holding him to northern Idaho after Xavier graduated from high school.

If Xavier ever graduated.

Juni O'Neill was the key to getting his brother out of his funk and into his cap and gown.

"Hmm, I guess I do have advice." Mitchell tipped the hand cart back and wheeled it a few inches. "Two pieces, come to think of it."

"Lay it on me."

"First, man, you've got to pray. If God's not in it, you don't want it. And if you can't honestly say that, pray some more. Because that's the absolute bottom line."

Zadok nodded. He understood. He didn't have to like that advice — yet — but he knew it. "And the second piece?"

"Become the man God wants you to be. Nothing to do with her or anyone else, just between you and Him."

He palmed his jaw. "Makes sense. How did you get so wise?'

The other man chuckled. "The school of hard knocks.

Is there any other way to learn anything?" He wheeled the hand cart toward the farmhouse.

School of hard knocks. Zadok had kind of hoped he'd already graduated from that one, but possibly not. He made his way back to his station to pack up his instruments.

Mitchell Ackerman's advice seemed to stack up with God's word in a way that Grant O'Neill's had not, but Zadok hadn't been asking or listening back then.

Now? First and foremost, he needed to be the man God wanted him to be. The man Quincey and Xavier needed.

He needed to let his dream of a future with Juni drift to the bottom of Galena Lake with that metaphorical ball.

NINE

S quash soup? Yum." Juni hovered in the basement suite's kitchen door. If she tried to hide, her sister would only come drag her out. That didn't keep her from wanting to avoid the coming conversation at any cost.

Almost any cost, but not at driving a wedge between her and Arleigh. They'd spent years distant in miles and distant in relationship, and Juni wasn't willing to go back there. She needed her sister. Needed their mom.

"Yeah, I snagged a loaf of sourdough bread from the Risen booth at the market, too. One of these days I should figure out how to make it." Arleigh wrinkled her nose. "Bread is intimidating."

"If either of us could figure it out, it would be you."

Arleigh scoffed. "You're more patient than I am, doing things with your hands. Me, I just throw dirt and seeds around."

"And grow gorgeous flowers. But what I meant was,

your schedule is more adjustable. I'm not around all day long, so making bread couldn't fit in."

"There are weekends."

"Market on Saturday, and church on Sunday."

"Whatever." Arleigh laughed. "People who want to bake homemade bread figure it out, I think. I heard Claire over at Green Acres is having a sourdough workshop in a week or two, but it's all day Saturday."

"Hmm." Juni contemplated. "It's not like I'm selling tons at the market every week. It wouldn't hurt to skip once. Or you could even sell my stuff."

"You've done it for me a time or two. But, a minute ago, you said you weren't interested in learning to bake bread... so I'm wondering if you're just trying to avoid the market. Or perhaps trying to avoid Zadok Shirkowski."

Juni should have known the conversation would spiral in. It wasn't like her sister hadn't warned her. She braced herself.

"So... tell me why you abhor Zadok."

She hesitated. Abhor seemed like a strong word. Also, possibly the right one.

"I'm waiting. Because you met him before you moved here in March, right?" Arleigh stirred the soup and skewered Juni with her eyes.

"You'll make a great mother. You've got *the look* down pat."

"Talk."

Was Juni required to tell the truth, the whole truth, and nothing but the truth? A perusal of her sister's expression assured her that Arleigh would not let it go until she knew everything... or thought she did.

But what was the point in holding back a tiny sliver here or there? Even Tracie didn't know the whole story, only that the blind date she'd set up had not been a dream come true. If her roommate hadn't been dating Zadok's friend John at the time, Juni might have gone into more detail, but there had been no point.

Juni let out a long breath. "We both attended SIU. He was a senior when I was a sophomore."

"Uh huh." Arleigh began slicing the bread but glanced up when Juni was silent too long.

"We didn't have many classes together with that big a gap, plus different majors, though he took theater as an elective in fall semester."

"Uh huh."

"I wasn't there to goof around. Dad made sure I knew that his funding of my education was dependent on me taking school seriously."

"Of course."

"It seemed reasonable." It still did. Kids who got a free college ride rarely appreciated the sacrifices their parents made on their behalf.

"My roommate that year was Tracie Dunham. She studied, but she also dated quite a lot. Just before Christmas, she began dating John, who happened to be Zadok's roommate."

Arleigh set the bread knife down and gave Juni her full attention.

"She kept saying, you should go out with this guy. Or,

that guy's really nice. How about that one over there? And I was like, no, no, no. Not interested."

"Why didn't you date? Lots of students do and still get good grades. It's not an either-or situation."

Juni sighed. "In a word, Dad. He's a theology prof there, not that I was in any of his classes. But I knew he was watching everything I did and, well, judging it. I wanted to get my degree and then get away from him."

"And he was paying the bills."

"Yeah. Until the last semester, when he punished me for daring to take an elective not related to my degree. And suddenly Galway's desire to play hockey overruled my education."

"Because he's a boy, so he's more important." Arleigh ladled soup into two bowls.

"Plus, he's Genevieve's son, and she's so much better than Mom ever was."

"I pity Genevieve."

"Me, too." Juni bit her lip. "I tried to talk to her a couple of times, but she won't hear anything against Dad. She's the perfect, demure, loyal housewife he always wanted."

"That makes me pity her even more. Here. I'll pray, and let's eat. Don't think you're done telling your story, because you're not."

Juni slid into the chair across from her sister and listened to Arleigh's thankfulness. Then she picked up her spoon and had a slurp of soup. "This is great, sis. Thanks."

"It is pretty good. Mitchell has tons of squash in the

storeroom where that came from, so you might be seeing this meal a lot in the next few months."

"Bring it on."

Arleigh slathered butter on her bread. "Eat, but don't stop talking."

"Yes, boss." Juni had a bite of bread. It was warm, tangy, and amazing. Maybe she *would* take that workshop. Arleigh was right. Women had figured out how to manage both work and domestic life decades ago.

Right, *women* had. It was still their job. Dad would be proud.

Juni shook Dad out of her head. She couldn't let him rule her life from 500 miles away. But... wasn't she doing that by punishing Zadok for something he'd done four years ago?

"Tracie begged me to let her set up one blind date for me. She said she'd stop if I'd only give it a try."

"So, you agreed, to get her off your back."

"Yes. I was to meet the mystery man at the campus coffee shop on Friday evening. I was to set a box of salted taffy on the table, and the guy would bring a red rose."

"Oooh, romantic."

Juni pushed the bowl away. Two bites, and her stomach was roiling too much to enjoy the delectable soup. "So I sat there and waited, and Zadok came in. He glanced around, came straight over, and laid the rose beside my teacup."

"He knew whom he was looking for?"

"He did. I was the only one who was *blind*."

"I don't understand. Did you already dislike him? Would you have told Tracie no if you knew who it was?"

"No, I thought he was kind of cute." Juni huffed a laugh. "And when an upperclassman notices a lowly soph, you're honored. I knew he was in the theology track, though, and I knew all about men who were overly religious. Dad taught me well."

Arleigh studied her. "You do know that there are lots and lots of men in ministry who aren't like Dad. Men who believe women are gifted and qualified for many positions in churches. Even preachers and senior pastors."

"Those men exist, in theory."

"Talk to Pastor Ron. You'll find—"

Juni chopped her hand to cut her sister off. "It doesn't matter. I've come to peace with it, since I'm not cut out to be a preacher, anyway."

"Back to your date."

"Right. The date." Why couldn't Arleigh have been sidetracked? "It wasn't five minutes in, and we're talking about life goals — as college students do — and he spouts off with his desire to have a traditional marriage with a woman who will be the perfect hostess, housewife, and mother. While not having a day job, because isn't that every woman's dream?"

"Uh oh."

"And I knew he'd been drinking Dad's Kool-Aid. Indeed, he was one of Dad's protégés. Should have seen that coming."

"So... you walked out?"

"After telling him exactly what I thought of his views."

"Which was...?"

"That women today have a voice. They don't need a man to fulfill them, and they definitely weren't put on this planet to be men's servants."

"How did he take that?"

"He was still sputtering when I left the coffee shop. I was furious, but there was no one to dump on. Couldn't talk to Dad. Couldn't talk to Tracie, since she thought Zadok was almost as wonderful as John. I didn't really have anyone else I was close to back then."

Arleigh's hand covered Juni's. "I wish I'd known. I'd have understood. I'd have been there for you."

"I know that now." Juni swallowed the sobs that wanted to surge out. "But then, I felt very, very alone."

"Can I practice driving?" Xavier raised his eyebrows at Zadok as they sat at the lunch table.

Finally! There was something Zadok could use as leverage. "Maybe? Is your homework done?"

The teen scowled. "I've got until Monday morning to do that."

At least he wasn't insisting he had none. Progress was progress. "How much do you have? How are things working out with Ms. O'Neill?" Zadok had been dying to ask.

"She's okay, I guess."

"Ms. O'Neill is amazing!" Quincey put in. "You're lucky she's your tutor. I had Mr. Weebly, and he was convinced the female mind could never understand math."

"Was he wrong?" Xavier smirked.

Uh oh.

Quincey narrowed her gaze. "I'll have you know I got an A in his class to prove him wrong. You be the judge."

Time to intervene. "Girls can be just as good at math as guys. Lack of a Y chromosome has nothing to do with brain cells." Or with a lot of things, Zadok had come to realize. "Tell me what homework you have, and we'll negotiate driving time."

Xavier eyed him suspiciously. "What do you mean, negotiate?"

"I mean that for every hour you spend studying today — and I mean studying, not gazing out the window — I'll take you driving for an hour tomorrow afternoon." How he'd get his own weekend chores done, Zadok wasn't sure, but he'd figure it out.

Ha. Maybe he'd need to take a page out of the play-book he was giving his kid brother. While Xavier was studying, Zadok should be working on his own stuff. Then they'd both have tomorrow free.

"I probably only have two hours of homework. I want to drive more than that."

Quincey bounced on her toes. "Maybe Zay will take you longer if you work ahead. He said studying, not just doing assigned work."

Right. Trust his sister to spot the loophole. "She's right. If you study for four hours today, and you can prove it to me, we'll take all afternoon tomorrow. Where do you want to go?"

Xavier brightened. "Can we take the mountain road into Montana?"

Huh. Not what Zadok had expected. "I don't see why not. Quincey, want to come?"

"Oooh, sibling bonding time. Yeah, no. I want to prep some dinners for next week. We talked about doing the meal planning thing at Green Acres, but I looked at the agenda and figured I could easily do something similar without paying the extra. I just need to figure out five or six dinners, get the ingredients, and do whatever prep I can ahead of time to make it quicker when we all get home after work."

"I should help with that." If he didn't, Juni would accuse him of chauvinism. Not that she'd ever find out unless one of his sibs told tales.

"I could use some ideas," Quincey admitted. "But what were your plans for the weekend before Xavier started making his own demands?"

"Hey!" Xavier sputtered.

"The gutters need cleaning, and the leaves need raking. Most of the trees are bare now."

Quincey raised her eyebrows at Xavier. "I'd offer to come help you rake, but someone probably needs to keep an eye on the kid, or he'll only pretend to do schoolwork."

"I'm not a baby. You don't have to stare at me while I'm studying."

This conversation had more twists and turns than a

Mario Kart game. Zadok sorted through the basics. "Okay, here's the deal."

Both siblings looked at him expectantly.

"Xav, what homework do you have? Is it one class or more than one? Show me where you're at and what you plan to get done this afternoon. You're right. Neither Quincey nor I can watch you every minute, so you've got to be responsible."

Trusting Xavier hadn't turned out too well in the past, but it sounded like he was willing to give it a try. Who knew driving hours would be the key to the teen's cooperation?

"I can do that." Xavier stuck out his tongue at Quincey. "I don't need a babysitter."

Zadok turned to Quincey. "Go ahead and start on a meal plan while I clean the gutters. Then we can rake the yard together and figure out more details about the menu. Does that work?"

"Sure! I want to do Meatless Monday and Taco Tuesday and—"

"Nooo!" Xavier fake-gagged. "Don't take away my meat. Don't you listen to health news? We're all starving for protein."

"But it's a thing!" Quincey insisted.

"Sorry, I'm with Xav on this one."

His sister's face fell. "But..."

Zadok held up his hand. "We can talk about it. Xavier, show me your homework. Quincey, find an idea for a vegetarian meal so amazing we won't miss the meat."

Xavier clasped his throat in a chokehold and slowly slumped in his chair.

Quincey glared at him. "I can do that."

Zadok looked at the remains of lunch on the table. While they'd talked, they'd also demolished a pot of soup and grilled cheese sandwiches. "Maybe Soup-and-Sandwich Saturday is a thing."

Quincey brightened. "If not, it should be!"

"So long as there's *meat*," groused Xavier.

Now was not the time to point out how few specks of chicken Zadok had noticed in his bowl. It might as well have been vegetarian for all the protein there'd been. He pushed back his chair. "We all know what we're doing. I'll get the table cleared while you grab your textbooks, Xav. Let's execute this plan."

But the day didn't seem so grim, even with hours of outdoor labor in front of him. It finally seemed as though his siblings were ready to pick up their own slack. Working together to make their household operate would make everything go more smoothly.

Zadok stacked the bowls and plates and carried them into the kitchen, where Quincey was already ladling the leftover soup into a fridge container.

Now, if only Juni O'Neill hadn't taken his heart and tossed it into the depths of Galena Lake along with that figurative ball, life would be nearly perfect.

He winced at the thought. Wasn't his joy and happiness supposed to come from serving the Lord, not in a romantic relationship? That's what he'd been taught in divinity school. God came first, then his wife and family, then ministry.

Right now, Zadok's family consisted of his siblings.

Whatever you do in word or deed, do all to the glory of God.

And that included managing this household. He might not have asked for this job, but it was his, all the same.

He'd laid it out for Juni. It was up to her what happened next. Her and God. Zadok's only recourse was to ask God to lead her. To lead them, if there were to be a them.

But Quincey and Xavier? He had no doubt of his responsibility to his siblings. They had to be number one. Well, number two, behind his personal relationship with Jesus.

But leaving Juni in God's hands was going to prove a challenge.

TEN

A re you a vegetarian?"

Juni blinked at the teenage boy sitting across the study hall table. "Um, no. Why do you ask?" As far as she knew, Xavier wasn't in foods class this semester.

"Quincey has decided we're having Meatless Mondays." The boy rolled his eyes. "Can you convince her growing guys need real protein?"

Juni leaned across and tapped his textbook. "Is this part of your homework?"

"No, but it should be in biology. Our bodies are biological, right?"

She laughed. "You're not completely wrong, but I'm pretty sure this isn't part of your current unit."

"Humor me."

"Finish the math questions on page 237. Then we'll talk."

Xavier eyed her for a moment before nodding and turning back to his schoolwork.

Juni hadn't thought about reducing the amount of meat in her diet since college, and then it had been for economic reasons. Rice and beans were cheap and a complete protein. She'd eaten that basic combination so many times after Dad cut her off that she never wanted to see them again. Surely there were actual tasty recipes, though. She'd basically dumped canned pork-and-beans over instant rice back then. She glanced up as someone entered the room. Quincey Shirkowski? A quick glance at Xavier proved he'd noticed his sister but was pretending not to. Was this some sort of ambush?

"Hi, Juni." Quincey spoke quietly as she slid into a chair at the end of the table. "How's my little brother doing? Studying hard?"

He shot her a scowl.

Quincey wasn't Xavier's guardian, but maybe Zadok had sent her for an update? That way, he wouldn't have to talk to Juni himself. Nah, he'd look for any excuse he could.

"We're doing fine," Juni replied cautiously. "What's on your mind? I'm sure you didn't accidentally wander into the high school."

The girl snickered. "Not so random. I wanted to talk to you about meal planning."

"*Meat* planning," mumbled Xavier.

"You're such a dude." Quincey punched his arm.

"Thanks for the compliment."

Juni managed not to smirk at their snark, but it was

hard. It must be fun to have a brother or two... although Quincey might disagree. "I'm no expert in meal planning."

"You have to know more than I do." Quincey pulled a notebook out of her bag, opened it, and pushed it across to Juni, narrowly missing a stack of felt pieces. "I thought it might be helpful to have themes to work with. What do you think?"

Juni glanced at the list. Meatless Monday. Taco Tuesday. One-Dish Wednesday. Pizza Thursday. Foreign Friday. Soup-and-Sandwich Saturday. Pasta Sunday.

She looked up. "Sounds good, but why are you doing this instead of Zadok?" She knew why, and Quincey would confirm it any second now. Planning and cooking meals were women's work. Right? Right.

"He's been doing everything, and it seems like it's time for me to pick up some of the slack. I get off work earlier than he does, after all."

Juni's eyebrows angled up. "Everything?"

The girl sighed. "Nearly everything. I've been fixing lunches on the weekends since he's busy both mornings. But honestly?" She leaned closer. "I'm getting bored of the same old stuff all the time. We get far too much take-out, but Zay's tired at the end of the day. I get it. I am, too. I work harder physically out at the farm than he does."

"Then... why?" Juni tapped the notebook.

"Because I figure if we have a plan for the week and do some prep on weekends, teamwork can help us get ahead of this. The teenager over there is getting fat from too many burgers and French fries, if you know what I mean."

"Hey!" Xavier glared at his sister. "I am not fat. These are muscles. I work out."

Quincey smirked then looked back at Juni. "My parents taught us that teamwork rules. That there are some things that one person or the other prefers doing or are more physically capable of doing. But all the rest of the chores should be divvied up or rotated. Even Fat Boy is capable of cleaning bathrooms."

Xavier glowered at her.

"By the way, the toilet needs a good scrub." Quincey batted her eyelashes at her kid brother.

Didn't they always? But this was new information about Zadok. If that's what he really had been taught and believed, why had he come across like a caveman on their date?

Because he'd trusted his prof. Dad. Negative points for gullibility.

Quincey turned back. "Do you and your sister split chores, too?"

"Sort of." Juni contemplated. "She does more of the cooking because she's around in the afternoon, and I do more of the cleaning. We don't have any outdoor chores since we live on Ackerman Farm, so Mitchell and his brother handle all that."

Quincey nodded. "So, my list. Carnivore Boy over there can't handle the thought of Meatless Mondays, but there are great options, right? I mean, millions of vegetarians can't be completely wrong."

"Sure, they can," Xavier mumbled.

"Okay, I'm no expert on all this." Juni glanced at the

clock. Fifteen minutes still remained in the period. "We should be doing this off the clock. Right now, I'm being paid to input knowledge into your brother's brain."

"Like an old-school flash drive." Xavier mimed plugging a device into his temple and made beeping noises. "Awesome."

"You're done soon? Can we talk then?"

Didn't look like Juni was getting out of this without being rude. She pushed the notebook back to Quincey. "Sure. Why not flesh out some ideas while you wait? Xavier, how's the algebra coming?"

He rolled his eyes. "Fine. This is dumb baby stuff."

"Then you'll have no trouble finishing the page before three o'clock."

Xavier sighed and picked up his pencil.

The kid was much brighter than his recent grades suggested. He simply didn't do the work. Didn't want to put in any effort. Did he not see the point? Was there any way to turn his attitude all the way around? Because he was improving... with a long way to go for autonomous operation.

Quincey nudged the notebook over and pointed at the words she'd scrawled: *Rice and beans???*

Juni was being sucked into this whether she wanted it or not. She pulled out her phone and ran a search on rice and bean recipes then tilted the device at Quincey.

Your favorites???

She sighed. Did the trio like spicy food or not? Shirkowski sounded Polish — wasn't that cuisine more potato-based than rice and beans? Which didn't matter one speck. It wasn't like the O'Neills only ate Irish fare which, incidentally, was also based on potatoes.

Cuban, she wrote back. *Don't forget your veggies.*

Quincey beamed at her and tapped into her phone.

Juni looked at the felt creatures on the table in front of her. She could probably make more progress looking at recipes as Quincey was no doubt doing than on the lion's mane for her new safari set prototype.

She might get some meal ideas of her own. Maybe Arleigh would like a bit of a break from cooking at times, too.

"You what?" Zadok scowled at his sister.

"Dude, she barged right into study hall and stole my time with Ms. O'Neill."

Quincey elbowed Xavier. "As if. You didn't need every bit of her attention. In your own words, it was so easy a dumb baby could have done it."

Zadok held up his hands. "Back up a minute. You left work early, went to the high school, and asked Juni—" he glanced at Xavier "—Ms. O'Neill to help you plan menus?"

"Sure. Why not? We need fresh inspiration around here. And look!" She pointed at the counter where a bag of hamburger buns sat beside a bowl of salad and another bowl of... he wasn't sure what.

"I want a real hamburger, not a fake one." Xavier

slumped against the wall and crossed his arms in front of him.

"If it's a round patty in a bun, it's a burger."

"Is not."

Zadok gave his head a shake. "What exactly are we talking about here?"

"Meatless Monday." Quincey raised her chin. "We are having bean burgers, and you—" she pointed between him and Xavier "—are both going to like it."

It wasn't going to kill him to have a meatless meal. It wouldn't kill Xavier, either. But weren't burgers sacred ground? Maybe the ones from the diner weren't amazing, but Quincey could have made patties from ground beef herself. That would have been enough to elevate the meal. But here stood his sister wearing an expectant expression.

"I'll try anything once." He held up a hand. "Almost anything. I draw the line at crickets."

Quincey blinked.

Xavier's lip curled. "Crickets? Who'd eat them? Some jungle tribe, maybe?"

Zadok laughed. "You'd be surprised. They're a thing. Good, cheap form of protein."

"Did you say good? Have you tried them?" Xavier couldn't have looked more horrified if he'd tried.

"No, I meant 'good' as in they're dense with absorbable protein. Look, kid, your sister has gone to a lot of trouble to make us dinner tonight, so let's go along with it, okay?"

"If it's terrible, will you grab us takeout?"

Zadok tried to hide his grin. Failed utterly. "I promise."

"Grr. It won't be terrible. This is a time-tested recipe. You're going to love it! I just need ten minutes to cook the patties, and we can eat. Then tomorrow is Taco Tuesday!"

How many ways were there to make tacos? Zadok wasn't sure he wanted to ask. There wasn't a Tex-Mex café in town, and he did miss that style of cuisine. He was letting Quincey run with this week, and they'd assess results on the weekend together. Xavier would have a say, for sure.

Zadok turned to his sister. "Need a hand?"

"I've got it this time, but thanks." She pivoted to the sink to wash her hands.

When she started forming the dark goop in the second bowl into patties, he turned to the youngest Shirkowski. "How was school, other than your sister hijacking your tutoring hour?"

Xavier shrugged. "Okay, I guess. We're starting on a Thanksgiving play."

"Oh? What part do you have?"

"He's the turkey!" Quincey yelled.

"I am not!" Xavier's eyes shot daggers at the back of Quincey's head.

That girl lived to get a rise out of her brother. "What kind of play is it?" Probably a Mayflower enactment or something. It was smart of Juni to reinforce history in theater class.

"It's about some people who help at a homeless shelter and learn to be grateful for what they have."

Zadok blinked. "Not what I thought you'd say."

"Yeah, Ms. O'Neill wrote it herself." Xavier shrugged. "It's a bit preachy, but whatever."

"Preachy? Like from Bible verses?" She could get in a lot of trouble in a state high school for pushing biblical themes.

Xavier shook his head. "Nah. I meant preachy about thankfulness. She made the point like a gazillion times."

"Gotcha. So what part are you playing?"

"A homeless guy."

"Oh?" Zadok bit his tongue.

"Practicing for when you flunk out of school?" Quincey taunted.

"That's not funny." Xavier glowered at her.

"Sorry!"

She definitely didn't sound repentant. Man, these two. Zadok was either going to be gray before he turned thirty or bald from yanking all his hair out.

The frying pan sizzled as she plopped patties into it.

Zadok turned to Xavier. "Wash up and set the table."

"Yeah, whatever."

"And tell us more about your part in the play over dinner."

"It's no big deal. Just school stuff."

"I'd like to hear about it."

Xavier eyed him. "If I tell you, will you take me driving?"

"The table isn't setting itself!" Quincey wielded her flipper.

"We can probably fit in half an hour after dinner if we

all pitch in with cleanup. You haven't had much practice after sunset."

"Yes!" Xavier pumped his fist and hip-checked Quincey from in front of the sink, which was beside the stove. "Move over, Veggie Girl."

She smirked. "If you're trying to insult me, you're going to have to try harder, Fat Boy."

Fat Boy? Zadok blinked. Xavier was gangly, nearly as tall as Zadok's six-foot-two, and probably weighed less than a hundred and twenty pounds. The kid was all lean muscle, just like Zadok. They both took after their dad in that way.

"Back at you, Fat Girl."

She wrinkled her nose at him. "You can do better. Try harder."

Was this everyday sibling stuff, or should he interfere? How should he know? He had more than eight years on Quincey. They'd never had this kind of relationship.

Did Juni and her sister call each other names and poke each other constantly? He couldn't imagine it, not in their mid-twenties, anyway. Maybe as kids?

Likely not with a man like Grant O'Neill as their father. The stocky middle-aged man took everything too seriously to roll with kids bickering like this, even in good fun.

Zadok's memory dropped him back in theology class that term. Professor O'Neill seemed to have such a deep understanding of scripture that all the students, mostly impressionable young men, were amazed. He was their hero, a man they looked up to.

What had the half dozen female students thought of

the prof? Zadok tried to remember, but he had only a vague vision of a cluster of young women sticking together in a male-dominated track. He didn't recall them joining in placing the man on a pedestal, but he also hadn't been watching for it. The only girl he'd been interested in at the time was the professor's daughter.

He stifled a groan as he refocused on the kitchen, where Xavier was setting plates on the table and Quincey was placing cumin-scented patties inside buns.

Had he been interested in Juni only because she was related to his personable teacher? He didn't think so, but it hadn't hurt.

Now, though? He could see Professor O'Neill in a different light... and it wasn't nearly as flattering.

"Zadok?" Quincey stared at him. "Are you here or somewhere else?"

"Here," he said grimly. He really needed to dissect what he'd learned in that class sometime soon. Didn't he have all his notes in a box in the attic somewhere?

ELEVEN

"Can I ask you a question?"

Juni paused beside her car as Mitchell stood in the doorway of the greenhouse. "Um, sure. What do you want to know?" So long as it wasn't anything to do with Zadok.

Mitchell glanced around.

He was worried about being overheard? What was going on? Arleigh had planned to pick the boys up from school for a friend's birthday party, so her wildly painted hippie van wasn't in the driveway. Who else could Mitchell be concerned about?

"I, uh, I love your sister."

He looked so adorable and bashful at the admission that Juni's heart melted a little. She grinned at him. "I may have figured that out all by myself."

"I want to ask her to marry me. Is it too soon?" He jammed his fingers through his hair. "What if she says no?"

"She won't say no. Trust me on that."

He searched Juni's eyes. "Are you sure? Because—"

"I'm sure. You're all she ever talks about. Okay, not quite. She talks a lot about Lincoln and Hudson, too." Also, Arleigh talked a lot about what she was learning from studying the Bible, but Mitchell probably already knew that.

"Would she hate it if I proposed at the market?"

Juni squealed. "She'd love it! I know she would."

"Okay, well, here's what I was thinking. You may have wondered why your booth is right across from the microphone, but I needed the proximity for this."

Her eyebrows tilted up. "*You* designed the market layout, not Paula?" Or Zadok?

"Uh, yeah? That part, anyway. Paula didn't take much convincing."

"You've been plotting this for a while." Statement, not question.

"I have. Honestly, I know she loves me. I just don't know if it's too soon. Aren't couples supposed to date for years before being sure?"

"That's dumb. Sorry, Mitch, but it is. That might be good advice for college kids, but not so much for people who are more mature and settled in their life's work."

He let out a deep breath and nodded. "Okay, I have a ring picked out. I... I don't know her size."

"Same as me." Juni eyed her rings and tugged off one of them. "We used to swap when we were teens, but I had better taste." She smirked at him.

"Maybe I should get you to look at the one I've picked. Maybe she'd like something different."

"Mitchell?"

He straightened his shoulders and looked between her and the ring on the palm of her hand. "Yes?"

"Stop all that second-guessing. She'll be thrilled with anything you pick out. I promise. Take this for sizing and get it back to me later."

"Won't she notice you're not wearing it?"

"I have like eighteen rings I switch between. She's not going to notice."

He blinked. "If you're sure." He plucked it from her palm.

"Absolutely. Now, is there anything else I can do to help? What's your plan?"

"Well, Zadok will be playing..."

Of course, Zadok. She nodded.

"I was thinking your mom might like to be there, so I'm setting 11:00 as the time. She can just come and shop, like she sometimes does."

"She'll like that."

"I'll have Treyan bring the boys over at 11. And maybe some of the Green Acres folks. Noel and Claire and Keanan and Chelsea have been part of our journey."

"Don't forget to invite Pastor Ron and Wanda."

Mitchell snapped his fingers. "Yes, for sure."

She'd been semi-sarcastic, but whatever. "So, you'll do it over the sound system?" The guy was braver than she'd guessed.

"I am. I want everyone to know. But that's also why

I'm worried, because what if she says yes only because she feels pressured with everyone watching?"

Juni rested her hand on Mitchell's arm. "Do you really think that could happen, or is it just nerves? Because if you believe that's an honest possibility, then no, you shouldn't surprise her with a proposal until you're certain you're on the same page."

"We're on the same page." His gaze was steady.

"So, you're just a nervous wreck."

"I guess." He huffed a nervous chuckle. "I didn't think I deserved another chance at happiness after Lindsay died. And my hands were so full with the boys..." He shook his head. "I never expected Arleigh to blast down my walls and take my heart captive."

Whoa, the dude was all flowery now. Arleigh truly had rubbed off on him. Juni gave him an impulsive hug. "You two are awesome."

"It's God, Juni." He patted her shoulder and stepped back. "He's the awesome one, not us. He's so faithful. First Peter 1:3 has come to mean a lot to me: 'Praise be to the God and Father of our Lord Jesus Christ! In his great mercy he has given us new birth into a living hope through the resurrection of Jesus Christ from the dead.'"

New birth into a living hope. That went right along with the verse from James that Juni had been pondering lately. *Every good and perfect gift is from above, coming down from the Father of the heavenly lights, who does not change like shifting shadows.*

The merciful God of living hope. The giver of great and glorious gifts. A God who didn't change on a whim or sneakily try to achieve His own agenda or use His created beings as pawns.

A Heavenly Father not at all like her earthly father.

She swallowed the lump in her throat and gave Mitchell another smile, this one more emotional. "Arleigh's talked about that verse, too. If I ever get married, I hope it will be to a guy who cares about my spiritual growth the way you care for Arleigh's."

Mitchell's gaze softened. "Good guys are out there, Juni. I'm no great catch—"

"Tell that to Arleigh."

He grinned. "I have. She chooses not to believe me. But truly, she's helped me as much as I've helped her, probably far more. Neither of us was perfect when we first met, and I'm sure I don't need to tell you that we're still a very long way from it. So don't be looking for the perfect man. Be looking for one who loves you and wants to grow with you."

She angled her head and studied the guy who would soon be her brother-in-law. "You're a whole lot smarter than I thought you were."

Mitchell let out a guffaw that rang off the wall of the nearby barn. "Boy, you know how to use a compliment to cut a guy off at the knees."

Argh, she may have been a little brash with that. "I'm sorry?"

"Don't be. That's one thing I like about you, Juni. I never have to wonder where I stand with you. It's like you have some sort of gift."

"Right. Thanks." She rolled her eyes. "Well, I look

forward to many decades of gifting you with my unfiltered wit. And, oh! I get two nephews out of this deal. I shall spoil them rotten and teach them my way with words."

"They're already spoiled rotten. We're trying to turn them back into nice kids." He narrowed his gaze. "Wait, you got me on that one, too. But seriously, there's a God-fearing man out there for you. You may even have met him already." Mitchell's eyebrows tipped up as he grinned.

"Yeah, I doubt it. But thanks, I think. I should get dinner started before Arleigh gets home. It's my night."

"The boys begged for a bonfire tonight, so I'm planning hot dogs and sausages. Would you and your sister like to join us?"

"I have leftover potatoes I was going to panfry, but I could turn them into potato salad instead..."

"Please do. If you don't have other plans."

Nothing sounded more fun than basking in her sister's soon-to-be-family and wishing she had one of her own. Did God really have someone for her? Someone who was not Zadok Shirkowski, thank you very much?

THE PROBLEM and the benefit of music were identical. Zadok had played for so many years that he no longer needed to think about his finger placement. Didn't matter whether he had the violin under his chin or the guitar across his chest, the music flowed with little notice from his brain.

Which left him with far too much ability to watch who hung around Juni O'Neill's booth. Today it was Simon Melnychuk and, from the scraps of conversation Zadok could overhear in the lulls, the fire chief was trying to convince the crafter of the marketability of felt firefighter figures.

Zadok's eyes narrowed. Why did the man care? One look at the array of Juni's sets should tell Simon fire-fighters wouldn't fit. Cats. Trees. Ladders.

Well, maybe, but it seemed Simon had more than toys on his mind, the way he looked at Juni with bright interest.

The way Zadok wished Juni would look at him. The truth slammed into Zadok's chest, and he took a step back. His fingers danced on. What was he even playing?

"Every Good and Perfect Gift," a song by David Glenn.

What if Simon was God's gift to Juni? No. Zadok didn't want to believe that. Still, it could be true. Would he be able to accept that scenario? He'd have to.

Juni's gaze slid past Simon and collided with Zadok's for a brief instant.

Did she feel that crackle of connection like he did? She was resisting it, that was for sure. And maybe he should, too. He'd spent a bit of time digging through his college notes the other night. The teachings on relationships he'd eagerly absorbed back then looked suspect in the cold light of day four years later.

They were blended with scripture in ways that made

the odd bits look like they belonged, but Zadok needed to take a step further back and examine them the way the Bereans in the Bible had, by eagerly receiving the teaching but also examining it against scripture to make sure it was true... and discarding it if it were not.

Zadok became aware of Mitchell's approach, and he glanced at the clock. Almost eleven. He nodded at the other man, easing back into the corner as Mitchell stepped up to the microphone. The greenhouse owner had some kind of announcement to make.

The place was packed. Where had everyone come from? It seemed half the town had appeared. Mrs. O'Neill. The pastor and his wife. Most of the folks from Green Acres, Quincey among them.

Something was going on, and a quick glance at Juni showed what he'd begun to suspect. She knew. It was...

"Anyone here believe in hope?" Mitchell cleared his throat.

Everyone in the greenhouse stopped what they were doing and turned toward the minstrel booth. Zadok's fingers kept moving, but slower. Quieter. Why couldn't he blend into the background? But the sun shone through the sparkling glass, no doubt silhouetting him as well as Mitch.

The guy must be nervous. Mitchell talked on and on, quoting scripture about hope and love before finally getting to the point.

Zadok couldn't take his eyes off Juni. Hopefully anyone who glanced his way would think he was watching her sister who stood beside her with shining eyes as Mitchell declared his love for her.

But Juni caught him looking and met his gaze for a long few seconds before she swallowed and looked down. She moved a couple of packets of toys one way, then the other, before sneaking another peek at him.

Zadok's heart warmed. She wasn't immune to him. She wasn't stealing secret looks at Simon or anyone else. Just him.

Hudson and Lincoln darted around the end of the massive greenhouse table and tackled Arleigh's hips, begging her to be their mama. She crouched and pulled the boys close while Mitchell stood awkwardly in the gravel path with a velvet box in his hands.

The greenhouse exploded with applause, whistles, and laughter as Mitchell closed in and offered the ring to Arleigh.

Zadok didn't want to watch the embrace or the passionate kiss, but he couldn't help himself. He wanted this kind of joy. This kind of love. This kind of great and glorious gift from the Father of lights.

Juni looked at her sister and bit her lower lip before dabbing at her eyes.

Tears? Longing to wipe them away filled Zadok, but it wasn't his place. Wasn't his time. Would it come? He didn't know.

Mitchell presented Arleigh with one more gift, a banner with vibrant blossoms and assorted greenery all around the words 'Arleigh's Flower Farm.' It was wild and gorgeous and suited an O'Neill sister.

Zadok became aware of someone beside him and glanced over to see Keanan Welsh from Green Acres. "Hey." He nodded to the other musician as he kept playing. Who knew what song he was fingering now?

"Hello. Happy days for Ackerman Farm."

"Yeah, looks like." Mitchell's brother, Treyan, had been married back in May. He and his wife, Brittany, and their daughter, Scarlett, were here in the greenhouse right now, too. Part of the crowd wishing the couple — the family — well.

"It reminds me of life at Green Acres. Community, you know? So many people to care about what you do. It drew me here from California years ago now. I came on a bicycle, pulling my earthly belongings in a bike trailer."

Zadok chuckled. "The original hippie."

"I suppose that's true. I craved community, both in the physical sense and the spiritual one. I didn't think I needed a wife, though."

"God had other plans, I take it."

"He did. He sent me Chelsea. She was so annoying. So needy. Incredibly unsure of herself and her standing as a believer."

Was the man telling tales out of turn?

Smiling, Keanan shook his head as though he could read the unspoken question. "God is so, so faithful. He chased her down. Chased me down, too. I only thought I was totally committed to Him before I nearly died in a South African hospital."

Zadok blinked. "That's a story I need to hear sometime."

"Happy to tell it. God used that in my life. In Chelsea's. She proposed to me when I was barely conscious in that hospital bed." The man chuckled. "Nothing like this, that's for sure."

"Wait, *she* proposed?"

"She did. She came all the way to Johannesburg for that purpose. And to make sure I survived, I suppose."

"Huh."

The market had resumed its heartbeat of buying and selling, of sharing and laughing. Of community.

"God turned both our lives plum upside-down. I don't know if you need to hear that story— scratch that. I don't know *why* God wanted me to tell you all this, but He did. He's so much more amazing than we can ever ask or imagine. No matter what it looks like, He is a good, good Father and gives glorious gifts to His children. He doesn't change His mind or play tricks on us like a shifting shadow. No bait-and-switch."

"James 1:17." Zadok's mouth was dry as he met the other man's gaze.

"Amen and amen."

He looked across to Juni, who was chatting with Jean Stedman. Both women laughed, and Juni glanced his direction for a fleeting second.

Was she God's gift to him? Not in the patriarchal sense of owning someone else like he'd once thought, but in the sense where God could draw them together, make them better together than they could be apart, like Keanan had hinted at about his relationship with Chelsea.

It gave a guy hope.

TWELVE

I t's gorgeous." Juni admired the ring her sister had thrust within inches of her nose.

Arleigh sighed. "That was so romantic. I can't believe he invited everyone who's close to us to be there for the occasion. That he included the boys and just made the moment so extra special."

"It was roman—"

"And that banner! Did you see it?"

Of course, Juni had seen it. The thing was vivid enough to make her eyes bleed and something like eight feet long. Even flashing lights wouldn't have caught her eyes more. "It's... colorful. Vibrant."

"I know! I can't believe he did that for me. It's like he affirms who I am. He's validating my identity, not trying to absorb me into Ackerman Farm."

"I thought of that, too." Only a daughter of Grant O'Neill would understand how important that was. Mitchell had been wise to figure it out. Zadok had not.

Jeepers, why couldn't she get the guy out of her head for more than two minutes at a time? He'd been watching her throughout the whole proposal while he kept playing his guitar. It had been a little unnerving, honestly. He was so talented he didn't even need to pay attention to his music for it to sound amazing.

Might he have changed since that disastrous night? Matured?

There were a few shreds of evidence. His apology had sounded sincere. But he'd had the nerve to tell her to let him know when she was ready to date him. As if. He'd be waiting until the cows came home. Until the stars aligned. Until that imaginary ball popped up out of Galena Lake and splatted her in the face.

Basically, until never.

Then why couldn't she block him from her mind and forget about him? Why did his intent gaze feel more comforting than intimidating?

Arleigh tilted her left hand one way then the other, admiring the glisten of the princess-cut diamond.

Far be it from Juni to comment about the impractical style for a gardener. Mitchell had invited her opinion, and she'd turned him down. She'd had her chance for input.

"I want you to be my maid of honor, of course."

Juni's heart warmed. "Thank you. I'd be honored, for sure. And if you had chosen someone else, I'd be very, very cranky."

Arleigh giggled and threw her arms around Juni. "I know, right? I'm so glad you moved back to Galena Landing last spring. I'm happy we've had another chance to get to know each other as adults. You're my best friend, and there's no one I'd rather have beside me."

"Aw, thanks." Juni hugged Arleigh back. "Who else? How big a wedding do you want?"

"I don't know. I'm sure Mitchell will want Treyan." Arleigh's grin slid to one side in contemplation. "Will it be awkward for you being paired with a married man?"

Juni shrugged. "It is what it is. I can't see Mitchell asking anyone but his brother." Perhaps it was a relief, even. She wouldn't need to spend time with, say, Zadok. Not that he and Mitch were close enough for that sort of invitation to be made.

"I don't know if we'll want more than one attendant each. I guess we'll have to talk about that. All we've decided is January, which isn't very far away at all. Oh, Mitchell will ask Penny and Pete if they'd like to stay with the boys during our honeymoon."

Juni's eyebrows popped skyward of their own accord. "Will they be up for that?" Mitchell's former mother-in-law had recently had colon cancer surgery.

"Mitchell seems to think they will be, and Treyan and Brittany will be around, as will you, so they'll have a community to help if needed. Right?"

"Yeah, of course. Thanks for not assuming I could do it as well as teach that week."

Arleigh laughed. "No, those boys are a lot, even now that they've settled down so much. And who knows how they'll be from all the excitement of a wedding."

"You're getting married!"

"I *know*! Isn't it crazy?" Arleigh gave Juni another big squish as they danced awkwardly in a circle.

There was likely to be an abundance of hugging and squealing for the next few months. Juni might as well get used to it.

"I guess I'll start looking for an apartment in town for the new year."

Arleigh frowned. "You don't have to do that. There's no reason you can't stay living right here."

"Um." Juni pointed upward. "Have you ever noticed how much sound comes through from the kitchen? When the boys run across the floor? When they holler at Mitch?"

"Yes? Your point?"

"My bedroom is directly below Mitchell's."

Arleigh's face turned fluorescent pink in two seconds flat. "Oh. I hadn't thought of that."

"So, yeah, pardon me if I'd like to live somewhere else."

"Pardoned," Arleigh mumbled. "Um, want a cup of tea?"

Juni laughed. "Sure, sounds good. I'll put my felties away and be right out. I baked cookies yesterday." She lifted the box she'd set on the table, carried it into her bedroom, and stashed it in her closet.

She dropped to her bed and stared up at the ceiling.

Juni could hear the sound of running water in their kitchen down the hall and the sound of running feet upstairs. Hudson yelled at Lincoln. Linc yelled back. A door slammed. Yeah, she didn't want to live here after her sister married Mitchell. There'd be too many reminders of what her sister had that she did not.

She could call Zadok.

No! She surged upright on her bed. Why would she even think that? Just because her sister was now engaged didn't mean she had to be. Just because Zadok was the only guy to show interest... no, that wasn't even true.

Simon Melnychuk made a point of stopping by her table at the market often. Of chatting with her after church. He hadn't ever asked her out, but it could be coming.

She'd consider him, right? Simon was a nice guy. A believer. He was gainfully employed.

Too bad she didn't feel a single spark of attraction toward him. Not even the tiniest flicker.

The tea kettle's whistle shrieked from the other room.

Juni sighed and pulled to her feet. Men. Why did they need to be so complicated? And why did she even care? She was a teacher with a decent job in a town she liked. Why couldn't she be happily single for the rest of her life?

It wouldn't be so bad. Plenty of women led that life and were content. The apostle Paul even talked about how much more ministry single people could do than those whose attentions were split between ministry and family. Of course, Paul was talking about men, but the principle still stood.

She should volunteer to help lead Alpha in January. That would set her on the right path of ministry.

"Juni? Tea's ready."

"Coming!"

Yes. Juni was going to embrace singleness. She'd put

both Zadok and Simon out of her mind and stop eyeing other men, wondering if they were single and suitable.

She ran her brush through her hair, straightened her sweater, and headed to the kitchen.

"There you are!" Arleigh poured two cups of tea. "I thought you'd fallen asleep or gotten lost."

"Lost in thought, maybe." Juni opened the cookie tin and set it on the small table. They didn't need to be fancy with extra plates to wash.

"Oh? Dreaming of a certain musician? A double wedding would be all kinds of fun."

"What? No!"

Arleigh giggled. "Sure, it would, but I agree you should date for a little longer first. Or, you know, start dating at all."

"I've come to believe that God has called me to be single."

"You came to that conclusion when?" Arleigh eyed her.

"Two minutes ago, but it's been a long time coming." Juni tried to keep her voice even and firm.

"Two minutes ago," Arleigh repeated.

"Yes. Have a cookie."

"So, you came to this conclusion right after your one and only beloved sister became engaged."

"Um... yes." *Put a little more determination in your voice, Juni.*

"How are those two events linked?" Arleigh spooned a dollop of honey into her cup.

"They're not."

"I don't believe you. Didn't we agree to be open and honest with each other?"

Juni sighed. "Okay, fine. I just don't see how God has anyone for me, so it's time I stopped looking."

"At the ripe old age of twenty-four? You're hardly an old maid." Arleigh dunked a gingersnap into her tea and took a bite. "Mmm. Good cookie, by the way."

"Thanks." Juni turned her teacup on the table. "Romance is one of those things you can't force, so isn't it better not even to look for it or pursue it?"

"Hmm." Her sister nibbled the cookie. "Yes and no. You're right that it can't be forced, but that doesn't mean you should give up on it and assume it will never happen for you."

"The apostle Paul was single."

Arleigh rolled her eyes. "Your point being?"

"God called him to that because He had other things for Paul to focus on."

"Like?"

"Like ministry."

Arleigh gave her head a little shake. "So, you're going to do what? Go overseas as a missionary? Join a convent? What exactly are you thinking of here?"

"I thought I'd start by helping lead Alpha. You heard Pastor Ron ask for volunteers at church last week."

"Alpha. Okay. You promise me you'll volunteer?"

Why was there a gleam in Arleigh's eyes? "Yes, I give my word. Why?"

"Because I heard Zadok is leading a team."

"Wasn't that the most romantic thing ever?" Quincey sighed in rapturous glee.

Xavier grunted. "Romance. Ugh."

Their sister rounded on him. "Mitchell proposed to Arleigh during the market today. It was so swoony." She clasped her hands together in rapture.

Swoony, huh? Donna O'Neill's expression had matched the one Quincey had just adopted. It had not been identical to Juni's, though she'd given her sister a hug once Lincoln and Hudson had darted away again. What did she think of her sister's engagement?

Didn't matter. "It was very fitting, since Mitch and Arleigh met through the market. Anyone want food?"

Xavier perked up. "Me!"

Quincey tapped on Xavier's thigh. "Hollow, as I suspected."

"Hey!" The teen scowled at his sister. "I can't help being hungry. You guys left me with only a sandwich when you went to the market this morning."

"It's not like you can't open a can of something."

Zadok followed Xavier's guilty gaze to the open cereal box on the counter. He stifled a chuckle. "Well, don't get too stuffed now, because Quince put soup in the slow cooker this morning." They'd bought one after having lunch at Juni's mom's that day.

"And I have fresh sourdough bread from the market for our sandwiches to go with it." Quincey set her bags on the counter.

"Soup-and-Sandwich Saturday is dumb. It's not filling enough."

She rounded on her little brother. "You don't like my plan? Make your own. No one is preventing you from cooking around here."

"Hey, I helped!"

"You got a bag of mixed vegetables out of the freezer, which I appreciated, but it's not like you were indispensable or saved me more than two minutes of time."

Xavier inhaled sharply, obviously ready to defend himself.

Zadok held his hands between them. "Peace, fellow humans. There are cinnamon rolls from the market for our snack. And Quincey's right, Xav. Soup and a sandwich is a filling enough meal. We can't eat pizza every night."

"Would a burger now and then kill you guys? I'm a growing adolescent!"

"You'll grow sideways, Fat Boy," Quincey muttered. "Cinnamon rolls are a terrible snack. We need protein and vegetables."

"I'll eat yours." Xavier pounced on the bag. "You go ahead and eat my veggies."

"I'll have my cinnamon roll, thank you very much." Quincey scowled at Xavier. "And a carrot stick."

"Where's your protein?" He held the bag out of her reach.

"Zadok..."

"I think you brought that on yourself, sis. It's a good question. Hand me mine, Xavier?"

"Sure." The teen pulled out a large cinnamon roll and passed it to Zadok before turning his back to Quincey and clutching the bag dramatically to his chest.

"Pass. Me. My. Cinnamon. Roll."

"You offended it. You said it was terrible. It doesn't want you. It wants me. It knows I have proper appreciation."

"Zadok! Speak to the child."

It was all he could do not to laugh out loud. "No can do. Xav has a point."

His sister's eyes narrowed and burned into his own.

"I mean, you also have a point. But you're a grownup—"

"Thanks for noticing."

"—and you are not required to eat the snacks I provide to the household. You are welcome to bring more appropriate foods into this house and offer to share them if you wish."

"Please, no." Xavier made a gagging sound. "Meatless Monday is going to kill me as it is."

"Hey!" Quincey rounded on him. "You had seconds of the Cuban-style rice and beans we had last week. You said it was not bad."

"Of course, I had seconds. I'd have starved to death if I hadn't. Meat fills a guy up faster. Like, you know, a burger."

Quincey snarled something.

Zadok escaped the room. Let them fight it out. He

provided food, and Quincey was helping big time with implementing her weekly plan. A couple of times a week they all pitched in to fill the slow cooker before going off to their day. He had to admit they were eating better and possibly even saving a little money. Maybe he could suggest they alternate between pizza and burgers on Thursdays. Call it Takeout Thursday instead. One wasn't necessarily any healthier than the other, after all.

"Do you think you'll ever get married?"

Zadok closed his eyes and turned slowly to face his sister. Guess she'd followed him after all. "Um... no idea."

"Isn't that what old people in their late twenties think about?"

"Old, huh?" He swatted toward her, but she danced away.

"Well, yeah. Practically a fossil."

"Thanks." He sobered. "I've been kind of busy the past couple of years with you two, and it's not like Galena Landing is oozing with single Christian women."

"Xav and I could handle you dating, you know. We're not babies." She chuckled. "Actually, if those cyclones of Mitchell's could handle it, anyone could. And you're not even responsible for us that much longer."

He studied her. "And you, not at all now."

"Yeah, I know I'm an adult." She fluffed her hair. "I just wanted to stick around for a bit and make sure you and Xavier weren't going to murder each other."

"Right. I appreciate it." And he did, but not for that reason, as well she knew. "It's been great having you around this fall."

"And taking over the meal planning, because you were terrible at it."

Zadok dipped his head in acknowledgment. "I was. But I'll do better in the future, even when you go back to college. You're still planning to in January, right?"

"Yeah." Quincey sighed. "I wish I could just stay at Green Acres. They're doing such amazing things there, but I don't want to be like you."

He blinked. "Like me?"

"Ancient with no prospects." She offered a cheesy grin. "Except for one you seem disinclined to pursue."

If Quincey only knew... scratch that. She should never find out how thoroughly he'd messed up... and how thoroughly Juni had shot him down.

THIRTEEN

Good job on your schoolwork, Xavier. What turned things around?"

The teen smirked at Juni. "My brother promised me driving hours if I caught up and stayed there."

"Smart thinking." Because Juni had no such carrot to dangle in front of him.

"I'd do even better if I had the lead in the Christmas play."

Juni wagged a finger at him. "Oh, no, I don't think I heard you just try to bribe a teacher."

"Definitely not." Xavier leaned onto the table and held her gaze. "Just saying I'm a good actor. Maybe the best in our class."

"You acted like you didn't care for a long time."

He curled his nose. "That wasn't acting."

"Driving time can't change your attitude down deep.

It's bribery — smart bribery — but can only affect the surface."

"So?"

"So, you tell me." Not that it was any of her business, other than tutoring the teen at the principal's request. Or had it been an order?

"I got tired of it." Xavier shrugged and looked down. "And besides, my parents aren't coming back."

Her heart squeezed. "I'm sorry."

"Yeah, I know. Everyone's sorry." He exhaled. "Doesn't change anything."

"It does and it doesn't."

"How do you figure that?"

"Well, if you feel like nobody else has ever experienced hardship, and nobody cares what happens to you, then I'd think that would be far more depressing than if people express care."

"Mrs. Bowerchuk." Xavier grimaced and put on a quavering, little-old-lady voice. "You poor growing boy without a mama or a papa."

The kid was right. He voice-acted really well. Juni could almost see the elderly lady leaning on her cane and peering up at the teen. "But she cares. She prays for you." She prayed for Juni, too. For dozens if not hundreds of people, by name, every day, if reports were to be believed.

"Yeah, I guess that's cool. Do you think God actually cares? Because that doesn't make sense."

Suddenly Juni remembered where they were. "This isn't an appropriate conversation during school hours."

Xavier rolled his eyes. "Yeah, whatever. Easy out."

"No. Want to talk about it? I'll meet you after school at Bella's Bakery. But here and now is all about your classes and your grades." Even if those topics were only superficial compared to the deeper questions he was asking.

"Seriously?"

"Sure. Treat's on me."

He grinned. "Deal. A guy's gotta eat."

Juni nudged his physics textbook closer. "Now, how about the questions at the end of Chapter 8?"

"Right. Those kinematics equations I'll never need to understand in real life."

"Driving lessons."

Xavier's sigh sounded like it came from a subterranean cavern.

"Why don't you sweep Ms. O'Neill off her feet and marry her?"

Zadok jerked as he looked toward his kid brother. Good thing Xavier was driving, not him. The kid looked as cool as a cucumber. "Where did that come from?" Not that the thought had never occurred to him.

Xav shrugged as he flexed his hands on the ten-and-two of the steering wheel. "I know you like her."

"What makes you think that?"

"Puh-leeze. How stupid do you think I am? I'm not even flunking physics anymore."

"Pretty sure this has nothing to do with physics."

"Well, she's my tutor, and now I get it."

"You could have gotten it without her help if you'd only applied yourself."

"Whatever. When are you going to make a move?"

Back to that, were they? His siblings were nothing if not insightful and dogged. "Tutoring went okay today, then?"

"Zadok."

"Xavier."

Xavier rolled his eyes. "I had a question about God, and she told me to meet her at Bella's after school. Bought me a Danish and a gingersnap hot chocolate."

Should Zadok offer to repay Juni? Better to leave well enough alone. She'd never accept, anyway. "Uh huh. What did you talk about?"

"About why God lets horrible things happen."

"Like Mom and Dad's accident."

"Yeah." Xavier stared out the windshield into the growing dusk.

Finally, Zadok couldn't wait any longer for his brother to carry on. "What wisdom did she impart?" It might be something he needed to hear, too.

"Just that it doesn't mean God hates us. He uses situations to help us grow. She said plants can't grow strong stalks if they're sheltered all the time. You know, from wind and rain and storms."

Zadok blinked. "So... we're like plants?" His brain might not be capable of jumping with Xavier's words.

"Kind of? She said God works everything for our good."

"Romans 8:28."

"Yeah." Xavier shot a glance at Zadok. "But did He work everything for Mom and Dad's good, too?"

A fresh pang of grief pierced Zadok. "I think He did."

"How do you figure that?"

"Oh, buddy. It's hard on this side. It really is. I get that. But it's partly because we have no concept of how amazing heaven really is. Our parents would have chosen to stay with us if they could have, but I can't wish them back now that they're in God's presence. We only have a feeble understanding of what it's like on the other side, but we know enough to know it's everything we could ever hope for, probably with a magnitude of a hundred. Or hundred million."

"Only old people should die."

"I hear you, but it's not like that. Babies die, kids die, teens die... there's no age out of bounds."

Xavier navigated a left turn onto a farming road. "It's not fair."

"We don't get to decide what's fair. We're not the rulers of the universe."

The teen harrumphed. "You and Ms. O'Neill are *so* on the same page with all that. I know you like her. I don't get why you're holding back."

So much for diverting the conversation, but maybe Xavier needed some time to think about that whole concept. "Kid, you're right about Juni. She's really nice, and I like her."

The boy smirked.

"But it doesn't go both ways. I need to understand that God may have an entirely different plan for me. And for her."

"What do you mean, it doesn't go both ways?"

"She doesn't like me in a romantic way." As much as it pained him to admit it.

Xavier snorted. "Yeah, right."

"Seriously. And we're not in the Dark Ages anymore where a knight would literally grab a damsel in distress and rescue her by riding off into the sunset with her draped over the back of his saddle."

"Wow, dramatic, much?"

"It was a thing in bygone days." Days which Professor O'Neill seemed to think still existed.

"That's dope."

"Not so much, because everyone deserves the right to make their own choices."

"But the damsel was in distress... didn't she want to be rescued?"

"Possibly? Probably? But a gentleman doesn't take it for granted. He asks and then respects her reply."

"Are we still talking about Ms. O'Neill? Because, like you said, this isn't the Dark Ages."

"Yeah, we're still talking about her." Zadok's heart felt heavy. "A long time ago, I hurt her and, while she says she's forgiven me, she doesn't want anything to do with me."

"Wait a sec." Xavier frowned. "She only moved here at

spring break. That's not a long time ago, even in old-people talk."

Drat, Zadok had gone and done it now. "We knew each other a little in college."

"Dude!"

He didn't want to talk about it, especially to his nosy, perceptive sibling. Either one of them. "Focus on the road."

"I'm focusing. I saw that deer, and I bet you didn't."

There had been a deer? Xavier was right — Zadok was doing a lousy job of supervising his driving. "It's time to head back home. Quincey should have dinner on the table by the time we get there."

"Yeah, we're on One-Dish Wednesday. Scary thought there."

"You have to admit we're eating better than we were."

Xavier slowed and slipped on the turn signal as he approached a four-way stop. "Too few burgers and fries, too many veggies."

"Too bad you're getting a healthier body out of the deal."

"Is it worth it?"

"Do you have fewer zits?"

The boy touched his cheek then glowered at Zadok before making the turn. "Maybe?"

"More energy?"

"I doubt it."

Zadok knew differently. Xavier's mood shift had to be a reflection of diet as well as the gentle lure of driving time and the not-so-gentle threat of academic probation.

"Do we seriously have to eat vegetarian on Mondays? I can handle the rest, more or less, but that is killing me. How is it better for me and for the planet?"

"Do some research. Present it to your sister."

"Seriously?"

"Sure. Why not? You've taken essay-writing in Language Arts, right? Put your skills to good use in a real-life situation."

"Huh." The kid looked thoughtful. "Maybe I will."

Zadok gave himself a mental high-five.

JUNI PULLED in at the driveway to Ackerman Farm to see Quincey standing beside Mitchell's boys' teeter-totter, holding her bike upright. "Hey! I didn't expect to see you here."

"I probably should have called first. I guess I assumed you came straight home after school."

"I usually do, but today your brother and I met at Bella's to talk over some things." Too late, Juni remembered that the teen might wish to keep their conversation private.

Quincey's grin overtook her face as she squealed. "Finally! You and Zadok!"

"Um, no. Xavier."

The girl threw her head back dramatically. Her younger brother hadn't inherited all the thespian genes in

the family. "Oh, you've got to be kidding me. When —
never mind. That's not why I'm here."

Whew. "What's up?"

Quincey tapped her backpack. "I have a mockup to
show you."

"Oh, the website? Come on in." Juni pointed to the
door that led into the house. "I'll grab my messenger bag."
She rounded the car and lifted it out.

Quincey followed her down the stairs and into the
suite. She glanced around and nodded. "Sweet digs."

"I've lived in worse. Arleigh and I painted the whole
place before we moved in, and Mitchell found some vinyl
plank flooring on sale. Plus, he upgraded the appliances by
a couple of decades."

"Cool." Quincey swung her backpack off, pulled out a
laptop, and set it on the small table. "Wi-Fi? Then I can
show you what I've done."

Juni rattled off the password.

The girl tapped it into the keyboard. The Wi-Fi symbol
solidified. A few keystrokes later, she turned the laptop to
face Juni. "What do you think?"

Juni settled into the wooden chair and studied the
homepage. "That's... amazing. *Feltie Fun?*"

"I can change that. You didn't give me a business
name."

"It's cute. And I like how you made the lettering look
like stuffed felt with running stitches around them. They
match my toys."

Quincey visibly exhaled. "I thought so. But again, I can

change anything. Everything. I needed to start some-where, that's all."

"These are the photos Zadok took?" Juni scrolled down the homepage with photos of each of her sets. She clicked a side arrow and took in the complete page for the mermaids with all the pieces listed, along with the price.

"Yeah. My big bro has his talents."

"He does." Not that Juni wanted to get into a litany, especially with his sister. She clicked the *Bio* page and blinked at her own headshot. Did she really look this good? The reflection in the mirror didn't offer this perspective. Mind you, the lighting in the bathroom wasn't the greatest. But really?

"Do you like that one? It's my favorite. Zadok caught great lighting. And you're so pretty."

Juni's head was already shaking. "I'm not pretty, though this photo... He must have spent an hour touching it up so I'd look better."

Quincey giggled. "I'm not going to deny he spent a lot of time on your headshots, but I don't think he improved you any."

Juni wasn't sure she wanted to know what the girl meant by that.

"You're pretty, Juni. I like your makeup style. It's not over-the-top but it brings out your features. So does the way you do your hair. Simple, but attractive."

"Thanks." Juni clicked away from the Bio page without even reading the text. Doubtless the girl had just copy-pasted what Juni had given her. Now she studied the various sales pages.

They looked great. And they'd had so much fun taking them that Sunday afternoon. Quincey had come with great ideas, but Zadok's skills with his camera were what made the felties look alive and inviting.

"Did you see the reviews? Scroll down."

"Reviews?" She clicked back to the mermaid page and read two reviews.

I love my mermaids Ms. Juni made. They live in my 'quarium and have adventures. I play with them every day. Scarlett A, age 6.

My dad made a glass box for my mermaid set. I have to share with my little sister. I'm asking Santa for a second set of mermaids for Christmas so we can play together without fighting. Dad says fighting is bad and he'll take the mermaids away, so I think the solution is more mermaids. Are you reading this, Santa? Sophie R, age 8.

Juni swiped at her damp eyes. "I don't know what I expected, but this... this is above and beyond. What do I owe you?"

"It's for my college portfolio."

"That doesn't mean I can't pay you."

"Well..."

Juni met the girl's smirk. Uh oh. It looked like she was up to something.

"There is something you could do for me."

Anything but that. Not that Quincey had said the words yet. Juni waited.

"You could go out with my brother. Just once. Then I'd never bug you again."

"I don't want to go out with your brother." She could

make a joke about how Xavier was way too young for her, but there was no point in pretending she didn't know exactly which brother Quincey was talking about.

"Why not?" Quincey's eyebrows tipped up as she studied Juni. "He's a pretty nice guy, if I do say so myself."

"I'm sure he is." Now. Too bad he hadn't been in the past.

"Then why not? Just once. Give him a chance."

"No."

Quincey sighed deeply and snapped her laptop closed. "Then I have no choice but to keep this website to myself."

Juni's hand stretched to the device before she knew what it was doing. "You can't do that! It's beautiful. Perfect."

"So, you agree?"

"That it's a great site? Yes." That wasn't what Quincey meant. She knew it.

"Nice try."

"I don't want to date him."

"Call it dinner with a friend."

"He's not my friend." Never would be her friend. Definitely he'd never be more, though her devious heart sent a timid *why?* into her stubborn mind.

"He could be. Juni, seriously. Give me one good reason why you hate him so much."

Not a chance. She wasn't going to be the one who talked about that ill-fated evening.

Quincey rose and tucked the laptop into her backpack.

"Don't go."

"You'll do it?"

Juni licked her lips while her heart hammered so loud it drummed in her ears. "That's really your condition?"

"It is. One hour with Zadok, and I'll port this website over to your own domain. I'll even help you set one up if you haven't reserved a URL yet."

"I haven't. I didn't know what to choose."

"Feltie fun dot com. Or feltie fun by Juni dot com if the other is taken. I haven't looked." Quincey slowly shouldered her backpack, gaze never leaving Juni's.

Drat. Juni was cornered by a nineteen-year-old matchmaker. She needed that website. She needed those glorious photos of her mermaids and cowboys and forest creatures and dragons. She needed those headshots. She needed to believe someone saw her as beautiful.

Quincey turned for the kitchen door.

"Wait." She sucked in her dry lips. "Okay. I agree."

The girl spun, and her face lit with a smile. "Great! You won't regret it."

"I already do."

"No, you don't." Quincey laughed. "I'll get Zadok to phone later to set up a time."

"About that. He won't call."

"Sure, he will." The girl studied her. "Why wouldn't he?"

"Because..." Oh, man. This was embarrassing. "He told me the ball was in my court." Juni held up both hands. "I can't call him. I just can't. I don't want him to think..."

"Two more stubborn people I have never met. Do I have to do everything for you?"

A tear trickled out of Juni's left eye before she could blink it away.

"Fine. Friday night at seven at The Sizzling Skillet. Meet him there. If anything changes, I'll let you know."

"Okay." Juni could barely get the word out. How had her life come to this? She only had to survive one hour, but surely he'd understand his sister's coercion, and that Juni's presence had nothing to do with changing her mind.

Was she really as stubborn as Quincey thought she was?

FOURTEEN

And to think it had taken his sister to set things up with Juni.

Zadok wiped his damp hands down his new black jeans and leaned against the log wall in The Sizzling Skillet's foyer, waiting for the hostess to seat him. Or for Juni's arrival, whichever came first. Quincey had even called for a reservation. She was serious about this date.

It wasn't a date. Not really. Juni had agreed under duress, and Zadok's attempt to let her off the hook had resulted in a firm head shake from Quincey, along with crossed arms.

Nope, she'd said. *The deal was she got the website if the two of you spent an hour together. Without that date, I won't turn it over to her.*

It wasn't fair to Juni, but far be it from Zadok to help his sister hold that cute website hostage. It wasn't going to be his fault if Juni didn't get the files. And, yeah, Zadok wanted to spend time with her. Sue him.

The door opened, and his head wrenched up, but it was only Treyan and Brittany. They must have a babysitter for Scarlett tonight. He managed a smile. "Hi there."

"Hey, Zadok." Treyan thrust out a hand to shake his. "Waiting for someone?"

"Uh, yeah."

Brittany grinned. "Anyone we know?"

This non-date was going to be the talk of the town in no time flat, wasn't it? He could only hope their reserved table was far from the Ackermans' table. In case discussion got heated. With Juni, it was entirely possible.

The door opened again, and there she was.

Zadok straightened and blinked. She was gorgeous in leggings and a long sweater beneath her open coat. "Hi, there."

Juni seemed to steel herself. "Hi."

Brittany giggled.

Juni noticed her neighbor. "Hi, you guys. Oh, we could do a table for four!"

Not so fast, girl.

The hostess appeared with two menus. "Ackerman, table for two? Right this way."

"It's our date night," Brittany announced as she waggled the fingers of her free hand at Juni. Her other fingers were twined around Treyan's. "Have fun!" They followed the hostess, leaving Zadok and Juni behind.

"You look great." Zadok couldn't help the words. After all, they were true.

"Thanks." Her gaze bounced off his.

This was going to be an awkward evening. Or, at least,

an awkward hour, since that's all Quincey had demanded. They'd be lucky to have their dinner in that short a time on a Friday evening, though. The place was hopping.

"Shirkowsi, table for two? This way, please."

Juni moved first, and Zadok's hand found the small of her back as he followed them both. Then he dropped his touch. He needed to play this cool. Or at least not make her any more angry with him than she already was.

They were escorted past Treyan and Brittany's table into the far reaches of the dining room before the hostess stopped and set down two menus. "Here you go. Can I get you anything to drink while you consider your options?"

"Ice water for me, please." Juni shed her coat before he could reach for it then slid into the booth's leather seat.

"Same for me, thank you."

"Sure. I'll grab those for you. Beatrice will be your server tonight. She'll be with you shortly."

"Thanks."

"Interesting decor." Juni looked up.

The ceiling lights were contrived of antique-looking wagon wheels with old-fashioned lanterns hanging from them. "Yes. Have you eaten here before?"

She shook her head and looked off to her right where some gold-panning equipment hung on the log walls. "They're doing the theme up big."

Zadok leaned back into the padded bench and fiddled with the saltshaker, a tiny canning jar with a perforated lid. "I don't think it's a theme. I think they've kept it just the way it's been for fifty years."

"Fifty?" Her gaze bounced off his.

"Probably something like that. Maybe longer. This is one of Galena Landing's original buildings from when the paddle-wheelers came up the river. This might have been their docking station, actually, since it's right on the water."

The half-moon glinted off the lake in the late October evening but didn't illuminate much.

"The post office is made of logs, too."

"Similar vintage, I'm guessing." Were they going to spend an hour discussing the town's history? Better than sniping at each other, probably. Zadok opened his menu. "Would you like to share an appetizer?"

"I... um..." She opened hers. "The riblets look good."

"They do. So do the zucchini sticks. Let's do them both."

"I'll pay for my own meal. It isn't fair that Quincey forced you into this."

"She's somewhat underhanded, my sister."

"Exactly."

The hostess set down their water glasses and took their appetizer order. Zadok hadn't even peeked onto the next page yet.

Juni looked out the window again. Right. Anywhere but at him. "It's me who's getting a website out of the deal. I wanted to pay for her time, but she refused."

"She told me."

"So, she forced this dinner. I'm sorry."

"I'm not. You know I'd take you out every single Friday if you wanted to." And possibly a few evenings in between.

She pulled her lips in for a few seconds. "Anyway, I'll pay. Actually, I'll pick up the whole tab."

"You'll have to arm wrestle me for it." He set his elbow on the table and held his hand in position.

Her gaze held a few seconds longer this time. "I'm not arm wrestling you."

Zadok smirked. "You'd lose. I torque lug nuts for a living."

"I thought you pushed pencils."

"I know my way around the garage as well. My father would have it no other way."

"I'm sorry. I'm sure you miss your dad. Your mom, too."

"I do. And I wasn't ever planning on owning and operating a tire shop. God works in mysterious ways."

"No." She stared into her water glass as she twisted it in circles. "You were going to be a minister of music."

"That dream is on hold." Perhaps forever, though he cringed at the thought.

"Galena Gospel Church doesn't employ one of those?"

"It's not big enough for two pastors. Besides... I'm not sure I'm cut out for ministry, after all."

Juni's eyebrows tipped up. She was looking directly at him for once.

"A few years ago, I realized I needed to reevaluate my beliefs." She'd know what he meant, right?

"Oh."

"I was being groomed to be a certain sort of person." Zadok held her gaze. "I realized two things. That I wasn't actually that kind of guy, and that it wasn't who God wanted me to be."

"I see."

"Do you?" he asked softly. "Because I think you believe I'm still the guy who messed up so badly back then."

She swallowed hard. "My dad..."

"Your dad was wrong. I'm only starting to figure out how many ways he was wrong."

"Do you know what narcissism is?"

"Someone who thinks they're right, no matter how wrong they are."

"Pretty much. That's my father. He's never wrong, no matter how hard the evidence slaps him in the face. He just carries on in his own little dreamworld, thinking that he's better than everyone else and they're just around to serve his ego."

That explained a few things.

"Which leads to gaslighting the people around him." Juni's eyes were full of pain when she looked at Zadok. "You can't tell him things are different. He just keeps on assuming he's right and ignores any evidence to the contrary."

That sounded like the professor Zadok had known. The man had been suave and genteel and well-respected. He'd been everything a naive Zadok thought he wanted to be.

"In Dad's world, women's only role is to support men. Specifically, to support *him*. It took a long time for Mom to realize how damaging their relationship was and then to find the courage to leave him. She knew everyone would believe him and not her, and that's exactly what happened. He was the victim. She was the disrespectful hussy who didn't know when she had it good."

The appetizers arrived at the table, and neither had even looked deeper into the menu. Zadok asked for five more minutes.

"Mom got clear of him. Arleigh did, too, though it was harder for her. After all, Mom's first twenty years — her formative years — didn't have Dad in them, but Arleigh and me... well, Dad was present our entire lives, feeding into our impressionable brains."

When she paused, Zadok asked, "How old were you when they split?"

"Fourteen." She opened her menu and slid her finger down the list of options.

He should probably pick something, too. If only she'd keep talking. This hadn't been part of Quincey's bargain. For all his sister cared, he and Juni could sit in silence for sixty solid minutes.

But, no. That wasn't Quincey's hope at all. She wanted Juni for a sister-in-law, and Zadok didn't know if Juni would ever be in a place to accept him in her life. Or any guy, really. Her dad had truly messed her up, and Zadok had taken the worst possible advice to get her attention back in college.

JUNI TOOK LONGER than required to choose an entrée. The lemon-crusted salmon looked amazing, but the longer she stared at the menu, the less time she'd be required to talk to the man across from her.

The man who claimed not to be like her father. Who, honestly, really wasn't. He was a victim, too.

She didn't know what to do with that information, so she turned the last page of the menu and studied the desserts. Not that she'd be hungry for sweets afterward, after sharing two appetizers.

Which were getting cold.

She closed the menu, laid it on the end of the table, and reached for a zucchini stick.

"Mind if I pray?"

Juni yanked her hand back. "Sure. Go for it."

"Father God, thank You for this evening. I pray that You will bless this food to the use of our bodies and bless our time together. In Jesus' name, amen."

At least he hadn't gone on and on. Dad would have.

Zadok wasn't like Dad. She needed to get that through her thick skull. But she didn't want to.

Why? Because with that piece of armor stripped away, she'd be vulnerable. How could she protect her heart if she let it go?

"Good choice on the riblets. That's a tasty spice rub."

Juni forced her mind back to the present and reached for a piece of the pork. "Umhmm."

Beatrice cruised past to take their order and refill their water.

Both appetizers were likely very good, but they tasted

like cardboard thanks to Juni's nerves. Didn't stop her from eating a couple of each.

They probably had another 45 minutes to go before their hour was up. Would they even be done eating by then? Also... did it matter?

Zadok's a nice guy. He likes you. Why watch the clock? Why not enjoy the evening?

Because it was hard to let her assumptions go. It was painfully difficult to admit she'd jumped to conclusions and then clutched them tight regardless of recent evidence.

"I'm sorry," she blurted.

"You're forgiven. I'm also sorry for hurting you."

She looked across the table into his hazel eyes. "I don't usually hold grudges." Although, she might have to ask Arleigh if that were true.

Zadok offered a lopsided smile. "I don't, either. Can we... can we start over?"

Juni sucked in her lip. "I... it depends on what that means."

Was that disappointment on his face? "Can we pretend we met this past March and became friends?"

"Friends." She exhaled. "I can try that."

"If we've been friends for seven months, I'm pretty sure I'd have asked you out by now. Would you have said yes?"

Her shoulder muscles tightened. "There's no way to know, because that's not what happened."

"I'm sorry. Again. I don't want to push you."

Well, he was, regardless of intention. Juni took a sip of

her water and glanced around the rustic restaurant. Treyan leaned forward on their table, his adoring gaze fixed on Brittany's face, which Juni couldn't see. There were a few other people she knew. The math teacher, Dennis Weebly, and his much younger wife. Gary and Emma Waterman sat across from Matt and Connie Santoro, all of them laughing.

Beatrice settled two large plates on their slab table. "Thanks for your patience. Here's your medium-rare steak, sir, and here's your salmon, ma'am. Is there anything else I can get you? No? Enjoy your meal." She bustled off to greet newcomers.

"Mmm. Smells good. That salmon looks great, too."

"It does. Thanks, Zadok." She'd never dreamed those words would come out of her mouth. Or that she'd mean them.

"You're welcome." He chuckled. "I'm missing Foreign Friday over at the house. Xavier was muttering at Quincey's attempt to make Chinese beef-and-broccoli from scratch."

Finally, a topic they could discuss. "Quincey was very excited about her meal plan. It's been going well, then?"

"Other than Meatless Mondays. Xavier isn't the only one who thinks we need more protein." He carved a piece of his steak and put it in his mouth.

"He whined about it in our tutoring session a couple of days ago."

Zadok's fork poised halfway to his mouth, and his eyes met hers. "Oh?"

"Well, not whined exactly." Although the word was

accurate. Was she breaking the boy's confidence? "A few minutes later, he complained about the essay he needs to write for English. I suggested he combine the two aggravations."

The man across from her chuckled. "I told him the same thing, and now he's spouting statistics at Quincey every chance he gets. The kid is actually researching something."

Juni tried not to smile as she flaked a bite of tender salmon. The delectable aroma of fish and lemon in a creamy dill sauce reminded her she was, in fact, hungry.

"I'm impressed, by the way," Zadok went on. "His attitude has turned right around in the past few weeks."

"I can't take credit for that."

"Sure, you can."

She shook her head. "It's you and the driving lessons. He'll do nearly anything for a chance behind the wheel."

"It's the first time since our parents passed away that he's actually wanted to spend time with me."

"Funny how that works."

"I know, right? I was the same way when I was sixteen. My dad could have asked me to do anything at all, dangling the carrot of driving hours in front of me."

"For me it was my mom." Juni forced a tight smile and stirred the cream sauce into the risotto. "She'd always said it was in the fine print of their marriage contract that Dad had to teach their kids to drive. Then they split up weeks before Arleigh was old enough to start."

"It's not the same as my siblings—"

"I know. Their parents died."

Zadok shook his head. "That's not exactly what I meant. They weren't betrayed by their parents. They couldn't blame them. It was an accident that no one could foresee or control." He searched her eyes. "How long was your dad single?"

Juni snorted. "A few months? Which made us all wonder if he'd already been seeing Genevieve before the divorce. Men like him can't stand not being the center of someone's attention. They crave the limelight, the adoration."

Zadok stared into the corner of the ceiling.

Juni glanced up, but there was nothing to see, not even a cobweb. "What are you thinking?"

He shook himself. "My mind was wandering, but it was probably nothing." He pointed his fork at her plate. "That looks good. Is the flavor what you expected?"

"Better." For one thing, she hadn't expected to have an appetite at all.

"This whole evening — so far — has been better than I expected." Zadok's gaze warmed when he looked at her. "I'd really like to do this again without my sister's inter-ference."

Why did she keep fighting her attraction to him? Hadn't he proved to her he was nothing like Dad, that he'd been a misguided kid back then but had seen the error of his ways?

"Maybe we could try that," she said softly.

FIFTEEN

Zadok would never have believed that a forced dinner together could possibly have such a positive outcome. He owed Quincey one, and she'd never let him forget it. If things went well in the future, he wouldn't even mind if she crowed over him all the time.

Because, truth? All the sad-puppy-dog eyes he'd sent Juni for months had had zero results. All the attempts at apologies, attempts to have a civil conversation on any other topic, attempts to get her to even look at him directly, had all been for naught.

Until Quincey. Yeah, he owed his kid sister big time.

He and Juni lingered over a shared dessert of rich gingerbread cake smothered in whipped cream, each with a cup of cinnamon-apple tea. Around them, most of the other diners had left, with fewer to take their place.

Beatrice stopped by oftener now. Was she hurrying them along? A glance at the polished burl clock on the wall showed it was past 9:30. The Sizzling Skillet closed soon.

Not that Zadok wanted the evening to end, even though she'd agreed to another one. Even though he'd see her at the market in the morning and at church the day after. Those weren't dates. This, tonight, had turned into one.

Finally, reluctantly, he slid his credit card into the bill holder Beatrice had set on the table a while back. "Would you like to go for a walk along the lake? The pathway is lit for a half mile or so." He pointed through the window.

"That sounds... nice."

He helped her into her coat, resisting the urge to let his hands linger on her shoulders. If he didn't rush her, there'd be plenty of time for touches like that. Patience would indeed be his friend.

Beatrice stopped by with a portable card scanner and completed the transaction for dinner. He gave her a hefty tip for allowing them to tie up a table for the entire evening.

Zadok shrugged into his leather bomber jacket and followed Juni out to the foyer and into the chilly late-October evening. A stiff breeze had come up while they were inside. Would she still want to walk? Because he wasn't ready for the evening to end.

"The path starts across the beach parking lot there." He leaned closer as he pointed.

"I walked it a few times in the summer."

"You and your family had some picnics here." He touched the small of her back, not as satisfying as he would have liked with her thick coat between them.

"We did. Mom loves the ritual of Sunday afternoons

together." She darted a glance at him. "I seem to remember you and your brother playing Frisbee down here."

Xavier had nearly collided with Juni that one time. "I try to spend time with him when he'll let me."

"Teens are hard."

They walked across the parking lot, and Zadok turned up his jacket's collar. It felt like they'd be getting snow in the not-too-distant future, but it rarely stuck around this early in the season. He wasn't looking forward to it, whenever it came. It meant teaching Xavier how to handle the truck in adverse conditions.

At least they had good tires.

Juni's shoulder brushed against his arm. And, oh look, she had *not* tucked her bare hands into her coat pockets. Was that an invitation? Only one way to find out.

Zadok let his hand touch hers. "You're cold." When she didn't pull away, he twined their fingers together. "The moon is pretty on the lake tonight."

"It is."

He ran his thumb over hers. Slow, slow, slow. He didn't want to go slow. He wanted to kiss her.

Way too soon, Shirkowski.

Zadok cleared his throat. "So, uh, when will you and Quincey launch your website?"

"Tomorrow after the market, I think."

"You work on a laptop, right?"

She glanced up at him, barely discernible in the shadows. "Yes?"

"Why not bring it over and have soup and sandwiches

with us? We've got lots of room for the two of you to work." And then he could be around, too. If the girls met in the basement suite, he couldn't exactly invite himself. It would be way too awkward.

"I could maybe do that."

He gave a mental fist pump. "Sounds like a plan. Quincey is cooking tomorrow."

"She does all the cooking?" There was a bit of an edge to Juni's voice.

"Not all, but quite a bit. She's off work earlier than I am. But we all pitch in with prep on the weekends and on mornings we're loading the slow cooker. Having lunch at your mom's that day reminded us how helpful one of those appliances could be for a household where everyone is gone all day."

She'd relaxed a little at his explanation.

Zadok had a feeling she'd have him rethinking every gender role he'd fallen into if they dated long enough.

Were they dating? He shouldn't get ahead of himself.

One day at a time.

And tomorrow he'd sing and play and exchange furtive glances with her at the market, and then she'd come over to his house and hang out with him and his siblings. That would be a big day.

One day at a time.

He could do that. It might require a conscious effort to remember every five minutes, but it was possible. He cast around in his mind for another topic of conversation. "Have your sister and Mitchell chosen a wedding day?"

"Yeah, it's crazy soon. First Saturday in January. Lindsay's parents are coming for Christmas and then staying to watch the boys while Arleigh and Mitch are away."

"That's over two months from now." How was that defined as crazy soon? If it were him, he'd think that was forever away still.

"Barely. There's so much to do, and there's Christmas in between, too. Arleigh says she wants to keep things simple, which is a good thing, as I don't think she'll have a choice. I hope she can find a dress she likes off the rack."

Zadok should be paying attention. He'd never wondered how long it took to plan a wedding. Round about the time his college and seminary friends started getting hitched, he'd found himself an orphan with two siblings dependent on him. Not the stuff of romance, that was for sure.

But now... maybe?

"I should get home. Tomorrow will be a big day." Her words were punctuated by a yawn.

One day at a time.

But could he blame himself for thoughts that raced way ahead? He and his sibs were finally settling into some sort of workable rhythm. Juni was finally talking to him. There was hope for a future, and it truly didn't need to happen with the snap of his fingers.

He kept her hand wrapped in his as they turned back on the pathway and ambled toward their vehicles. He couldn't even drive her home.

Just as well.

At her car door, he caught both her hands in his.

"Thanks for a great evening. Sweet dreams, and I'll see you at the market in the morning."

She searched his eyes for just long enough he was tempted to go for it, but the kitchen door opened nearby and several of the wait staff erupted, talking and laughing.

"Good night, Zadok." Juni pulled away and turned to open her car door. "See you."

He stood and watched until her taillights signaled the turn north across the bridge before he clambered into his truck.

This was an evening he'd never truly expected. What a gift God — and Quincey — had given him. Now, if only he could manage not to mess things up again.

"Oh! I wasn't expecting you to wait up for me." Juni backed up a step at the sight of her sister, clad in her floral bamboo pajamas, curled up in the corner of the sofa.

Arleigh raised an eyebrow and peered above the wedding magazine in her hands. "I wasn't expecting you to be this late. Wasn't the deal for one hour?"

"It was." Juni turned to hang up her coat and toe off her boots.

"Who did you hang out with afterward?"

"We, um, stayed in The Sizzling Skillet until almost closing."

Arleigh looked at the clock.

So did Juni. 10:30.

"*Almost* closing? We're like eight minutes from town."

"And then we went for a walk along the lake path."

Her sister closed the magazine, laid it on the end table, then drew her knees to her chest and patted the sofa beside her. "I think you've got some sharing to do."

"He apologized."

"He's done that before."

Juni sighed and dropped onto the other end of the sofa. "I may have judged him too harshly."

"You think?"

"Maybe?"

"So, you spent nearly three hours at dinner and then went for a walk. I assume some talking was involved?"

"Quite a lot. I heard more about his parents' deaths. That must have been so hard for him and, of course, for Quincey and Xavier. It changed his life, really, since he came back here and took over his dad's business for at least as long as it would take to get both kids through high school."

"Was there some kissing involved, too?"

"No!" Juni shot back to her feet. "I barely know him. Barely even like him a tiny bit."

Arleigh snickered. "Tell yourself that, but I don't believe you on either count. Sure, you knew him way back when, but you've also known Zadok 2.0 since last spring. You may not have talked to him much, but you couldn't help but know who he is and what he stands for."

"Right. You win."

"It's not a competition. But you've also been fighting your attraction to him the whole time."

"How would you know? You've been so wrapped up in pushing Mitchell away for just as long—"

"Have not."

"Almost. When you started nannying for him and we moved into this suite, you practically hated the guy's guts. When have you had time to scrutinize my love life?" Too late, Juni realized her mistake.

Arleigh's eyebrows shot up. "Uh huh?"

"That's not what I meant."

"Sure, it's not." Arleigh hugged her knees to her chest. "You know something? It's okay to admit that you like the guy, sis. You don't have to keep pretending he's a jerk. We both know that was just your way of denying everything, but you already admitted an attraction, so can't we just go with that now?"

"I don't know how."

Arleigh began singing "Let It Go" from the "Frozen" movie.

Juni tackled her sister, tickling her until she collapsed in a giggling heap. It was infectious. It felt good to let off a little steam, laughing with her sister.

Too soon, though, Juni straightened. "I don't know what to dooo," she wailed.

"Enjoy the moment?"

"How can I? I don't know what will happen next."

"Um, earth to Juni, that's sort of how life goes. We pray, we make the best decisions we can, and then trust

God to keep leading us. We can never see the whole path spread out in front of us. Life's an adventure!"

"I don't like adventure."

"Says the woman who's inspired dozens, no hundreds, of kids with your magical felties. All those mermaids and dragons are inspiring imaginations for quests. Who wants to live in a safe box all the time?"

Juni dropped to the other end of the sofa and eyed her sister. "You. You wanted to. We were alike that way."

"I didn't want to. Not really. I was afraid."

Afraid? Not Arleigh. "But you risked everything to start your flower farm. That's not what a fearful person does."

"And you saw how well that worked out for me. I lived in an ancient, musty trailer that collapsed in a winter rainstorm while the river swept my rented greenhouses away."

"If all that hadn't happened, you wouldn't be sitting here with that ginormous rock on your left hand."

Arleigh held up her ring and smiled as the facets glinted light around the room. "That happened in spite of my fear, not because I was brave. And I'm thankful."

"I'm happy for you." It was even true.

"It was hard to set aside fear and choose hope instead."

"I know." Juni rubbed her temples. So much had happened. Had she made a mistake forgiving Zadok?

No. The Bible commanded forgiveness. Seventy times seven, Jesus had said, maybe in hopes people would have stopped counting by then. Could a person forgive someone and still stay cautious around them? That only made sense. God didn't expect people to invite repetitive pain, just forgive it.

There was something messed up in there, but it had been a really long day. Plus, she hadn't slept much the past couple of nights as she tried to figure out how to get Quincey to hand over the website without going for dinner with the girl's brother.

Dinner had been nice. Much nicer than she'd thought possible.

"Penny for your thoughts?"

Juni shook her head. "There isn't anything to say." The instant Arleigh found out about the hand-holding, she'd be back to planning that double wedding. Best to keep her in the dark as long as possible. Perhaps forever. "I should go to bed. Market tomorrow."

"Where you can gaze at your gorgeous boyfriend for four hours straight with no one even noticing. Except me. I'll notice."

"He's not my boyfriend." But... wasn't he? Hadn't she held hands with him and agreed to go out again? There wasn't anything official, though. "Also, I'll be too busy selling to gaze at anyone." Juni reached over and picked up the magazine. "Find any great tips tonight?"

"Oooh, I'm happy to share them with you."

"For you, dingbat, not for me."

Arleigh faked a pout. "You can't blame a girl for trying."

"Look, you haven't been engaged for a full seven days yet. How about we focus on your wedding and not worry about me?"

"I can't believe I'm marrying Mitchell." Arleigh went back to smiling at the ring.

Mission accomplished. "Have you asked Mom about walking you down the aisle?"

Arleigh grimaced. "She thinks I should ask Dad."

"No way."

"She said it would be a nice gesture."

"And when you told her you hadn't even planned to invite him at all? Never mind Genevieve and their five perfect children?"

"Only three are perfect. The other two are girls."

"Right." Juni rolled her eyes. "Poor kids. Their mother isn't as smart as ours was."

"I feel sorry for Genevieve, too. She's been brainwashed. Even if she had any independent thoughts, she has no place to share them."

"Yeah, I know. That one time I tried to talk to her about Dad's controlling nature, his narcissism, she shut me down faster than I could blink."

"We should pray for her. For the kids, who I guess happen to be our half-siblings."

Yeah, they should. Mostly, Juni tried to pretend they didn't exist, which wasn't that much different from how Dad treated her, come to think of it. "Are you going to invite him, after all?"

"I don't know. I wanted Mom to do the honors."

"You don't have to have a parent walk you down the aisle at all, you know. It's not like you're an object changing ownership."

"I thought of that, too, but I like the tradition of the parents' blessing and all that."

The day Dad blessed either one of them would be one to remember, for sure.

Juni pulled to her feet and stretched. "Well, I vote for you going solo if Mom won't escort you. Tomorrow I'll be able to show you my new website. You'll love it. I know! You should get Quincey to make you one, too."

Arleigh waved a hand. "I don't need one. Floral arrangements don't travel as well as your felties do. Quincey is coming over after the market, you said?"

A flush crept up Juni's neck. "About that. I think I'll take my laptop over to the—her house, instead. More room to spread out."

"How much room do two laptops need?" Arleigh eyed her. "Also, doesn't she live with her brothers, including that really tall, hot, musical one?"

Busted. "She does. I'm going over for the afternoon and dinner."

"But you're not dating."

"Hello? I'm working on the website with Zadok's *sister*."

Arleigh smirked, jumped to her feet, and squeezed Juni. "I'm happy for you, and I can't wait to see the website. Also? That guy's a keeper. Don't put him off too long."

And she darted off into her bedroom and shut the door, leaving Juni standing in the middle of the living room, staring after her.

Nice Arleigh was so excited about the dawn of this

relationship, because Juni was not all that sure it was a good idea, even now. But Arleigh was right on the first three counts. Zadok was tall. He was hot. And he was musical. Whether he was a keeper or not remained to be seen.

SIXTEEN

At the market, Zadok switched between his guitar, ukulele, and violin. He sang along when the lyrics begged to be shared. Most of the time, those were the peppy praise songs he was practicing for leading worship Sunday mornings with Keanan Welsh. Then he morphed into some of the older hymns.

Paula hurried by his spot, humming along under her breath. Rosemary Nemesek had been chatting with Nila, the potter, and the two turned and focused on him. Rosemary's boot tapped along.

Several townspeople engaged the O'Neill sisters at their booth across the way. Looked like Juni had sold several sets so far. She seemed more relaxed than usual. Was that on account of their date last night?

They'd had a date.

Yeah, it hadn't started that way, but it had definitely become one. And, yes, Quincey had been exactly as smug as Zadok had expected. His "I owe you one" had elicited a long list of ways he could repay her. Starting with cooking every night in November, only days away now.

How hard could it be? He didn't even have to follow her menu plan. They could have Meaty Mondays. Xavier would love him forever.

What was he playing, anyway? He had to focus for a few seconds to realize he'd been picking out Fanny J Crosby's famous hymn, 'To God Be the Glory.' He stepped to the microphone to sing: "To God be the glory; great things He has done! So loved He the world that He gave us His Son, who yielded His life an atonement for sin, and opened the life-gate that all may go in."

He let the guitar sing the refrain without his voice.

Praise the Lord! Praise the Lord! Let the earth hear his voice! Praise the Lord! Praise the Lord! Let the people rejoice. O come to the Father through Jesus the Son and give Him the glory; great things He has done!

Zadok's heart was full. God had indeed done great and glorious things, and the little bit of joy He'd given Zadok last night and the hope of more to come was only a blip on the eternal radar. And yet, the blip was Zadok's. It was his life, and he felt the blessing.

He glanced across at Juni and saw her mouthing the words to the chorus, so he played it again. This time her gaze met his, and she offered a little smile to acknowledge the lyrics. Or him. Or maybe both.

Zadok grinned back then looked away. Everything was too new, too fragile, for random market visitors to catch him making googly-eyes at Juni. Or worse, one of the other vendors or Paula. He'd never hear the end of it.

As it was, Arleigh nudged Juni, and Juni elbowed her sister back.

He shouldn't be surprised Arleigh knew what had gone down. Not after the way Quincey had gone after him last night when he'd finally arrived back at the house. But did Arleigh's nudge mean she was okay with him and Juni? He wasn't about to ask her. But maybe he'd ask Juni later.

Zadok shook his head. He'd played that refrain like five times in a row. Time to pay better attention. He set down the guitar, picked up his ukulele, and launched into a jig.

It seemed the mood in the entire greenhouse brightened with the peppy music. Chatter seemed louder, laughter more often. Hopefully sales would increase, too.

"Nice repertoire today." Paula appeared at the edge of his space.

"Thanks." His fingers danced on as he nodded at the market manager.

"I don't know if you realize what a difference live music makes to us every Saturday. It's just so inviting."

"I appreciate hearing that."

"Want a coffee or something? You haven't taken a break in a while."

"I, uh..." His gaze flew to the clock. She was right. "Maybe I'll take a few and do my own shopping. Quincey sent me with a list."

Paula laughed. "I bet she did. That sister of yours is something else."

"Oh?" Zadok closed off his current song and laid his instrument in its case. "You know her?"

"I've been hanging out at Green Acres some. I know they really appreciate her there. She's full of youthful enthusiasm, and that's contagious."

He laughed. "I didn't know any of that crew were lacking in enthusiasm." Though, granted, the six couples who ran the place weren't as young as they once were. Some of them were probably pushing forty.

Paula smiled in return. "No, you're right about that. Still, I think she and the other interns and students are a reminder of their original mandate."

"Sustainable living." It seemed a mighty lofty goal for them to think they could produce nearly everything they needed on the eighty acres they operated — the forty Jo, Claire, and Sierra had originally purchased plus the forty the couples had purchased from Rosemary and Steve Nemesek a few years later.

"That and teaching others to do the same. They've had hundreds of students through that farm school over the years."

His eyebrows tipped up. "Hundreds?"

"I'm sure when you count up all the weekend work-shops as well as the seasonal courses it would come to that. Maybe more."

"Huh." Green Acres Farm had been established before his parents had moved to Galena Landing. He'd never thought much about the wide range of influence they'd had. Noble ideas, sure. And contagious, if Quincey was anyone to go by.

Paula patted his arm. "Go get that coffee. Jean still has plenty in her urn, and Brittany brought cupcakes. You don't want to miss one of those." She leaned closer. "Don't tell Jean I said Brittany's baking is better."

Zadok chuckled. "I think everyone knows, but there are plenty who want a one-dollar treat instead of paying five."

"True enough." Paula nodded and moved on to the next vendor.

What would Juni say if he brought her a cupcake and a coffee? He knew how she took her coffee — he'd been watching her at the market for seven months — but would that be too obvious in front of the current crowd?

But he was done pretending he didn't have feelings for her. She'd given him a green light last night. Not a glowing neon sign visible for a hundred miles, but certainly enough to give him a little confidence.

Yeah, he'd do that, but he wouldn't linger. He'd set it on her table then chat up some of the other vendors while he drank his own brew. Unless she invited him to linger.

A guy could hope.

JUNI PARKED her car at the curb of the address Zadok had given her. She looked at the single-garage bungalow reminiscent of the 1970s like this entire neighborhood of Galena Landing. The living room jutted toward the street with its large windows and vertical siding.

This would be way beneath Dad and Genevieve. He

deserved the newest, biggest, and best, which his tenure at the university afforded him.

Had Juni needed any further proof that Zadok wasn't cut from the same cloth Dad was? Of course, this property had been chosen by his parents, not by him.

She shook her head to dislodge any and all comparisons. They were only habits now. She knew better than to continue believing what she'd clung to for so long.

Zadok is not like Dad. Zadok is not like Dad. I know that.

A figure appeared in the wide glass panes and waved.

Great. Quincey had caught her sitting in her car as though she were going to rethink this and drive away without coming in. Juni absolutely had enough nerve to grab her messenger bag, exit her car, and stride up that sidewalk.

Any second now.

"God?" she whispered. "I'm going to need some help here, please. And a little wisdom wouldn't go amiss." She took a deep breath, pushed the door open, and reached for her bag. Here went nothing.

Quincey flung the door open wide as Juni arrived on the sheltered front step. "Yay! You came!"

"I did." As though the younger woman hadn't pretty much forced her.

"The guys are in the kitchen making chili and corn-bread for dinner. It's not exactly what I had in mind when calling it Soup-and-Sandwich Saturday, but I guess it's close enough."

"That sounds delicious." Juni removed her jacket, and Quincey hung it in the nearby closet.

Zadok appeared at the archway to the living room. "Hey, good to see you."

"Hi." The remainder of her words fled at the sight of him. Not that he was dressed so differently from at the market in worn jeans and a navy Henley with the sleeves pushed up his forearms. Somehow he looked more... domestic?

"I thought we'd work at the table," Quincey said. "It's just off the kitchen around here, if you want to bring your bag."

Quincey's laptop was open facing the backyard, leaving options for Juni.

She knew she ought to sit with her back to the kitchen, but she absolutely couldn't force herself to. She'd constantly be tempted to glance over her shoulder, and that would be far too obvious. No, she set her own laptop with her back to the wall, the kitchen shamelessly in front of her.

"*More* mushrooms?" Xavier grimaced as he wielded his knife at the peninsula. "I don't even like the dumb things."

Zadok winked at Juni. *Winked.*

She was in such big trouble being here.

"Your palate won't grow up if you don't let it," he advised his brother then turned back to the stove where ground beef and onions already sizzled, if the aroma wasn't steering Juni wrong.

She forced her gaze back to Quincey, who leaned back in her chair with a wide grin, her arms crossed over her chest. "So, teach me everything I need to know."

Quincey's eyebrows ratcheted up.

"About the website."

"Of course, the website. You couldn't possibly have meant anything else."

Was that heat creeping up Juni's neck? Great. "Absolutely the website."

"Okay." Quincey leaned forward and tapped at her keyboard. "Here's the website host I recommended the other day. Are you set up there?"

Juni nodded and navigated to the portal on her own laptop. And then she spent the next hour focusing as tightly as she could on Quincey's words and actions as they worked together to set the pages up on Juni's own domain.

But it wasn't easy ignoring the two guys — okay, one, specifically — working nearby as well as the delectable aroma they'd concocted. After a while, Xavier disappeared down the basement stairs while Zadok turned the element on low and dropped into the chair across from Quincey.

"How is it going?"

"Good." Quincey didn't glance up.

But Zadok wasn't looking at his sister, anyway. His warm hazel gaze was locked on Juni's, his lopsided grin and — wait, was that a dimple? Why had she never noticed?

Because she'd been too focused on ignoring him. Avoiding him. Casting him in a negative light. But now? She noticed. Took in his slightly tousled brown hair, the slight scruff on his chin. What would it feel like to touch that?

To be kissed?

No! She did not want to be kissed. Not by Zadok Shirkowski. Not by anyone.

His warm gaze faltered a tiny bit.

Juni was doing it again. Saying she forgave him. Saying they could be friends, maybe more, but second-guessing herself every minute of the day. The guy had the patience of a saint not to run for the hills and never look back. She managed a smile.

His expression softened immediately. Like she had some power over him. It was… heady. How could she trust herself to treat him right with their history?

One step at a time. One minute at a time. And if he did end up running, she could scarcely blame him. She'd hopefully learn something from the experience for next time.

Next time? There wouldn't be a next time. She'd practically vowed never to marry — but then, so had Arleigh, and look at her, head over heels in love with Mitchell Ackerman and counting down the days until their wedding. But could Juni lay everything out for her sister and get her advice? Truly everything?

It didn't matter what Arleigh thought of her. They'd been through a lot in their childhood, in their teens, and now this summer. Her sister had her back, no matter what. But could she be trusted to see Juni's situation without her rose-colored glasses on?

"Deep thoughts?" Zadok's murmur was quiet.

Juni blinked and refocused on him. She managed a smile. "It's okay."

"Just okay?" Quincey didn't look up. "I thought you loved it."

"The website?" Juni wrenched her focus back to what Zadok's sister was doing. "I do. I love it. You're doing an amazing job."

Quincey glanced between them then pointed a finger at Zadok. "You're distracting her. Go away. Give us another hour."

He chuckled and lifted both hands in the air. "Wow, I know when I'm not wanted. Maybe I'll take Xavier out for a drive. One hour, you say?"

Xavier popped his head out of the stairwell. "Did someone say my name and driving in the same sentence?"

Zadok chuckled and winked at Juni. "It's either that or you let me beat you at Mario Kart."

"As if you could. I'll grab my jacket." Xavier darted past him toward the door.

"I'll see you in a bit. Maybe you wouldn't mind giving the chili a stir after a while, though it should be fine."

"I can do that."

"Shoo." Quincey waved her hand but didn't look up from her screen. "Enough, already."

Juni shared a smile with Zadok at the girl's focus, but it was on her behalf, so she couldn't exactly complain. "See you soon."

His gaze lingered on hers for a long moment.

What was he seeing in her eyes? On her face? Was it the same thing she was seeing on his?

Hope, maybe. A little attraction... panic reared its ugly head once again, but she shoved it back down. No! She was done with that. Did the guy have to do cartwheels to prove he wasn't like her father? She knew he wasn't. *Knew it.*

It was just that she'd been steeped in her stinking thinking for years and years. It was hard to simply let go.

He gave her another smile before heading out of the room. A moment later, she heard the front door close and, shortly after, the rumble of his truck starting up and then fading down the street.

"Finally," Quincey murmured. "Now, see this piece of the shopping cart? I need some banking info from you to finish setting it up."

Juni felt like part of her had driven away with Zadok and Xavier, which was all kinds of ridiculous. She barely knew him.

There she went again. She knew him better than she allowed herself to realize. She'd seen him in action for more than half a year in a variety of settings.

"You with me?"

Juni met Quincey's questioning gaze. "Um, yes. What exactly are you looking for?"

Time to wrap up the website. In an hour, Zadok would return, and who knew where the evening would lead them? Could she let herself get even a little excited to find out?

SEVENTEEN

W ould you stop looking at your watch?"
Xavier's voice was tinged with impatience.

The kid was right. It would be less obvious
if Zadok checked the dashboard clock, but that wasn't
what his brother was talking about. Xavier knew Zadok's
mind wasn't on the driving lesson. It was true, but Xav
was doing pretty well. They were mostly logging hours
now, at least until the snow flew and the teen would need
to learn to navigate slush and ice. Plus, at some point,
Zadok needed to let him drive around Coeur d'Alene or
even Spokane and get some interstate and city driving in.
That sounded all kinds of terrifying.

"You've got it bad, dude." Xavier sighed. "It's like
you're not even here, just dreaming about my teacher."

Zadok blinked and sat up straighter. How had he
forgotten that link? Would anyone think it was weird for
him to date his brother's teacher? Surely there wasn't a
rule about that in modern Galena Landing?

"You could do worse, you know."

Man, he needed to rein in his thoughts. "You like her?" Xavier shot him a look.

Eyes on the road, buddy. But it had only been a quick glance.

"Duh. She's a way better teacher than Weebly or Donovan."

"*Mister* Weebly to you, kid. And *Miz* Donovan."

"Yeah, yeah. I do have one problem, though."

Zadok braced himself. "What's that?"

"I never know what to call her. At school, she's Ms. O'Neill, but at home you and Quincey are constantly talking about Juni."

Oh, was that all? "Just remember where you are, that's all. So, you like her okay?"

"You already asked me that." Xavier smirked and flexed his hands on the steering wheel.

Ten and two, buddy. But Xavier knew that.

"You gonna marry her or what?"

"Uh..." Zadok's brain scrambled to catch up. "We started 'dating' like yesterday." He air-quoted the word. "Planning a wedding already might be a tad premature."

His brother shrugged. "Like you and Quince are always telling me, I'm just a kid. How should I know how long these things take?"

"More than twenty-four hours, I can tell you that much." Of which spending an entire one sitting in the passenger seat with a newbie driver behind the wheel asking questions about his love life seemed too high of a percentage of his time.

Yeah, okay, he was chafing at the bit to get back to the house. Who knew what all Quincey might tell Juni about him? Or what would Juni figure out from being in the house the siblings called home? She'd know the decor was his parents' style, right? It wasn't like he'd put his personal stamp on anything in the public areas.

It had been hard enough taking over their bedroom. He'd slept in the basement family room for months before bracing himself and sorting out their personal space. He'd struggled more during that week than he had the week of the accident and the double funeral.

Screech.

Zadok sat bolt upright as the truck lurched to a stop and a five-point buck bounded across in front of them with mere inches to spare.

Xavier let out a trembling breath. "That was close. He came out of nowhere. I barely saw him before he was in front of the truck."

"Good job." Zadok needed another moment to catch his breath and even out his tone. "They do that, for sure. It's one of the hazards of driving in the north. You handled it just right." At least the road hadn't been covered with ice or snow, making stopping on a dime impossible. At least there hadn't been an oncoming vehicle to make avoidance trickier. At least...

"You drive. I'm shaking."

Zadok had to get a hold of himself. He couldn't get lost in the memories of the crash that had taken their parents. "Keep driving, Xavier."

"Didn't you hear me?" His brother's voice crackled like it hadn't in a few years.

"I heard you." Zadok steadied his voice. "I understand. I do. But you need to keep going, or fear will paralyze you, and who knows when you'll be ready to drive again. There's an intersection up ahead. You can turn around there and head back to the house. But you are doing the driving, not me."

Xavier eased onto the accelerator, signaled to turn onto the side road, then stopped. "Are you sure? Because..."

"I'm sure. You've got this. You know how to turn around, so check for traffic, then do it. You're a good driver. You can manage."

"I'm a good driver?" Xavier's voice was plaintive. Needy.

"You are. Deer are a fact of life around here. You definitely don't want to hit one, but you're not likely to be badly hurt from it. The truck would sustain damage, and, uh, so would the deer, but you'd be okay." Probably.

Xavier focused on getting the vehicle turned around and pointed back toward Galena Landing. "How was that?" He glanced over as he accelerated up the highway.

"Very nice. And see? The buck is long gone. Now you know it pays to keep being watchful."

"Yeah. That was intense." Xavier's fingers flexed as he drove. "What did Dad and Mom hit?"

"An elk."

"They're a lot bigger."

"And their car was a lot smaller." Which was why Zadok had traded his junker car in on a truck when he moved north as guardian of his siblings. If he could have bought a *tank*, he would have. Safety first. Hot-looking wheels, second. Or tenth.

"People who live in cities don't need cars, right?"

"That's true in the bigger cities, at least, if public transportation is well laid out. But a lot of places, having your own makes life a whole lot easier." He eyed his brother. "Why do you ask?"

"That deer thing was scary."

"Yeah, but we can't let fear rule our lives. You know that, right?" Did Zadok know it himself? Did he live like it?

"I guess."

"It might sound cliché, but we have to remember that God's got it. Whatever it is, He's got it."

"He didn't have Mom and Dad."

Zadok closed his eyes for a quick prayer. "He did. He never let them down."

"Funny way of showing it."

"There's a verse in the Bible that says, 'for my thoughts are not your thoughts, neither are your ways my ways,' declares the Lord. 'As the heavens are higher than the earth, so are my ways higher than your ways and my thoughts than your thoughts.'"

"Yeah, I don't think so."

Zadok cringed inside. "Faith in God and believing He knows best is the only thing that held me together two years ago."

"Nothing held *me* together," Xavier muttered.

"God wants to. It's why Jesus came." Had Zadok even realized how much his brother struggled? Well, there'd been clues like the lack of schoolwork, but that it went this deep? Right into the strata of faith?

Then again, how deep had his own personal faith been when he'd been Xavier's age? And he hadn't suffered the trauma of losing his parents then.

"I get it. That's your pat answer."

"It's not just that. Jesus is real. His love and care are real." If he hadn't been watching, he'd have missed Xavier's eyeroll, and his heart hurt. "Being a teen is hard. I remember."

"Everything is hard."

"I know."

"And pushing it off on God is... I don't know. Simplistic? And what I expect of a guy who thought God wanted him to be a pastor. So what about that now, huh? Did He change His mind?"

Zadok stared out the windshield for a long moment. "Like I said, God's thoughts aren't the same as mine. I'm sure I heard Him correctly, but sometimes there are detours."

Xavier scoffed under his breath. "You call our parents' deaths a detour?"

If Zadok couldn't even answer his own brother's questions, how could he expect to have been a decent pastor? Sure, he'd planned on heading up the music ministry in a large urban church with a full staff, not winging it on his own. He didn't think God had called him to be a senior minister or the only one in a smaller, rural congregation, like Ron Wilson.

He'd taken classes in oration and homiletics and apologetics, but didn't a man need a lot more life experience to be the primary preacher?

It didn't matter. Not for now, anyway. Galena Gospel Church was blessed to have Pastor Ron and Wanda at the helm. They were a godly couple, and the congregation was flourishing.

But Xavier was still waiting for him to answer as they entered town limits. "That wasn't exactly what I meant," Zadok said. "But Dad and Mom have fulfilled the mission God gave them, even though it doesn't seem like it to us. The detour I mentioned was mine, not theirs. And moving to Galena Landing to hang out with you and Quince probably wasn't a detour at all. God has done a lot of growing in me in the past two years. I see it in you and Quincey, too, but there's no denying it's been crazy hard."

Xavier muttered something under his breath as he flipped on the signal for their street.

"Plants in a greenhouse look pretty." Zadok considered Arleigh's lush blooms. "But they often have such weak stems that a big storm would break them. Gardeners have to expose them to the elements little by little so they become strong enough for the big winds."

"If you're trying to be comforting, you're missing the mark. We had the big storm already, and I, for one, wasn't ready for it." Xavier looked across at Zadok for a long few seconds. "My stem broke."

WHERE WERE THE GUYS? Juni and Quincey had wrapped up the website and created a Facebook business page along with an ad account. They'd stirred the chili and set the table and now sat in the living room where Quincey told Juni all about her business classes in college and what she hoped to do in the future.

It wasn't that Juni wasn't interested. She was. But the hour had come and gone, and this wasn't the way she'd envisioned the day going.

It's not all about you, Juni.

She knew that. She knew that she was only responsible for herself, while Zadok was basically a single parent to two teenagers. His responsibilities might ease in a couple of years, but they would never end.

Arleigh was taking on two little boys. That was a big job, too, but she'd been their nanny before she began dating their dad. It was different for Juni. The kids were older, and they weren't technically Zadok's.

The truck grumbled into the drive. The garage door rattled as it lifted, and the truck disappeared into its nether reaches.

Now that Zadok had returned, she could breathe. Which was a little crazy, because only 24 hours ago she still hated his guts. Or, at least, had been determined to keep him at a distance.

The door from the garage opened, and a moment later Xavier shot down the basement stairs while Zadok came into the living room. He gave her that lopsided grin she'd come to love — no, like, or at least appreciate — but there was sadness in his eyes.

"Sorry we're a little late. We had a close encounter with a whitetail buck, but Xav didn't hit it, so all is well."

Juni grimaced. "They're everywhere these days, especially at dusk. Don't they know it's hunting season?"

"Apparently not." Zadok glanced toward the stairwell and shook his head slightly. "I'll get the cornbread in the oven. That qualifies as our sandwich for tonight."

"You're playing fast and loose with the rules." Quincey bounded to her feet. "I'll fix a salad."

"When is a better night for chili and cornbread?" Zadok jostled his sister lightly as they headed through the entrance into the kitchen. "Your system doesn't allow a lot of leeway."

"Maybe Saturday should be Zadok Day," she mumbled.

"Fine by me." He grinned at Juni, who'd followed them. "Did you hear that? I have a day named after me."

"I have an entire month."

He laughed. "So you do."

Quincey opened the fridge and pulled out a bag of greens, but Juni stepped around her as though magnetically drawn to the tall man over by the stove.

Zadok searched her face. "Did you miss me?" he asked quietly.

"To my utter shock and astonishment."

He chuckled and caught her hand for a brief moment. "I'll take that answer. I'm still a little amazed myself."

"That cornbread isn't making itself," Quincey muttered.

"She's a hard taskmaster," he said to Juni.

She laughed. "I know it. Here, let me help you. Where's the recipe? Or is it a box mix?"

"As if." He chuckled as he pointed at a photo-album style recipe book lying on the counter. "Right there. The mixing bowls are in the bottom cupboard by your knees. I'll start getting out the ingredients." He reached past her and turned the oven on before doing so.

It didn't take the two of them long to mix up the batter, pour it into a 9x9 pan, and pop it in the oven. By then, Quincey had set the bowl of salad on the table with three kinds of bottled dressing and disappeared.

Zadok leaned against the cupboards and reached for Juni's hands with both of his.

How could she resist? She stepped closer and let him pull her into his arms. It seemed strange and yet safe and familiar to feel his hands caress her back. Finally, she leaned all the way in and rested her cheek against his chest with her arms around him.

Please, Lord, if this isn't right, take away this attraction.

But hadn't she been praying that for seven months now? And the only answer seemed to be the opposite. That it *was* right. That she was, in fact, safe with this man. That he would guard her and not steamroll over her the way Dad had done to Mom and was now doing to Genevieve.

Juni breathed in the unique blend that was Zadok Shirkowski. The woodsy aroma might be from his stringed instruments, but there was a hint of chili powder and musk.

"Are you sniffing me?"

Heat surged up her neck and flooded her face. "Sorry."

He chuckled, and she felt the rumble under her cheek. "I might be guilty, too." His hands rubbed her back soothingly. "You smell like... hmm. Something floral."

"Umhmm."

"It seemed like a safe guess." Zadok rested his cheek on the top of her head. "Jasmine?"

He was seriously trying to figure out her perfume? "There's jasmine, yes. And some gardenia and other scents."

"I like it."

Had he just kissed her hair? What would happen if she leaned back a little and looked up at him? But... did she want to be kissed? Yes? But also possibly no. It was too soon. Yesterday at this time she'd been grumbling and whining around the basement suite as she prepared for dinner out. Quincey's edict had been so unfair.

And now she wanted Zadok to kiss her? She needed to slam on her mental and emotional brakes. Did that mean she should step out of Zadok's arms? Yes. In a minute or two. A little longer wouldn't hurt. After all, she was already here.

"When's food?" Xavier asked.

"About ten minutes, when the timer goes off," Zadok answered, not loosening his hold on her.

The teen mumbled something else, and his footsteps padded away.

"He's having a rough time," Zadok murmured in her ear. "Still blaming God for taking our parents."

"Aw, I'm sorry to hear that." She angled back a little to look up at him. "I'm not surprised, from some of the things he's said in tutoring sessions. Not that I can talk to him about his relationship with God on school property."

"Yeah, that complicates things." Zadok's hazel eyes looked into hers. "He was pretty shaken up about that near-miss with the deer and all this stuff came bursting out. I thought we were past it."

"I think grief is like a spiral. It feels like you've come full circle, back to the starting point, but it's not exactly true. You've moved a little in or out even with that circling around thing going on."

"You might be right. Thank you. I needed to hear that."

How did she answer? It's like he thought she held the keys to wisdom or something. She so did not.

Zadok straightened and pressed his lips to her forehead before releasing her and picking up the wooden spoon he'd been stirring the chili with. "I'll get this dished up. Thanks for keeping an eye on it while I was out with Xav."

"No problem."

Another way he was different from her father. If Dad knew how to do more than boil water, she wasn't aware of it. Zadok could cook — from scratch, even. Suddenly her tummy rumbled. Yep, she was hungry for this delicious-smelling dinner, but maybe, just maybe, she was also hungry for this man.

And maybe that was all right.

EIGHTEEN

Z adok marveled at how well Juni fit in with his siblings. She'd coaxed Xavier out of his bad mood while chatting with Quincey about websites and shopping carts and search engine optimization. It was almost like a foreign language, other than that all the words were English, but their meanings didn't seem to be.

Still, he could sit back, relax, and let the conversation flow over him which, not incidentally, gave him the opportunity to watch Juni without it feeling creepy. She'd told him the chili was amazing and polished off a second piece of cornbread and a bowl of salad.

A woman who didn't shy away from food? Sign him up.

He was already signed up. He'd signed up months ago — years ago — only now she was on the same page. *Thank you, Lord.*

"Zay, didn't you get some cookies from the market?" Quincey asked.

"Uh, yes, I did." He surged to his feet and went into the kitchen. "Brittany had butterscotch-chip cookies today, and I snagged a couple of dozen." He arranged eight of them on a plate and set it on the table.

"Thanks." Xavier rose, snagged two of them, and glanced at Juni. "I guess I've got some homework to do. Catch you all later."

Juni gave him a brilliant smile. "Soon you're not going to need tutoring anymore."

The kid hesitated. "Yeah, I will." Then he bounded down the stairs.

Hopefully to his textbooks and not the Nintendo Switch, but hey, why distrust him? Sounded like Xavier couldn't get enough time with Juni, either.

A few minutes later, Quincey began gathering the dishes, and Juni jumped up to help. "I've got it." Quincey waved Juni back to the table. "Zadok cooked dinner, and it's my night for cleanup. Xavier did it earlier."

"Oh. If you're sure." Juni leaned back in her chair and took her second cookie.

"We have a chore chart based on our daily schedules." Quincey returned to the table for the leftovers. "It all works out, more or less."

"I'm sure you and Arleigh do something similar." Zadok studied Juni.

Was that a flush on her cheeks? "Arleigh does most of the cooking. She's home, and I'm not. But I do most of the cleaning."

He hadn't meant to make her feel bad. "Teamwork is what it's all about. It doesn't always look the same."

The dishes clattered as Quincey slotted them in the dishwasher.

"Want to go for a walk?" Zadok asked. Anything to get Juni's undivided attention for a little while. That hug before dinner only made him want more. Like... kissing.

Was she ready for that? Because he was totally on board, but he'd been yearning for a relationship with her for a whole lot longer than she'd been amenable.

Maybe no kisses tonight.

"Sure. Then I should probably head back to the farm soon. I've got homework, too... to grade."

He rose, and she did, too. He got her jacket from the closet and held it for her, letting his hands settle on her shoulders for a brief moment. Was it his imagination, or was she leaning into his touch a little?

Maybe there'd be kisses.

He pulled on his own jacket and stepped into his tennis shoes while she tugged on her low boots. Then he opened the door and ushered her out.

"Brr." Juni turned up the collar on her jacket. "When does Galena Landing usually get snow?"

It felt cold enough, and a faint crisp smell lingered in the air. "Could be anytime, but this early, it will probably melt again. It doesn't usually stick until closer to Christmas. But, you never know."

"I should have brought gloves."

"Let me borrow Quincey's." He ducked back inside and returned a few seconds later with a pair of knit gloves. "Here." He held one out for Juni to slip her hand into, then the other. He squeezed them both. "Better?"

"Much." She smiled at him.

"Good. Because I can only warm one at a time if we're walking." He wrapped his fingers around hers as they wandered down the block.

The streetlights illuminated the sidewalk well enough. Rectangles of light glowed from windows in the houses along the street. A few folks had Halloween decorations out — orange lights along the eaves, with skeletons and wispy, ethereal ghosts fluttering in the yards.

"You into Halloween?" he asked.

She shuddered. "No, not really. We weren't allowed to participate when I was a kid, and that made me angry. I didn't want to be different than my friends. I wanted to dress up and go trick-or-treating, but my dad..."

Right. Zadok should have guessed Professor O'Neill would have considered it wholly a pagan holiday. He squeezed Juni's hand. "You didn't miss much but an overdose of sugar. My parents had a more lenient view than yours, but they were careful what events we were allowed to participate in." His thoughts meandered down memory lane for a minute. "I've got a few years on Quincey and Xavier, but I'm pretty sure it was the same for them. Our parents used to host a bonfire complete with hot dogs and marshmallows and games. Our friends loved it."

"Was that here in Galena Landing?"

"No, we lived near Great Falls when I was a kid. My parents bought Tires and Treads and moved here after I left home."

"Right. I knew that. A bonfire sounds fun. Sometimes it was hard being my father's daughter." She huffed.

"Most of the time. He didn't explain anything, just made rules we had to obey."

"That's not the kind of parent I want to be," he said softly. "There definitely have to be rules. I get that, but blind obedience isn't healthy for anyone. It's how cults operate."

Was it his imagination, or had her fingers tightened around his?

"Yeah. My dad... can we talk about something else?"

"Sure." They could skip the Halloween talk. If they married — and that was still a huge, huge if — they'd need to circle back to these topics eventually. Or spiral to them. He couldn't help smiling at the reminder of their earlier conversation. Thankfully, it was too dark for her to catch his grin during a difficult conversation. He swung their hands between them. "Santa Claus?"

She snorted. "Do you have to ask?"

This time, he chuckled out loud. "Sure, I do. How do you want to raise your kids on that topic?" Oops, he'd nearly said *our* kids.

"Are these your usual first-date questions?"

"Third date."

She blinked up at him. "Third?"

"Date one was nearly four years ago. It... wasn't my finest moment."

"You're right about that," she muttered.

Maybe he shouldn't have reminded her. "Date two was last night. Yeah, my sister set it up, but it was still a date, right? If I'm being very truthful, which I try to be, Quincey set this one up, too. But it's still our third date."

"How many girlfriends have you had in the past few years?"

"None that made it to the third date, that's for sure. I might have been a little cautious."

"Because of me." She sighed. "I may have overreacted."

Zadok turned and caught both her hands. They stood near a streetlight, and he could see her face. Hopefully, she could see his. Read his sincerity. "You did not overreact."

Her eyebrows pulled together. "I didn't?"

"I was totally out of line that night. I didn't recognize it then, but I certainly do now. I'd ask again for you to forgive me, but..."

Juni let out a chuckle. "But we've covered that. You're forgiven."

"And so are you. But, here we are. Third date. So, yeah, I want to know how many kids you want and whether Santa will play a part in their Christmases."

Was that what he really wanted to know? Maybe a little. What he really wanted to know was if she'd welcome his kiss. Santa seemed a safer topic.

Santa.

Zadok had lured her out into a cold Idaho night to talk about the jolly red-suited elf.

Perhaps it was a valid discussion. They'd already covered Halloween, even if not in detail. She could get onboard with his hot dog roast for their kids and their friends.

Now that he'd pried her mind open enough to let him slip inside, the future was full of glorious possibilities. A wedding. Babies. Growing kids — gangly little boys with tousled hair and little girls twirling gleefully. Children free to be themselves, to live with two parents who loved each other, loved them, and loved God.

Whoa.

Juni needed to put the brakes on her imagination. "This is not our third date."

He looked down at her and laughed. Not a cruel laugh, but just because he found those words hilarious. Apparently.

"I'm serious. Dates are on purpose. That one years ago was a blind date and, um, it didn't end well. So, it doesn't count. Also, 'dates' your sister engineered are also not actual dates. Sorry. The Santa discussion has been tabled."

"Will you go out with me for dinner tomorrow? I hear the Bluebell in Wynnton is great."

She pursed her lips and caught his gaze drop to her mouth. Oh, boy. She needed to be super careful here. If this were a third date, kissing might be in order, but not on a pre-date. A woman had to have standards, after all.

Yeah, she could hear the double-talk in her own head, but she'd given the ultimatum out loud and couldn't very well back down. She turned and stared at the nearest street sign as though it was vitally interesting. "Dinner in Wynnton sounds very nice, thank you."

"Can I pick you up at four? We could go for a walk along the river before dinner."

"Four is good," she said primly. "At least, if I get my English papers marked tonight."

"Is that a hint to head back now?"

She sighed. "I'd better."

They turned toward his house and began to stroll, hand in hand. She might have homework to grade, but that didn't mean she was in a hurry to leave this man's side. Today had been... nice.

Only nice? Okay, a lot more. She'd go to sleep tonight remembering his lips on her forehead in his kitchen, his arms holding her close, his amazingly masculine scent.

"What do people discuss on first dates?" Zadok asked after a minute. "I want to be sure I understand all the rules."

Juni poked his side with her elbow. "You mean, besides the weather?"

He snorted. "That's a non-date topic."

She pretended to think. "Let's see. Family background. Educational background—"

"What if we've covered all that in our pre-dates?"

"Fine. If we must talk about Santa tomorrow, I'll deal with it."

Zadok let go of her fingers only to wrap his arm around her back and settle his hand on her waist. He tugged her close and chuckled. "I'm so confused. First date, but third date topics. I'll try to keep up with the program, but if you have an agenda to share, it would be helpful. Do you have my email address?"

She couldn't help laughing in return. He was too much. Too funny. Pushy, but in a good way. She would never have thought that possible. What else had she closed her mind to all these years because of her dad's narcissistic behavior? Because she'd assumed every man was like him if they exhibited even a tiny hint of sexism?

"If I get a few minutes between papers, sleep, church, and our date, I'll make a list."

"You do that."

Was it her imagination, or were they meandering more slowly than before? It was like neither of them wanted to arrive at his house, because she needed to go home. Did she really?

Yeah, she was a grownup with responsibilities. She couldn't just blow off her actual job because she wanted to linger near this intoxicating guy.

"While you're making that list..." Zadok cleared his throat.

"Umhmm?"

"There's one thing I hope you put on it."

"Oh? What's that?" And why was her heart hammering?

"I was wondering on which date a kiss is acceptable."

"Oh." Her voice kind of squeaked on that.

"I'll be honest. I was hoping for the third date. But with this new set of standards, that seems to be at least next Tuesday."

He had a point. Three whole, entire days, at a minimum. And if they went the more usual route of a date a week, that was right up to Thanksgiving before she'd feel his lips on hers. Daily dates sounded mighty good at the moment.

Or possibly she had too many rules.

"Pre-dates might count for something." She moistened her lips, hoping he wasn't looking right that second.

Zadok turned to face her. This time there was no streetlight, but the gleam in his eyes still shone bright enough to see. Both his hands rested on her waist as he gazed at her. "What do they count for? Help a guy out here. Does each pre-date count for a real date in this scenario? Or is there some other formula I've missed?"

Once she answered him, there was no going back. The big question was why would she even want to. Hadn't she decided she was all in? It wasn't like she didn't know him fairly well from the past seven months.

He searched her eyes. "Or I might have missed something else, because I haven't heard yet whether the third date is the magic one, whether it's a pre-date or a real one."

The hopeful tone in his voice from a minute ago was less strong now. All because Juni was trapped inside her head, quadruple-guessing herself. A kiss was just a kiss. Lots of women kissed men they didn't wind up marrying. It wasn't like this was a big deal.

Yeah, it was. Because Juni wasn't that sort of person. She couldn't kiss and forget. Not with Zadok. Not with anyone.

He tugged her close to his chest as he had earlier, only now their bulky jackets wedged between them. As he pressed her head against his chest, she realized he'd given up on her ever making a decision. Or, at least, in the next five minutes.

Juni leaned back so she could look up at him and lifted her hands to his cheeks. If it weren't for these gloves, she'd be able to feel his face. Feel the slight stubble there. Goals for next time, because there would be a next time, right?

"Kiss me," she whispered.

"Are you sure?" he whispered back.

In reply, she lifted to her tippy-toes and pulled his face closer. Goodness, he was tall. But that was her last thought for a while. How long? She had no idea, because time wasn't a real thing while his soft, warm lips caressed hers.

Zadok's kiss felt better than she'd ever imagined, which, okay, didn't take much because she'd blocked any romantic daydreams until just yesterday. But still, the few kisses she'd participated in before were barely-there vanilla compared to luscious salted caramel.

She never wanted this kiss to end. It warmed her to the core of her being and awakened her in a way she'd never dreamed of. How had she blocked this kind, gentle man from her life — her mind — for so long? Because, wow. Just wow.

He eased back, but her lips were starved for more, and she refused to release him for another few minutes. Or hours. No one was counting.

But the next time he pulled away, he groaned and clutched her close, pressing her head to his chest in a way she couldn't fight. Maybe she didn't want to.

Because that had been a lot to process.

She held him, too, just inhaling his essence and struggling to get her heart rate and airflow back to something related to normal.

"Thank you, Juni," he murmured into her hair. "I'll always remember this moment. Always treasure it."

"Me, too." She let out a long, shaky exhale. "Me, too."

NINETEEN

Zadok couldn't recall what songs he and Keanan had led worship with this morning. He couldn't recall Pastor Ron's sermon, but it had maybe been a little longer than usual. Or perhaps it had just seemed like it because Zadok had been so anxious for 4:00 to arrive.

Then the afternoon had lagged interminably. He'd finally challenged his siblings to a Mario Kart tournament. Zadok's spectacular loss had made both Xavier and Quincey inexplicably happy, so it had been worth it.

Finally, he sat in the truck for five minutes along Thompson Road around the bend from Ackerman Farm. Yeah, idling was bad for the environment. He got that, but at least no one from Green Acres Farm had driven, walked, or cycled by to give him a disapproving frown.

A guy didn't turn up for his date early... but also not late. He waited until his truck clock, which he'd made sure to align with his smart watch, ticked over to 3:57 before putting the truck back in gear and driving the remaining distance.

He'd been to the farm several times since the Farm Fresh Market started operating out of Mitchell's greenhouse a few weeks back. But now he parked behind Juni's car. Mitchell's truck was home, as was Arleigh's flower-adorned hippie van.

The O'Neill sisters lived in the basement suite, but where was the access? He didn't see an external stairwell, didn't see a door he could be certain led to the right place.

Zadok scrunched his eyes shut for a second, trying to remember if he'd ever seen either of the sisters enter or exit the house. Only by the door over there by the porch swing. But didn't that lead into Mitchell's residence? That wasn't exactly whose door Zadok wanted to knock on this Sunday afternoon.

It was 4:02, and he was late. Text Juni and ask her? He could do that, but before he'd done more than pull his phone out of the cup holder, the door opened and she popped out wearing jeans, short boots, and her long, puffy coat.

Zadok bounded out of the truck and hurried toward her. "I wasn't sure which door led to your place."

"Oh!" She looked startled and then smiled. "That door leads into an entryway with Mitchell's kitchen door to the left and the stairs to the basement suite on the right."

"Good to know." He slid his arm around her and guided her to the passenger side. "We should have planned an all-day date."

"Oh?" She looked up at him with sparkling eyes.

"Yeah. This afternoon dragged on and on *and on*. Even Quincey beat me at Mario Kart. My head was so not into the game. I'll never live it down."

"Poor you."

"Such sympathy." He held the truck door while she clambered inside.

"I try."

Oh, the flirting. Zadok couldn't help grinning as he rounded the vehicle and jumped in. "How does time do that?" He started the engine and began backing out.

"Do what?"

"Drag so utterly when you're anticipating something? And I'm sure the next few hours will just zip by because I'll be with you."

He glanced sideways to see her tiny smile at his words. He pulled onto Thompson Road and reached over to gather her hands in his. "Maybe you weren't as impatient for four o'clock as I was?"

"Fairly eager." Juni glanced his way with a shy smile.

Now she was cautious? Well, it beat being ignored, that was for sure.

Zadok needed both hands on the wheel to navigate over the bridge and through Galena Landing before the southbound highway stretched in front of them, but then he reached for Juni's hand again.

Maybe this *was* a first date, because he had those sorts of jitters. What if he said or did something wrong again? No, he and God had talked about this.

"So, about Santa."

Zadok's eyebrows shot up as he glanced her way. "I'm confused. What date are we on?"

She peeked at him, her cheeks reddening. "Does it matter?"

"Not to me, but yesterday you said..."

"That was Fearful Juni speaking."

She was right about that. But, still. "She's the one I kissed last night. I like her." Not, maybe, as much as he'd like Carefree Juni, but he was willing — mostly — to proceed cautiously.

"She likes you, too, but she's afraid of her own shadow, and she's terrified of the future."

There were two futures he could see at the moment. One cloaked in gray fog and interminable rain and one with bright sunshine and flower-strewn mountain meadows. One had no Juni in it. The other was filled with her vibrancy.

"It will surprise no one that Arleigh and I grew up in a Santa-Claus-free zone. It's interesting to hear Arleigh and Mitch navigate that one these days. It does seem like something coup—" Her voice broke off.

"That couples should discuss," he finished for her.

"Before things get serious. In case there's a deal-breaker in there."

Zadok squeezed her hand. "There's no dealbreaker in Santa for me, either way. We could, uh, do him with our kids if you wanted. Or not do him. I have no skin in that game."

Their gazes mingled for a few seconds. Man, her cheeks were such a bright pink he'd feel like teasing her if she weren't so clearly uncomfortable. So clearly expecting to be let down.

He softened his tone. "So, that's how you were brought up. What do *you* think about Santa?"

"Well, I don't want to lie to my kids. I don't think that's a good thing."

Zadok nodded. "And?"

Juni pulled away from his grasp and twisted her fingers together. "I understand that Saint Nicholas was a real person, and it's silly not to believe in a real person."

He nodded. Waited.

"I don't know. What do you think?"

He thought he needed to tread carefully, that's what. "My biggest issue with Santa is from the viewpoint of kids in underprivileged families."

Juni's brows pulled together as she turned to face him. "What do you mean?"

"Kids from wealthy families get big presents from Santa. Kids from poor families are lucky to get a candy cane from him. For a legend who apparently gives gifts to every child who's been good, what are they supposed to think?"

He could see the light dawning in her eyes. "Right. That rich kids are inherently better than poor kids. That's an absolutely terrible thing to teach children!"

"I agree. And that's the main reason I'd prefer not to give my kids the classic American Santa upbringing. Acknowledge him? Sure. Like you said, Saint Nick was a real person, and his legend is worth passing on. But it's a sideline compared to the birth of our Savior. *That* is life-changing and equally available to everyone, regardless of economics."

Juni studied him. "How did you get so wise?"

Wow. Zadok nearly choked on his own breath. "I don't think of myself as wise, and my siblings would definitely argue with that designation. But... I guess I think a lot."

JUNI TRIED to imagine her parents having this sort of discussion about Santa Claus and failed. It seemed unlikely that Dad would ever have considered Mom's opinions to be worthy of discussion. He'd totally run the show in that and every other way. Maybe Juni should find out what Mom thought.

If Grandma Rykerts hadn't gotten through to her daughter, the three of them would probably still be right there under Dad's thumb.

Just the fact that Zadok was willing to ask her opinion and carry on a rational discussion about things had to prove he wasn't like Dad. Which she already knew. Why did her mind keep circling like this?

It wasn't circling. It was spiraling, like she'd told Zadok about Xavier's grieving process. A person could spiral into the depths of despair or they could spiral toward the light. She was headed for the light, but the path wasn't flat or straight.

Juni forced her mind to stop its whirlwind and looked

back at Zadok, who glanced her way uncertainly. "How do you and your siblings celebrate Christmas now that they're older?"

He exhaled audibly. "The first year was the hardest. Keanan and Chelsea invited us out to the farm for dinner, and that helped for a few hours. I'm not sure how we'd have navigated without the church Christmas Eve service and then spending Christmas afternoon at Green Acres."

That first holiday after they'd left Dad had been brutal, not that the previous ones had been precisely joyful. It was hard to find joy when Dad had nothing good to say about anyone's way of celebrating. Everything was too commercial. Even good church people sidelined Jesus in favor of lavish parties and gifts and decorations.

He wasn't completely wrong, but his pious, restrictive attitude wasn't the answer, either.

Juni realized she hadn't replied. "They're great people out at Green Acres. Did you go again last year?"

"Pastor Ron and Wanda invited us then. I'm not sure what we'll do this year. With Quincey working at the farm, they might expect us there, but it's early yet."

She chuckled. "My mom isn't leaving anything to chance. She's made plans for Arleigh and me, and that includes Mitchell and the boys. And because Treyan is Mitch's brother, he and Brittany and Scarlett are invited, too, but they're probably going to Spokane to Brittany's mom and step-dad's house. I'm sure she'll invite you guys once she..."

"Figures out we're dating?"

"Yeah. That." How was she going to tell Mom? Or

maybe Arleigh already had. Not that Mom wouldn't love Zadok or his siblings. It was more that Juni had made such a huge deal of why she didn't like him. Words she now needed to eat.

Zadok's large, warm hand reached across the console and enveloped hers, calming their twisting.

She closed her eyes and reveled in his touch. How the calloused tips of his fingers slid along hers, warming her by his contact, awakening so many feelings she'd never had before yesterday. Never allowed herself to consider.

"Having second thoughts?" he asked quietly.

Her eyes sprang open as she turned to look at him. "No! Definitely not."

He angled his sideways grin her direction, but his eyes still looked wary. "Whew. You had me wondering for a minute."

"No. I'm... glad you were patient with me. I don't know why, but I'm thankful."

"Hey, now. I was only patient because my feelings refused to go away. Every time I saw you, I couldn't get over the idea of how much I liked you and that we could be so good for each other."

"If I quit pushing you away."

He flashed a bigger grin. "Yes. That." Then he sobered. "But it's okay. God has everything in His time. Did I want it to happen sooner? Yeah, sure, but God knew what He was doing."

Juni leaned against the headrest and studied the man beside her. "My stubbornness was God's plan?"

"He can use anything and anyone." Zadok winked. "He's the giver of good and perfect gifts, remember?"

Juni scoffed. "I'm not God's gift to anyone."

"I wouldn't be so sure about that."

She felt herself stiffen. What was going on inside her? Ah. Gifts were something to give away, which meant ownership. That was the problem, right there. But didn't God 'own' her? She'd put her trust in Him. She'd acknowledged His gift of salvation and how He'd redeemed her. She claimed to trust Him like a sheep with its shepherd. There was definitely an element of ownership going on there.

She and Arleigh had talked about that with the whole 'who gives this woman to be married to this man?' question in a marriage ceremony. It denoted a change of ownership. The father had owned his daughter and now he gave her away to her husband.

A gift.

But gifts weren't free. Someone, somewhere, had to pay for them. If not with money, then some other way.

"Hey, Juni." Zadok's voice was soft. "Isn't every good and perfect gift given and received from God above? The apostle James talked about that."

"We were bought with a price," she quoted slowly. "Where's that?"

"First Corinthians chapter six, I think." He hesitated. "Okay, total change of subject. What's your favorite color? I think that's a first-date question."

Bless him for not continuing to push her out of her comfort zone. Her comfort zone that might be full of questionable theology — thanks, Dad — and definitely was full of landmines.

"Hmm, hard question."

His eyebrows shot up. "How so?"

"You first."

"Blue."

"That's what guys always say."

"From the vast dating experience you told me about. And your many brothers."

Juni laughed. "You got me there. What shade of blue?"

"Your eyes."

She blinked in surprise. So much for the conversation feeling less personal. "My favorite color varies by my mood, but it's safe to say it nearly always includes a shade of pink."

"And you called my choice cliché." Zadok chuckled.

"You're right."

"It kills you to say that, doesn't it?" he teased.

He had no idea. Well, maybe he did, a little. "Favorite subject in school?"

"Duh. Music."

Juni rolled her eyes. "I mean academics."

"If I can't say music, you can't say art or drama."

"That's fair. But you first."

"Hmm." He drummed his fingers on the steering wheel. "History."

"Really?" She studied him. "I wouldn't have guessed that."

Zadok waggled his eyebrows in her direction. "That's

why this is date one... or maybe four. We still have things we don't know about each other."

She chuckled. "True, that."

"Your favorite?"

"English Literature. Where I got to study William Shakespeare's plays along with Oscar Wilde's and George Bernard Shaw's."

"I think you just cheated. Didn't we agree it couldn't be drama?"

Juni batted her eyelashes at him. "But English Lit is about the language, not about performance."

"You're sneaky. I can see I'm going to have to keep an eye on you." Zadok smirked. "Which won't be much of a hardship, since it means I can gaze into your pretty blue eyes. My favorite color, you know."

"Too bad yours aren't pink, so I can't reciprocate the sentiment."

"What, hazel isn't your favorite color?"

"Is that what color they are? I wasn't sure. I thought they were golden brown but then they looked green, and I thought I'd been mistaken." And then she'd closed her eyes because they were kissing, and you didn't stare into a guy's eyes while your mouth was so busy with his. Why? She didn't know, but it seemed to be a rule that eyes knew to follow. Like there would be one too many senses involved if they were busy on the job, too.

"That's the definition of hazel."

The original question had fallen out of her head. "I... forgot."

"I think you're saying my presence turns your brain to mush."

"I might be saying that, but don't let it go to your head. Besides music, what hobbies do you enjoy?"

"My dad left a decent woodworking shop in the shed out back. I've started playing around in there some, when I've had time. Lately, though, my 'hobby' seems to be sitting in the passenger seat while Xavier drives. How about you?"

"I guess I can't say creating things with felt, huh?"

"It's a given, like my music."

"Right. I like to paint things. Not walls so much, but like those little wooden birdhouses you can buy at Hobby Lobby and other stuff like that."

"Do you now?" He flicked the signal light. "Here's the riverside park, if you're still up for a walk."

"There's a park here? Sure, let's see it."

He parked the truck and turned off the ignition before turning to her and tapping her nose. "You like painting wooden things? Well, isn't it convenient to have a boyfriend who likes to *make* wooden things? We should collaborate."

Juni caught his hand before he could pull back. "That does sound convenient. I'd like to see something you made."

"That can be date number two. Or five. Not that anyone's counting, mostly because they aren't sure where the starting point is."

He leaned slowly over the console as he spoke, gaze

intent on hers, until their mouths were only a breath apart.

Once again, Juni's eyes knew something she didn't, as they fluttered closed at the touch of Zadok's lips.

All the better to focus on kissing him, she decided, but the moment ended much too soon.

He cleared his throat. "Let's walk. And maybe do some kissing without this console in the way."

She could get onboard.

TWENTY

Xavier eyed Juni in study hall the next afternoon then shook his head and looked down at his textbook.

"What?" she couldn't help asking.

"You and my brother... I don't even want to know."

"Oh?" Her heart leaped. Was Zadok walking around in the same daze she found herself in? She'd given her drama students the wrong page number — one for a totally different play than the one they were currently rehearsing — this morning. She'd laughed it off as she apologized and focused really, really hard through the rest of her classes. As far as she knew, that had been her only blunder. Only humiliating one, at least.

"Never mind," Xavier mumbled.

Had he said something further? Juni needed to keep her head in the game even during the teen's tutoring hour. Not that he needed her help anymore. He'd managed to turn in all his overdue work and pass his midterms, though some of them by a bare squeak. But that had been a couple of weeks ago now, and his grades were still improving.

One of these days Ms. Atkinson would call her in and dissolve this assignment. Honestly? She'd miss her time with Xavier when that happened.

"Math homework the trouble?"

The teen rolled his eyes. "Always. It's stupid. When I'm an adult, I'm never gonna need to know this stuff."

"I guess it depends on what you plan to do for a living."

"Not change tires on peoples' cars, that's for sure."

"Was that your dad's dream?" Juni knew it hadn't been Zadok's.

"Who knows? He wanted his own business, that's all. He'd have been just as happy with... I don't know. A health food store."

Stuart and Barb Smith had owned Nature's Pantry for, what, ten years now? They might be nearing retirement, but it still seemed like they were having the time of their lives whenever Juni wandered in. She was possibly addicted to the organic chocolate they sold. It was sugar-free, but didn't taste like it. Must be some kind of sorcery.

"...stupid..."

And there she went, daydreaming again. *Focus, Juni.* "Do you want to own a small business? Or maybe a larger one?"

Xavier shrugged. "I doubt it. Business owners probably need math."

She chuckled. "There are spreadsheets and programs

to help them run their numbers, but yeah. They need to have a working knowledge of it."

"I want to build things."

Now they were getting somewhere. "What kinds of things? Zadok showed me the desk he's building in the workshop."

"It will be cool, I guess. But I mean houses."

"The actual hammering of nails, or designing them?"

The teen slumped lower in his chair. If he did that another time or two, his boneless body would slither right onto the floor. "Architects probably need math, too."

"I'm sure they do. It would be hard to design spaces without knowing their size relationships to each other. Without being able to figure out how many two-by-eights and sheets of plywood you need."

Xavier jabbed his textbook. "None of which is in here. It's dumb."

"There are basic principles that form a foundation."

"Yeah, I learned those in grade school."

She was headed out on a limb here. What did she really understand of the construction trade? Not much. "Do you know Brent Callahan at Green Acres?"

"Yeah? A bit. He owns Timber Framing Plus. Have you seen the cool houses he's built?" Xavier pulled himself up in his chair and leaned over the table, his eyes glowing. "Those wooden beams are massive! And everything fits together like a giant jigsaw puzzle. It's amazing."

No doubt numbers were involved. "Maybe you should talk to him about what it takes to run a company like that.

They build all over the Inland Northwest, from what I've heard."

She didn't know much, but her sister had lived in Green Acres' student housing — in a renovated grain bin, no less — for a few weeks last spring, and Juni had toured the premises and met the couples who operated the sustainable farm. Allison had showed her around the farm school her husband had built, and Xavier was right. The wooden beams were massive, the entire structure stunning. Pleased at Juni's response, Allison had then invited her into their timber frame house, and Juni's respect had only grown.

They had some very interesting structures at the farm as they'd experimented with various sustainable building materials from straw bale to log to timber frame and insulated grain bins. Sierra and Gabe's family lived in an earth ship built into the hillside with exterior walls of recycled tires.

They'd probably cleaned Desmond Shirkowski's tire shop of all the old rubber out back, come to think of it. Or maybe that had been earlier, when Roger Sharp still owned it.

"He's a busy guy." Xavier had slumped again.

"Maybe you could get a summer job with him. He must need laborers on his builds. Gofers."

Xavier's eyebrows raised quizzically. "Gofers?"

"You know, grunts who can go-fer this and go-fer that."

"I don't want to be a grunt."

Juni reached across the table and tapped his unopened

textbook. How much of the hour had already disappeared? "Two things, buster. One, studying hard, getting good grades, and choosing your college major are key to having options down the road. And, two? It's a rare job that anyone gets to do without being a grunt for at least a little while. That's how people learn what their job requires. You need to study, but theory will only take you so far. After that, you have to actually *do* the things, and you will probably make mistakes. Hopefully, you will learn from them."

He flipped his textbook open listlessly and found his page with a dramatic sigh. "Joy."

"Life's not all about joy, you know."

"It ought to be." He picked up a pencil and stared at the page.

She longed to remind him exactly where joy could be found, but she could be fired if anyone happened to overhear her proclaiming Jesus on school grounds. "Any questions before you get started?"

"Yeah. What do you see in my brother?"

Juni's heart stuttered. "I meant about math. Because the clock is ticking by, and you haven't begun your assignment."

The teen had quite the repertoire of exhalation. "No, I know how to do this. I just don't want to."

At least he was being honest. That went a long way, didn't it?

"Want a coffee while you wait?" Zadok gestured toward the single-brew coffee pot. He'd upgraded to that unit last year when he realized how bitter drip coffee became after sitting on the burner for hours.

Keanan Welsh stared at the unit with a frown. "No, thank you."

What was that face for? "There are lots of flavor options, and it makes good coffee."

"I'm sure it does. It also generates a lot of waste."

The light began to dawn. Of course, that would be Keanan's first thought. Green Acres' members prided themselves in minimalism. "Most of the time I refill my own pods. I do have a few specialty factory-filled pods, too." A guy had to be honest.

Keanan sat in the guest chair across from Zadok's desk. "Either way, I don't need a coffee right now. It seems I hardly see you except at music practice. How are you doing? Is the tire shop treating you okay? How are the siblings?"

"The business is doing okay. October is always super busy with everyone swapping out to their winter tires."

"Yes, I'm somewhat behind this year. We use Chelsea's car as little as possible, so it had escaped my notice that the tires were worn."

The man had to have been married nearly a decade

and yet considered their car as belonging to his wife, just because she'd owned it before they met? Zadok needed to wrap his mind around that.

"We will miss Quincey when she goes back to college in January."

Zadok blinked. "I will, too, but there aren't many opportunities around here for her without her degree. Although I'm not sure she plans to live here afterward."

"She's bright and enthusiastic. She'll do well wherever she goes."

"I think so." His heart swelled with pride for his sister. "Everything has been a lot better since she came home in April. Last school year with Xavier was really hard. We were both struggling, and he couldn't seem to snap out of his funk. Truth is, without you welcoming me to the worship team at Galena Gospel, I might have been hanging out in the doldrums with him."

Keanan eyed him. "You have real talent and a passion for Jesus. We're glad to have you, and it's nice to get an occasional break from leading without fearing everything will fall apart."

"Thank you." Zadok's throat tightened.

"Ever thought of preaching occasionally? I believe Pastor Ron feels the same way I did, like he can't take a vacation because there are so few people to fill in."

"I took classes in homiletics, but preaching wasn't really my focus. I was planning to head up a church music ministry. Maybe work with youth... back before I realized I couldn't even get through to my own teenage brother."

"You should talk to Pastor Ron."

Hadn't Zadok just told the other man he had no interest in speaking? It wasn't that he got stage fright, although hiding behind an instrument was easier than not. He just wasn't sure he had anything to say that would bless or challenge others. Seemed like he'd been barely hanging in there on his own.

"Will you?"

"Why?" Zadok studied Keanan. "If he is looking for an occasional break, why don't *you* step in?"

"I have enough on my plate with leading worship, organizing and leading Alpha for 11 weeks twice a year, and my work on the farm. Keeping my wife and children happy." The man offered a sappy smile. "I asked God and did not feel like this was something He wanted me to add."

"Oh." When the man put it that way, he really did have a full life already. Zadok had volunteered to help with Alpha, but he didn't have a wife, though he did have two 'kids' to look out for. Maybe someday he'd have a wife. Someday soon? He couldn't help hoping.

"Something to pray about, anyway."

"Uh, sure." Except, had he just agreed to seriously consider preaching? That wasn't his call, but what it was seemed a vague, distant dream now. His actual life was so different from anything he'd ever planned, and yet it was the life that God had distinctly led him to after his parents' death. His siblings were a responsibility he couldn't simply walk away from to pursue his own goals.

Had this been God's plan for him all along, and he'd just read the signs wrong? He couldn't see that. He'd felt so certain that God was leading him into his chosen career.

Which was not operating Tires and Treads, yet here he was, putting in time until Xavier graduated from high school. And then what? Uproot the teen to an urban center where there was an opening for a music minister? What if Quincey chose a career at Green Acres? That would mean she'd stay in Galena Landing. Could he be the one to separate what was left of his family?

Zadok glanced around the dreary tire shop reception area with its once-white walls, not-so-sparkling windows, rusty file cabinet, and third-hand desk with one corner propped up on a brick to keep it more-or-less level.

Where was his pride in his workplace? He was putting in time as though it didn't matter, so long as he had an exit strategy.

God had given him this gift — a mortgage-free home and business — in a town with few employment opportunities when he needed an instant job after the funeral. Had he thanked God for that gift? Had he treated it as valuable?

No to the second question. That had to change. Even if he did sell the business in a couple of years, Galena Landing deserved a business owner who took pride in his building and served them with a joyous heart in the meantime.

"I need to paint this room."

Keanan pulled back and stared at him before starting to laugh. "I would like to hear how you came from considering preaching to painting a reception area."

"Right. It's convoluted, but the bottom line is that I've been treating Tires and Treads as a stopgap measure and not as a worthy enterprise on its own. I haven't treated it as a gift from God."

"Every good and perfect gift is from above," Keanan mused.

"I never thought of this gift that way." Zadok gestured around the dingy space. "But if it's from God's hand, it is, isn't it?"

"Indeed. Paint, you say?" The man studied the walls. "Chelsea would have some good ideas for you. In fact, she's been itching for a project and talking about repainting Andi's room, which doesn't need it, I assure you. This, however, does."

"Oh, I couldn't ask Chelsea. I hardly know her."

"You are not the one doing the asking." Keanan laughed. "Consider this a gift exchange. You receive the gift of an experienced painter, Chelsea receives the gift of a project to brighten a week or two, and I receive the gift of a happy wife."

"Well, when you put it that way..." Zadok couldn't help chuckling in response. "Next time she's in town during business hours, tell her to stop in and give me some advice."

"She lives to give advice. Another gift."

"And then we'll go from there."

"That sounds like a good plan." Keanan checked the clock on the wall. "Since we still have some time before my wife's car is ready, tell me what God has been teaching you lately."

"In the past few minutes, He's shown me another angle to James 1:17."

Keenan smirked. "This was on top of other lessons on God's gifts?"

"Yes. When I was at South Idaho U, I may have seemed quiet and shy, but really, I thought myself above many of the other students. I was called into ministry, after all, and they were only going to be doctors and lawyers and teachers."

"Only," Keenan murmured.

"I know, right?" Zadok wasn't going to talk about that ill-fated blind date. "And yet here I am, operating a tire shop. All those things I prided myself in slipped away."

"How do God's gifts come into play?"

It was a good question. "I didn't think they did for a long time. I mean, I was grieving. Struggling to take care of two teenagers. My entire life's course had been uprooted in a single car crash. Everything was a tragedy. Nothing was a gift."

"And?"

"I guess it was Romans 8:28 that sank into my thick skull first."

"And we know that in all things God works for the good of those who love him, who have been called according to his purpose."

"Yes, that one. I had to ask if I loved God. If I had been called at all."

"Because you couldn't see the good."

"Exactly. Then we've been leading the song 'Good, Good Father.' The one by Chris Tomlin."

Keanan nodded. "God *is* a good, good Father. It's who He is."

"And I'm loved by that Father. That's my identity. But it took quite a while for those lyrics to sink all the way in. His undeniable love and unexplainable peace are great and glorious gifts I hadn't been looking for. Hadn't noticed when they arrived. Hadn't thanked Him for their existence."

"Then there are the gifts the Holy Spirit gives to believers. To some He gave the gift of apostles, prophets, evangelists, pastors, and teachers. These equip believers for works of service, so that the body of Christ may be built up until we all reach unity in the faith and in the knowledge of the Son of God and become mature, attaining to the whole measure of the fullness of Christ." Keanan smirked. "Ephesians 4:11-13."

Zadok forced a chuckle. "Back to that, are we?"

"I felt God nudging me to open your eyes to that opportunity. What you do with it is between you and Him."

"Thanks." What else could he say?

Austin opened the door from the work bay and poked his head around. "Your car is ready to go, Mr. Welsh."

Keanan rose to his feet. "Thank you very much."

"My pleasure." Austin disappeared.

Keanan paid his invoice and exited the reception area with a wave and a promise to have Chelsea stop by. A minute later, he drove off the lot.

Zadok watched him go, mulling over the man's words. Was there truly opportunity here in Galena Landing?

Should he keep the tire shop and accept that music and maybe preaching at times were to be lay positions and not his career?

This isn't what I signed up for!

No, but maybe it was God's gift to him, even so.

CHAPTER
TWENTY-ONE

J uni stared at her email. She had an order for six sets of felties! All of them from the same person who wanted mermaids, each slightly different, for her granddaughters.

She didn't have six sets of that style, let alone in different colors or embellishment styles. The forest creatures and dragons had become more popular at the market lately, so she'd been focusing on those while introducing the new safari series.

Quincey had put in a lot of work, but Juni hadn't really believed a digital storefront would do anything. She'd allowed the teen to build the site as a favor. And so she could spend some time with Zadok, though she'd done her best to deny that reason until she'd been cornered.

Now he was the best part of her days, and they had a date tonight, *and* she needed to hand-sew dozens of felt seashells. Aargh. What was she going to do?

She couldn't blow off her business, but she wanted to

spend time with Zadok. They'd only been dating for a week. He wouldn't understand if she canceled their evening.

Perfectly submissive Genevieve would meekly set aside her own interests and defer to Dad. She'd stay up until the wee hours stitching mermaids so it didn't interfere with taking care of her husband and children. Anything Genevieve wanted came last. And she didn't seem to mind, from what Juni had observed.

Well, Juni wasn't that sort of woman. And Zadok said he wasn't that kind of man. Guess he'd have a chance to prove it, because Juni was independent and had her own small business aside from teaching at Galena High.

Given a choice, she'd much rather linger over a decadent dessert at a candlelit table in The Sizzling Skillet than gobble a fast-food burger at home in her sweats while stitching tiny felt pieces together.

Grownups had to do grownup things.

Since when were mermaids more grownup than kisses?

Juni sighed. Since today.

She glanced at the clock. Zadok would be at Tires and Treads for another hour and pick her up in two. Could she get enough done before 6:00 to take a couple of hours out? Then stay up late tonight?

That wouldn't work. She had classes to teach in the morning, and stumbling in unrested was not in the best interests of her job. But she'd also promised to fulfill the orders through her website within 72 hours, and it would take every minute of her spare time between now and then to sew up all the mermaid sets.

Did she even have enough of the beads she used? How had she let herself get low?

Sheesh, Juni. Can't you do anything right?

She slumped against the cushions on the sofa and cradled her face in her hands. Dad might be an egotistical, narcissistic jerk, but he wasn't completely wrong. She was flighty. She took on more than she could handle. She was disorganized. She was attracted to the new, bright, and shiny.

Squirrel! Or, in this case, giraffe! Because the new safari set was so fun.

What had she been thinking last spring when Arleigh had suggested she make a little extra money with her felt creations at the market? Just because Scarlett had been so thrilled with that first mermaid set didn't mean it was something she should do as a business.

And just because she'd sold dozens at the local market didn't mean she should launch an online storefront, too.

Idle hands are the devil's workshop.

Dad again. A girl should never sit around with nothing to do, or she'd get into trouble. She should always be doing, always be striving, always be working.

Except on Sundays. Then she should fold her hands in her lap, read the Bible, and pray.

Today was Tuesday, not Sunday. She'd run her devotional reading through the car's speakers this morning via Bluetooth and prayed while she drove. She'd been three minutes late leaving for school as it was. Thankfully, the line at the drive-through for her coffee and doughnut had been shorter than usual.

Today, she needed to work. She reached for her cell phone to call Zadok, but... maybe she *could* get enough done in two hours to feel good about taking a little time off? If they didn't linger over dessert... it was worth a shot.

Juni jumped up, pulled the bin of craft supplies out of her closet, and dumped it out on the table. Arleigh and Brittany had gone to Spokane for a couple of days to look at wedding gowns, so no one would need the table for anything else.

Would Juni have liked to join their excursion? Sure. But substitute teachers were in short supply at Galena High, and she couldn't justify taking two days away. Besides, Brittany was married to Arleigh's fiancé's brother, so they were practically sisters now. Arleigh wasn't going to need Juni anymore.

She shoved the depressing thought aside along with the embellishments that clearly weren't part of the mermaid collection. She needed to keep everything sorted better, except both the mermaid and dragon sets shared some of the sparkly things, while the forest creatures and ranch sets shared other motifs.

Okay. She sent a Hallmark movie from her laptop to the big screen and cranked up the sound.

Now, mermaids.

ZADOK PULLED into the Ackerman farmyard. Whew, Juni's car was home. He'd called her several times, but she hadn't picked up. He'd begun to worry, but she must be okay. Right?

He stepped into the common vestibule and tapped on the door to the basement, but no one answered. The volume of a TV show or movie from below would be enough to drown out the sound of an approaching train, though. Whistle and all.

He frowned. Knocked again, harder. Still nothing.

The other door opened and one of Mitchell's boys poked his head around. "Hi! What are you doing?"

"Hi, Hudson." It *was* Hudson, right? "I'm here to pick up Ms. Juni for dinner, but I don't think she can hear me knock!" Hopefully, he'd managed to curb the impatience he felt. The last couple of times he'd picked her up, she'd been watching for him. What was different tonight?

"Ms. Arleigh's gonna be my mom."

Zadok managed a smile at the boy. "I heard that! I bet you're excited."

"Yeah." The kid nodded enthusiastically. "And Ms. Juni is gonna be my auntie. And Mrs. O'Neill is gonna be my grandma, just like Grandma Penny. Except she lives in a 'partment in Galena Landing, and Grandma Penny and Grandpa Pete live far away."

"Right." Keep the kid reined in. "Is Ms. Juni home?"

"Yeah. She came home from school after the bus. She said hi. But Ms. Arleigh isn't home. She and Auntie Brittany went to Spokane."

Juni had mentioned that on Sunday. Zadok pulled his phone out of his pocket and tapped Juni's number again. After three rings, it went to voicemail. And, no, he couldn't hear her phone over the volume of the TV.

"Oh, Mac! I'm so happy. Kiss me again."

He glared at the door. Why was she watching that sap when she could be kissing him for real?

No, she was probably sick. Quincey complained of terrible cramps with her monthlies. Maybe Juni was like that, too, and hurting right now. She'd struggle with hearing loss later in life if this was indicative of her coping strategies, though.

How was he supposed to know what the problem was if she didn't answer her phone or her door? Should he barge down the stairs without invitation? Or just go home and wait for her to phone or text with an apology?

Juni couldn't have forgotten, could she?

No, not with the way her eyes had shone when he kissed her goodnight on Sunday. He'd gone 45 hours without seeing her, and that was long enough.

He was going in.

Zadok put his hand on the doorknob and hesitated.

"Whatcha doin'?"

"Maybe Ms. Juni is sick and needs help."

The boy's face brightened. "Do you think she puked all over her bed? Or maybe she cracked her head on the side of the bathtub and she's bleeding! Dad always tells me to slow down or that will happen to me."

Zadok hadn't even thought that she might be unclothed. He couldn't just barge in there. He eyed the kid. "Do you want to run down and see if she's okay?"

"Me? Can I?"

"I think that's a good idea." Better than her boyfriend rushing in without an invitation, in case she was in the shower or something. Why would she be in the shower with a movie blaring? How should he know?

"Okay." Hudson darted to the basement door and looked up at Zadok. "I won't puke if she did. That other time it was because the dog puke stank so bad."

Zadok's own stomach was roiling by now. All he could envision was the golden-haired beauty face down in her own sickness. "Run back up and tell me how she is, okay?"

"Okay." The kid slipped through the door and disappeared.

Juni shrieked.

The movie went silent.

Everything went silent for a long moment. Where was Hudson? Should Zadok go down there and see for himself?

Footsteps pattered upward and the boy burst back into the entry, eyes wide. "She's okay." Then he darted into the Ackerman kitchen and shut the door.

More silence. Now, what?

The basement door opened one more time, and Juni stood there, white as a sheet.

"Are you okay? Do you have a fever?" If she did, he

should probably keep his distance. No point in spreading a virus.

Juni blinked. "A fever? No. But I'm so sorry, Zadok. I had this order come in on my website and I totally lost track of time. I meant to call you, but... I didn't."

He studied her face. She looked to be telling the truth. "I called you four times."

"You did?" Her face blanched further. "I didn't hear it."

"How could you have, over that movie?" *Kiss me, Mac.*

"I said, I'm sorry." Her chin came up a little. "I like my movies loud, and Arleigh isn't here to object."

This was a silly thing to fight about. Wasn't it? But there was a principle here. He glanced at his watch. "I can call The Skillet. Maybe they'll let me postpone our reservation for half an hour, since it's too late now to be there by six."

Juni winced. "I don't think I can take the time tonight. I'm so sorry."

Zadok opened his mouth and closed it again. Most anything he could think of to say would not make things better. How would Jesus want him to respond? And did he *want* to take the high road here or not?

He shoved his hands deep into his pockets. "Big order then?"

"Six mermaid sets. I have to have them in the mail by Thursday."

"I see." So, no dates for a couple of more days. *Zadok, don't be a jerk about this.* "That's great for you."

"Yeah. It is." She looked at him, obviously relieved. "So, are we good?"

Just like that? But hadn't God forgiven him for far more than losing track of time and forgetting to call someone? Still, Zadok, not fictional Mac, was the guy she kissed like he held the keys to heaven and earth.

How could she forget?

Let it go.

He didn't want to. He wanted to make sure she understood, but then he'd be turning into Grant O'Neill, and he wasn't that man. Right? He wasn't. He definitely wasn't.

"Uh, is there anything I can do to help?" Not that he could sew those tiny stitches like she did, but maybe he could keep her company. Quincey and Xavier weren't expecting him home for a few hours, anyway.

Juni's face brightened. "Would you mind grabbing some burgers and fries from the diner? There isn't much you can do to help, but we could hang out while I sew."

"Sure. I can do that after I cancel our reservation." He hated how stiff his voice sounded. Maybe twenty minutes apart while he drove to town and back would be a good thing right now. He'd have time for an attitude check with God.

Juni was quick and creative and fun, all things he was not. He loved how she complemented him. He'd known how amazing she was four years ago in college, and he'd totally blown it back then. He didn't want to mess up again now.

JUNI DASHED into the bathroom after Zadok's truck drove away and looked at herself in the mirror. Man, she was a sight. She hadn't bothered to unpin her bun after school, but it was partially down, plus she seemed to have smudged her mascara. She looked like one of the raccoons in her woodland sets.

She took down her hair, brushed it, and gathered it into a ponytail, then cleaned up her face and changed from her pencil skirt and ruffled blouse to jeans and a cute T-shirt. Why hadn't she changed before diving into sewing? She'd been way too focused.

So focused she'd forgotten the time completely. Juni cringed. She'd forgotten *Zadok*.

How could she have? He was her boyfriend, and they had a date. She should have called him hours ago. He would have understood.

Now? She hadn't missed the tight lines around his eyes and mouth. He was angry or, at least, extremely frustrated. Of course, he was. She'd brushed off their third date. Or sixth. However one counted these things.

Juni ran back to the living room and turned the volume down on the paused movie. On second thought, she found an instrumental playlist and put it on barely loud enough to hear. Dad would approve.

Um... Dad wasn't here. Except he was, inside her mind,

shaking his head with disapproval in his eyes. He'd raised her better than this. Raised her to be put together and certainly never to forget appointments.

Dates. She'd been so focused on those stupid mermaids that she'd forgotten a *date*. She really was a loser.

She emptied her lunch bag, which she usually did when she walked in the door. Did a quick tidy. Glanced at the clock. She probably had another five or maybe ten minutes before Zadok returned. Good. She could get another fish or two sewn before pausing to eat.

Or not, since she heard his knock on the upstairs door before she'd finished stitching one. "Come on down!" she called.

This time she pressed a kiss to his lips before taking the bag from him and setting it on the counter. "Thanks so much." She glanced at him sidelong. Had he truly forgiven her?

Zadok fingered the felt scraps on the table. "This is quite the operation you have going on here."

Possibly forgiven. "Yeah, I'm going to need to place an online order for more embellishments." As soon as she'd shipped these sets. Juni pulled the burgers and fries out of their packages and set them on plates. "We can eat at the coffee table."

"I'll grab the sodas." He followed her to the sitting area, and they set everything down before taking seats side by side on the sofa. Then he took her hand and prayed a brief blessing over this meal.

Zadok really wasn't like Dad. She'd be punished with

the silent treatment much longer by her father. Slowly, Juni relaxed a little and bit into her burger. She was hungrier than she'd thought.

Her cell phone rang from the bedroom where she'd tossed it when she came home from school. "Excuse me a sec." Juni darted into her room and pulled the device out from beneath the green felt roll she used for the woodland sets. A list of missed calls scrolled by. Zadok. She cringed then stilled when she saw her father's number.

Did she even want to answer this? But one of the missed calls was from him, too. Best to get it over with.

She tapped the accept button just before it would have gone to voicemail. "Hi, Dad," she said nonchalantly as she walked back into the living area. She wouldn't let him rattle her. She was done with that.

"It's Genevieve." And the woman was sniffling.

"Genevieve?" Juni blinked. Right, they still had an old-school phone attached to the wall in the kitchen. This wasn't Dad's cell phone number. He only used that for college stuff. "Um, hi. What's up?" Because if Dad had asked his wife to call and see if Juni would come for Christmas — or worse, beg to walk Arleigh down the aisle — the answer was a big fat no.

"I just wanted you to know some silly girls at the college are trying to smear your father's good name."

The only parts of Juni able to move were her eyes. She fixed them on Zadok's questioning gaze. Not that he could likely hear Genevieve's words. "They *what*?"

"They've gone to the dean and made up some tall tale about how he touched them inappropriately. Someone leaked the lies to the press, and I thought you should know before you heard about it on the news." Genevieve hiccupped. "Why would they do that to Grant?"

Unable to remain upright unassisted, Juni braced herself against the doorframe. "My father is being charged with sexual misconduct?"

"Those words are so ugly."

"I... wow." She scrubbed her free hand across her face.

"You know he'd never do anything like that, right? Maybe you could testify in his defense if it goes to trial. But I'm sure it will all be dismissed as soon as they realize how silly and unfounded it all is."

"I doubt the judge would want a close relative's character reference."

"Just in case. Like I said, I'm sure nothing will come of it, but what if it does?" There was a note of hysteria in Genevieve's voice.

"I'll pray about it."

"Oh, that's good." The woman sounded relieved. Of course, she thought Dad would be vindicated.

Juni wasn't so sure. She closed off the call and stared at Zadok. "I can't believe this. You heard?"

"I heard your side." Zadok bit his lip and didn't look directly at her.

What was all that about?

TWENTY-TWO

Z adok's heart had all but stopped as his mind raced through the college corridors once again. There hadn't been many females in his ministerial classes. Not many women aspired to pastoral positions, which hadn't surprised him at the time. It tended to be a man's field.

Hadn't Professor O'Neill pushed back against the college admins when they opened enrollment to women? He'd cited scripture to stave them off and been told there'd been cultural situations in the first-century church that had nothing do with men's innate authority.

Had there been any reason to suspect...

"What are you thinking?"

Zadok pulled to his feet to face Juni, who still stood in her bedroom doorway, holding her phone, and staring at him with a tinge of suspicion. "There weren't many women in class back in my day."

"Of course." She tossed her phone onto the pile of felt

scraps on the coffee table. "And they likely aspired to get a degree in matrimony."

Didn't that sound just like the professor? The man hadn't forbade female students from attending class — he didn't have the authority — but he'd belittled them in slight ways, all the same. Been condescending. Made a few jokes.

Allegations of sexual misconduct went significantly deeper. The man would be vindicated, though. He hadn't actually crossed any lines. Right?

"I can't believe he'd do this to Genevieve."

Zadok blinked. "To Genevieve?"

"His wife." Juni waved her hand impatiently. "He's a married man, a pillar of his church, of his community, of his department at the college. Why would he chance his reputation?"

Did Juni believe the tales? "Just allegations, at least, so far. Right?"

She scowled at him. "Allegations don't usually get fabricated from thin air."

"It wouldn't be the first time it happened." Zadok tried for an easy smile. "People have invented stories before, if they thought they had something to gain from it."

"You mean *women* have invented stories."

"This type of tale, yes." Too late, he saw where she was going with this. "But men have invented other sorts. It's not unique."

"You don't think he could have done it."

Zadok held up both hands. "I didn't say that. All I meant was that they are only allegations at this point, from what his wife said to you, right? The college ethics committee will look into it. There are protocols for this sort of investigation, and we need to let them progress. There will be time later to evaluate the evidence when it's all come to light."

If there was anything to see. Also, was there a frosty tinge to the air? Because Zadok could have sworn the temperature in the basement suite had just dropped ten degrees and was still plummeting.

Juni stared at him so long he wasn't sure she actually saw him anymore. Then she shook her head. "I should have known."

"Should have known what?" Zadok was lost.

"That you'd side with him."

"I didn't," he protested. "What I said was, let the system do its job. We don't know anything yet other than accusations were made. Or did I miss something?" Because that could be. He'd only heard Juni's side of the conversation.

"They wouldn't accuse him of something if he were innocent."

"You do know that's not a given, right? History is full of people trying to sabotage other people's reputations with no substantive evidence. It wouldn't be the first time a prof or minister or someone else in authority was accused simply because someone wanted to smear them. Even if or when he's proven innocent, the taint often remains."

Where had the loving, laughing Juni gone? Because the icicles from her eyes were daggers.

"You're sticking up for my father."

"I'm not. I'm only saying—"

"You are."

Man, she was not looking at the situation rationally. Not in the slightest. But Zadok was in the right, and he knew it. "Our society is founded on people being assumed innocent until proven guilty. You're jumping to 'he's guilty' without letting due process occur."

"You don't know him like I do."

His blood chilled. "Did he sexually abuse you?"

Juni stalked closer, eyes blazing. "I would never have let that happen."

"Did he try?"

"It's none of your business."

It would be his business if their relationship continued. If they married. Yesterday, he'd thought that's where they were heading. Maybe not in the next couple of months, but surely in the next couple of years. Now? Nothing seemed clear except one thing. If he weren't extremely careful, he'd find himself on the outside once again, this time for good.

He moistened his lips. "Juni, you're my girlfriend. I care about you: past, present, and future. I'm not the enemy here."

"My dad is."

"He isn't, either."

Juni's arms remained crossed over her chest, and her toe tapped out a rhythm on the concrete floor. "So, who is?"

"Does there have to be one?" It might be the girls, if

they were lying. But if they told the truth — Zadok's brain scrambled to catch up. Could the allegations actually be true?

She made a snort of disbelief and turned away from him.

If only he could take her in his arms and comfort her, but somehow he'd become a foe. Because he hadn't immediately condemned her father? But he couldn't jump on that bandwagon in good conscience. It wouldn't be the first time girls — yes, usually females — had banded together to bring down a professor they didn't like for some trumped-up reason. And, yes, sometimes there had been misconduct at the heart of it, but not every time.

"Thank you for bringing burgers. Maybe you'd better leave. I have a lot of sewing to do before Thursday."

"Juni, don't—"

She whirled to face him. "Don't what? Don't fulfill my promise on my website? Which I will edit and change as soon as I have this order done, I assure you. But I *do* have responsibilities, and I *will* meet them."

"Let me help."

One eyebrow tipped up. "Do you know how to hand-sew? Can you do a blanket stitch? How about a French knot? A chain stitch?"

"No. Something else? Or I could just keep you company." He had a sinking feeling that if he left now, it would be a long time before he would be welcome in Juni's life again. It might already be too late.

"I need to focus." She picked up the plate containing

her burger and fries and set it on the counter. "Would you like yours back in the takeout container?"

"Are you kicking me out?"

"No." But she didn't turn and look at him, either.

Zadok softened his voice. "Juni."

Her shoulders lifted as though in defense. "Yes?"

"Let's not leave things like this."

"I don't know any other way to leave it."

"Your dad and whatever he's done or not done doesn't define our relationship. Those days are long past."

"They don't feel long past. They feel like they're right here in the room with us."

"We don't have to let them. We can turn them over to God together and let Him calm our hearts. Let the law do what it is designed to do."

"So sanctimonious."

His anger flared. Had he heard her muttered words clearly? She was accusing him of self-righteousness? Zadok pushed down the irritation. She was too emotional about this whole thing with her dad and not seeing straight. Maybe a little time apart would be a good thing. She'd remember that she'd forgiven him for his attitude on that blind date, that he was a new person in Christ.

Was he new? Was he falling back into old patterns? How did that old saying go again? That ruts were just graves with both ends knocked out.

But, no. This wasn't a rut. This was him trying not to dog-pile on a man who might not deserve the accusations. On the other hand, he might, but it wasn't Zadok's job to ferret out the truth. Thank the good Lord for that.

He rested his hands on Juni's hips, but she stiffened and didn't turn to face him. He kissed her temple. "I'll see you in a couple of days, okay? I'll be praying for you."

"Yeah, sure. Maybe pray they'll find the evidence they need."

Zadok wasn't going to restate his position again. Not tonight.

He let himself out.

JUNI LISTENED TO HIS SLOW, heavy tread on the steps. Heard the house door then the truck door close. Heard the engine rumble and fade down Thompson Road.

The absolute nerve of that man.

She blinked back hot, angry tears. How could Zadok defend Dad after all they'd gone through and talked about? Yeah, he kept saying that wasn't what he was doing, that he was trusting the process, and it sounded good, but why couldn't he see the truth?

It only made sense with the kind of man her father was. She'd used the word sanctimonious on Zadok, and maybe she shouldn't have, but it suited Dad to a tee. He held himself above others as though he were superior to everyone else. Rules didn't really apply to him, because he was better than that.

If some of his students reported him for touching them inappropriately, odds were mighty good that others would come out of the woodwork with accusations of grooming or even forced sex. This was only the tip of the iceberg.

Zadok was right in that there wasn't any real evidence yet, but it would come. She knew it beyond a shadow of a doubt.

Genevieve would live in denial for a while, but then she'd begin to connect the dots until she couldn't dismiss the evidence, either. If she ever stopped blindly holding her husband on his pedestal.

The only people Juni felt sorry for were their kids. Not that she'd ever really viewed them as her half-siblings, even when she'd occasionally babysat for Dad and Gen's date nights back in her college days.

They were Genevieve's offspring.

They were nothing to Juni. Shared paternity? Apparently, but her only sibling was Arleigh, not those children. How old were they now? Gregory must be eleven or twelve. Grace would be ten. Galway, eight, Gannon, six, and the littlest girl, Glory, would be... two? Three?

Juni knew what it was like to have her beloved father stumble, fall, and bounce back. He'd bounce back from this, too — unless he ended up in jail.

She wasn't hungry. She dumped her leftovers and then Zadok's into the chicken scrap bucket. At least someone would get some benefit from this ill-fated meal.

About those stupid mermaids. She glared at the mess on the dining table and the neater stacks on the coffee table. Why was she in this ridiculous predicament? She should never have tried to take her felties beyond the

Farm Fresh Market. Should never have promised a 72-hour turnaround.

The temptation to stuff all the felt, embroidery threads, and embellishments into a large garbage bag and haul it out to her car to put in the dumpster behind Galena High nearly overcame her.

No. She was a grownup. She'd made a promise, and she'd fulfill it. It wasn't like she'd have anything else to do in the next few days with Zadok angry with her.

Well, she was angry right back at him. He was so... obtuse. So male. Yeah, she'd liked the manliness of him before, but now? Not so much. Guys always stood up for each other. Old boys' club or something. They were all alike, after all.

Back to her movie — but Mac and Sherry's simpering words and kisses were more than she could bear. Fine. Not a movie at all, unless it involved car chases and shoot-outs where the bad guys got what they deserved.

Juni closed her eyes and took a deep, cleansing breath. In. Out. In. Out. A few more times.

Okay, music then. Arleigh had a worship list queued up on their shared Spotify. Maybe that would calm Juni in a way that explosions and gunfights couldn't.

She washed her hands, sat back on the sofa, and reacquainted herself with the completed felties and the half-done ones. She picked up a neon orange fish and the white stripe she'd sew on top with a black chain stitch.

A while later — she couldn't have said how long — Arleigh skipped down the stairs and burst into the suite carrying a large garment bag. "Hey! I found a dress! It's gorgeous. You'll love it."

Juni forced a smile onto her face. "That's great."

The stars faded in Arleigh's eyes. "What's wrong?"

"Wrong?" Juni gestured toward her mess. "Nothing. Just a big mermaid order I need to get done in the next couple of days. Let me see the dress!"

"You've been crying."

Since when was her sister this observant? Juni didn't want to intrude on Arleigh's happy bubble with her own woes. On the other hand, Dad was Arleigh's father, too.

She pulled to her feet and reached for the garment bag. "First things first. Let me see!"

Arleigh held it out of reach. "What's going on?"

"Um... well..."

"You didn't break up with Zadok, did you?"

Juni glared. "Why would it be me doing it, not him?" But Arleigh wasn't far wrong. Zadok had made a certain amount of sense. Juni could have agreed with him, and they wouldn't have fought over it.

"I know you."

"Thanks." Juni pivoted toward the table and began shoving felt into the box from whence it came.

"Juni." Arleigh touched her arm gently. "You're terrifying me."

Juni gritted her teeth. "Genevieve called tonight."

"What did she want?" Finally, there was an edge to Arleigh's voice.

"She played it off as nothing, as though it couldn't

possibly be true, but some students have accused Dad of touching them inappropriately."

"Touching them... oh, boy."

"Apparently someone leaked it to the press, and she wanted me to hear it from them first, because of course it's just a slander campaign against Dad's good name."

Arleigh rounded the table and pulled Juni's gaze to her anguished face. "Do you think he could have done such a thing?"

"Of course, he could. He thinks he's light years beyond manmade rules."

Arleigh dropped into a chair and rubbed her temples. "What happens next?"

See, why couldn't Zadok have asked that question instead of assuming it was all a hoax?

"I don't know. The college ethics board is looking at the allegations. I guess if they are proved to be founded in reality, then they'll turn it over to the police to charge him? I didn't ask Genevieve."

"What a mess."

"At least you have a good reason to give Mom now about why you don't want him to walk you down the aisle."

Arleigh shrugged. "I already told her I wasn't going to. Does she know about this?"

"I haven't talked to her. I just found out myself about an hour ago."

"Didn't you have a date tonight?"

Juni finished clearing the surface of the table. "I did,

but then I got the order for six mermaid sets, and I only had two completed. Now I have three."

"I bet Zadok was disappointed." Arleigh grinned. "That guy is totally smitten."

"I... forgot to phone him to cancel."

"You didn't."

A tension band tightened around Juni's skull. "He wasn't impressed."

"And then?"

Why did Arleigh have to be so perceptive? Why couldn't this all just be about Dad and mermaids? Two things Juni would never have thought to put in the same sentence before.

She sighed. "Then he sort of forgave me and went to get takeout instead, but then Genevieve called."

"And?"

"We might have argued about Dad."

"Don't tell me he stuck up for him."

"Not exactly, but he's not convinced Dad's guilty, either. He seems to think he'll be exonerated after due process."

"I guess that's a possibility. I mean, we don't *know* Dad is guilty. It's not like we witnessed him doing something wrong."

Why did it sound so sexist when Zadok said it yet so reasonable when Arleigh did? "There will be evidence. And there will be more students coming forward. This whole thing is going to snowball."

"You can't know that." Arleigh studied her. "Not unless you know something you haven't told me."

"Call it intuition."

"Intuition isn't the same thing as evidence."

"Now you sound like Zadok."

Arleigh managed a smile, but it didn't reach her eyes. "Smart guy. I knew I liked him for a reason."

Juni huffed, grabbed the box, and strode to her bedroom. She shoved the box in her closet and whirled around to find her sister standing in the doorway studying her.

"Did I touch a sensitive spot?" Arleigh asked.

"You think?" Juni glared at her.

"When is your next date?"

"I'm not sure there will be one." Juni may or may not have let her bedroom door smack her sister's nose as it closed. Why did no one understand?

CHAPTER
TWENTY-THREE

He'd never been so tempted to phone Paula and tell her he couldn't make it to play at the market. He did have a scratchy throat, after all. It might have something to do with all the pleading he'd done to God on Juni's behalf over the past few days.

Had he been wrong to suggest — okay, insist — that the legal system be allowed to run its course in determining Grant O'Neill's guilt or innocence? It seemed like women today were all too eager to smear a man's name in the mud.

And the man might be guilty. Zadok couldn't know. He hadn't seen his former college professor for several years. But the man might also be innocent, something Juni wasn't willing to contemplate. She was out for blood.

Zadok dragged himself into the kitchen, where Quincey met him with a guarded look. Great. Not only had he alienated Juni, his own siblings were tiptoeing around him. He tried to find a smile somewhere. Failed.

"Coffee's made." Quincey glanced at the clock. "And you're going to have to hurry if you want something to eat, since we need to leave for the market in twenty."

"We?" He poured coffee into a travel mug, cringing at the thought of food on his roiling stomach.

"I told you I was helping with the Green Acres Farm booth this weekend."

Right. She had.

Zadok took a sip of coffee and nearly spat it out. "We need to buy that Redband Roasters stuff Brittany sells at the market. It's way better than this."

"Up to you, bro. I don't drink coffee. Sierra has converted me to herbal tea."

"Of course, she has," Zadok muttered. Should he dump the brew down the drain? It was bitter. Just like his soul.

Man, he needed to get a grip on himself.

He stopped in front of the sink. No, he needed to get a grip on God. Where were all the platitudes about God's wonderful gifts now? Same place they'd always been, in the Word. The Word that had tasted like sawdust in his mouth the past few days.

Taste and see that the Lord is good.

Where was that found? Somewhere in Psalms. And David's life had been far messier than Zadok's could ever be. After all, he wasn't about to become king of anywhere, and no one was trying to kill him. Stab him through the heart, yes. Murder him? Not so much.

He took a long, deep breath and let it out slowly. Again.

God, help me.

His position at the minstrel booth was to minister. To provide background music that might remind shoppers of God's love and mercy.

To serve, just like his namesake in the Bible, who'd been a high priest of Israel and whose descendants also served for many generations.

He had a higher calling than to woo Juni O'Neill. He'd thought that would involve ministering in a church somewhere. His only current way to do that was as a lay person. Keanan had suggested he preach occasionally, but that would still be unpaid.

Could he keep operating that tire shop until he retired, believing he'd met God's call in lay ministry?

"Zadok! Are your instruments in the truck?"

He blinked at his sister. "Uh, no. They're by the door."

"I'll take one. We need to roll."

"Right." He hadn't grabbed anything for breakfast, but maybe one of the vendors would be serving muffins or something. He picked up the ukulele and violin while Quincey hoisted the guitar case, and they headed to the truck.

Once they were driving, Quincey glanced his way. "She's still not talking to you, huh?"

Zadok shook his head and slowed for the stop sign at the highway.

"Want me to give her a piece of my mind? Because I can, you know."

He mustered a chuckle at the thought. "No, it's okay."

"I've already done enough, you mean. If I had any idea she'd turn on you like this—"

"Quincey, stop. It's not like that."

"Then what is it like?"

He deliberated. "There are other things going on, outside of Galena Landing, that I can't talk about. It's just... hard right now. You could pray for her. For us."

"It doesn't seem like praying does much."

Zadok swung to look at his sister. "What do you mean? Prayer is everything. It's our phone line to God that's always connected. He always hears."

"And then ignores."

He hadn't dreamed Quincey's doubts ran this deep. "He doesn't ignore us, sis. It's just that His timeline is different from ours. That, and He sees the big picture, and we only see what's right in front of us, smacking us in the nose."

"Is that really what you believe? Deep down?"

"Yes, it is."

She pivoted to look into his face, but he needed to focus on navigating through town. As he crossed the bridge on the north side, he glanced back at her. "What? Do I have something on my face?"

"Listen, Zay. I'm only going to say this once, but if that's what you truly believe, then act like it. You say God hears and answers prayer and that He has the best for us in mind. Act like it."

She flounced back to face the windshield with her arms crossed.

And... she wasn't wrong. He'd joyfully claimed the blessings he wanted as presents from a good Father, but what about the harder things? Weren't those from Him, too? They might be the gifts no one ever wanted, but that didn't mean they weren't worthy. Didn't mean they didn't bring blessing down the road.

"Thanks, Quince."

She quirked an eyebrow at him. "You're welcome."

"I'm not sure when you got so wise."

"I'm not sure when you got so dumb."

Well, then. Guess he'd been put in his place. "Wow, your tact knows no bounds."

"I've met tact." He caught her eyeroll. "I've even been known to employ it on occasion, but sometimes it's just not worth the hassle."

"Hmm. You might be right." Although, at other times, it was needed in spades. And he might not have called upon it the other evening like he should have. Why couldn't Juni see he was only trying to provide a counterbalance? She hadn't allowed him to be neutral but insisted he take her side.

And he was going to be facing the booth she shared with her sister for the next four hours. A trial? Or an opportunity?

"No mermaids? I specifically came to the market for a mermaid set for my niece's birthday."

Juni rubbed her temples with both hands. "I'm sorry.

I'm sold out right now, but I could have a set ready by Tuesday."

"But her birthday is Monday."

Was this where she said something about not putting things off until the last minute? Hard to say when she was so often guilty of the same thing herself. "I'm sorry. That's the best I can do, but a lot of little girls enjoy these other sets, too."

The woman sniffed, offered a cursory glance at the dragons and forest animals, and shook her head. "No, that's not what I want. Emorie has been crazy about seashells since her parents took her to Sanibel Island at spring break. She's told me a dozen times about the mermaids she almost saw. Nothing else will do."

"Then I'm sorry." How many times did Juni need to say that? She'd said those words to Dad so many times growing up. She could never please him. She couldn't please anyone, it seemed. Tears stung her eyes, but she kept her smile in place as the woman huffed and turned away.

Arleigh nudged her with a gentle elbow. "Don't let her ruin your day."

"Easier said than done. How can I call myself a businessperson if I can't even keep basic inventory in stock?"

The elbow dug a little deeper. "A successful one? Since you *sold out* of your most popular set, you must be doing something right."

"And can't get more sequins until Monday. That's if my order comes in like the tracking number says it will.

Sometimes living in a small town on the backside of beyond really stinks."

"I hear you." Arleigh straightened and faced the aisle. "Good morning, Rosemary. How are you and Steve doing today?"

"Grateful for God's blessings." The older woman offered a gentle smile. "Those fall bouquets are stunning. May I buy three?"

"Sure. Any preference of which ones?"

Rosemary Nemesek pointed out her choices, and Arleigh began to wrap them. The woman turned to Juni. "How is business for you?"

"Good. I've had several orders through my online store and, as you can see, I'm completely sold out of mermaid sets for the time being."

"Those are so darling. The little girls in my life love them, so I'm not surprised to hear you're having trouble keeping them in stock. You must be sewing your fingers to a bone."

"I definitely had hand cramps this past week." To go along with the heart cramps, not that she'd mention those.

"Is it worth it to you?"

Juni blinked. "Pardon me?"

"You know. The time you spend, the money you bring in... is it worth it?"

"Not this week," she muttered. If she'd been out with Zadok on Monday, she'd have let Genevieve go to voicemail. She wouldn't have found out about Dad's indiscretions — alleged indiscretions — in front of him. Maybe things would have been different.

She didn't dare glance across the greenhouse corridor to where he played "Good, Good Father" on his violin. Nice someone was a good father. It certainly wasn't Grant O'Neill.

"If it's not, why do it?"

Such a simple question. One with no simple answers. "I'm not sure." But she did know. It felt good to be popular, to be wanted, to be successful, even if it was just with a tiny store making things that brought smiles to children's faces.

But worth it? She'd had so much fun the day she'd created the first set for Treyan's daughter, Scarlett. The little girl's glee had been infectious and her ideas for embellishments as inspiring as they'd been impossible. It had been so gratifying. Now it was drudgery.

Rosemary patted Juni's hand before cradling the bouquets in the large market bag she brought every week for that purpose. "I'm praying for you, sweetheart."

Why Juni? Was this something Rosemary said to just anyone, anytime? Juni turned wide eyes to Arleigh. "What was all that about?"

"She's intuitive. That's all I can say."

"How can she even think of other people when her hands are so full taking care of a disabled husband and with all her grandkids and...?"

"Because she's that sort of person. She cares." Arleigh gave a slight chuckle. "I want to be her when I grow up."

"Three bouquets. Is their house that big?"

Arleigh shook her head. "She keeps one at home occasionally, I think, but mostly she takes them up to Galena Hills Care Facility and gives them to whichever resident needs cheering up."

"That's... amazing."

"I know. She's awesome, always thinking of others."

Gina Zima paused in front of their table. "Oh, good! You have some sets left. I was worried I'd miss out."

Juni gave the woman her full attention. "Good thing Emma already has mermaids, since I'm sold out of those."

"No, I'm looking for a gift for a little boy in Emma's class. Justin is in the hospital in Coeur d'Alene, and I thought some felties might help cheer him up. His mom is a friend of mine."

"I'm sorry to hear that."

"Yeah, it's nasty when cancer attacks kids. He's doing pretty well at the moment, and they're hoping he'll be home by Christmas. Still six weeks, right? So that's what we're praying for."

As far as Juni knew, Gina and Rosemary weren't related to each other, but both had the same heart, one in tune with helping cheer up people who needed it.

She swallowed hard. "What are Justin's interests? I have the dragons, the ranch sets, the forest creatures, my newest, a safari set."

Gina studied them, shaking her head slightly. "I don't know him that well."

"I tell you what. Take one of each. Let me donate them to the cause."

"Oh, I couldn't. I mean, I wasn't asking for a donation."

"I know, but I'd like to."

"At least let me pay for the one set I'd meant to buy."

"Okay, that's fair." Juni tucked four packets into a paper bag before accepting Gina's cash.

"Gina, please take a bouquet for Justin's mom, okay? I want to give something, too, and his mom will probably appreciate the flowers more than a little boy would."

"Arleigh, that's too much." Gina blinked back tears.

"It's not. It's what community is for. What friends do." Arleigh began wrapping stems.

"Thank you. Stacy will be grateful. I know I am."

Gina turned toward the Ackerman Farm booth, which was laden with squashes of all kinds, along with garlic, apples, and beets.

Arleigh nudged Juni. "You're awesome."

"I'm not. Anyone would have done that. *You* did it, too."

"Not everyone."

Business was fairly steady for the next hour, and Zadok's music laid underlying notes beneath the hum of chatter and laughter throughout the greenhouse.

Juni's sister was right. This was what community felt like. Not like the woman who'd been rude when she couldn't get the last-minute gift she'd wanted. Not even like the grandmother and her online order which would doubtless delight her granddaughters. It hadn't been personal.

But this was. Rosemary still chatting with Jean

Stedman over coffee a few booths down. Quincey crouching in front of a little girl by the Green Acres booth. The child was obviously telling her a tale, complete with a multitude of gestures that nearly bopped Quincey on the nose more than once. Keanan picking up Zadok's guitar and joining in for a few songs with nothing but nods exchanged between the two men. Paula bustling around, clipboard in hand, chatting with vendors and customers alike.

"You okay?"

Juni hadn't even realized the deep sigh she'd uttered had been audible. She glanced at her sister. "Yeah. I think so."

"Deep thoughts?"

"I'm not sure I can leave Galena Landing."

"Who said anything about leaving?"

Right. She hadn't verbalized that. "You know, with things the way they are with Zadok."

"You can't let him determine your life choices."

It had been hard enough to evade him for the first few months, remembering the kind of guy he'd revealed on their blind date. Except he'd apologized for that — explained, even — and she'd forgiven him. Seventy times seven, the Bible said. Was that all for one offense, or for multiple offenses? Either way, Juni was nowhere near that number yet.

This was a new problem, him sticking up for Dad, but was that really what he'd done? It had sounded like it, but his words had looped through Juni's mind for five days now, and she wasn't as sure as she had been.

"Mom took the news pretty well."

Juni glanced at her sister. "It didn't surprise her. I don't know how she can keep such a neutral attitude, even if she doesn't have specific memories that would bolster the girls' claims."

"God." Arleigh shook her head. "God has absolutely helped Mom set everything aside and forgive. One other good thing — she's accepted that I don't want Dad walking me down the aisle. Don't even want him at the wedding."

Juni breathed out relief. "Good." Forgiveness was one thing. Giving someone the ability to hurt you over and over again was something else entirely.

She looked between the throng of shoppers to find Zadok watching her. Could she forgive him again? That didn't mean she needed to resume where they'd left off. Those were two completely different things.

Right? Right.

Was there any chance she'd misunderstood him?

He broke eye contact, turning to say something to Keanan.

If she wanted to make Galena Landing her permanent home, she was going to need to figure this out. But maybe, just maybe, she could depend on God to help her. It was worth a shot.

TWENTY-FOUR

T hanks for inviting us for Thanksgiving." Zadok leaned back in his chair beside the very long table in the Green Acres' main house.

It had been two long weeks since he and Juni had exchanged any words. She'd come to the market the next Saturday but missed the week after. He hadn't dared ask Arleigh why, but Xavier still met with Juni three times a week for tutoring or, more to the point, homework supervision. He hadn't said anything about a substitute, so her absence at the market didn't mean Juni was sick or out of town.

"You are welcome here." Keanan smiled at him from across the table. "We try to hold an open-door policy for our friends."

"We appreciate it." Zadok was maybe also a little tired of being the needy one. He'd dreamed of the hinted-at invitation to Mrs. O'Neill's apartment for Thanksgiving, but it hadn't materialized. All because he couldn't keep his opinions to himself.

Which he still had a hard time regretting, honestly. If Juni was one to jump to conclusions like that — something he already knew about her from four years back — then she wasn't someone he could trust with his heart.

Except he *had* trusted her. He'd — dare he admit it even to himself? — begun to love her. Yes. Loved, against his better judgment.

Down the table, Xavier had wrangled a seat between Brent Callahan and his son Finnley. Xavier peppered Brent with questions about timber-frame construction. Maybe coming to the farm for turkey dinner was worthwhile for that connection if nothing else.

In the adjacent kitchen, Mason and Noel seemed to be on cleanup duty, while Quincey helped Liz and Claire serve pumpkin pie. Then the men returned to the table and conversation resumed.

It had been a while since Zadok had felt quite this stuffed.

Finnley Callahan and Christopher Waterman invited Xavier to shoot baskets with them as the meal closed. The boys were younger than Xavier by several years, but he appeared willing when he went outside with them.

Brent leaned onto the table to meet Zadok's gaze. "Your brother asks good questions. Think he might be interested in learning on the job over the summer?"

Zadok couldn't stop the first real smile he'd formed in weeks. "I'm sure he would. Feel free to ask him."

"I will." The man nodded. "I wanted to run it by you first, though, in case you had objections or other plans."

"I appreciate that, but no. We've talked about construction some. I know he doesn't want to spend his life changing tires."

Brent chuckled. "Do you?"

"I can't say that I planned for this to be my life, no. But I can see God's hand in it, for now, at least."

Chelsea turned to him. "Keanan mentioned you might want a hand painting your reception area."

Zadok rubbed his temple. He'd forgotten about that with all this stuff with Juni. "Yeah, it's way past time."

Mason laughed. "Man, I worked there for Roger for a few years, and I'm pretty sure that place hasn't been cared for, let alone painted, since it was built 30-some years ago."

"I hate to admit what sad shape it's in." Why hadn't Dad fixed it up any when he'd bought the business? Too late to ask. "But it's time."

"Just paint?" Chelsea asked. "How about window coverings? The floor?"

The floor? Zadok had to think a minute to even remember what was on it. Commercial vinyl tile. Chipped. "Might as well go all in." Or maybe he should contemplate the cost before he committed.

"If you're considering vinyl plank, I have a dozen boxes in my warehouse," Brent put in. "I had a client change her mind about one of the rooms in a recent build after we'd ordered. You could have it for cost if you want it."

"Vinyl plank?"

"Yeah. Wood look in a grayish brown. The stuff is waterproof and nearly indestructible."

"Sounds like an offer I can't refuse."

Brent chuckled. "You haven't seen it yet."

"It has to be a huge improvement over what's there now." Zadok turned back to Chelsea. "What color would you recommend on the walls?"

"I'd have to come have a look." She tapped her jaw. "It has a huge window, right? Faces south?"

Zadok nodded. "There's a reflective shade when the sun is a problem, but it probably needs replacing, too. It keeps coming off the rail."

"A soft green might be nice," Brent's wife said. "It's warmer than blue but not as warm as yellow."

Chelsea nodded thoughtfully.

"I'm kind of partial to blue," Zadok objected. Like the cornflower of June's eyes.

Both women raised their eyebrows as they looked at him.

"Or, you know, green might be nice." His resolve weakened along with his voice.

"You're learning." Brent laughed.

What good would the lessons do if Juni refused to give an inch? Was it up to him to grovel? He hadn't done anything wrong! In fact, he was in the right. Which was not an attitude that would facilitate a reconciliation. But did a reconciliation even make sense when the other party was so unrelenting? Yeah, he was just as confused about that as he had been two weeks ago, and it wasn't for lack of praying.

"I'll stop in Monday, if that works for you," Chelsea said.

Zadok nodded. "I have nowhere else to be. It definitely works."

"Perfect. I'll have a look around and then give you some recommendations. How many rooms are we talking?"

He stared at her. Hadn't they been discussing the reception area? But there was also a restroom and small staff room where the guys stashed their stuff during the work day. Zadok cringed. It was full of junk and old files he'd never got around to sorting.

He took a deep breath. Might as well go all in. "Three, including a restroom." There was inheritance money if Tires and Treads couldn't pay for the upgrades on its own. Zadok would get the return when he sold the business and, meanwhile, it would be a far more welcoming environment.

Did it even matter? It wasn't like there was another tire shop in Galena Landing. The nearest competition was in Wynnton.

But... it still mattered.

Zadok became aware that his cell phone, which he'd silenced upon arrival at the farm, was vibrating in his hip pocket. He should probably ignore that... but what if it were Juni, wanting to talk and rebuild their relationship? He should at least check who was calling.

He pulled out the device and glanced down. Then stared at the display. John Leslie. Man, he hadn't heard from his old college roommate since the condolences John had sent for the funeral.

"Excuse me. I need to take this." Zadok surged out of his chair and turned away as he thumbed to accept the call. "Hello?" He hurried outside into the cold, sunny November day.

"Zadok, my man! It's John."

"I saw your name. Nice to hear from you, and I hope you're having a good Thanksgiving."

"Sure. All good..."

But there was hesitation in the man's voice. "What's up?"

John sighed. "I don't know if you've heard, but do you remember Professor O'Neill from seminary days?"

Zadok's blood chilled. "I do remember him." How could he not, but John couldn't possibly know he'd reconnected with Juni.

"He's been charged with sexual harassment by five women ranging over the past ten years. Including Tracie. She didn't want to come forward, but she broke down and told me everything a few weeks ago, things she'd never told me before, and... she had to do it, man."

Zadok dropped into an Adirondack chair on the deck and ran his free hand through his hair. "He came on to Tracie?" Tracie had been Juni's roommate back then, and she had married John a year or two after graduation. But, this...

"You wouldn't believe the stuff she told me."

He hadn't believed Juni, either, but that wasn't entirely fair. She'd had no proof, just jumped to conclusions. Conclusions that, apparently, were founded on truth, even though she hadn't known it.

Zadok felt sick to his stomach, suddenly aware of how much turkey dinner he'd eaten. "How far did it go?" Maybe he didn't want to know.

"Innuendoes. Touching her breasts *accidentally*. Making sure she noticed his, uh, bodily reactions to her."

"That's disgusting."

"I know. I can't believe she never told me. I'd have — I don't know what I would have done, but something. Man, I hope they lock him up for life."

"Is it... is it going to trial?"

"I'm going to make sure of it. Tracie and the others, they deserve to have him suffer for what he did to them. I can't believe it. All those years. All those classes of his I sat in, how much I looked up to him, thinking he was God's voice to aspiring pastors."

"Yeah." Zadok cleared his throat. "Me, too. Has he been suspended?"

"Yup." John sounded smug about that. "Until his name is cleared, but it won't be. The man is as guilty as sin. It will take a while to come to trial, though. The attorney we've hired is building a watertight case."

"Wow." Zadok didn't know whether to congratulate John or not. His former roommate sounded vindictive, but then, his wife had been wronged by Grant O'Neill.

So had Zadok's girlfriend, if Juni was still that. She'd suffered at least as much as Tracie and the others, though possibly — hopefully — in a different way.

"Let me know how things pan out, okay?"

"Sure. Hey, how are things going for you these days? I heard of a church in Omaha looking for a music minister. Want me to send them a recommendation for you?"

A reminder that John was actively employed in the field Zadok had aspired to for so long. "Thanks, but no. I'll be in Galena Landing at least until my brother finishes high school, and that's a year and a half away still."

"He'd probably survive a move."

"I won't ask it of him."

John sighed. "Your call."

"Yes. Yes, it is."

"Maybe there's another reason you're staying there? Have you met someone?"

This was absolutely not the time to catch John up on Zadok's love life, or lack of it. "Maybe. Early days yet."

"Well, I hope it works out for you, my man. Keep in touch."

The line went dead, and Zadok lowered the cell to his lap and stared out across the valley. He could hear the basketball bouncing on the concrete pad over near the farm school building and hear the boys laughing. He could hear muted voices from inside the house, too.

Mostly, he could hear a thrumming in his head. What was this going to do to Juni? Was it his responsibility to tell her John had called? Why did the hope of reconciliation feel farther off than it had since Juni's stepmother had phoned her?

God, help. Please help.

IT HAD BEEN years since Juni had sat at a Thanksgiving meal with her sister and her mother. Since before the divorce, actually. She'd never have guessed then that the next time would have included Arleigh's fiancé and his two young sons. And, only a few weeks ago, she'd assumed Zadok and his siblings would also be present. Mom's apartment would have been crowded with nine people, two of them unable to sit still for 20 seconds, but Mom would have loved it.

Juni would have, too. If only Zadok hadn't stuck up for Dad.

He hadn't. Not precisely, but it had come too close for Juni's comfort. In just the blink of an eye, his veneer had been scraped enough for her to see he was still, at heart, attuned to her father's teaching for all that he'd said his eyes had been opened. When push came to shove, he still defended Dad.

Sort of.

Zadok could try to talk his way out of his initial reaction, but the longer he remained silent, the less likely it would be that she believed him. She needed to face the fact that he hadn't repented, or he'd have let her know by now.

Was she in the wrong? Nope. Not at all. Not when it came to Dad. There might not be any real evidence — not yet — but there was zero doubt in her mind that plenty would come to light.

If only she could reach out to her former roommate, but when Tracie kept dating John after setting up that disastrous blind date, Juni had stopped talking to her. Rumor had it that Tracie had married John, which made her a forever traitor.

Even inside herself, Juni cringed. That whole seventy-times-seven forgiveness thing... did that apply to Tracie, too? How could Juni claim to follow the Lord if she held onto her bitterness?

Tracie's attempt at apology back then had been more of an, 'oops, sorry,' than anything fervent. She'd said the words, though.

Juni had shut her down.

"You okay, Juni?" Mom offered a concerned expression.

Great, now she was spacing out in front of everyone. Juni forced a smile. "Sure. I'm fine."

Though where were the others? Mitchell and Arleigh's voices came from the kitchen along with the clatter of dishes and the sound of running water. The boys had a puzzle out on the table across the room.

"Is this about your father?"

Wasn't everything? She shrugged. "I'll get over it."

"Only if you let God handle justice."

"I don't understand how you can forgive him."

Mom shook her head with a slight smile. "Only through Jesus."

Yeah, Juni was a Christian, too. But so was Dad, or so

he said. Words were cheap, but Mom actually lived them. So did Arleigh. Juni? Not so much. "But, *how*?"

"Oh, honey. I spent years trying to tell God how to run His universe."

That was a relief, because some days, it didn't seem like the Creator was doing that great a job. Look at all the wars. The modern slave trade. The floods and famines.

"Do you know what Eve's sin was?"

Juni blinked. Where was her mother going with this? "God told them not to eat the fruit of the tree of the knowledge of good and evil. Eve disobeyed." And Adam was right there with her.

"That was the result of her primary sin."

"Pardon me?" Juni gave her head a shake.

"Eve told the snake that God had told them to not even touch the tree, but God hadn't said that."

"So... her first sin was lying." Made sense.

"Her first sin was believing she knew better than God how to run His creation."

"I'm not following."

"The tree of the knowledge of good and evil. Eve wanted to understand good and evil on her own terms. She wanted to create her own definitions."

Juni bit her lip and contemplated her mother's unsettling words.

"Eve thought she could do a better job of defining them than God could." Mom squeezed Juni's arm. "I've been there. I think we all have. Even the psalmist, David, begged God to hurry up and smite the evildoers."

Juni was totally into smiting if that would take Dad out.

"What David didn't understand — what none of us truly understand — is that God is still in charge. He knows what He's doing, even when everything around us looks like absolute chaos. He still has a plan. He's still working His plan."

"But..." Juni zipped her mouth shut. It was hard to argue with Mom's logic.

"I know. I get it. But it's only when I give everything over to God, over and over and over again, and remind myself that He defines good and evil, and I do not... that's when I can let go and find peace amid all the trials."

Peace sounded good. Juni couldn't remember the last time she'd really felt that in her life. She'd blamed Dad for her constant feeling of being off-kilter. And, yeah, he definitely was a problem, but she was using him as an excuse. Pointing at him meant she didn't have to face her own failures.

But, he'd sexually abused young women under his authority! How could she pretend that hadn't happened, now that she knew?

That wasn't what Mom meant. Mom wasn't flippantly excusing him. She wasn't saying the girls shouldn't prosecute their professor.

She was admitting that she, personally, was accepting God's authority in the matter. She knew judgment wasn't on her.

There was a balance in there somewhere, and Juni had been riding the Ferris wheel round and round. Now soaring above and ignoring all the problems as she had while dating Zadok, now plummeting to the bottom and wallowing in all the injustices.

All of it based on feelings. All of it based on her own concept of right and wrong.

Ouch. Juni was just like Eve.

TWENTY-FIVE

M ay I have a word with you, Zadok?"

Zadok turned to Pastor Ron as Keanan and the other musicians tidied up the platform after practice on Saturday. They'd been preparing a set of songs featuring Thanksgiving and the beginning of Advent. He took a closer look at the older man. Was it his imagination, or maybe the lighting, or did Ron Wilson look a little paler than usual? The man had played the drums for practice — had there been less energy than usual?

"Sure. What's up?"

"As you know, we're coming into Advent, so I know this is a terrible time to ask you this."

Now the man was scaring him. "Ask me what?"

"Between you and me and a few, select, other people, I need to go to Boise for some medical testing this week. They were able to get me in this quickly only because of a cancelation." The man winced. "Which was because of a death, actually."

Zadok's brows furrowed as his gut turned sour. "What kind of testing?"

"They're unsure whether my lungs or my heart are the primary problem, but it's better to be safe than sorry, or so I've heard."

"I'm sure it is. So, what's the request?" Although, he had a sinking feeling he already knew.

"Would you be willing to preach next week? It's the second Sunday of Advent, the Sunday of peace. I know it's not much notice."

"Preach?" Zadok hated that his voice came out with a squeak like a boy in the first throes of puberty. Even Xavier was well past that.

Pastor Ron nodded, studying him. "Not to corner you, but there's no one else I can ask, and I know you've completed seminary."

And his parents had died shortly after commencement, diverting his plans. "*Music* ministry, with all due respect, sir."

"You have a degree in music and then a postdoc in ministry, right?"

Zadok tried not to sigh out loud. "Yes, but..."

"Can you pray about it for a couple of days and let me know by Monday? Tuesday, at the latest? Wanda and I are headed to Boise Wednesday, and I'm admitted Thursday. Depending on what they find, we may return by Sunday, but it would set my mind at ease to not have to worry about the timing."

"What's your backup plan?"

The pastor's smile looked a little thin. "Honestly? I don't have one. I know that sounds manipulative, but it isn't meant to be. Ed Graysen used to pinch hit for me occasionally, but he's declined a lot since his wife's death and then his stroke. He's now a resident of Galena Hills."

Zadok closed his eyes and took a deep, bracing breath. How could he say no? It wasn't like he hadn't been warned. "How about Keanan Welsh? Noel Kenzie?"

Pastor Ron shook his head. "God has laid your name on my heart."

Trust God, even when it's hard. Especially *when it's hard.*

That's what Dad used to say. Dad had been a smart man. A devoted follower of Jesus.

Zadok braced his shoulders and looked at his pastor. "I'll do it, sir. But I don't know how."

"Thank you, son." The man's relief was palpable. "If you want to pop by the office, I'll give you the notes I've made so far. You may use them or not, but they might give you a launching pad."

"Sounds good." He could do a lot of the prep at the tire shop. Being the boss had its perks. It wasn't like he had tasks to keep him busy every minute, especially now that most everyone in the valley had switched to their winter tires. The rest would flock in after the first significant snowfall, and that wasn't scheduled for this week. Besides, Austin and Bobby could handle the influx if it came.

Oh. Wait. Chelsea would be in on Monday to figure out a plan for the facelift. That didn't mean she'd start right away, though. Zadok could put her off so that he could focus on writing a sermon.

A sermon on peace.

Maybe first he needed to figure it out for himself.

"TIME TO DECORATE!"

Juni stared at her sister. "Decorate?"

"For Christmas." Arleigh frowned at her. "Don't tell me you are a minimalist on this one. Mitchell and the boys picked up a tree for us at the fire hall. He even found us a tree stand."

At least Juni didn't need to go and worry that Simon would take her presence as encouragement, though why? He was a nice enough guy. But, he wasn't Zadok.

She needed to get over Zadok. Or... maybe talk to him. Make things right. Shouldn't he apologize first? Wouldn't they just have the same argument all over again if she approached him first?

Aargh.

"Juni? I picked up a few strands of white lights when Brittany and I were in Spokane, but I don't really have any decorations. Maybe we don't need any. Unless you're against having a tree at all."

"Against it?" Dad, of course, was certain people worshiped Christmas trees and that all the baubles were commercialism at best or idols at worst.

"I know Dad doesn't do Christmas," Arleigh said apologetically.

But Juni was done with Grant O'Neill and everything he represented. "A tree sounds nice." Not that she'd ever lived in the same house as one. Student dorm rooms were no place for individual trees, and Juni hadn't bothered last year when she'd been on her own. She'd still gone to Dad and Genevieve's for dinner and the reading of the Christmas story.

"Any ideas for decorating it? Besides the lights." Arleigh grimaced. "I didn't have much, but what I did have got wrecked in the flood last winter."

"We could whip up some felt ornaments."

"Aren't you tired of sewing?"

Juni shuddered. "I'm shutting the shop by the end of the year, like I told you. But mermaids and dragons and hippos aren't exactly festive ornaments."

Arleigh laughed. "I think they'd be kind of cute, if you have any extras."

"Only if you hang some of your neon felt flowers on the tree."

"Ha! It's a deal. I have a dozen or so of those from when I used to babysit Scarlett. Who says we have to have the same decorations as everyone else?"

"Mom might have a few extras."

"Maybe, but she bought a pre-lit artificial tree and tends to minimalism and simplicity."

"Maybe the boys would like to make some paper snowflakes."

Arleigh's eyebrows arched. "Have you *met* Mitchell's

kids? And you would trust them with sharp scissors?"

"Um, no. You're right, but we can think of some way for them to contribute, right?"

"Maybe. You're the one with all the crafty ideas." Arleigh twirled in their tiny living room. "I love Christmas. I think it means more to me because I never got the whole experience of it as a kid. The wonder of Jesus' birth never gets old, and I love all the symbols that remind me of it."

"And the gifts."

Arleigh grinned. "I haven't had many of those, but it's different now. Mom and I usually exchanged something small, but this year there's Mitchell and the boys and Treyan and Brittany and Scarlett..." Her voice petered to a stop as she looked at Juni. "Sorry."

Juni took a deep breath. "Sorry for having people who love you? No, that's great."

"You miss Zadok."

She shrugged. "Sort of, but I'll get over him."

"Why?"

"What do you mean, why?"

"Why get over him when you could talk to him and clear things up?"

"Or he could take the initiative."

Arleigh bit her lip. "From what you said, you shut him down pretty hard. And besides, why is it the man's job to do that? We're all about equal opportunity around here, right? Don't let Dad get in your head about that."

"It's not Dad." Juni felt her hackles rise.

"Sounds like him to me. Remember, I lived with him for a lot of years, too. I recognize his voice in my head."

And Juni didn't? Could she be guilty of clinging to traditional roles only when it suited her? Ouch. That hurt. And then there was the whole talk Mom had had with her on Thursday about Eve's sin of thinking she knew better than God.

Juni didn't like to be wrong. More than that, she didn't like to admit it and have others see her fallibility. If she apologized — not saying she was going to, of course — that made her vulnerable. Zadok might not accept her apology. He might decide he'd had enough of her nonsense and self-righteousness...

She really was a lot more like her father than she preferred to admit.

Enough. Juni surged off the sofa. "Where is this tree? Where do you want to put it? I think people usually put them in front of windows, but all we've got is those small ones way above the sofa."

"There's really no other place to move the sofa, anyway," Arleigh mused. "We could put the tree between the TV and the table along that wall over there."

"If it's not too big."

"Mitch said he got a skinny one for us."

"Well, let's have a look. It can't really fit anywhere else that I can figure out."

"You're right." Arleigh tapped on her phone. A few seconds later, it chimed. "He'll bring it down right away."

Which meant Arleigh and Mitchell hadn't been sure how she'd respond. Was she really that stuck in her old ways — Dad's ways? She didn't want to align with him in any respect, especially after Genevieve's call two weeks back. He'd merely been pompous before. Now he seemed slimy. Icky.

Footsteps thudded on the basement stairs, and Arleigh flung the door open to reveal the trunk of an evergreen coming through, followed by a smiling Mitchell and then his kids.

"It's a fir tree," Lincoln announced. "See? The needles are flat and not in bunches. Isn't that right, Dad?"

Mitch grinned at his son. "You've got it."

"You gots lights?" Hudson asked.

Arleigh squished the younger boy to her side. "I do have lights! What kind does your dad have? All colors or white ones?"

"Not all the colors. Just red and yellow and blue and green."

The kid was cute when he wasn't wrecking things.

Mitchell tore his gaze from Arleigh long enough to glance at Juni before refocusing on his fiancée. "Would you like to come up later this afternoon and help decorate ours? We can make popcorn and hot chocolate."

"Um..." Arleigh glanced at Juni.

"Both of you, of course."

But he was only being polite. "I've got... um... papers to grade. You go ahead. We can do ours this evening, or even tomorrow."

"Are you sure?" Her sister looked torn.

Arleigh's future was with Mitchell, Lincoln, and Hudson. Of course, she needed to make memories and new traditions with them and leave Juni behind. "Yeah, no problem."

It wasn't like she'd had any expectations at all until a few minutes ago, but she should have known Christmas would come up. After all, indications were everywhere. The town's streetlights had magically sprouted festive banners overnight, and strands of lights suddenly surrounded many storefront windows. Others had been painted with snowflakes or wintery scenes.

Of course, the holiday was going to invade her own home, too.

It needed to invade her heart. Hadn't Jesus come into a strife-filled world to bring peace to all? He was the original good and perfect gift. No one could deny that, if they believed in anything good in this world.

"Here, hold the tree as straight as you can," Mitchell instructed as he angled the trunk into the base Lincoln had carried. "Then I'll clamp it tight. Ready?"

Arleigh grasped the trunk. "Ready."

"Me, too." Hudson grabbed at the tree, and the whole thing swayed.

"You gotta hold it still," Lincoln informed his brother.

Hudson stuck out his tongue, and the tree wobbled.

"Either hold still or let go." Mitchell's muffled voice came from beneath the boughs at the base.

"I'm helping."

Juni stifled a laugh. The kid was *so* not helping but making it harder for Arleigh to steady and for Mitchell to clamp.

Was that how she helped God, too? Enthusiastically, but with little value to recommend her offerings?

Why did He even want human help? Like

Mitchell, God could do a way better job without their feeble interference. But, also like Mitchell, He knew His likenesses would be better for their desire to learn and grow. They'd be better with His gentle guidance.

It wasn't about getting the job done better or faster, not in the slightest. It was all about relationship.

She'd need to think on that.

"I'M sorry you don't feel well." Arleigh eyed Juni on Sunday morning. "I can stay home with you and make a pot of chicken soup."

"No, please don't. I'll be okay. I just need more rest."

"Are you sure?"

Well, Juni definitely wasn't going to tell her sister she was half making it up. But there was the other half, where her gut really was churning. Who knew? She might barf yet.

"I hate you missing the first Sunday of Advent. The Zima family is lighting the hope candle this morning."

Juni didn't want to know how Arleigh was privy to that information. "I'm sure Ethan and Emma will do a great job with their parents."

"Watch online?"

Juni rubbed her temple. And get a closeup view of the worship team leading songs of thanks and hope? Nope.

"I'll probably be asleep." She yawned and leaned back on her pillow.

Arleigh rested her cool hand on Juni's forehead. "Dear Heavenly Father, please heal my sister. Please heal her gut and her heart, in Jesus' name, amen."

"Thanks."

"Love you, sis."

"Love you, too." And, man, if that wasn't causing tears to prickle at the corners of her eyes. "Have a good time."

"Oh! I just remembered there's chicken soup in the freezer! I'll get out a package. Heat it up if you're hungry, or we'll both have it for lunch. Whichever."

"You're having lunch with Mitchell."

"I hate for you to be alone when you're not well."

Arleigh was as hard to dislodge as a bush full of burrs. "Don't disappoint Mitch and the boys on account of me. I'm a survivor."

"It's time to leave for church. I'll quick grab that container of soup. If you're sure you're okay—"

"I'm sure."

"All right then."

Arleigh's footsteps faded. Juni heard the fridge's freezer door open and close and then a clunk as a frozen object landed in the metal sink.

"Bye, Juni!"

Juni was done answering. She waited until Arleigh's footsteps on the stairs receded and Mitchell's truck engine rumbled away. Then she threw off her blankets and trundled into the bathroom where she started filling the tub. Sometimes a girl needed a little pampering.

And, because she was a good Christian girl, she'd put on a worship playlist in the background. Arleigh had a whole bunch set up in their shared music app. That would almost be the same as going to church.

She poured bath salts into the tub and lit a couple of candles before sinking into the soothing depths.

The strains of Matt Redman singing "Blessed Be the Name of the Lord" rolled into the bathroom. Of course, she knew that was one of her sister's favorite songs. Hers, too, at least once upon a time. The songwriter talked about blessing God's name whether in easy times or hard.

What had God ever done for her? Even as the grumpy thought circled her brain, she knew He had done a lot. Yes, He'd allowed her to be raised by a narcissistic father who'd — probably — turned out to be a sexual predator, but God had also protected her from him.

He'd given her a safe place to retreat to here in Galena Landing, near her sister and her mom and their unwavering faith. He'd provided a job and a place to live and a purpose. He might even have given her a godly boyfriend whom she'd pushed away.

It stank like crazy to admit Zadok was smarter than she was. More levelheaded. More forgiving.

More like Jesus.

She could admit it in her head, but out loud? To Zadok's face?

"I was wrong." She practiced it out loud. Cringed.

The thing was, she hadn't been wrong. Not entirely.

Were semantics worth hanging onto? How could she simply let it go?

TWENTY-SIX

Z adok sat at his desk, listening to the lift creaking as it raised a car into the air in the work bay. His Bible was open in front of him beside Pastor Ron's hand-scribbled notes and his laptop with 'advent peace' open as a search term.

Why was he here? Why had he agreed? Could he still say no?

He closed his eyes. Ironically, the first thing he needed was God's peace in the midst of this preparation. How could he talk about tranquility if he had none of his own?

God had settled his heart after his parents' funeral. He'd felt certainty about giving up his own plans and staying on in Galena Landing to see his siblings through school and into adulthood. Had resentment ever reared its head? Sure, it had, but he'd kept bringing it back to God, who had been faithful.

Zadok read through the Christmas story in Luke again, watching for the word.

The angels said to the shepherds, "Glory to God in the highest heaven, and on earth peace to those on whom his favor rests."

Was it anywhere else?

Simeon in the temple... was that part of the Christmas story? The old man had said, "Sovereign Lord, as you have promised, you may now dismiss your servant in peace."

That couldn't be the part Pastor Ron wanted highlighted. It wasn't in the notes at all, only the angels' visit to the shepherds.

What must it have been like to be part of a group of obscure shepherds, watching their flocks as they did every night, suddenly surrounded by angels proclaiming God's announcement?

The door to the parking lot opened with a rattle of chimes and a whoosh of cold air, and Zadok looked up.

Chelsea Welsh closed the door behind her then set her hands on her hips and slowly turned, studying the area while completely ignoring him.

Zadok watched her, and a smile began to form on his face at her focus. She was taking this mighty seriously. He cleared his throat. "Good morning, Chelsea."

She gave him a startled look then blushed. "Oh, I'm sorry. Good morning, Zadok. Also, Keanan was right. This space needs help, and you've come to just the right person."

He hadn't come to her at all. Her husband had offered up her services in an effort to keep her from redecorating their own home. *Good luck with that, Keanan. This one looks born to change her world.*

Zadok smirked. "Good to know. The restroom and staff area are right through there." He pointed to the alcove beside the door to the work bay.

"Mind if I have a look?"

"Be my guest." He'd taken the time to scrub the restroom first thing this morning. Might've been him procrastinating working on the sermon, but it might also have been him remembering a woman was coming to snoop in all the corners. He'd even wiped the staff room table... the part not covered with boxes and junk. The guys usually went home or to Bella's Bakery for lunch. Zadok did the same or ate at his desk. The table back there was mostly for show. Or, more to the point, to collect clutter.

Chelsea scurried into the other spaces then back, nudging her glasses up her nose. "Wow."

Didn't sound like a good wow. Her reaction might not be a huge shock, but his heart still sank.

"Beyond hope?"

"Not at all." She straightened. "But you really need to organize that back room. It's... quite something."

"Yeah. I think most of the collection is from before Dad bought the business. He never quite got around to dealing with it."

"It's time."

Zadok leaned back in his chair and nearly tipped it. The springs or pistons or something were totally shot. "I don't have time. Not this week, for sure." Not with a sermon looming over him. About peace, of all things.

She crossed her arms, tapped a foot, and looked

around again, a thoughtful expression on her face. "Are you open through Christmas week?"

"I usually shut down between Christmas and New Year's... because I need a break."

Chelsea nodded decisively. "That will work. We'll tackle this place first thing in the new year, once you've had a chance to go through everything."

Had she even heard him say he needed time off?

She kept talking. "Any records older than seven years can go. If you don't have a paper shredder, buy or rent one. Then go digital and save a few trees."

"We are digital now," Zadok said stiffly.

"Good, good. I'm not sure if there's anything here that the thrift store could use—" she eyed the brick holding up the desk corner "—but keep that in mind as you go through things."

He couldn't help a murmur of agreement at her assessment.

"I'll see you soon with some paint swatches. I know we talked about green, but now that I'm in here, I think a warm, sunny yellow would be more welcoming."

"No." That would remind him too much of Juni and Arleigh's apartment. "I voted for blue."

"No." Chelsea studied him for a moment. "I'll compromise with green, if I must."

"Green is okay, I guess." It didn't seem like he'd get to voice many opinions over this project. He'd go along with Chelsea for the most part. It would be worth it in the end, but meanwhile? It was going to add a ton of stress to his already not-very-peaceful life.

Peace. He'd get back to searching for that as soon as Chelsea left. Then contemplate whether there was any hope of reconciliation with Juni. She hadn't been in church yesterday. She'd almost certainly skip next week, too, if she found out he was preaching.

Could Zadok find an anchor in the midst of all this turmoil? Was fighting for Juni even worth all this?

There was nearly always a guarded expression in her eyes. Her dad had not fought for her when she was a child. Her mom might have tried — Zadok couldn't know — but they'd been separated much of the past eight or nine years.

Juni had mentioned she hadn't kept in touch with anyone from SIU days. Had her friends tried? Tracie might not have because Juni was Professor O'Neill's daughter. Others?

He tried to remember the people she'd hung out with back then, but his memories kept seeing her entering the student union alone. Exiting the classroom building alone. Studying in the library alone.

She hadn't trusted anyone.

Zadok leaned back, pondering, and he leaned just a smidge too far. The chair tipped, and he crashed to the floor on his back, thunking his skull against the tile.

He blinked the stars away and turned his head from side to side. Nothing seemed hurt but his pride.

The first thing he was going to do the next time he had a few hours free was buy a new office chair. Go big or go home... yep, and a desk. There'd be no options in Galena Landing. He'd have to drive to Wynnton or find something online. It would have to wait until this sermon was in the bank.

"What are you working on?" Xavier leaned across the study hall table. "I thought you weren't going to sell any more of those toy things."

Juni poked her needle in and out of the felt piece in a running stitch before securing the series of stitches. "I'm not, once Christmas is over. I still have orders to fill for another couple of weeks."

"I don't recognize that one."

Had they spent so many sixth periods together that the teen knew all her feltie sets? Could be. Or he'd studied her website. The one she'd be taking down soon.

So much for impulsiveness. Why couldn't she ever think things through and do anything right the first time?

Dad. She was getting faster at recognizing his voice. How about God's voice?

Every good and perfect gift is from above, coming down from the Father of the heavenly lights, who does not change like shifting shadows.

Well, she wasn't much like God, either, it seemed. Who was queen of shifting shadows and changing priorities? Juni O'Neill.

"I don't recognize that one."

She glanced at Xavier and sighed. "Because this is a

Christmas tree ornament. Arleigh and I didn't really have any."

"Yeah, her place flooded last winter." Xavier narrowed his gaze at her. "Why don't *you* have any?"

Did she have to delve into this with Zadok's brother? The kid was supposed to be doing his math homework, after all. Not that he still needed Juni's oversight, but she was in no hurry to give up this time. Ms. Atkinson would clue in soon enough.

But it had been an honest question and deserved a thoughtful reply. "I told you before that my parents divorced when I was a teen."

Xavier nodded, focused on her.

She glanced around, but they were alone in the room. She lowered her voice, anyway. "My dad thought Christians were a bit excessive about Christmas, and that it was all a huge distraction from remembering Jesus' birth."

"I can see that," Xavier said. "It's all about buying stuff and going to parties."

Hmm. "We can turn it into that, but it's not what it's really all about."

"Yeah." He sighed. "It's about Jesus. But I guess we're not supposed to talk about Him at school."

"You can. The rules are for staff."

"That's dumb."

"It is what it is."

"Life is full of stupid rules. Do this. Don't do that. Why do we care if people like us or not?"

"It's not just about conforming to society's expectations. Some things are actually right or wrong."

"Like not talking about God at school?" Xavier scoffed.

"You were talking about rules. Some seem arbitrary, but others are foundational to our society. They keep civilization, well, civilized. They keep us from devolving into anarchy."

"I suppose. I mean, I get why we should always drive on the same side of the road."

Juni pounced on the distraction. "Are you getting many driving hours in these days?"

The teen shrugged. "Zadok's always busy. Plus, he's not that fun to be around lately. He's such a grouch. Who wants to hang out with a stick-in-the-mud like that?"

Juni stopped herself from shooting her hand into the air. Her. She'd hang out with him.

She *could* hang out with him. She could call him and apologize. Or she could go by Tires and Treads. He wouldn't be able to send her to voicemail if she walked into his place of business.

"I'm sorry he's grumpy," she said cautiously.

"And you haven't come by in a couple of weeks." Xavier studied her. "Did you guys have a fight? Because that's dumb. Get over it. It's killing me."

"It's not about you." Had she managed to keep her voice even?

He pushed out a huge sigh. "You say that like you're this ancient, wise person, like Yoda."

"No. Then I'd say, about you it is not."

"Har har." Xavier did not look amused.

Well, she'd tried. "You've got homework, right?"

"I'll get it done." He pushed the still-closed textbook

to the side. "I need you to fix this thing with Zadok. Don't treat me like a child and tell me it's not about me. I know it's not, but it's still stupid and you guys need to get over it. Have you ever, like, heard of talking to each other?"

Juni glared at the teen. "This is none of your business."

He crossed his arms and stared back. "I think it is. Also, I told Zadok the same thing."

Heat and cold washed over Juni like waves. "Oh?"

"He said it wasn't up to him. Which means it's up to you."

"There's more to it than that."

"Try me."

"No." *You're not my counselor or psychologist.* Somehow, she managed not to say the words out loud. But maybe she should avail herself of counseling services. Who in this town offered that from a Christian perspective? Because no one else would understand her history.

Wanda Wilson, but the woman was married to Pastor Ron, and Zadok was tight with the man from his involvement with the worship team. Maybe Juni should keep trying to muddle through this on her own.

Like that was working out so well for her.

It wasn't just Zadok. He'd only semi stuck up for Dad. It was all the baggage from her own childhood and right up to last year, quite honestly. She needed to ditch it all. Somehow Mom and Arleigh had managed to kick that albatross aside. Why couldn't she?

But had they done it alone or with help? Juni didn't know. Didn't want to ask. Might not want to know if she was the only defective one who couldn't get beyond Dad's clutches without expert help.

The man had a lot to answer for.

Guilt stabbed her. He'd physically wronged several young women. He'd never done that to her. They had a legitimate reason for the shackles that they were trying to shed, unlike her. Her ties were all in her head.

But weren't they real, all the same?

Yeah, she needed guidance. When the school bell rang, she'd call Wanda and see if the woman thought she could help.

Xavier must have given up on Juni, because he'd actually opened his book and was scribbling out an equation of some sort on a scratchpad.

Juni looked at the little felt pieces she was stitching together. She'd decided to make a dozen three-dimensional presents with scraps of lace and rickrack as the ribbons around the felt.

Every good and perfect gift is from above.

What would God put inside a tiny gift box like this one just for her?

Salvation. Check. She already had that gift.

Purpose. Hmm. She didn't have that one, did she? Kind of. She liked teaching. She liked crafting things. Was that her purpose?

Love. No, not a man's love, but God's. She knew God loved her, for sure. So maybe other people's love could be a gift from God, too? Arleigh thought Mitchell's love was. Juni had thought Zadok's might be. Maybe it still was?

Hope. That was another gift Arleigh talked about from

First Peter. How did it go? *In his great mercy he has given us new birth into a living hope through the resurrection of Jesus Christ from the dead.* The word 'given' nailed that as a gift.

Forgiveness was a gift God had given her. Juni was so not perfect. She was impulsive and judgmental. Dad might deserve her reaction, but others might not. And yet God forgave her every time she asked Him to. Seventy times seven... but that was for humans. Pretty sure God wasn't keeping score.

Peace. She could use that gift.

Hope. Joy. *Please, Lord. I need these in my life.*

She'd give Wanda a call.

TWENTY-SEVEN

ow's it going, son?"

Tears pricked Zadok's eyes. Man, he missed his dad. He'd give nearly anything to hear his father's voice, but he never would again. Not on this side of eternity, anyway.

He swallowed hard and managed a smile for the pastor. "I'm not sure how it's going."

Pastor Ron motioned for Zadok to take a seat then folded his hands on his desk. "Tell me."

"Peace. Does a man need to know it to speak on it?"

A smile crinkled the older man's eyes. "I've found I learn to know the topics on a deeper level when I study them and preach on them."

"But to start with?"

"Are you a child of God, Zadok?"

"You know that I am." He'd shared the story of his salvation with Pastor Ron as they'd prepared for Zadok's parents' funeral.

"Philippians four says, 'do not be anxious about anything, but in every situation, by prayer and petition, with thanksgiving, present your requests to God. And the peace of God, which transcends all understanding, will guard your hearts and minds in Christ Jesus.' It's there for the asking, son. You may not understand it. In fact, you likely won't, at all, but that doesn't stop it from filling you and guarding your heart and your mind."

"I know there's a lot of trouble in the world. Wars, famines, earthquakes." Zadok shook his head. "The list goes on."

"It is not simply the absence of war. It's wholeness, completeness, where once there was splintering and fracturing. Like joy, it's found deep within the human soul and then bubbles out to impact the world around us."

"I never thought of that." He still wasn't sure he understood what the pastor meant.

"A peacekeeping mission doesn't actually keep peace. It might offer a temporary truce, perhaps even a long-term one, but it's always fragile. The fractures are still there. Though there is a band holding the two sides together, hostilities still simmer beneath the surface. Is that peace, just because they are not actively fighting?"

"No. I see what you mean."

"Some fractures, like that between the Jews and Arabs, have been there for millennia. There have been times when there has been an uneasy truce, but peace?" Ron shook his head. "That can only come when there is a oneness, a wholeness. Then the splinters would be healed completely over."

Zadok shook his head. "I don't see that happening anytime soon." He kept an eye on the news. The Middle East was a mess, and it wasn't the only region.

Ron studied him. "So, the angels' proclamation to the shepherds was really big news."

"Glory to God in the highest heaven, and on earth peace to those on whom his favor rests." Zadok tried to picture the dark night. Had the sky been blanketed with stars or with clouds? How cold had it been? How many shepherds had been on watch? Were they young or old?

And — bam! — an angel, shining with God's glory, appeared out of thin air in their midst. Suddenly the night was not just like any other. A message of divine birth, and then the angel was joined by a multitude of angels — mind-boggling — with the proclamation of peace.

The shepherds' world needed that gift as much as today's did. The way Pastor Ron described it, that inner hush wasn't something that anyone could just decide to have.

"If it is possible, as far as it depends on you, live at peace with everyone." Pastor Ron chuckled. "Romans 12:18."

"But it's not possible. Right?"

"True, but, clearly, we are to do our best. We are not to be the ones to cause deeper splinters but do our best to hold onto wholeness for the sake of everyone around us."

"We shouldn't cast the first stone."

Ron nodded. "You've got it."

The pieces were fitting together. "How do you preach the same four topics every Advent?"

"Bringing hope, peace, joy, and love in a fresh way annually is a challenge, for sure. It requires me to keep digging, to not assume I've already learned the topics and fully applied them."

Another spiral, just like Zadok and Juni had talked about. Sometimes it seemed they were back in the same place, but it was a little different. Lessons had been learned. Progress had been made.

He and Juni were back to a stalemate, but it wasn't the same one as before. Not exactly. They'd made a great deal of progress in between, but this spot in the spiral had the power to derail them. Each time they made it past this nexus, they would be a little bit stronger.

Which meant, they needed to talk things out. If only Zadok knew the status of Professor O'Neill's investigation.

But that wasn't the problem. Not really. The problem was that Juni had slid right back into defensiveness against the way the man had raised her and brainwashed her as a child.

No. She hadn't slid back. The spiral brought her near, but not to the same place.

And was her reaction the real problem? Oh, it was part of it, but Zadok had also slid back into his own pattern of defending the man he'd held in high regard years ago. He'd have tried to soften John's response if John wasn't married to one of the victims. Would Tracie make all that up and convince John of her story's truth?

Hardly.

Not completely impossible, but not likely.

"You're deep in thought."

"There's a lot going on." Should he seek his pastor's counsel? Maybe, but not today. "Please pray for me. Not just for the sermon, but for peace to fill my own heart, too."

"I will." Pastor Ron ducked his head and began to pray out loud.

Zadok's heart warmed as the man brought his name before the Lord. Brought Quincey's and Xavier's. Brought Juni's. Wait, how did Ron know about that? He wasn't going to ask.

When the 'amen' came, Zadok launched into his own prayer, asking God to give Ron and Wanda safety in their travel and to give the medical team wisdom over the next few days.

"Thank you for that." Ron rose behind his desk, wincing. "I'm trusting the Lord for a good outcome, but mostly, I need God's presence. A little more oxygen when I breathe would also be good."

Zadok stood and shook the pastor's hand. "Thank you."

"You know who you could talk to if you need more? Steve Nemesek."

"The man in the wheelchair." Zadok hadn't chatted with the older man much. Steve's wife, Rosemary, was a regular at the market, but the gravel paths were too difficult for Steve to navigate.

"He's had a difficult path in the past decade or so since the onset of Guillain-Barré. But there is a man who accepts pain as a gift from the Lord. And that brings him peace that radiates out to anyone who's in his presence. Steve lives and breathes Jesus."

"I'll keep him in mind. Thanks." But maybe Zadok had enough to ponder for the moment.

ARLEIGH WAS WRINGING her hands and pacing the suite when Juni arrived at home near 5:00. "Where were you?"

Juni paused in the middle of unwinding her scarf. "What happened?"

"Dad happened. I thought you'd be home right after school."

Her gut soured. "What do you mean, *Dad happened*?"

Arleigh stopped with her hands on her hips. "Where were you?"

"I had an appointment after school." Juni hung her jacket and scarf before prying off her tall boots.

"What appointment?"

Apparently, Juni wasn't going to get out of telling her sister. "With a counselor, okay? Now tell me about Dad. Is he insisting on coming to the wedding? Because you don't have to let him."

Arleigh's eyes narrowed. "A counselor? We're coming back to that. No, *seven* former and current students have named him in the sexual harassment case. Dad will be lucky if he's not in *jail* on my wedding day."

"Seven? That's... a lot. Genevieve only said 'some.'" Juni studied her sister. "Where did you hear this?"

"Someone leaked it on social media. They tried reaching out to Mom, but she says she told them the divorce was final years before the allegations started, and that she had no knowledge of or comment on his current situation."

"They'll be after us next."

Arleigh shook her head. "I don't think so, not as complicit, anyway. In their eyes, we'd be considered victims, too. Of course, mob mentality being what it is, they could turn on us, I suppose."

"Great. That's just what we need." All the tentative progress Juni had made with Wanda Wilson vanished.

"Don't worry about it until it happens, because it might not."

She forced a chuckle. "Who are you, and what have you done with my sister?"

"I've learned a bit about hope over the past while. I've learned God holds us in the palm of His hand. I've learned God cares."

Juni slumped into a chair at the table. She needed to learn those things, too. She desperately needed to feel God's presence.

Arleigh took a seat across from her. "Tell me about the counseling."

"I talked to Wanda. You know, Pastor Ron's wife."

"And?"

"I've been struggling to cope with all this stuff with Dad. It's uncovered all the lies he told and the lessons he pushed on me. I don't know what's true and what's his exalted opinion. And with every revelation, like this one, it feels like I'm in a teacup in a tsunami, and it's tipping me out."

Arleigh rounded the table, crouched beside Juni, and wrapped her arms around her. "God's got it. He does."

"I know." At least, Juni understood the words. "But it's a never-ending struggle."

"He says we should cast our anxieties on Him because He cares for us."

"The storm keeps growing."

"No matter how big it gets, our God is even bigger."

"I wish I had your faith."

"You don't need mine. You have your own."

Juni shook her head. "Mine is wimpy and weak."

"And you know what to do with a weak, wimpy body, right? Push the muscles day after day until they're stronger."

She glared at her sister. "I'm not a fan of exercise. Of any sort."

"That doesn't negate the fact that the only way to strengthen muscles is to move them over and over."

"Yay. I wonder what else God will throw at me."

"I don't think that's how it works."

"Why can't we just learn something like in school? Study it for a few days or weeks, write the exam, and move on to the next thing?"

"Right?" Arleigh sighed.

Juni's cell rang, and she stared at it. Same number as before.

Arleigh bit her lip. "Dad?"

It rang a second time. "The house number." Who was it, Dad or Genevieve? Or maybe even one of the kids? Did she dare answer? Did she dare not?

Third time. Juni snatched it up. "Hello?"

"Juni!" It was Genevieve. "Do you know where your dad is?"

"Pardon me?" Juni stabbed the phone and put it on speaker. Not that Genevieve's voice was hushed.

"Your dad. Do you know where he is?"

Juni and her sister exchanged wide-eyed glances. "I haven't heard from him for a few months, no."

"You were my last hope."

That remark didn't bode well. "Why don't you tell me what's going on?"

"I don't know where he could be. He hasn't been home for a few days. I realized last night that some of his clothes were missing. And it looks like our bank account is nearly empty. I don't know where he is, and no one seems to have seen him."

Juni found no help on Arleigh's pale face. "Oh, wow. He was suspended from the college, right?"

"It was all slander and lies. You know that, don't you? Grant would never..." Genevieve began to sob.

Innocent men didn't drain their bank accounts and run for the hills. "I'm sorry." What an insipid response. And yet, Juni *was* sorry. Sorry for so many things, including ever looking up to her father. Including thinking perfect, meek Genevieve deserved Dad. No one deserved him.

"I don't know what I'm going to do."

"What do you mean?" Juni glanced at her sister.

"There's only enough money in my account for a few weeks of groceries. These boys eat a lot."

"In *your* account?"

"My household account. Only Grant has access to the rest. He transfers funds for groceries and incidentals into it on payday. This was a larger sum than usual." Genevieve's voice broke. "Does that mean he isn't coming back?"

As if Juni could read her father's mind. The man was a dirtbag, and keeping his wife and kids on an allowance was only the tip of the iceberg. "I'm sure you've called his cell phone."

"So many times. It just goes straight to voicemail, over and over."

"I see."

"Maybe you could try? He'd answer you."

Juni doubted it. "I can try, but I wouldn't hold out too much hope for success."

"Phone me back, okay? Please, Juni?"

"Sure." Not that there would be anything to report. She ended the call and shook her head. "Oh, boy."

"He's made a run for it."

Juni sucked in a long breath and let it out slowly. "Sounds like it."

"The creep."

"Yeah."

"Is she going to lose the house if he doesn't come back?"

"Dad told me the house was paid for."

Arleigh's eyebrows rose. "And you believe him?"

"I thought I did. Now, I'm not so sure."

"It would be a bummer if Genevieve and the kids suffered on account of Dad's ego."

"They already have. They will some more, as we have."

"But they're not homeless yet. That's more suffering than she deserves just because she trusted her husband."

Juni spread her hands. "I'm not sure what we can do about it."

"Invite them to Galena Landing for Christmas, at least. If Dad's still AWOL then."

"Are you out of your mind? Where would we put them? She has five kids!"

"And they're our brothers and sisters."

"Half," Juni muttered.

"The half that counts right now." Arleigh shrugged. "They're victims, too. It's not their fault their mom married our dad, any more than it's our fault"— she toggled her finger between the two of them —"*our* mom married him. All his kids are victims."

"I know, but..."

"First things first. Call him and see if he picks up."

"I doubt he will." But she had promised, if only to get Genevieve to stop blubbering for a few minutes. Juni sighed, reached for her phone, and tapped Dad's cell number.

One ring. Two. Three. And then voicemail. "You've reached Professor O'Neill..."

"Blah, blah, blah," Juni muttered over the rest of his pompous greeting. Finally, the beep signaled her turn to leave a message, but before she could say anything, a robotic voice said the mailbox was full.

No surprise there. Not if he was trying to vanish when under investigation.

Juni sighed and looked at her sister. "Figures."

"Yeah, it does. Poor Genevieve."

Thinking of Dad's second wife as a co-victim wasn't anywhere Juni's mind had gone before. Juni tapped the house phone number.

It rang only once before Genevieve's eager voice came. "Hello?"

"It's me, Juni. Dad didn't pick up, and his voicemail is full, so I couldn't leave a message."

"Oh."

How one short syllable could deflate from beginning to end was an anomaly Juni couldn't understand. "If I hear from him, I'll let you know. You do the same, okay?"

"Okay." Genevieve sounded bleak.

"Hey, are you going to be okay?" Drat Arleigh, anyway. Her concern was wearing off on Juni.

"I... I don't know. I can't believe this. What do I tell the children?"

That their dad was a narcissistic jerk who would throw anyone under the bus, even his own kids, to save his own neck? Maybe too soon to say all that to Genevieve. "Whatever you think is best."

"I can't lie to them."

"I wasn't suggesting you lie. But they're young, and

you don't have to give all the details to pre-teens. Or to Glory. She's only... three?"

"Four." Genevieve sighed. "But you're right. Gregory's only 12. Too young to bear this burden."

So was 24, but Juni held her tongue.

"I'll tell them Dad's gone away for a bit. I don't know when exactly he'll return, but he will, right? Don't you think?"

"I'm sure he will be back." When the law caught up with him.

"That's what I thought." Genevieve's voice held relief. "It's only a matter of a few days. He just needed to catch his breath with these girls slandering his good name."

Sure, believe what you want. That's why he took his clothes and left extra in the allowance fund. Juni would bet real money on him having drained any other accounts he had, then skipping the country. So, maybe he wouldn't be back. God only knew.

"I'll let you know when he's home. Meanwhile, please pray for him."

"I'll pray for you and the kids." Hopefully Genevieve wouldn't notice the lack of the promise she'd asked for.

"Oh, thank you. Talk to you soon, I'm sure."

Juni tapped to close the call and laid the cell on the table. "Well, look at the big, brave man facing the penalties for his sins."

Arleigh rubbed her face with both hands. "Running away is not the act of an innocent man."

"Ya think?"

"We need to help Genevieve."

Of course, that's what Arleigh got out of the scenario.

Also, so much for the flicker of peace Juni had attained in Wanda's office earlier. Now the woman was away for a few days, so Juni couldn't even fill her in, other than via email. It could wait. Right?

TWENTY-EIGHT

She was in church, seated, as usual, between her sister and her mother about halfway back.

Zadok had been certain she'd skip again. She'd find out he was preaching and make sure she was nowhere nearby, but that hadn't happened.

Now she was going to hear his sermon. The one that still felt like he was pretending to be someone he was not, regardless of how much he'd prayed over it. He had not achieved peace, though he'd glimpsed it a time or two over the past week. He'd reached for it, but it had slipped between his fingers with barely any sensation to cue him of its presence.

Keanan and the rest of the team led worship this morning, the carols focusing in on the shepherds. Keanan glanced Zadok's way with a quick grin as the others left the stage. He leaned into the mic again.

"As many of you know, Pastor Ron and Wanda have been away in Boise this past week and expect to be traveling home soon. Our brother Zadok Shirkowski will be sharing today in a message entitled 'The Gift of Peace.' Please come up, Zadok, and let me pray for you... and for us, that our hearts might be open to receive what God has for us on this second Sunday of Advent."

This was it.

Zadok's rubbery legs carried him up the steps and to the center of the stage where a portable lectern awaited him. He bowed his head as Keanan prayed. Then his friend took a seat beside his wife and offered a thumbs-up.

This didn't feel like peace. Not exactly. Zadok took a moment to gather his thoughts and look out over the congregation. Were there typically this many people in the sanctuary? He was no stranger to standing up front, but every eye in the audience was not usually staring expectantly straight at him.

Lord, You've got this. It's all for You.

He glanced down at his notes. "When Pastor Ron asked me to share with all of you a few days ago, I told him no. You can see how well that worked out for me." He waited for the ripple of laughter to subside. "Because peace is elusive, isn't it? Every time we think we see it over here, it fades like a rainbow. Then maybe it's over there, but a wisp of fog slips between, and it's gone."

Zadok took a deep breath and let his gaze pass over Juni. She was looking down. "A wise man once told me that peace isn't merely the absence of conflict. There can be a ceasefire, but the sides are still splintered. Still mistrustful. Still ready to pick up arms again at the slightest provocation. That's not peace. True peace is when the fractures are healed so completely that there's no evidence there ever were rifts at all.

"In John 14:17, Jesus says, 'Peace I leave with you; my peace I give you. I do not give to you as the world gives. Do not let your hearts be troubled and do not be afraid.' So, let's dig into the Christmas story this morning and examine this gift God brought to us through the birth of His precious Son."

Zadok felt his nerves settle as he proceeded into the story of the shepherds and the proclamation the angels declared over them. All his study, the talk with Pastor Ron on Tuesday plus their phone call last night, the prayers and the writing... all melded together as he shared the words God had surely given him.

He found his seat at the end of it and sang along with the congregation as Keanan led them in "Silent Night." Now *that* was peace.

After the benediction, Dan North turned in the pew in front of Zadok and gave his hand a firm shake. "Thank you for that message today, Zadok. We should hear from you more often."

"Thank you, but I'm happy for preaching to be Pastor Ron's job." Although, it hadn't been as bad as he'd expected.

"Don't get me wrong. I appreciate our pastor's insights. I do. But a fresh perspective from time to time is welcome."

Should Zadok tell Dan North how much input Pastor Ron had provided? Still, the man wasn't completely wrong. Their pastor might have guided Zadok's study, but the message had been filtered through Zadok's own life experiences. "Thank you," he said simply.

Steve Nemesek clapped his hand on his shoulder as Zadok started to rise. Instead, he turned to see the wheelchair-bound man behind him.

"Good word, son. 'Glory to God in the highest heaven' indeed. Thank you for allowing God to use you this morning."

An unexpected tear pricked Zadok's eye. "Thank you, sir."

Steve chuckled. "You are a man of many talents. I'm sure God will continue to bless you as you offer those to Him."

No words could pass the lump in Zadok's throat, so he just nodded.

Zadok gathered his notes — it felt strange not to have an instrument to carry — and made his way to the back. By the time he reached the foyer, over a dozen congregants had stopped to thank him, and nearly everyone else was gone. Juni and her family were no longer present.

Disappointment poked him, but wasn't that silly? Had he expected Juni to be so impressed she'd line up with others to offer her appreciation? Well, not expected, exactly, but he'd have accepted it. Been grateful for it, as it would have signaled the end of their impasse.

But, no. The crevasse between them was too deep for mere words, one-sided at best, to fill it in. They needed true peace, the kind he'd preached about, not merely an absence of disagreement. For their rift to be mended into perfect wholeness would require an act of God.

Didn't everything?

Wearing his parka, Xavier lounged against the window, poking at his phone. He glanced up at Zadok's approach. "You finally ready?"

If he'd expected any awe from his kid brother, he'd assumed incorrectly. "Sure. Where's Quincey?"

"She got tired of waiting and walked home, but she's nuts. It's snowing like crazy out there." The teen brightened. "Can I drive?"

Welcome back to planet earth, preacher.

"Let's head outside and take a look before I make any promises."

"THAT WAS a lovely sermon this morning, don't you think?" Mom ladled corn chowder into bowls in her apartment kitchen.

"Very nice." Juni sliced a loaf of sourdough bread her mom had picked up at yesterday's market. The one Juni had skipped, as she would the remainder of the season. She had several more orders to fill from her website — a notice on the homepage said she wouldn't accept any more after next week. Hopefully, she'd be able to keep up until then.

In the other room, Lincoln and Hudson played a raucous game of Go Fish with Arleigh, while Mitchell set the table. At least that pair hadn't remained mired in traditional roles.

"When can I invite Zadok and his siblings for Sunday lunch again?"

Juni stilled then shot a glance at her mother.

"What?" Mom smiled innocently. "I thought you two were getting somewhere."

Mitchell almost managed to cover a guffaw then exited the kitchen with a few glasses of water.

"It's complicated."

"It always is, but a relationship with someone who loves and honors Jesus is worth sorting through."

"Like you did with Dad?" Juni clapped her hand over her mouth as her eyes widened. Those words should not have come out.

Mom bit her lip. "I was deceived, which is not much of an excuse."

"I don't want to be conned."

"What about Zadok gives you pause?"

What, indeed? And did Juni really want to discuss this with her mother? "Last we talked about the situation, Zadok seemed to think Dad might be innocent."

Mom managed a watery smile. "Innocent until proven guilty and all that."

"Yes. And Dad hasn't come up roses, has he?"

"Zadok's right, though. Leaders have been accused of scandalous things they never did for a variety of reasons. You and I had a gut feeling from the beginning that these weren't trumped-up charges, but justice doesn't have the luxury of going on intuition. They require facts. Grant's disappearance doesn't look good for his innocence, though."

No kidding. "But Zadok was Dad's student and looked up to him..."

Mom sighed. "Your father can come across very likable, very pleasant and agreeable. The faculty and students in his classes would have seen the very best version of himself he could create."

"All the while he was doing *this* to the women around him."

"Again, we need to separate facts from intuition."

Aargh, Mom sounded too much like Zadok. Not that she didn't have a point, but...

"Don't tell me you don't reserve your very best side for the students at Galena High. You want them to like you. You want Ms. Atkinson and your fellow teachers to like you."

"Of course, I do. But I'd never abuse one of them!"

"I didn't say you would. All I'm saying is it's natural to put your best foot forward on the job. Of course, Zadok and the other students liked your father. He made sure they only saw the side of him he wanted them to see."

Juni pounced on that. "So, you agree that he's guilty."

"I can't agree to that. I wasn't there. I didn't observe any misconduct. I agree that I'd be surprised if they couldn't pin anything on him, but I'm not the judge or the jury." Mom looked at Juni with sad eyes. "I'm thankful for that, honestly."

That made one of them. If Juni could influence the outcome, she'd be on it in a heartbeat.

"God is the final judge. Even if your father is guilty and gets away with it, ultimately, God will not let his sin go unpunished."

"He'd better not get away with it."

"But then there's God's grace. Oh, sweetheart, don't you see it? If your father repents before God — truly repents — God will forgive him. Jesus has already taken his punishment."

"But... that's not even fair."

"We will continue to pray for two things. One, that justice will be served and, two, that your father will see the error of his ways and make things right with God and those he's wronged."

"You're a better Christian than I am."

Mom shook her head. "No. Maybe more experienced, but not better. Bitterness doesn't help. I had to learn that back fifteen years ago or so. Don't think I didn't fight it, too, especially when your father remarried so quickly after the divorce. When Genevieve seemed so starry-eyed like she'd won the lottery."

"She's still starry-eyed," Juni muttered.

"She's tried so hard to be the perfect wife and mother."

Juni narrowed her gaze. "How do you know this?" Had she talked about Genevieve to Mom since she'd moved to Galena Landing in spring? She didn't think so.

"I still have friends in the old neighborhood. It took me a while to make sure they understood I didn't want to hear the gossip." Mom let out a rueful chuckle. "Because, at first, I did want to hear it. I got some sort of weird pleasure from seeing her struggles, even second hand. Your father held me up as an example to her, if you can imagine."

Juni couldn't believe her ears. "A good example?"

"Good at times, bad at others. Apparently, I was a better cook. The thing is, focusing on him and the marriage I'd thought we had didn't do me any good. It kept me tethered to the past, to a place I couldn't return to and didn't truly want to return to. But as long as I kept thinking about it, I couldn't move forward in my walk with the Lord and in my new community. Your father still defined me until I shed the bitterness and anger. Only then could I embrace my future."

Juni studied her mother's calm face. Peace like Zadok had preached about. She hadn't wanted to listen, but there she'd been in church, wedged between Mom and Arleigh with no escape route.

Not only had he spoken about the gift as though he had embraced it for himself, his entire demeanor radiated serenity, even in the first few minutes when he seemed a little nervous.

How had he managed to find that gift when it eluded her? It didn't seem fair. What verse had he quoted at the beginning?

Peace I leave with you; my peace I give you. I do not give to you as the world gives. Do not let your hearts be troubled and do not be afraid.

Had Juni been trying to live it both ways? Jesus offered her tranquility, but He didn't give the way the world gave. Nothing else — no one else — could give it to her. Even justice for Dad wouldn't. It might give her smug satisfaction for a bit of time, but it wouldn't give peace.

Only Jesus could do that. He said He'd come to give life, abundant life to the fullest.

But, could she give up hoping for Dad to be caught and punished? Could she have it both ways? Could she pray for justice without being sucked back into the vortex of bitterness? Mom thought she could. Mom prayed for justice and for Dad's relationship with God to be renewed, an example Juni would do well to follow.

"I wonder where Dad went off to." Juni had finished slicing the loaf a long time ago. Now she tucked the bread into a beautiful basket her mom had had as long as she could remember.

"I've been wondering the same thing." Mom ran her finger over the fine reeds that made up the basket. "We picked this up in Bali on a mission trip years ago. Your father wanted to return, but we never did. I was pregnant with Arleigh soon afterward, and life took a different turn."

"Bali? Like, in Indonesia?"

Mom nodded. "We did a bit of traveling back then. It's been so long."

"Hmm. I don't remember that."

"It was before your time." Mom shook her head. "It's of no consequence now. He could be anywhere. I just thought of Bali because of this basket. We spent a few days in the village where these are made. It was one of the few things I took when I left your father. I felt it meant more to me than to him."

"Is lunch nearly ready?" Arleigh poked her head around the doorway from the other room. "The boys are getting antsy."

"Yes." Mom lifted a pair of bowls and handed them to Arleigh.

"Sorry, sis. We got sidetracked in here."

"I overheard a little." Arleigh offered a tight smile. "Mom, I've got a question for you."

Uh oh. Did Juni know where this was going?

"I've been thinking about Genevieve and the children. If Dad doesn't come back before Christmas, they'll be all alone."

"They don't do much for Christmas anyway," Juni cut in. "It won't be that big of a deal for them."

"Then this is a great opportunity for them to experience a real celebration of Jesus' birth." Arleigh arched her brows at Juni and turned back to their mother. "I was thinking of inviting them to Galena Landing for a week or so, only I don't know where they could stay. Juni and I don't have room, nor does Mitchell, and you certainly don't."

"Not that Mom would want Dad's second wife as her company."

Mom silenced Juni with a look. "That's very compassionate of you, Arleigh. Let's think on that and pray."

Juni felt like she was in class with her least favorite teacher heaping impossible amounts of homework on top of all the other assignments.

Did God really want her to forgive her father and

welcome his second wife and their children? When was enough, enough?

God gave His one and only Son to a world He knew would kill that Son.

And Juni was complaining about a little discomfort?

Oh, God. She needed help.

TWENTY-NINE

I need you to be on board with this."

Juni stared at her sister. "I don't see how it could possibly work. We've already established that no one has room for six extra people."

"Maybe you and I could bunk out at Mom's for a few days, and Genevieve and the kids could sleep here."

"Uh... you do recall Mom has a one-bedroom and that her sofa isn't even a pull-out? And it's horribly uncomfortable?"

Arleigh sighed. "I remember all that."

"Also, it's hardly fair to inflict them on Mitchell."

"That's the worst part. If I've done the math correctly, Galway and Gannon are about the same age as Lincoln and Hudson. That sounds like a lot of trouble under one roof."

"Dad's kids wouldn't dare."

Arleigh grimaced. "You're probably right. But I feel we

have to do something. They're all innocent victims, too, and here's a chance to show them a God of grace."

"Funny Dad named his third daughter Grace when he's never demonstrated it in any other way."

"I forgot that. How old is she?"

"Ten? Eleven?" Juni shrugged. "Somewhere in there."

"Do you remember your ten-year-old self?"

Juni snorted a laugh. "You bet I do. I knew by Glory's age — and she's four now — that I couldn't do anything to gain Dad's approval and love. By ten, my head was down, hoping not to be noticed."

"And then puberty."

"Ugh. Don't remind me." In Dad's world, female cycles were no excuse for variable moods.

"I think... I just can't sit by and do nothing for those kids — our siblings — to show that God loves them no matter what."

Her sister was a better Christian than she was. Everyone was.

Juni took a deep breath and let it out slowly, remembering her long talk with Wanda on Tuesday. The pastor's wife had gently reminded her that bitterness didn't go away without a purposeful action to counteract it. Prayer, yes, but more than that. She needed to actively forgive and step outside of her comfort zone to act on that, regardless of how it would be received.

Or, Juni could keep clinging to the bitterness, allowing it to strangle her relationship with Jesus.

Lord, I choose You. I can't even imagine what my sister is asking for, but I choose to trust You to help me be hospitable, however that looks.

She opened her eyes and met Arleigh's gaze. "Okay."

Arleigh took a step back. "Okay? Seriously?"

"If Genevieve agrees, we'll figure it out. Maybe Green Acres has a guest accommodation we could rent for a few days. Or... Pastor Ron and Wanda have space now that their kids are grown and gone, right?"

"I can't believe you are okay with this."

Juni rubbed her temple. "I'm not, really. But I can't keep blocking what God is trying to do in my life through this whole mess."

"Because all things work together for the good of those who love Him."

"Yeah. That. Is it still okay to say I'm scared? I really don't want them here, but all the things you said about those little kids being innocent... even Genevieve... you're right. I've been guilty of judging them all, lumping them in with Dad."

"So, I'm going to phone now, before I lose my nerve." Arleigh pulled her cell out of her purse. "I... I don't have the house number."

"I'll share the contact with you." Juni navigated to her contacts list and stared at it. She sighed, tapped 'edit,' and changed the name from 'Dad' to 'Genevieve' before sharing. Seemed more accurate under the circumstances.

"Thanks." Arleigh squeezed Juni's hand. "Can we pray about this first?"

"Good idea."

Arleigh offered a brief prayer and tapped the number. She set it on speaker and laid it on the table.

It rang twice before a breathless voice answered. "Hello?"

The sisters exchanged a look. "Hi, Genevieve? It's Arleigh."

"Oh. Hi, Arleigh." The woman's disappointment was palpable. "I thought maybe... never mind."

"I take it you haven't heard from my dad yet?"

"No. It's been over a week. I think... do you think he might not be in the US anymore?"

"We wondered that ourselves."

Would Dad really have abandoned his family and escaped overseas? Yeah, probably. Facing the investigation and trial, especially if he knew he was guilty, would not sit well with a man of his pride. Mom said he'd loved Bali.

"Listen, Genevieve, we were wondering, Juni and I..." Arleigh's eyebrows rose as she glanced at Juni, who nodded. "We were wondering if you and the children had plans for Christmas. Maybe you'd like to visit us in Galena Landing for a few days? I don't really know my younger siblings, so I thought—"

"Oh, we couldn't."

"We'd really love to have you. We have friends with extra space, and—"

"I really appreciate the thought, Arleigh, but no."

"My mom also extends the invitation."

"Donna?" Genevieve's scoff was mingled with a sob. "No, really, it won't be possible. My parents are planning to visit. We haven't seen them during the holidays for years, and Grace is excited to decorate cookies with her grandmother. The boys want to take their granddad ice skating. So, we'll be fine here."

"If you're sure."

"Yes. I'm sure." Genevieve hesitated a moment. "But I'm grateful you reached out. I understand you're getting married soon. I... I wish you all the best."

"Thank you. Mitchell is amazing. I'm so thankful God brought him and his sons into my life. I was at the end of my rope last winter — I'm sure you heard about the flood that wiped out my business and my home — but God extended his extravagant mercy and gave me a new and vibrant hope. He has been so good to me."

"That's... nice. Truly."

"I'm praying for you, Genevieve. Juni and I both are. I know this is an extremely difficult time for you, but lean on God. He has a plan for you and the children through this experience."

"Hope is in short supply at the moment."

"But not with God. With Him, it's on tap all the time. There's a limitless supply."

"I'm not sure of anything right now." Their stepmother's voice broke.

Juni leaned toward the phone. "Genevieve? Arleigh's right. I know she is. I've had so much bitterness toward my dad — honestly, at you and the kids, too, because it seemed you could do nothing wrong while I could do nothing right. But I'm learning, slowly, that huddling in self-righteous anger wasn't doing me any favors, that it only kept me from wrapping myself in God's grace. His mercy and love are a great and glorious gift, like the breaking of a new dawn."

"If you only knew how little I could do right."

Juni could make some guesses. "Please know we care about you and feel for you all."

Arleigh leaned in. "Are you okay financially? Is there a mortgage on the house or anything?"

"We'll be okay for a few months, I think. Grant seems to have paid another term of hockey for Galway." Genevieve sounded disbelieving. "I don't know about the house. Grant always took care of everything."

"Do you know anyone you can call to look into it?"

"I'll add it to my list."

A list that a pampered wife of Grant O'Neill had never needed before. If Juni had access to her father right now, she'd throttle the man. But then, she'd likely fall back into her old habits, right after she'd spouted a good line about bitterness and grace.

Lord, help me. Seems this will be an ongoing process.

Zadok stomped the snow off his boots as he entered the house a couple of days later. Winter had arrived with a vengeance amid plummeting temperatures and swirling snow.

Somehow, he was hanging onto his peace from the weekend even though he felt like his relationship with

Juni was just as tumultuous as the weather. She'd sat through his sermon, but she and her family had left the building before he'd made his way to the foyer.

The question toggled back and forth in his mind. Call her? Or not?

So far, 'or not' had won out. He'd taken Xavier to the community hall parking lot and taught him to spin doughnuts with the truck in several inches of snow. Xavier had loved it, but it had also taught the teen a few things about how a vehicle handled in those conditions. How an extreme reaction on the steering wheel could take the whole thing sliding sideways.

The experience had also taught Zadok a few things about his brother's temperament. The boy could focus and think clearly, which were excellent qualities in a driver in northern climes.

"Hey, you're home!" Quincey yelled from the kitchen. "Dinner's almost ready."

He was going to miss his sister when she returned to college in a few weeks. It was nice coming home to a hot meal. What of Quincey's ideas could he and Xavier morph to suit the two of them? Planning and prepping, for sure.

Zadok chuckled as he hung his parka. Meatless Mondays, however, would be a thing of the past. They'd survived, and some of the meals had been pretty tasty, but vegetarianism wasn't a lifestyle the Shirkowski guys were about to embrace.

Xavier came up the stairs from his basement cave. "What's that smell?" He wrinkled his nose. "Oh, hey, Zay."

"Hello to you, too. Smells good, huh?" Zadok wasn't

about to cut down Quincey's experiments in front of her, but the aroma was complex, to put it mildly.

"It's a recipe called Moroccan Medley I found on a blog. The combination of spices sounded so odd I had to try it."

Zadok followed Xavier into the kitchen.

The boy stared at his sister. "It sounded odd, so you thought you had to inflict it on us? What's wrong with you?"

Quincey wrinkled her nose at him. "Don't knock it until you try it. I've sneaked a bite or two, and it's great." She lifted a ladle and let the contents pour back into the pot. "There's chicken, so don't worry about it being meatless. It's not."

"It's not the chicken that smells like that."

She rolled her eyes. "No, it's the cumin and coriander and chili powder."

"I don't even know what all of those are."

"Then it's high time we expand your tastebuds. The coleslaw you made on the weekend is tonight's veggie. Care to get it out?"

"Sure, whatever." Xavier sent pleading eyes to Zadok. "Maybe we can top this off with takeout later?"

Zadok tried his hardest not to laugh but only managed to keep his response to a smirk. The boy never stopped trying, but he still had seconds of most of the meals he grumbled about.

He filled three water glasses while his siblings set out the rest of the meal. They sat down, and he offered thanks to God.

"Oh, Xavier, I was talking to Brent Callahan today." Quincey picked up her spoon.

"Oh?" Xavier's gaze swung to his sister. "What about?"

"Well, first, he says he uses a ton of math every day in his job as a contractor."

The kid shrugged his shoulders. "Math, schmath. No big deal."

News to Zadok. "I thought you hated it. That it was too hard and you'd never need it again."

Xavier shot him a narrowed glare. "Whatever. It's not that bad."

Another reason Zadok needed to talk to Juni, to thank her for the miracle she'd wrought in Xavier's attitude to school.

"*Anyway...*" Quincey had a bite of the medley.

"What?" Xavier asked. "Did he... did he say anything else?"

Quincey glanced at Zadok before turning back to her younger brother. "He says he'll be hiring a couple of gofers for the summer, and you should apply on his website. The one I updated for him in November."

"Yes!" Xavier leaped to his feet and pumped both fists in the air as his chair clattered to the floor.

Nice both siblings had bright futures to look forward to. Maybe, someday, Zadok's would get back on track, too. He'd once had a vision of leading worship in a megachurch in front of thousands. It was a good calling, one that would require him to keep his personal relationship with Jesus strong. That part would be the same anywhere. He needed Jesus to help him run a tire shop, too.

He paused with his spoon halfway to his mouth. Did he *act* like his current job was important to the kingdom? Did he treat it as a ministry? Not so much.

"Why are you frowning at your spoon?" Quincey glared at him. "You haven't even tasted dinner yet."

"What? Oh." Zadok eyed the combination. Chickpeas, sweet potatoes, tomatoes... and the spices. They combined into an enticing fragrance, actually. He took in the bite and savored it before pointing the utensil at his sister. "*That* recipe is a keeper."

"Are you kidding me?" Xavier asked.

"Try it," Zadok advised.

The teen took a tentative bite and wrinkled his nose. "I guess I'll live."

High praise. Zadok managed not to chuckle. "How hard is this one to make?"

"Cooking level two, and you're capable of at least level four."

"I am?" Now he did laugh.

"Yeah, you are. I worry about you two when I leave again. Maybe I should stay."

"You need to follow your dreams." Zadok thumbed toward Xavier. "The kid and I will be fine. And if your dreams lead you back to Galena Landing, well, that's good, too."

"But you won't be here."

What if Xavier worked for Brent at Timber Framing Plus after high school? What if Zadok didn't sell Tires and

Treads? He shrugged. "It's too early to know for sure. We — all of us — need to ask God continually what He's got for us, individually and together."

Quincey dabbed at a tear trickling down her cheek. "I'm so glad I stayed home this semester. I was floundering, not gonna lie. I felt so alone, but now I feel like the three of us are a real family, even without Mom and Dad."

Xavier stared at her. "You're crying about that? That's dumb."

Zadok socked his brother lightly in the arm. "It's not dumb. Family is a gift. One we shouldn't take for granted. I'm thankful, too, Quince. You've helped me see things in a new way and helped me get a handle on all this." He pointed at the food in front of him. "We're gonna be all right, though. Xavier, you, too, can aspire to be a level-two cook."

"He's still looking at level one from miles away."

Zadok grinned at his sister. "Everyone's got to start somewhere. And you've got a few weeks to get this boy whipped into shape."

Xavier held up his hands. "No whipping allowed."

Zadok's cell rang, and he glanced down at it. There weren't many people he'd allow to interrupt dinner, but if that happened to be Juni, he'd make an exception.

Not Juni, but Pastor Ron.

That might be the other person he'd accept a call from. "Hello? Zadok here."

"Zadok?" Wanda's unsteady voice came through the device. "I'm in Wynnton with Ron. He... he's had a heart attack, and they're transferring him to Coeur d'Alene. Pray for him, please?"

"Absolutely. Is there anything I can do? Let Paula know?"

"I called her first so she could notify the prayer chain."

Then... why not let Zadok find out when the prayer chain got to him? "Okay. She'll let everyone know."

"Zadok, I don't know how to ask you this, but can you handle things at the church for the next few days or weeks? Ron keeps worrying about it, and he needs to let it go and work on recovering."

"Will he be okay?" Ron couldn't be more than, what, 50? There was no scenario where Zadok hadn't expected the man to be his pastor for another decade or two.

"The paramedics got to him in time. He's stable for now, but he needs an echocardiogram he can't get in Wynnton before we know for sure what's going on." She gulped. "What his prognosis is."

Zadok closed his eyes and inhaled. Exhaled. "You tell him not to worry about anything at the church. I'll meet up with Paula and Keanan and... whoever else I need to, and we'll manage just fine while he recovers."

"I'll tell him." Relief flooded her voice. "Thank you."

"You're welcome, I think. We'll pray for you... but, Wanda?"

"Yes?"

"I'm going to need prayer, too. Because this is not within my comfort zone." Not remotely.

"I understand," she said softly. "I'll pray for you, too."

And just like that, Zadok's life flipped upside down.

THIRTY

D id you hear about the pastor?"

"I did! How awful."

"A blow for the community for sure... and so close to Christmas!"

Juni forced her feet to keep walking down the high school corridor past her fellow teachers. Was there another pastor in Galena Landing besides Ron Wilson? What had happened to him?

She ducked into the staff restroom and pulled up the email app on her phone. She'd been in too much of a hurry to check before school, and mostly, she didn't want to know. Emails these days mostly contained more orders for felties. How many times had her finger hovered over the button to take down her website?

Mom had forwarded an email from GGC Prayer Chain just minutes ago. With a feeling of dread, Juni tapped to see the message.

Dear praying friends,

Pastor Ron had a heart attack a few hours ago. He was taken by ambulance to Coeur d'Alene where he is stable and in good hands. Wanda is with him and requesting prayer.

I'll let you know more when I hear more.

Paula Dye

Secretary to Ron Wilson, Galena Gospel Church

How scary! Juni read it again and closed her eyes to send a swift plea heavenward for Ron's health just as the bell rang.

She needed to be in first-period English Lit two minutes ago. Tapping to close her email, she sucked in a deep breath and hurried to class.

Scenarios and prayers swirled through her mind as she tried to focus on Charles Dickens and *A Christmas Carol*. Her students deserved her undivided concentration, but it had never been so difficult.

She hardly knew the man, but she'd sat under his teaching for more than eight months and had come to appreciate his gentle wit and his way of sliding his point into his listeners' hearts. Even if he recovered completely — and he would, right? — he'd be out of commission for a while.

Wanda, on the other hand, had been so sympathetic yet down-to-earth last week when Juni had bared her soul.

She shot a prayer heavenward while listening to her students debate which 'ghost' they'd welcome the least. No surprise, it was the Ghost of Christmas Past. It seemed even teens had regrets while hoping the future would be rosy.

At her first break, she checked email again, but there were no updates. She glanced around and took a chance on calling Mom at the town office. No news on the pastor's status, but there was something else.

"You should know Ron asked Zadok to fill in over the next few weeks."

Juni's emotions swirled. "As in preach every week?"

"That, and keep everything running. With Paula's help, of course."

The market manager and the church secretary were one and the same, each position only part time. At least the market was shutting down for the winter after next Saturday's market. "That's a lot for him, with a business to run, too."

"It is. He'll be splitting his time between the two. His employees can probably manage okay for a while with minimal supervision."

The bell rang — were school breaks always this short? "I have to go. Let me know if anything else happens."

Zadok stepping in to fill Pastor Ron's shoes, even temporarily?

Juni took a long, deep, fortifying breath. She couldn't think of anyone who would do a better job. Zadok had all the qualifications, even though this wasn't what he'd planned. His message last Sunday had been on-point and well-delivered.

She'd been putting off talking to him, with the feltie orders still coming in and all this stuff with Dad. Maybe she'd subconsciously thought she could put Zadok off until the new year, when things had settled down a little.

But... she couldn't wait. It wasn't fair to him, and it wasn't fair to her own heart, either. Dickens' character, Ebenezer Scrooge, had turned things around immediately after realizing the great gift he'd been given. He hadn't waited. Maybe he'd been afraid those ghosts would come back and haunt him for good but, either way, he hadn't waited for a more convenient time.

But Juni still had classes to teach all day... and Xavier Shirkowski for sixth period tutoring. Hmm. How could she work with that?

Joy.

Zadok scrubbed his hands through his hair. In some ways, it was helpful to have themes set in place to guide his sermons through the remainder of Advent, but seriously, joy?

How could he preach on joy with Ron awaiting open-heart surgery to replace damaged valves? He'd FaceTimed with the pastor, who'd been too tired to sit up or talk for long. Wanda had held the tablet for her husband while they chatted.

Honestly, though, was there any such thing as joy if life was full of sunshine and roses? A person didn't really need it when happiness would suffice. It was when the giddy dance of momentary glee slammed into harsh reality that the undercurrents of joy were vital.

The good people of Galena Gospel Church weren't going to expect polish from Zadok under the circumstances. They would understand if his sermon was short and lacking, but he wasn't about to settle for mediocre when this task — was it a gift? — had been dropped in his lap.

God had something to say to Zadok about joy. Something for the congregation to hear. This Christmas season had the possibility of bonding them all together more tightly than ever before. Joy could do that. Next week, love.

Oh, boy. What did he know about love? The point was God's love, of course, as represented through the nativity. And there was the traditional Christmas Eve candlelight service to prepare for, too.

One thing at a time. This week's theme was the Gift of Joy.

Zadok scanned through Ron's hand-scrawled notes. What was Romans 15:13? He looked it up.

May the God of hope fill you with all joy and peace as you trust in him, so that you may overflow with hope by the power of the Holy Spirit.

If the Holy Spirit offered it, it was a gift, right?

Zadok bowed his head in prayer.

JUNI SAT in her car in front of the Shirkowski home. Xavier had told her what time his brother would be home and invited her to wait inside the house, but she couldn't do that. That invitation needed to come from Zadok, and only if he wanted to.

She'd passed so much judgment on so many people. On Zadok. Would he find it in his heart to forgive her?

Yes? She thought he would, but maybe it was the happy ending of *A Christmas Carol* rubbing off on her. Real life was different. Hers, anyway.

Wait, that wasn't God's voice running through her head. What did the Bible say?

Well, there was James: *Every good and perfect gift is from above, coming down from the Father of the heavenly lights, who does not change like shifting shadows.*

God, her good, good Father, so unlike her earthly one, extended great and glorious gifts. Was it too much to ask that one of those gifts might be Zadok's love?

Because there was a man who didn't change like shifting shadows, either. He wasn't one who'd tell a woman he was interested in her one day and then retract it the next. Or a few weeks later.

It was cold in the car, and daylight hours were fleeting this close to winter solstice. Galena Landing had a bylaw against leaving a vehicle running when not in motion, a statute she was sorely tempted to break.

Juni blew vapor into the frosty air and rubbed her mittened hands together. Maybe she should have called in advance. Maybe she should have stopped by Tires and

Treads instead. Maybe... maybe that was Zadok's vehicle rounding the corner a few blocks down.

She pushed her car door open and stood on the shoveled sidewalk as his truck turned into the short drive and the garage door automatically rattled up.

There was no connecting door for him to avoid her, so he'd have to come around to the door.

Why would he want to dodge her? Once again, she shoved that negative thought out of her head.

And then he stood in front of the garage door as it rumbled downward. He wore his down parka and a beanie and looked at her.

She looked at him.

Yes, she needed to make the first move. Driving here wasn't enough. She walked toward him but stopped ten feet away. "I'm sorry, Zadok. I was wrong." The words weren't quite as hard to say as she'd thought they might be.

"I'm sorry, Juni. I was wrong."

Was he parroting her? Making fun of her words? No. There was no mockery in his tone. Just sincerity.

Juni took a few steps closer. "But you weren't wrong. You didn't claim my dad was innocent. Just that I shouldn't jump to conclusions. And that was correct. It's exactly what I was doing and defending."

"I was wrong, too, though. I didn't act out of compassion but out of old habits. I was already annoyed..." He closed his eyes.

"Because I didn't call you to cancel our date or explain

what was going on. That night was one thing after another, and I handled it poorly. All of it. I'm sorry."

How was it they now stood within arms' reach of each other? Had she moved toward him, or had he moved toward her? Both.

He held out a hand. "You're forgiven. But please forgive me, too."

Those hazel eyes of his pierced hers and removed all air from her lungs. or maybe it was the grasp of his fingers around hers. "Forgiven."

"It's such a beautiful word, isn't it? Forgiveness. One of God's many gifts for us, whether we need it or not. And we all do."

"Because *all* have sinned and come short of God's glory," Juni breathed.

"We're not immune. None of us." Now Zadok clasped both her hands as he studied her face. "I'm human. I will mess up again. It's a given."

Juni let out a shuddering breath. "Me, too. I'm starting to see some things, how I've allowed my bitterness toward my father invade everything else in my life. I don't want to be that person. I want God's grace to flow through me, even if the recipient doesn't deserve it."

"If we didn't deserve punishment, there would be no need for grace."

She managed a tremulous smile. "This is why I need you in my life. Because you keep pointing me back to Jesus, time and time again."

Zadok winced slightly. "Too preachy? Because..."

"No. You're the real deal. There's no evidence you're a

different person in your private life than your public one. No one has anything bad to say about you." She let out a chuckle. "Even Xavier sings your praises."

Zadok shook his head as a small smile crept across his face. "Even my kid brother, huh? It wasn't so long ago that wasn't the case."

"I remember. But you loved him steadfastly, and—"

"You know whom I want to love steadfastly?"

"Who?" She looked up at him. He was so close now, their breaths mingling in the frosty air.

"You." His gaze dropped to her lips, and he swallowed before meeting her eyes again. "But there's something you should know before you answer that."

Had there been a question in there somewhere? She hadn't noticed. "What's that?" Not that there was anything in the world that could change her mind now.

"Did you hear about Pastor Ron's heart attack?"

"I did. Is he going to be okay?"

"I think so, but it will take time."

Juni nodded.

"The thing is, he and Wanda asked me to fill in for him indefinitely. And it's not like I can just shut up the tire shop for the time being, either. I have two other families depending on that income, to say nothing of drivers in the community who need access to good tires in a timely manner."

"You're going to be busy."

"I am. Although Tires and Treads always closes between Christmas and New Year's, so there's that. But..." He shook his head. "I'm going to have to put Chelsea off."

"Chelsea?" Juni's brows drew together. "Chelsea Welsh? What does she have to do with anything?"

"I've hired her to update the interior, everything but the work bays. And my dad left behind a lot of the mess that Roger Sharp left him. There are heaps of old papers and just plain junk in the back room I need to go through that week, but how? I can't do everything. And all I really want to do is be with you."

"I've got two weeks of winter break. Can I help you sort stuff? I doubt I can help with things at the church, though. Paula's got everything under control there, I'm sure."

"You'd help me with that?" Zadok's gaze intensified. "I was figuring on making Quincey and Xavier pitch in, but they probably wouldn't make it any easier or faster. You would."

"Of course, I would. What else would I do with my time?"

"Isn't your sister getting married at the beginning of January? I'm sure there's lots she'll want help with."

She could feel Zadok withdrawing, so she squeezed his hands. "It will all work out. Arleigh's on top of things, and the wedding will be small and not so complicated."

Zadok inhaled sharply. "Pastor Ron was going to marry them."

"Oh. My. Goodness. Yes. Are you qualified?"

He shook his head. "I'm not ordained, and I'm not sure I can figure it out quickly enough. But I'm sure the local judge would be happy to fill in." He shook his head. "Wow,

I feel so unprepared to step into Pastor Ron's shoes, even for a few weeks. How can I do this?"

"One step at a time, one day at a time. Lean on God. You'll do fine."

"Does this situation make you want to run away from me?"

"Why would it?"

"When we started dating... a couple of months ago... I was just Zadok from Tires and Treads."

"You were never *just* that guy. You've always been Zadok the follower of Jesus, the musician, the caregiver, the one others can depend on. Who you are hasn't changed."

He searched her face. "I want to have changed from four years ago."

"You just trusted the wrong role model for a time. When you figured it out, you did an about face. It's me who kept my blindfold on tightly. I didn't want to see who you really were away from SIU. The Zadok I know in Galena Landing has many of the same characteristics as the previous version with one important distinction."

"Hmm?"

"You're willing to learn, to admit failure, to make things right." Would her dad ever show this willingness? From what Juni knew of narcissists, she doubted it, but God was in the miracle business, so... maybe? It was a request worthy of prayer.

"I see that in you, too." Zadok's finger slid down the length of her jaw.

"You do?" Because she'd clung so fervently to her original beliefs.

"I do. But you haven't quite answered my question."

She was transfixed by his eyes. What kind of question mattered right now?

"I'm a minister, albeit temporarily. Are you okay with that? With dating a guy in that position?"

"I *did* answer that! Why wouldn't I be okay with it? Because you're you, Zadok, no matter the label or job description."

"I don't date for the fun of it." Now both his hands cupped her face. "I did back then, but not anymore. I don't want to waste time on someone who doesn't at least see the potential of going the long haul with me."

Juni slid her arms up around his neck. "There is distinct potential."

And then his lips were on hers, caressing, melting the entire atmosphere. It was a wonder the snow wasn't melting and the daffodils surging out of the ground in full bloom.

Oh, Zadok. She'd come home.

THIRTY-ONE

ow did Juni brighten every room she entered?

Zadok marveled at how much fun she made the whole sorting job. Quincey and Xavier and Juni tackled that back room like they were in training for an Olympic event, leaving Zadok to clean out the reception area. He'd removed everything but the ugly, broken desk and a few chairs — he and Xavier would take those to the landfill as soon as the replacements he'd ordered online arrived.

At the rate the trio was going, there would soon be a full truckload for the landfill. The women sorted, while Xavier shredded old records from decades gone by. The three of them talked and laughed in the back like it was party time in Tire Shop Central.

He should be back there helping them, but Juni had given him strict orders to stay out unless invited. His job, she informed him, was to write his New Year's sermon. Somehow, he'd managed the last two Sundays of Advent.

Pastor Ron's scrawled notes had helped immensely, but now?

Zadok stared out the plate glass window to the street beyond. Snow swirled, obscuring the business across the street. His own future looked about as clear. It was there, within reach, but impossible to see from where he now sat. There were too many unknowns in the way.

Should he plan on a series? The last he'd heard from Ron, it would be at least two more weeks before he'd be able to return.

Zadok had dropped by the house and been amazed how old and tired the man looked for all he wasn't close to retirement age. This heart trouble had kicked him in the teeth, but surely it was only a matter of time.

But maybe not within two or three weeks, though Zadok didn't want to step on the man's toes and make plans for much longer. What he needed to do was sit down with the pastor and try to get a clearer mandate. Not that Ron or Wanda knew what would happen, either, or they'd tell him. Wouldn't they?

There were three months until Easter, but Ron would be back long before then.

A bundled-up figure appeared out of the swirling snow and headed toward the tire shop.

Zadok frowned, surged to his feet, and headed to the door. Didn't the person see the 'closed' sign on the window? But, oh, it was Wanda. He opened the door. "What brings you out in this weather?"

"I needed to talk to you without Ron around." She unwound her scarf. "Do you have a few minutes?"

"For you? Absolutely." He pointed at the guest chairs. He'd only left those in place for his work trio's breaks. "I can't believe you drove down, though."

"I didn't. It's not too far to walk, and I needed some fresh air to clear my head. I'll stop and pick up a few things at Super One on my way home." She set a backpack on the floor, tucked her gloves into pockets, and unzipped her parka before settling in a guest chair.

"Can I make you a coffee? I've got half a dozen kinds of pods."

Wanda glanced at the machine. "Sure. Just regular coffee, though."

Zadok nestled a pod into place, found a clean mug — bless Quincey for making sure those existed — and started the machine before turning back to Wanda. "What brings you here?"

"Ever to the point." She smiled, but he noticed the smile didn't reach her eyes. "It's Ron, of course, as you suspected."

Zadok sat in his chair, careful not to lean too far back. "I thought as much."

Wanda sighed. "He's anxious about the church. About you. He's certain he's asked too much of you, dumping all the concerns of the congregation on you while you've got a business to run, a family to care for, and a girlfriend to date."

She wasn't entirely wrong. "It has been a lot, but I think the hardest thing right now is not having any idea how to plan for the future." And he wasn't talking about Juni.

"Ron keeps saying just another week or two."

Zadok nodded.

"The church board met last night."

His eyebrows surged upward. During Christmas week? That had to be unusual. Wanda studied him for a long moment, and Zadok's uneasiness grew. "Am I doing a bad job? Do they want someone else to fill in?"

"No, not at all." Wanda dabbed at her eyes. "I'm messing this up, and here I agreed to talk to you in their place. The thing is, Ron needs a much longer time to recover than he's willing to admit. He's exhausted and sleeps four or five more hours a day than he needed before. Then he chafes at the bit and begins to study for the next sermon series he planned but then I find him asleep again."

Zadok's heart went out to his pastor. "The spirit is willing, but the body is weak."

"Exactly. I'm not going to lie. I'm worried about him, but God keeps reminding me that He's got this, that all things work together for the good of those who love Him."

"Romans 8:28," Zadok murmured.

"The board would like to ask you to consider staying on for the next three months, not as a volunteer, but as paid staff."

Zadok stared at her, his mind nearly completely blank. "Me? But I'm not qualified."

"We're an independent church, so I guess we get to decide who is qualified, and the board unanimously agreed that you are their choice."

He shook his head. "It's not like they have a lot of options."

"Maybe not a *lot* of options, but some, including splitting up the position. Steve Nemesek could certainly preach, at least part-time, if someone built a ramp for his wheelchair. Matt Santoro is a people person. He's available for visitation, which he has already been doing for several years. Keanan Welsh is already in charge of our small groups, which includes Alpha, starting next week, as well as music."

Zadok's mind raced through the repercussions. "It all sounds good, but I can't just close this place." He waved a hand around the tire shop and realized he hadn't given Wanda the coffee. He got up and did so. "Austin's and Bobby's families depend on the income, and the whole town depends on their tires."

Wanda accepted the mug and took a sip. "Thank you."

He plugged the coffee maker with another pod for himself. "I'm sure the board had some thoughts on Tires and Treads."

"Well..." Wanda eyed him. "They did wonder if Mason Waterman might agree to run the tire shop for you over the winter when Green Acres Farm isn't so busy. He worked here under Roger for years."

Mason. Zadok dropped into his chair and leaned back, remembering just in time what a bad idea that could be. Leaning back, not Mason. Because Wanda was right. Mason knew the tire business and had a head for books. "Has anyone talked to him?"

"If you agree to see if all the pieces slip into place, Steve will talk to him. Mason is his son-in-law, after all."

"I..." Zadok leaned forward with his elbows on the desk and rubbed his temples. *Lord? What do You say?* His gaze landed on the open Bible in front of him, where he'd been contemplating a sermon to kick off the new year.

Forget the former things; do not dwell on the past. See, I am doing a new thing! Now it springs up; do you not perceive it? I am making a way in the wilderness and streams in the wasteland.

He stared at Isaiah 43:18-19 some more. Rubbed his eyes and read it again. And God brought another verse to mind from a bit later in Isaiah: *Before they call I will answer; while they are still speaking I will hear.*

Zadok could all but hear God chuckling amidst angels singing. Or maybe that was Quincey and Juni in the back room. But still, wasn't this his answer?

Peace settled over his heart as he looked up to meet Wanda's eyes. "Yes."

"I'm sure you need time to pray over it and talk to your family before you make a final decision. To Juni..."

He shook his head. "God has spoken. I'm in."

"Sнн." Juni put her finger to her lips. "Is someone out there with Zadok?"

The Shirkowski siblings glanced between each other as though doubting her sanity.

"I smell coffee."

"Maybe Zay is begging the coffee machine to work faster?" Xavier suggested.

Juni rolled her eyes. "Be right back."

"Unless she gets so busy kissing she forgets all about us," Xavier muttered as she left the room.

Now there was an idea. Kissing was so much more fun than musty papers from the 1990s. Seriously. Who kept stuff for 30 years? Not just fun things like mementos, but invoices and receipts from ancient history.

"I'm sure you need time to pray over it and talk to your family before you make a final decision. To Juni..." Wasn't that Wanda Wilson's voice?

There was a very brief silence. "God has spoken. I'm in."

Juni ducked into the tiny restroom, just out of sight. What on earth were they talking about? What was Zadok so confident about that he didn't need to talk to her about it when Wanda clearly thought it was warranted? Was this another case of Zadok assuming he knew best because he was male?

No. She couldn't react to everything in life — to everything Zadok did or said — with that filter. Hadn't he proved by now, time and time again, that he wasn't that guy? He wasn't like Dad.

She had to trust him. Starting by not waltzing into a private discussion, no matter how badly she wanted to find out *right now* what was going on.

Juni locked the restroom door and stared at herself in the mirror. Quincey had scrubbed this room until it reeked of disinfectant. Thankfully, the odor had dissipated some in the past few days.

Did Juni trust God? Or not?

Did she trust Zadok? Or not?

She met her own gaze in the mirror. "God's word says, 'And we know that in all things God works for the good of those who love him, who have been called according to his purpose.' It also says, 'Every good and perfect gift is from above, coming down from the Father of the heavenly lights, who does not change like shifting shadows.'"

Juni let out a long breath. Those were excellent reasons to trust God. But Zadok was not God. He was a man, and he was fallible.

Zadok's eyes lit up when he talked to her about the Bible, about what he'd been studying for the Advent sermon series the past few weeks.

Had Dad ever looked excited about the Word of God? The gleam in his eye was more about vindication. About judgment. The 'God's going to get you if you don't behave' mindset.

"God?" It seemed weird talking to her Heavenly Father out loud in a tiny restroom while staring at herself in the mirror. "God, I see no reason not to trust Zadok. I know he loves You, and I know he loves me. Whatever is going on, whatever Wanda and he are talking and agreeing about, I trust You. Zay doesn't need to ask my opinion about every little thing. He needs to be exactly whom You called him to be. I accept that."

Even if it means I ask him to move forward without you?

Ouch. Juni scrunched her eyes shut. God wouldn't ask that of them, would He? But hadn't she prayed all along that God wouldn't let them keep moving toward a long-term relationship if it wasn't His best will for their lives?

She opened her eyes and bit her lip. "Yes, Lord. Even that. Though it would break my heart. I love him, God."

Peace I leave with you; my peace I give you. I do not give to you as the world gives. Do not let your hearts be troubled and do not be afraid.

Juni slipped out of the restroom and back into the storage room.

"Who was it?" Quincey asked.

"I didn't go out there, just to the restroom, but I think it was Wanda."

"Pastor Ron's wife?"

Juni nodded. "Now, which shelf were we going to tackle next?"

"The stupid paper shredder is jammed again," Xavier muttered. "It's overheated."

"Only because we have mountains of shred," Quincey replied. "We need to get all that out of here. It's encroaching on our elbow room and has to be a fire hazard." She scrunched her nose. "I wonder if it could be used for rabbit bedding? I'll ask Noel. He'll know."

"Why don't you kids call it for today?"

Juni glanced toward the door where Zadok leaned against the frame, hands in his jeans pockets.

"It's 3:30, and you've been at it all day. Besides—" his

gaze slid to Juni "—I need to talk to Juni without you two hovering."

"Oooh, I always wanted to witness a proposal!" Quincey pulled her phone from her hip pocket. "Are you sure you don't want this recorded?"

Juni held her breath. That couldn't be it, could it?

Zadok stared at his sister impassively for a long moment before thumbing over his shoulder. "Out. Meet you at home in a while."

"If you've got special plans, don't worry about it."

"Yeah, it's Meatless Monday," Xavier whined. "Someone might as well avoid it if he can."

Quincey rounded on her younger brother. "Oh, shush. It's good for you."

"No, it's not. Haven't I explained to you like a thousand times why meat is the most efficient form of protein on the planet?"

"Out." Zadok raised his voice. "You guys can fight about it on your own time."

"Fine, fine." Quincey jammed her elbow into Zadok's ribs on her way past as she put on her jacket.

Xavier followed her, shrugging into his. "Bring me a burger and fries?" he stage-whispered to Zadok.

Zadok's eyebrows flickered as he obviously tried to rein in his amusement, but as the door chimes rang out, his face sobered as he reached both hands to Juni.

"You're scaring me." But that didn't stop her from stepping into his arms and pressing a quick kiss to his lips. "What's up?"

"You know I've wondered how long Pastor Ron would

be out of commission. He looks terrible — well, you've seen him — but he keeps insisting he'll be ready to come back in a week or two."

"And?"

"Wanda just came in with an official request from the church board."

Juni searched Zadok's gaze and saw only peace. She knew what had to be coming.

"They've asked me to take on the pastoral position — paid — for three months, and we'll see how Ron is doing toward the end of that." His Adam's apple bobbed as he swallowed hard. "It might be for longer. It might be permanent."

She offered him a tremulous smile. "That's amazing. I'm so happy for you."

"Are you?" Zadok's hands rubbed her upper arms. "It means you'd be dating the pastor. No doubt, everyone will have opinions. Are you up for that?"

"Are you?"

"I'm all in. For both."

"Then so am I."

His voice broke as he clutched her close to his chest and murmured, "thank you," into her hair. "I love you so much. I can only imagine how hard it might be for you living in a fishbowl like this."

"Zadok?"

"Hmm?"

"I said I was *all in*. I mean that."

"Are you sure?"

She grabbed the lapels of his shirt and looked him in

the eye. "I'll tell you how sure I am. Zadok Shirkowski, will you marry me? I want to spend the rest of my life with you, whether you are the pastor of Galena Gospel Church, the minister of music at some big-city church, or the owner and operator of Tires and Treads." Her eyes widened as she gasped. "The tire shop!"

"Never mind." Zadok leaned so close their breath mingled. "Did you mean that question?"

"Absolutely. I want to marry you, if you'll have me."

"I want nothing more." He crushed her tight against his chest. "I planned to ask you in my own time and in my own way."

"Sorry-not-sorry." Juni tilted her face toward his. "Now kiss me, please. And let's figure out the details."

THIRTY-TWO

J uni had meant to keep her secret for a little longer. After all, she didn't want to draw attention away from her sister's wedding, which was in just a few days.

But Arleigh took one look at her when she walked in the door and said, "Spill."

"Me? I don't know what you're talking about." Juni rolled her scarf, tucked it in the basket, and finger-combed her hair.

"Lying does not become you."

Ouch. And Arleigh was right. Especially not if Juni was going to be a preacher's wife. And she was! She hung her parka and toed off her boots before looking her sister in the eye.

"I'm marrying Zadok."

Arleigh shrieked and threw her arms around Juni. "I'm so excited! Show me the ring! When's the big day?"

"I don't have a ring, because I'm the one who did the asking. Spontaneously."

"No way!" Arleigh laughed then covered her mouth with her hand, though her eyes still danced. "Did you really?"

"I did." Juni giggled, too. "I can't believe it, either, but Zadok planned to wait until—" Was this supposed to be a secret? But the whole church board knew, plus a few others, plus it would be announced Sunday... and Arleigh and Mitchell would be away on their honeymoon.

"Until?" Arleigh prompted.

"This is sort of a secret," Juni warned.

"Okay?"

"The church board has asked Zadok to take on the pastoral role for a minimum of three months, to be reevaluated at that time. And he's nervous."

"Oh, Juni! He'll do such a great job. He shouldn't be worried."

"I know. He really puts a lot of study time and prayer into each sermon, but filling in part-time, week-by-week, was one thing. Everyone's expectations will be much higher for a longer term."

"What about the tire shop?"

"There are options, but we're not sure. Anyway, with all that upheaval, I wanted Zadok to know that whatever the future held, I'm in with him, 100 percent."

"I'm thrilled for you both!"

"We're looking at maybe July, when school is out for the summer. We'll see if Pastor Ron is well enough by then to marry us, otherwise we'll be going your route and asking the local Justice of the Peace."

"It's not how Mitch and I planned it, but it will be fine. I can't believe I'm going to be married in just five days. It doesn't matter who performs the ceremony so long as someone does."

"What more can I do to help?"

"I think we're good. Mom flat-out told me I wasn't creating the floral arrangements. She ordered those out of Wynnton and will pick them up Saturday morning."

"Good for her. The bride has other things to take care of, like herself. However, you can go all kinds of crazy for flowers for my wedding, okay?"

"Oh, that will be fun. How many attendants? Me, of course!"

"Of course, you and Quincey. I'm not sure if I'll ask anyone else. Zadok might ask Keanan, but then who will do the music? We haven't decided." They'd been too busy sealing the deal with a few dozen kisses to focus on mundane details like that. There was plenty of time.

Juni's phone rang, and she glanced at it. Unknown number? Not a chance was she going to answer so some scammer knew this was a live number.

It chimed for voicemail.

"Who's that?" Arleigh asked.

"I don't know." Juni scowled. "But I guess I'm curious." She tapped to listen to the voicemail.

"Hey, baby." Juni's eyes widened and she stabbed to put it on speaker. "You forgot to give me your sister's number, so I can't call and wish her a happy wedding day." Dad laughed, but it sounded hollow. "I hope she'll be happier married than I ever have been, but I doubt it."

Arleigh dipped her head, raised her eyebrows, and stared at Juni.

"I don't know when I'll be back in the good old US of A, but not anytime soon. Sorry about that. Give me a call back?" There was a pause. "This is your father, of course."

Click.

"Let me get this straight." Arleigh's hands found her hips. "He's sorry he won't be stateside soon. *That's* what he's sorry about? Not about making sexual advances on a bunch of female students? Not about leaving his wife and five kids high and dry with almost no money? Not about... sheesh, I can't believe the nerve of that man."

And to think Juni had once believed Zadok Shirkowski had anything at all in common with Grant O'Neill. They both carried XY chromosomes, and that was about it.

How had she not seen the zillions of differences years ago? How had she been so blind?

Well, her vision wasn't limited anymore. Zadok was a thousand times more honorable than Dad had ever dreamed of being.

"I'll email him later and tell him he can email me in the future, that I'm blocking this phone number."

"You don't have to do that for me."

"I'm not doing it for you. I'm doing it for my own sanity. Because I'm done letting him speak into my life."

Arleigh's eyes misted over. "He doesn't think anyone can be happy when married."

"See? That's why I'm blocking him. Because he's

completely wrong. Narcissistic people like him can't be happy married or single or any other which way because, sooner or later, the other person forgets to give him the honor that is due him, and then he's unhappy about it."

"You think Genevieve messed up?"

"Are you kidding me right now? Of course, she did! She's human. No one can be perfect all the time."

"No one but Jesus."

"Exactly. We can't let any human determine our worth. Not Mitchell. Not Zadok. Not Mom. And definitely not our dad."

"Thanks for the reminder." Arleigh hugged Juni. "You're going to make a great pastor's wife."

Juni stepped back and eyed her sister. "What expectations do you have for that position?"

"Um... is this a trick question?"

"Only if you think it is."

"Okay, well, Wanda has an office at the church. She hosts a ton of events for women's ministry and heads up the kitchen for Alpha."

Alpha. That was starting next week, and both Juni and Zadok had volunteered to help out. Could they still find time to do that?

My peace I give you.

Short answer, yes... but only if they leaned on the Lord.

Juni looked at her sister. "I'm not Wanda. I'm not a trained counselor. I already have a job teaching at the high school. Also, I'm not certain hospitality is my gift."

Would the church give her room to be herself, or would they expect her to be Wanda 2.0?

Know who she could talk to about that? A counselor. Wanda, herself.

ZADOK SAT through Arleigh and Mitchell's wedding from a pew near the back, flanked by his siblings, but he barely noticed the bride. She was beautiful, most likely, since she shared some features with Juni. There were candles and flowers and two cute little boys, each carrying a ring pillow. There was a beaming little girl — Mitchell's niece — carrying flowers.

The bride and her mom walked the aisle together, and Zadok squirmed in his seat. Would Donna walk Juni at their wedding, too? It sure wouldn't be Grant doing the honors.

He couldn't believe Juni had proposed to him. He'd thought it was way too early in their relationship, especially with all the unknowns in front of him. And that was precisely why she'd asked him to marry her.

Keanan's hands stilled on the piano keyboard as the local magistrate began the marriage ceremony. She didn't ask who gave this woman to be married to this man. Unusual, but he got it. The traditional wording reeked of ownership, and the O'Neill sisters had fought too long and hard to escape their father's influence to let the wording stand.

Finally, Mitchell and Arleigh were proclaimed

husband and wife. While they kissed, Juni looked at Zadok for the first time during the ceremony.

He tried to pour all his love into the smile he offered in return. This woman. She was coming to him as a partner, as an equal. She'd come to realize there were some things he was better at than she was, and also vice versa. There were going to be times of adjustment, for sure, but they weren't going to let things fester.

Please, Lord.

The members of the wedding party made their way to the church foyer, and Zadok waited impatiently amid the line to greet the newlyweds. Not that he cared about them — much — but...

Finally, Juni stood in front of him, resplendent in a knee-length black dress, her hair in an updo with curls framing her face.

He couldn't help himself. Zadok slid his arms around her waist as she flung hers around his neck. "You're beautiful," he murmured against her hair.

"Thanks. You look mighty good to me, too. I can't wait for this to be over so I can put on comfy clothes." She sighed against his chest. "I'm happy for them. I am, but I'm happier for us. Is that terrible?"

He clutched her tighter. "If it's bad, then I am, too. Because one day soon, that will be us. I love you."

Someone coughed.

Right. Zadok was holding up the receiving line with his PDA. And his fiancée still didn't have a ring on her finger to point to as a reason the interim pastor might act this way.

They'd all understand soon enough. He kissed Juni's cheek and let his fingers trail down her arms and hands until the touch broke. "I'll see you in a few."

"I'm counting on it." Juni held his gaze for a long moment before turning to the somewhat patiently waiting people behind him. "Hi, Chris. Hi, Gina! Good to see you guys."

"Anything going on we should know about?" Gina Zima asked in a stage whisper.

Zadok tilted his head back toward them to hear Juni's response. "That's for me to know, and for you to find out!"

"Oooh, that sounds intriguing! Your sister is such a beautiful bride. I'm sure you will be one, too."

A flush crept up Zadok's neck as he shook hands with Mitchell's brother, Treyan, and his wife, Brittany, before reaching the bride and groom. Arleigh winked at him before hugging him, and Mitchell smirked. Whether that was for having his wife by his side or for Zadok, Zadok didn't know. Didn't care. He waited across the room until the last of the folks made their way past the wedding party.

At last, Juni came over to him. "Now photos. Then the reception. It all takes so long. How about we elope?"

He laughed as he hugged her. "Now there's an idea. I'm sure that would go over well with the church board and all the members here."

Juni offered an exaggerated sigh. "Life in the public eye is going to be *so* fun."

Zadok searched her face. "Regrets?"

"Not even a little bit. All of it will be worth it a hundred times over when I can call you my own."

He glanced around the foyer. Only a few people remained. The photographer chatted with the bride and groom as he gestured to an area with banks of white poinsettias.

"I have something for you."

Juni tilted her head toward him, fully focused.

Zadok loved that about her. Loved everything, actually. He dug into his suit jacket pocket and pulled out a small velvet box. "Quincey and I made a trip to Wynnton yesterday. She helped me pick this out. I hope you like it. We can exchange it if not—"

Juni squealed. "Show me already!"

Right. Wasn't this supposed to be accompanied by the guy dropping to one knee as he proposed? What happened if they'd already covered that part? Zadok shifted on his feet, preparing to lower himself, but Juni pulled the box from his hand and opened it.

Her eyes widened. "Zadok, this is gorgeous. It's so, so beautiful. I'm so happy!" She flung her arms around his neck.

He rocked her close, once again inhaling the fragrance of her perfume and bouquet. "Are you sure?"

"About the ring? Or about you?"

Zadok tried to swallow the emotion clogging his throat. Failed, because a little of it seemed to be leaking out of his eyes. "Either. Both."

"No regrets, Zadok Desmond Shirkowski. None. Nada.

You are the very best thing that has ever happened to me, and I'm so grateful for you."

"A great and glorious gift from God." Not that he felt like he measured up to that lofty ideal, but this precious woman certainly did.

"Yes. That." She eased back. "Put the ring on my finger?"

He reclaimed the velvet box as she offered it, then slid the gleaming diamond onto her finger.

"How did you guess my size? It fits perfectly!" She tilted the ring this way and that, catching the glint from the lights.

"Quincey talked to Arleigh."

"The sneaks." Juni chuckled and looked back up at him, love shining from her eyes. "Thank you."

"I see congratulations are in order." Paula stood beside them, shifting awkwardly from one foot to the other. "I can't think of two nicer people to spend their lives together." She offered a tremulous smile.

"Thanks, Paula." Juni hugged the market manager. "I'm sure you saw this coming months ago."

The woman smiled. "Maybe. I did notice how you two managed never to look at each other at the same time though your booths were across from each other all season."

"At the same time?" Zadok's eyebrows shot up. "You paid a lot of attention."

"I did." Paula gave him a brief hug. "And I also hear congratulations are in order for your job change."

"Temporary job change," Zadok corrected.

"We'll see how things play out." Paula bit her lip. "I'm sorry to see Ron sidelined, but I have every confidence you'll manage well, because I know you'll depend on God to get you there."

"Thanks, Paula. That means a lot."

"Juni! Time for photos!" Arleigh called.

Juni flashed her ring toward her sister.

Arleigh squealed and darted across the foyer as fast as she could in a gown that seemed snug down to her knees. Quincey had called it a mermaid cut.

Juni met her halfway, and the sisters rocked from side to side as they hugged.

Zadok's gaze lifted to see Mitchell watching him. The man grinned and dipped his head. Zadok smiled back. They were going to be practically brothers in a few short months.

Then Arleigh was in Zadok's arms. "I'm so happy for you and Juni! You take good care of my sister, or you'll have me to answer to."

He hugged her back then set her on her feet. "I'll keep that in mind, but I don't think you need to worry."

"I know." Arleigh beamed at him then whirled back around. "Pictures! Let's get the show on the road."

The photographer leaned over to Zadok. "If you stick around, I'll make sure to get a few engagement photos for you and your fiancée."

"That would be amazing. Thank you. I have nowhere else I'd rather be than right here."

Nowhere but about six months in the future. But for now, this was a day he'd remember forever.

EPILOGUE

- July -

I 'm so proud of you, sweetheart."

Juni's eyes misted at her mom's words. "Thanks. That means a lot."

"I never thought one of my girls would marry a pastor."

"I know, right? But Zadok wasn't a pastor when I fell in love with him."

Mom smoothed her hair as they waited outside The Sizzling Skillet for the rest of their group to arrive for brunch. "You knew he wanted to be a minister of music."

"I did." Juni smiled in memory. "God works in mysterious ways, right? Even at New Year's, we had no idea that Pastor Ron would accept a medical retirement and that the church would offer Zadok the permanent position."

"And then Austin and Bobby joined forces to buy Tires

409

and Treads from him. That took a big load off his shoulders."

"It really did." Juni remembered the relief and joy Zadok had experienced as his employees made him an offer back in April. It seemed especially fitting since Austin's dad had once owned the tire shop, but Austin hadn't had the resources to take over when Roger wanted to sell five years ago. Now it was back in their family. "It didn't hurt that we'd cleared out all the old junk, and Chelsea did such a great job redecorating it. It's so much more welcoming now."

"Pride in one's workplace is always of benefit." Mom smiled. "I love working at town hall. I never dreamed I could be so independent and so happy with it."

"Still no dating?" Juni gave an exaggerated sigh. "Now that you've got your daughters married off — well, in a few hours — you should start looking around for someone to share *your* life, too."

"God's going to have to drop him in front of me, gift wrapped with a card saying, 'For Donna.' Maybe then I'll pay attention."

Juni laughed at the mental image as several cars entered the parking lot. Arleigh and Brittany arrived together, Brittany's baby bump practically exiting the car ahead of the rest of her. Genevieve clambered out of the backseat.

Juni glanced at her mother, but of course Mom only had a smile for her ex's second wife. Genevieve and the children had come for the wedding and were staying at Gina and Chris's for a couple of days.

Genevieve offered Juni a hug and managed an awkward smile for Mom.

"I'm so glad you're here." And Juni meant it. "Are you doing okay?"

"Yes, fine. I've filed for divorce, not that it makes any difference since your father is still in Bali hiding out from what he's done." She pursed her lips tightly. "Apparently Indonesia doesn't extradite to the US, so he's safe enough there for now. Coward."

That was a good way to describe Dad. "And everything worked out with the house?"

"Yes, thankfully, it was paid for. And the banker found an account your father neglected to drain, which has sustained the children and I for the past few months. However—" Genevieve took a deep breath "—I've got a number of resumes out. I never thought I'd need to support five children by myself, but here I am. At least Glory is ready for kindergarten, so I won't have to pay much for childcare."

"I'm so proud of you." Words the old Juni would never have dreamed of saying to her stepmother.

"Thank you. I don't feel worthy of that, but I'm learning to trust that God will take care of the children and me. It's hard."

"I'm sure it is."

Arleigh slid her arm around Juni's waist. "Everyone ready? I think the restaurant staff is waiting for us by now."

Juni glanced across the parking lot to where the Farm Fresh Market was in full swing. Paula waved.

Juni waved back. She and Zadok had planned their wedding for late afternoon so Paula and all the vendors could attend once the market was done for the day. Plus, they needed full access to the park, since they'd chosen to have an outdoor wedding. An amazing number of townspeople wanted to attend their pastor's wedding. Thankfully, Pastor Ron retained the credentials to perform the ceremony.

"Any regrets?" Arleigh whispered, steering her toward the restaurant door.

"None. I'm glad I stopped trying to make the felties a business. It's enough to make a few here and there to give to local children in the hospital. But, it's fun to sub for Paula from time to time to keep the market running."

"And your job?"

Juni laughed. "If you're asking if I'm happy with the offer for next school year, I couldn't be happier. Splitting the position with Rachel Jones is perfect, especially since I get to keep the drama classes! I think I'll stay plenty busy enough."

Just as they entered the frontier-style café, Quincey rode up on her bicycle along with Chelsea from Green Acres Farm. Quincey was back for the summer, but this time she was living out at the farm 'to give the newlyweds space,' as she said. Xavier had taken over the basement a couple of years ago, and he was simply part of the bargain. One more year of high school, but he was pretty independent now with his driver's license and his summer job working for Timber Framing Plus.

Things couldn't have turned out better. All that

remained was marrying Zadok this afternoon. It couldn't come soon enough.

ZADOK STOOD at the head of the grassy aisle, Pastor Ron on one side of him, with Keanan and Xavier on the other. The men of the church, headed up by Simon Melnychuk, had set up rows and rows of folding chairs, which the women had promptly decorated with little bouquets on the ends of the rows.

Nosegays, Arleigh had informed him.

She could call them whatever she liked. They could be present or not. Zadok didn't care. All he needed was the woman who would soon be walking toward him.

Diana played her flute while Rylee accompanied her on a portable keyboard. Both women played with the worship team and had been nervous to provide all the music for the wedding without Zadok or Keanan to lead, but they were doing well.

Probably. For once in his life, music was not the focus.

Quincey strolled down the aisle carrying a vibrant bouquet from Arleigh's Flower Farm. No wonder Quincey — and now Arleigh — wore pale green dresses so as not to compete with the flowers.

Zadok shifted his weight to the other foot.

"She's coming soon," Keanan whispered. "It's all worth it."

"Thanks." Zadok glanced at his best man with a grin. "So much..." but his voice trailed off as Juni and her mom, arms linked together, appeared between the bushy rhododendrons that formed the other end of the aisle.

Juni's bouquet trembled slightly, but her radiant smile was focused on Zadok with not a shadow of doubt to dim it.

He felt himself relax as the duo paced toward him. She was so beautiful, and she was offering herself to him, as he was giving himself to her. Willingly, wholly, forever, together.

Thank You, Jesus, for this great and glorious gift of love.

Have you read all the previous Farm Fresh books? The original series is also set in Galena Landing as the women who homestead at Green Acres Farm fall in love! All six titles are available on Amazon and in KU as well as in paperback and audio.

You can find titles and details at
https://valeriecomer.com/ffr

SUBSCRIBE!

Are you subscribed to my email list? This bi-weekly newsletter is the best way to be kept up-to-date on what I'm working on, what's for pre-order, and what sales or promotions might be happening. Plus, you get a free e-copy of *Promise of Peppermint*, the prequel to the Urban Farm Fresh Romance series, as my thank-you gift.

https://valeriecomer.com/subscribe

If that's a fuller inbox than you prefer — but you're still interested in occasional news — follow me on Bookbub and/or Amazon to keep up with new releases.

DEAR READER...

Thanks for reading *A Great and Glorious Gift*! I'm so honored that you chose to spend the last few hours with Zadok, Juni, and me. You are appreciated.

I'm an independent author who relies on my readers to help spread the word about stories you enjoy. Would you take a few minutes to let your friends know? Facebook, Instagram, Goodreads... wherever you hang out online.

Also, each honest review at online retailers means a lot to me and helps other readers know if this is a book they might enjoy. I'd sure appreciate your help getting word out!

I welcome contact from readers. At my website, you can contact me via email, read my blog, and find me on social media. You can also sign up for my newsletter to be notified of new releases, contests, special deals, and more! Click here to subscribe. You'll receive *Promise of Peppermint*, the novella that introduces the Urban Farm Fresh Romance series, absolutely free as my thank you gift!

~ Valerie Comer
www.valeriecomer.com
http://valeriecomer.com/subscribe

ACKNOWLEDGMENTS

Writing this series has been hard. Paula Dye, whose namesake graces this series, passed away between the release of *A Wide and Pleasant Place* and the writing of *A Green and Vibrant Hope*. Paula loved helping me create the farmers market manager character while she was ill, the process providing her with a focus on the difficult days. Paula, you are still so very missed.

Thank you, dear readers, for loving the Farm Fresh Romance stories and bemoaning the end of the Urban Farm Fresh Romance series. I hope you've enjoyed this trip back to Galena Landing, where it all began in *Raspberries and Vinegar* back in 2013!

If you're an Idahoan, you may have wondered at my choice of the name South Idaho U for my Boise-set university. It was not an error but a deliberate choice, since I didn't wish to put any real school in a bad light with the handling of the situation with Professor Grant O'Neill.

Thank you to Lynnette Bonner. Not only did she mastermind this multi-image cover, but she's been a great motivational buddy as we spur one another on to meet our daily word counts! Check out her fun contemporary romances under her pen name, Brynn Stewart.

Thanks also to author buddies Elizabeth Maddrey and

Jan Thompson for keeping me accountable. I do the same for them. Read their books!

Many thanks to my editor, Nicole, for fitting in this (long!) manuscript during a very busy season for you. I appreciate you, your humor, and your keen eye. Thank you for making my stories better.

I'm also grateful for the Christian Indie Authors Facebook group. These folks make a difference in my life every single day. I'm thrilled to walk beside them as we tell stories for Jesus!

Thank you to my Facebook reader group, who had a lot of ideas helping me determine what, exactly, went wrong in Juni and Zadok's original blind date! I'm also thankful for their prayers, encouragement, and great fellowship. If you'd like to join the fun, please search Facebook for Valerie Comer Reader Group. There's a question for admittance!

Thanks to my husband, Jim, whose love for me never fails and who encourages me in every endeavor. Thanks to my kids, their spouses, and my wonderful grandkids for cheering me on. To them, having an author for a mom/grandma is "normal." Imagine that!

All my love and gratitude goes to Jesus, the One who is my vision, the High King of Heaven, the lord of my heart. Thank You. A thousand times, thank You.

Valerie Comer Bibliography

Farm Fresh Market Romance

1. A Wide and Pleasant Place
2. A Green and Vibrant Hope
3. A Great and Glorious Gift

Urban Farm Fresh Romance

0. Promise of Peppermint (ebook only)
1. Secrets of Sunbeams
2. Butterflies on Breezes
3. Memories of Mist
4. Wishes on Wildflowers
5. Flavors of Forever
6. Raindrops on Radishes
7. Dancing at Daybreak
8. Glimpses of Gossamer
9. Lavished with Lavender
10. Cadence of Cranberries
11. Joys of Juniper
12. Together in Thyme

Pot of Gold Geocaching Romance

1. Topaz Treasure
2. Ruby Radiance
3. Sapphire Sentiments
4. Amethyst Attraction

Miss Snowflake Pageant

1. More Than a Tiara
2. Other Than a Halo
3. Better Than a Crown

Farm Fresh Romance

1. Raspberries and Vinegar
2. Wild Mint Tea
3. Sweetened with Honey
4. Dandelions for Dinner
5. Plum Upside Down
6. Berry on Top

Sweet River Ranch Romance
(Montana Ranches Christian Romance)

1. A Surprise Wedding for the Cowboy
2. A Jilted Bride for the Cowboy
3. A Sunny Sweetheart for the Cowboy

Cavanagh Cowboys Romance
(Montana Ranches Christian Romance)

1. Marry Me for Real, Cowboy
2. Give Me Another Chance, Cowboy
3. Let Me Off Easy, Cowboy
4. Kiss Me Like You Mean It, Cowboy
5. Choose Me for Always, Cowboy
6. Trust Me With Your Heart, Cowboy

Saddle Springs Romance
(Montana Ranches Christian Romance)

1. The Cowboy's Christmas Reunion
2. The Cowboy's Mixed-Up Matchmaker
3. The Cowboy's Romantic Dreamer
4. The Cowboy's Convenient Marriage
5. The Cowboy's Belated Discovery
6. The Cowboy's Reluctant Bride

Garden Grown Romance
(Arcadia Valley Romance)

1. Sown in Love (ebook only)
2. Sprouts of Love
3. Rooted in Love
4. Harvest of Love

Riverbend Romance Novellas

1. Secretly Yours
2. Pinky Promise
3. Sweet Serenade
4. Team Bride
5. Merry Kisses   valeriecomer.com/books

ABOUT VALERIE COMER

Valerie Comer's life on a small farm in western Canada provides the seed for stories of contemporary Christian romance. Like many of her characters, Valerie grows much of her own food and is active in the local foods movement as well as her church. She only hopes her imaginary friends enjoy their happily-ever-afters as much as she does hers, shared with her husband, adult kids, and adorable grandchildren.

Valerie is a two-time *USA Today* bestselling author and a two-time Word Award winner. She writes engaging characters, strong communities, and deep faith into her green clean romances.

Please visit her website at www.valeriecomer.com, where you can read her blog, explore her many links, and sign up for her email newsletter, where you will find news, giveaways, deals, book recommendations and more.